The Getaway

When Maria Duffy left her career in the bank to become a stay-at-home mum, she never dreamed that writing, something she's always loved, would become her job one day.

She lives in Dublin with her husband Paddy and their four children.

Her bestselling novels include *Any Dream Will Do*, *One Wish* and *A Love Like This*.

ALSO BY MARIA DUFFY

Any Dream Will Do
The Terrace
The Letter
A Love Like This
One Wish
Falling Softly
In Search of Us

The
Getaway

MARIA DUFFY

HACHETTE
BOOKS
IRELAND

First published in Ireland in 2019 by
HACHETTE BOOKS IRELAND

1

Cataloguing in Publication Data is available from the British Library

ISBN 978 1 4736 7317 5

Typeset in Adobe Garamond Pro by Bookends Publishing Services

Printed and bound in Great Britain by Clays Ltd, Elcograf, S.p.A

Hachette Books Ireland policy is to use papers that are natural, renewable and recyclable
products and made from wood grown in sustainable forests. The logging and manufacturing
processes are expected to conform to the environmental regulations of the country of origin.

Hachette Books Ireland
8 Castlecourt Centre
Castleknock
Dublin 15, Ireland

A division of Hachette UK Ltd
Carmelite House, 50 Victoria Embankment, EC4Y 0DZ
www.hachettebooksireland.ie

For Paddy
My rock, my husband, my friend
For our 25th wedding anniversary

Author's Note

While the main character in this novel is a writer, that's where the similarities between her life and mine end. This book is entirely a work of fiction with no resemblance to real persons or places or events.

Chapter 1

It was the tampons that finally did it. Linda Costa pulled the car into the side of the road and wept. It hadn't stopped all day. 'Mum, can you drop me to school because I don't want the rain to make my hair frizzy?' 'Can you make a veggie lasagne for dinner today?' 'Mum, remember you have to pay for my school trip online by lunchtime today.' 'Linda, can you leave my grey suit into the cleaners and pick up some decaf coffee when you're in the shops.' And then from her dad: 'Linda, I need a lift to the physio and your mother is going to her bridge club. Can you be here at three?'

It didn't matter that she had a job. The fact that she had already written a best-selling book and was on a deadline for her next one didn't count. Because being an author was just something artsy. A fancy schmancy word for somebody who made up stories in her spare time and was lucky enough to get them published. And she worked from home. The kiss of death. Working from home meant that she could get up in the morning and make breakfast for everyone, bring the kids to school, do the housework, shopping and make the dinner. Her friends would say she was lucky that she had all that time to herself during the day and could go for coffees and lunches when they all had to go out to work. She'd often try to explain that managing a household and writing novels was work too. But nobody seemed to understand.

Most days she just got on with things. It was the way things were and it was never going to change. But today was different. She was coming off the back of four weeks of no sleep. Stressing every night about a deadline she was never going to meet and spending all day doing everything else except writing. When she'd brought her dad to the physio, he'd insisted she bring him to Aldi afterwards to get some cheese that was on special.

'I don't really have time today, Dad,' she'd explained, thinking of the rush-hour traffic she'd be bound to hit on the way home if she delayed another minute. 'Maybe Mum can pick it up for you later.'

'Forget I asked,' he'd said, his eyes welling up. 'I'll just have some bread and butter for my tea. I'm sorry I'm such a burden.'

And so she'd ended up walking around Aldi with a shopping list while her dad sat and had a cup of tea in the coffee shop next door. Ever since her dad's leg had been amputated ten years before, his personality had changed completely. He'd gone from being funny and lovable to a self-pitying martyr with no sense of humour and a very large bee in his bonnet. It was no wonder her mother escaped to play bridge three times a week.

Her journey home from her parents' house in Blackrock had taken her, just as she'd feared, right into rush-hour traffic so she was already stressed and agitated when Ben had rung half an hour later. 'Mum, when will you be home?'

'I don't know, love. The traffic is pretty bad so I'll be quite a while yet.'

'But the batteries in the Xbox are gone and I can't find any. Will you get some on your way home?'

She'd resisted the urge to scream but instead agreed and pulled into a service station a few minutes later. So with a mega pack of AA batteries and an extra-large Mars bar to make the journey a little more bearable, she was on her way again. The traffic was moving at a snail's pace so when her son had rung again and wondered what was for dinner, she'd snapped at him to work it out between himself and his sister. There was plenty of food in the fridge and cupboards so they could rustle up something between them. Satisfied that she'd exerted her authority, she felt a bit calmer. That was until her husband, Roberto, had rung to see if she could have his dinner ready by six thirty because he had to take a conference call soon after and it was likely to go on for a while.

'Ring the kids,' she'd said, her voice calmer than the turmoil going on in her head. 'They're on cooking duty.'

It was almost two hours later when she took the slip road off the N4 into Leixlip where she lived with her family. She was relieved to be finally close to home but she was still reeling from all the phone calls. Did they really think she was super-human? Honestly, how was she expected to meet everyone's demands while she was running a house and writing a book? Not to mention the numerous emails building up in her inbox that she'd never catch up on. She'd just got through the traffic in Leixlip village and turned up Captain's Hill towards home, when her phone rang again. It was Shauna, her sixteen-year-old daughter.

'Mum, get me some tampons on the way home, will you? Super plus.'

'I've passed the shops now, love. I'll be home in a minute. I'll pick them up tomorrow for you.'

'No, Mum,' came the whiney voice through the speakers of the car. 'It's an emergency. I need them *now*.'

Linda glanced in her rear-view mirror and saw the tailback of traffic behind her. It would take her ages to get through that again so Shauna would just have to wait until the next day. 'There's some in my bathroom. They should do you until tomorrow.'

'I've used them already. Just get them, for God's sake, will you?'

She winced at her daughter's tone. That had been the way lately with Shauna – she'd become very self-absorbed and treated her parents like cash machines and her mother like a slave. At first, Linda had blamed the behaviour on her friends. She was hanging around with a new group of girls these last couple of years, so maybe they were having an adverse influence on her. But she soon began to realise that the friends were decent girls and Shauna's behaviour was down to nobody but herself.

'Mum? Are you still there? Get me chocolate too. I need it

to get me through this time of the month. And can you hurry because ...'

Linda ended the call suddenly. She'd had enough. She must have taken her eyes off the road for a split second because her tyres clipped the edge of the pavement and she had to swerve to avoid hitting a street lamp. Her heart was thumping almost out of her chest as she veered off out of the traffic amidst a chorus of beeping and pulled into a side street to park the car. Once the tears started, she couldn't stop them. Big fat pools of water fell from the corners of her eyes as her body convulsed. She pounded her head off the steering wheel until it began to hurt and she was forced to sit back and try to catch her breath. She couldn't take it anymore. She was everything to everybody and yet who looked after her? Who cared how she was feeling? That she was on the verge of a breakdown? She closed her eyes and waited for the tears to subside and for her breathing to settle. And then she began to wonder what would have happened if she'd actually crashed into that street lamp. If the traffic hadn't been going so slowly and she'd hit it with force. Imagine she'd died. How would Rob cope? How would he manage the children with working such long hours? How would the children feel not to have a mother, her parents not to have their only child? She pictured the scene. A police officer calling to her door. 'Mr Costa, can we come in please? I'm afraid we have some very bad news ...' Would he cry? Would they all huddle together in shared grief? Would they realise how they'd treated her? How they'd taken her for granted? But it would be too late.

A knock on the window scared her half to death and she opened her eyes to see an old man staring in at her, looking very concerned. Shit! She must look like a raving lunatic. She wiped her eyes with the back of her sleeve and let the window down.

'Are you okay, Miss? I was just walking the dogs and noticed you there.'

'I … I'm fine. I've just had a bit of bad news.'

'Ah, sorry about that. I don't mean to intrude. I just wanted to check.'

'Thanks for your concern,' she said, mortified. 'But I just needed to pull in for a moment. I'm grand now.'

She watched as he walked on up the hilly road with his two Alsatians. She envied his state of oblivion. He looked like he hadn't a care in the world. She'd forgotten what that felt like. And she was angry too. Angry that he'd interrupted her wallowing and self-indulgent imaginings. She closed her eyes again and tried to regain her thought process. But it was no use. The moment had passed and all she felt was exhaustion. Exhaustion and shame. She really shouldn't allow herself to dwell on such negative thoughts and she definitely didn't wish herself dead. But sometimes she just wished she had a fairy godmother who'd wave her magic wand and transport her somewhere away from all her worries.

Her phone rang suddenly, startling her, and she was surprised to see her dad's name coming up on the display. Oh God, he'd better not be ringing with some excuse to get her back over there. Well, she'd just stand her ground for once and refuse.

'Hi, Dad. What's up?'

'Hi, love. I hope you got home okay.'

She thought for a moment before answering. 'Yes, Dad. Safe and sound.'

'Ah good, good. I just wanted to say thanks for today. I know you're a busy woman and I know I ask a lot of you, so thanks.'

She was speechless. 'It's okay, Dad.'

'Okay, love. I'm just going to get my tea. Bye bye for now.'

A click and he was gone. She sat for a moment, her head awhirl with thoughts. It was nice to be appreciated. Especially by her dad, who wouldn't make a habit of showing his gratitude. Maybe he'd noticed something about her earlier. Maybe he was more perceptive than she'd given him credit for. The phone call had thrown her, but the fact remained that she felt unhappy. Unhappy, unappreciated and stressed. And if she didn't do something about it soon, she feared she'd have a proper breakdown and end up in an institution. What would they all do then?

And then a thought suddenly struck her. She grabbed her handbag from the floor of the car and checked the inside pocket. Just as she thought, her passport was still there. She'd collected it from the depot the previous week and had forgotten to put it with the other passports at home. She took it out and stared at it. It was taunting her – willing her to use it. How easy would it be to just hop on a flight somewhere and disappear for a while. She had money, credit cards, motive. Just because she didn't want to end her life didn't mean she wouldn't like to check out for a while. Her heart was telling her she couldn't do it but her head understood. Her head knew she needed to escape, so ignoring her pleading heart, she turned the car around and headed back towards the N4. The traffic wasn't so bad going in the opposite direction and before she knew it, she was on the M50 heading towards the airport. For the first time in ages, she was buzzing with excitement. She was really going to do it. God only knew where she'd end up, but something was telling her it would be the start of her taking control of her life.

Chapter 2

Linda sat at the kitchen table, her laptop open in front of her, a cup of coffee by her side. This was her dream job. The thing she'd wished for more than anything. The thing that had given her a life for herself – something other than being a mum and a wife. She'd felt as though she'd won the lottery when she'd landed that book deal. It had been perfect. They were giving her money to fulfil her ambition of having a book published. It was almost laughable. But she wasn't laughing anymore. The dream was turning into a nightmare as she was finding it almost impossible to write the second book. She'd written a couple of chapters but she just couldn't seem to get into the zone.

She took a gulp of her coffee and poised her fingers over the keyboard. *Just let it flow*, she thought to herself. *Let the words come rather than forcing them.* And so she began to type. Sentence after sentence. Her fingers danced swiftly over the keys and very soon she'd filled pages with her thoughts. Two hours later, completely drained from her marathon writing session, she sat back to survey her work. But as she read it back, she could feel that old familiar disappointment well up inside her. It was rubbish. Complete and utter rubbish. So, with a heavy heart, she found the all too familiar delete key and deleted the whole thing. Snapping her laptop shut, she put her head in her hands and resisted the urge to cry.

She was still sitting in the same position some minutes later when the doorbell rang. It would be her best friend, Ger. Linda had rung her the previous night when she'd gotten home from her failed escapade and Ger had been very supportive.

'I'll come over tomorrow,' she'd said. 'Straight after my 12 p.m. yoga class. We can have a chat then.'

Ger greeted her with a hug and within minutes they were sitting at the kitchen table sipping coffee.

'I just couldn't go through with it,' said Linda, tucking into her second Jaffa Cake. 'I wanted to. I really did. But I just didn't have it in me.'

'So you actually got as far as parking at the airport and then bottled it?' said Ger. 'You must have really felt like you were on the edge.'

Linda nodded. 'I did more than just park actually. I went in and spoke to someone at the Aer Lingus desk. I asked her if there were any available seats on flights going out in the next couple of hours.'

'You did *not*!' Ger looked appalled. 'So what did she say?'

'She asked where I wanted to go and when I heard my own voice saying "anywhere", that's when I came to my senses. I thought maybe I was going mad or something. So I scuttered away quickly with whatever bit of dignity I had left.'

Ger shook her head. 'I can't believe you let things get so bad without telling me. Without telling anybody. I feel awful that you've been going through such a hard time and I didn't know.'

Linda smiled at her best friend's anxious face. 'I'm fine, Ger. I really am. First-world problems, as they say. Nobody has died, and everyone is healthy, so they're the main things. Other stuff is just trivial.'

'I don't agree,' said Ger, sipping her coffee and taking a chocolate biscuit from the plate. 'If things are making you feel this bad, well then it's serious.'

'What? This is coming from the girl who preaches "don't sweat the small stuff" and "live in the moment"? What happened to that? I thought you'd be telling me to just close my eyes, breathe deeply and let it all go.'

'God, Linda, do you think I'm that insensitive? Did you keep all this to yourself because you were afraid of what I'd say? That I'd dismiss your problems as trivial?'

'Well, I wouldn't say that exactly, but you do have a habit of making me feel as though my problems aren't really problems at all.'

Ger looked close to tears.

'I don't blame you for it,' said Linda, quick to reassure her friend.

'That's your job. It's what you do. And most of the time I appreciate the advice you give me.'

'But not this time,' said Ger, quietly.

'It's just that the more my stress levels were building up, the harder it was to say anything to anyone. It felt like I was moaning every time I opened my mouth about anything so I just learned to keep it closed and get on with it.'

'You poor thing. I really had no idea. But the important thing is you've told me now so we can do something about it. For starters, I think you should—'

'Honestly, Ger. I know you mean well but I just couldn't cope with a mindfulness session at the moment. I'm sure it would be good for me and would help me relax, but I need practical solutions.' Ger was a yoga instructor and mindfulness coach and she was so zen that nothing ever bothered her or got her agitated. Having said that, she lived alone, had no kids and worked at a job that required her to relax at all times.

'Well, if you had waited until I was finished, I was going to suggest no such thing. What I was going to say is that despite your failed attempt at escaping to a foreign country, I genuinely think you need to get away for a while. On your own. You need to put some distance between you and the things that are making you feel this way. You'll have time to think without things pulling you in a million different directions and it might be easier to work out how you're going to move forward.'

Linda reddened. 'I'm sorry. I just assumed. And it would be great if I could get away for a while, but the reality is, there's just no way.'

'There's always a way.'

'It's okay for you to say that when you've nobody else relying on you for anything and can go where you want when you want, but it's different for me.'

'So you keep reminding me.' Ger looked crestfallen.

'I'm sorry,' said Linda. 'Again. I seem to be saying that a lot lately.'

'I'll tell you what,' said Ger, rooting in her handbag and producing a pen and notebook. 'Why don't we make a list of the things that have you feeling like this and let's see what we can do about them. Right, fire ahead.'

'It's not as easy as that. I can't just—'

'It's as easy or as difficult as you make it, Linda. Just say what comes to your mind when you think about the worries you have.'

Linda relented. It would probably be good to get some of the stuff off her chest anyway. 'Rob.'

Ger raised an eyebrow. 'I didn't expect to hear you say that. I thought you two were solid.'

'We are,' said Linda. 'Well, we used to be.'

'That doesn't sound good.'

'I don't really know anymore, Ger. He's a good man and I do love him but…'

'Go on.' Ger reached out and touched her hand and Linda knew she'd feel better for saying the words out loud.

'I just feel fed up with him. He doesn't ever acknowledge how hard I work and he takes me for granted. I keep thinking back to years ago when he was so thoughtful and used to surprise me with little things like booking a meal out for us or a weekend away.

Things have just become very stilted. Boring, even. Oh God, does that sound awful?'

'No, it sounds perfectly natural. You've been together a long time. But how serious is it? I mean, are you fed up to the point of leaving him or do you just need time away?'

'I'm not going to leave him,' said Linda, aghast at the suggestion. 'It's not like that. I'm just fed up with the same old story day in, day out. It was his Sicilian values that made me fall in love with him in the first place. You know, the respect for women and how he used to look after me and treat me like a princess. But now those traditional values are the thing that could be the breaking of us.'

'How so?'

'It's just that he's so much happier when he's bringing home the money and I'm at home running the house and looking after the kids. It's how he was brought up. His dad worked in finance and his mum was mother earth. From what he's told me, she used to get up at six in the morning to bake bread and cook breakfast for her husband and six children. By lunchtime she'd have pasta made from scratch and sauce bubbling on the stove. By all accounts she was some sort of superwoman in the home.'

'And do you think he expects you to be like her?' Ger looked incredulous.

'Not exactly,' said Linda. 'But I do think that me earning so much money last year has made him feel a little inferior. In a way I understand. He works so hard and all of a sudden, something that was just a pastime for me became a job and I was handed more money than he earns in a year.'

'Yes, but that money is for both of you. For the family. Surely he gets that.'

Linda nodded. 'He does but it's just a big change for him, I suppose. He was used to the way things were – him bringing home the money while I ran the house and looked after the kids. And it worked well, really.'

'But not if you weren't happy,' said Ger, watching her carefully.

'I *was* happy. But there was just something missing. And when I got that book deal, it was like the missing part of the puzzle. I felt fulfilled. I had everything I ever wanted – a great husband, two wonderful children, a lovely home and the job of my dreams.'

'So what's changed?'

Linda thought for a moment. 'I don't know exactly. Maybe it's me. I want more now. I have this great opportunity to make a name for myself in the writing world but I'm pulled in so many different directions that I just don't have enough time to dedicate to my writing.'

'Ah, Linda. You just need to talk to Rob about it. He's a reasonable man. Surely if you explain things to him you can both come to a compromise. I'm sure he'd help out more if he thought you were feeling this way.'

'But it's not as simple as that. There's more to it. You know how he was planning on quitting his job to start up on his own?'

Ger nodded. 'Yes. And surely that's a good thing. Didn't he say he'd be working from home initially so that might free you up a bit to write? Maybe that's his way of acknowledging your writing career.'

'Yes,' said Linda. 'And it seemed like a good plan at first. In fact I was the one who encouraged him to do it. When I got the advance last year for *two* books, I told him that we'd have enough to pay off the rest of the mortgage so that would take pressure off him. He could leave his job and not worry if his start-up was slow to make money.'

'And he's changed his mind?'

'No, just the opposite.'

'Go on,' said Ger, leaning forward on her elbows.

'He's actually really into the idea. He keeps talking about when he's going to tell them in work that he wants to leave.'

Ger shook her head. 'I still don't get it. That's what you want, right?'

Linda sighed and continued. 'As I said, the advance I got was for two books, Ger. I worked on that first one for the last ten years so I'd perfected it. Made it as good as it could possibly be.'

'And it was brilliant. I actually cried when I saw it on the shelves of Easons and when you were on the telly talking about it.'

'You don't understand.' Linda winced as she took a sip of her now cold coffee and shoved the mug away from her. 'Everything has changed.'

'Changed how?'

'That money. I'll probably have to give a chunk of it back.'

'Why the hell would you have to do that?' Ger's mouth gaped open.

'I keep saying – the advance was for two books. The second one is due on my editor's desk in a few months and I have barely any of it written.'

'But I thought you were almost finished. You said it was going well. What do you mean you have barely any written?'

'I lied. I'm nowhere near finished. I'm scared, Ger. I'm really scared. I saw this fabulous life mapped out for myself, doing what I've always wanted to do. And now I'm worried that it's not going to happen.' She burst into tears and didn't pull away when Ger came and wrapped her arms around her.

'It's been awful,' she sobbed. 'I've sat at my laptop any time I had a moment free and looked at a blank screen. Sometimes I'd write a few sentences and sometimes even a chapter or two. But when I'd read them back, they'd sound ridiculous so I'd delete them. I'm not getting enough time to just sit down and let the words flow. And knowing I have a deadline just makes it all worse.'

'No wonder you're so stressed,' said Ger, sitting back on her stool but keeping a hold of Linda's hands. 'And keeping it all to yourself is never a good thing. I'm just glad you've told me now and we can try and sort it out.'

'But how? Nobody can write this book for me. And I certainly can't do it.'

'Well, for starters, you've written a brilliant book that was in the *Irish Times* bestsellers for weeks. Do you know how many people envy you for that? How many writers out there who are clamouring to get noticed by publishers?'

'Oh God, Ger. I'm sorry. Yet again. I wasn't thinking.' Ger had written a self-help book that she'd been trying to get published for years, but after numerous rejections, she'd given up and published it herself on Amazon.

She shook her head. 'This is not about me. I need you to realise how good you are and just maybe you have too much going on at the moment to let your creativity shine.'

'Thanks, but I still have no book and no book means no money. I can't have Rob leaving his job with the expectation that my money will keep us afloat for a while. But I haven't the heart to tell him I'm a failure.'

'Stop that right now. You're not a failure at all. You're a very successful woman who's just encountered a blip. You need to talk to him, Linda. Before he makes any decisions about the job. And you need to address what you're feeling about your relationship too. It's not just a matter of him helping out more, is it? You said you were bored?'

Linda nodded. 'There's just no excitement there anymore. No passion.'

'In the bedroom?'

Linda reddened and fiddled with her spoon.

'Come on, Linda. You can talk to me about anything.'

'Sex is just a part of it. It's become so routine. So stilted. But that's how it is with every aspect of our lives. I want to be surprised. To be whisked off my feet sometimes. It was so good when we were younger and life was unpredictable. So exciting. Nowadays I get excited if I get a new attachment for my steam cleaner or if Weetabix is half price in Tesco.'

Ger laughed out loud at that. 'Aw, Linda, you're just overthinking everything at the moment. You definitely need to get away. And is it just the writing and Rob? Or is there anything else that's bothering you?'

Linda thought for a moment. 'Well, the kids aren't helping with my stress levels either. Honestly, Ger, if Ben isn't sitting in his room reading, he's playing games on his Xbox. And I can barely get one word out of him these days.'

'He's at that awkward age though,' said Ger. 'I remember when I was thirteen and wasn't sure where I fitted in. I'm sure it will get better as he makes more friends in secondary school. And Shauna's doing okay, isn't she? She seems to have blossomed into a social butterfly.'

'And that's another problem.'

'What do you mean?'

'She's the complete opposite to Ben. She's sixteen going on twenty-seven. She speaks to me like I'm a piece of dirt and does what she wants when she wants. I really feel she's getting out of control. Do you know she came home drunk as a skunk the other night?'

'No! What happened?'

'I knew as soon as I saw her face that she'd been drinking. She tried to deny it but she was slurring her words. Her eyes were all bloodshot and her mascara was half way down her face.'

'So what did you do?'

'I dragged her into the bathroom and made her look at her face in the mirror. She promptly threw up in the sink and then collapsed on the floor bawling her eyes out. I swear, if I get a sniff of her drinking again, I'll kill her.'

Ger tried to stifle a giggle and Linda wasn't impressed.

'It's not one bit funny, you know. I honestly don't know what to do with her.'

'I'm sorry, Linda. I know it's tough for you but do you remember the time when you and I drank a bottle of vodka in your house when your parents were out? I honestly don't know how we got away with it because I don't remember going to bed that night.'

'I suppose we all did it,' conceded Linda. 'But it doesn't make it any easier. It's horrible to see your child like that. And I'm sure we were a lot older when we started drinking.'

'Are you serious?' Ger shook her head. 'We were fourteen when we first got drunk. You have a short memory.'

'Well, there's a lot going on in this head at the moment. I'm having trouble remembering what day it is, let alone what happened over thirty years— Hang on, was that somebody coming in the door?'

Linda stood up at the sound of the front door quietly closing and quickly opened the kitchen door. 'Shauna! What are you doing home? It's only three o'clock.'

'We got off early. I'm going for a nap.'

'Hold on,' said Linda, stepping out into the hall and closing the kitchen door behind her. 'School didn't finish early today. We would have been notified.'

'Well, it was just free classes for the last two. There was no point in staying. No biggie.' Shauna proceeded to head up the stairs but Linda grabbed the sleeve of her shirt.

'No biggie? You bunk off school but it's no biggie? When did you get to be so rebellious? Come on. I'm driving you back in.'

'Let go,' said Shauna, shrugging free of her mother's grasp. 'As I said, I'm going for a nap. I'm not feeling well. So chill, okay?'

She disappeared upstairs, leaving Linda wondering where it had all gone wrong. She could have done without that today. She leaned against the bannister and willed herself not to cry. The kitchen door opened suddenly, startling her, and Ger appeared with her bag over her shoulder.

'Sorry, Linda, but I have to fly. I have a class in an hour so I need to prepare. Is everything okay with Shauna?'

'Nothing I can't handle,' said Linda, forcing a smile. 'I'll give you a buzz later on.'

'Great. We can chat again then. And think about what I said about getting away. I really think it would do you the world of good. I'd come with you if I had the time but I have classes booked for the next six weeks. Why don't you talk to Rob and tell him what you told me today? He'd understand. You'll work it out – I'm sure of it.'

They hugged and Linda kept the smile plastered to her face until Ger's car disappeared around the corner. She closed the door and sighed before turning to head back into the kitchen. And that's when she saw it. Her reflection in the hall mirror. She always avoided looking near it, and in fact she hated having it there at all. But Rob's ninety-five-year-old grandmother had brought it over from Sicily and he'd insisted that they hang it for everyone to see. The mirror was oval in shape with a thin silver frame, and as she stared at herself, she was reminded of a cameo brooch that her mother used to wear. Except the face on the brooch looked regal, and there was certainly nothing regal about how she looked. She'd been quite a looker when she was younger but the years hadn't been kind. Her once bouncy hair had dried up into a long, dark frizz that refused to be tamed and her skin had become dull and lifeless. Even with her large-rimmed glasses covering a multitude, the black bags beneath her eyes were obvious, as were the many fine lines around her face. Tears sprang to her eyes suddenly as she mourned the loss of the pretty, carefree girl she used to be. But tears wouldn't get the dinner made or clean the house, so she took off her glasses and wiped her eyes with her sleeve, before turning away from the mirror.

Back in the kitchen she placed the cups in the dishwasher and set about making dinner. Was Ger right, she wondered, as she peeled potatoes and placed them in a pot of water. Would Rob understand? He'd hate to think she was unhappy, but would he understand the reasons why? She wasn't so sure.

Linda had met Rob when they'd worked together in an insurance company twenty-five years ago. Back then, they were colleagues. Both ambitious and both determined to rise up the ranks of the company. But as their relationship progressed, it had become clear to Linda that Rob was a traditional sort of guy and would expect her to stay at home if they had children. And she hadn't put up much of a fight. Insurance wasn't exactly her passion and as soon as she'd held Shauna in her arms, she'd been in love and had been happy to take on the role of housewife and mother. Rob had been promoted since on many occasions and now held a senior role in the company.

To be fair to him, Rob wasn't a dictator. He never bullied her into staying at home or forced her into a situation she wasn't happy about. He'd just grown up in a household where his mother stayed at home and his dad worked in an office, and theirs had been an idyllic life. He simply wanted the same for his family.

As the years passed and Ben came along, Linda was happy. Nothing ever fazed her and Rob hailed her as a natural-born mother and home-maker. She actually found the baby years enjoyable and relished her role. And they were good kids for the most part. She felt very lucky. It was only when the teenage years came along and messed with their heads that they became difficult. And Linda began to find motherhood more challenging.

It was when she was pregnant with Shauna that she'd discovered her love of writing. It had all begun with a diary. She'd set up a document on her laptop to write about how she was feeling every day. And then she'd wanted more. So she started to write stories. She loved reading crime books so the stories always had an edge to them. She'd even entered one in a short story competition she'd heard about on a local radio station and had come third. As the years went by and her confidence grew, she began to plot her first book. The book that would be ten years in the making. And then, after a lot of rejection and hard work, a publisher had finally said yes the previous year and had offered her a sizeable advance for a two-book deal. It had been more than she'd ever imagined. A dream come true. At last she was doing something for herself. Something that made her heart sing and on top of all that, she was being acknowledged for her work. She'd walked on air for a long time. That was until the book had had its time on the shelf and the publisher was shouting for the next one.

The sound of boiling water splashing out of the pot of potatoes startled her out of her reverie and she quickly lowered the temperature. She knew she couldn't go on feeling like this; she was going to have to talk to Rob later. She needed to tell him about the book situation so he could put the idea of leaving his current job on hold for the time being. They just wouldn't be able to afford for him to do it. And then once she knew his salary was guaranteed, she could stop pretending to be a writer. She also needed to talk to him about how stressed she was. She needed him to know that she was overwhelmed with so much going on in her life and was desperately trying to keep it all together.

But Ger was right. She really did need to get away for a while. Talking was good but her exhaustion levels were at an all-time high and she really needed to recharge her batteries. She'd never really thought it would be possible but now she was beginning to think that she could actually do it. Her writing buddy, Aidan, lived in Spain so maybe she could go and visit him for a while. He'd been asking her to go over and visit since he'd moved there five years previously and she'd always had some excuse not to go. A bubble of excitement began to form in her stomach. Could she really do this? Could she walk away from her responsibilities for a week or two and actually have time for herself for a change? It was a thrilling thought.

She took out a bag of carrots to chop and suddenly her heart felt lighter. Maybe her mini breakdown the previous day had been worth it after all. It had forced her to face what was happening and why she was so stressed. And now she was finding solutions. She felt very proud of herself.

Just then she heard Shauna's bedroom door opening. Maybe this would be a good time to have a little talk with her daughter. Just the two of them while it was quiet in the house. She was feeling more positive now than she had in days and suddenly the thought of talking to Shauna about her attitude and behaviour didn't faze her anymore. And then there was a loud bang followed by a shriek.

'Who the fuck left a fucking bag right in the middle of the landing. I could have broken my fucking neck!'

Linda flinched and went back to chopping the carrots. Maybe their chat could wait for another day.

Chapter 3

'I'd no idea, love,' said Rob, spearing a piece of beef on his fork and stuffing it into his mouth. 'I'll have a word with the kids and get them to start pulling their weight.'

Linda sighed. She'd spent the last half hour explaining to her husband how she was feeling. How she was overwhelmed with everything and how there weren't enough hours in the day. He thought it was as easy as getting the kids to empty the dishwasher or pull out the Hoover every now and then. Maybe he'd realise how much more serious things were when she told him about the book. Or the lack of it.

'It's going to take more than that, Rob. I don't think you realise how bad things are.'

'What are you talking about?' He smiled that smile. The one she hated. The one that said, *Who's a silly billy then?* The one that trivialised everything she said. 'They'll grow out of it, love. Everyone says the teenage years are difficult.'

'But it's not just the kids,' she said, exasperated. 'It's a whole lot more than that.'

'Well, tell me then.' He put his knife and fork down and she knew she had his attention, so she continued.

'It's about the book. The next one. I need to talk to you about—'

'I'm one step ahead of you there,' he said, tipping his index finger off the side of his nose. 'I wasn't going to say anything yet but now that you've brought it up …'

'Brought what up?' Linda was confused. 'What do you mean you're one step ahead of me?'

'I've done it, Linda. I've told them I'm going.'

'Going where?'

'Leaving. I told them in work today that I wanted early retirement and they're going to discuss terms with me over the next few weeks.'

'But I—'

'I know. You thought I wouldn't do it. And I wasn't sure myself at first. But I've always wanted to work for myself. And if I'm working from home initially, I'll be there to give you a helping hand. That's what you want, isn't it?'

'Well, yes. But giving up your job so suddenly. Starting your own business. It's a big step.'

He smiled and reached over to touch her hand. I know, love. But don't you worry. It might take a while to get going properly but I'll make sure I'm still earning enough. And having your book money there as a backup will ensure we won't go short.'

She didn't know what to say. There was no way she could tell him about the book now. He was so enthusiastic about his plans and the ironic thing was that she'd pushed him to leave his busy job. She'd been dazzled by her newfound status as a well-paid author and thought they were set up for life. She'd be writing a book each year from now on and raking in the cash. She'd quite liked the idea of Rob doing more around the house while she brought home the money. She'd even considered the possibility of renting a little office for herself away from the house. Somewhere she could go every day to write without having the breakfast dishes staring at her or feeling like she had to hoover the floors or sort washing before she began her writing. But that was never going to happen. How could she tell him she was a failure? How could she tell him it had all gone terribly wrong?

'So what were you going to say about your book, love?' he said, sitting back in the wooden chair, his plate wiped clean.

For just a moment, she toyed with the idea of coming clean about her failure, but she couldn't do it. 'It's just that I could do with getting away on my own for a while. Just a few days or maybe a week. Somewhere quiet so that I can finish my book and at the same time recharge my batteries.'

He looked taken aback. 'On your own? Away where?'

'Anywhere.' She realised again how that sounded, so quickly continued. 'I wouldn't mind visiting Aidan for a bit. He says the sea is very therapeutic for writing so maybe it would help me finish that book without any other distractions.'

'Distractions? What distractions? Don't you have the house to yourself all day while I'm in work and the kids in school? Surely that's plenty of time for you to get a bit of writing done. Didn't you manage just fine with the first one?'

Linda sighed. The little fact that it had taken her ten years to write the first one and the publishers were expecting the second in months seemed to have escaped his memory.

'And besides,' he continued. 'It wouldn't be ideal having the kids come home to an empty house every day. Ben would be straight on that Xbox and Shauna… well, God only knows what that girl would get up to. Who'd make sure they did their homework and had something healthy to eat?'

'I was sort of hoping you might take some time off,' said Linda, her dream of sipping pina coladas on the beach slipping through her fingers. 'But I suppose that would be asking too much. Just forget I said anything.'

Rob's face was stony and she felt tears prick her eyes. How could she ever have thought he'd agree to something like that. A lot of her friends took breaks away without their husbands but that wasn't them. Neither of them had ever been away alone since they had got married twenty years before. She'd just have to put the whole idea out of her head and try and get on with things. She was about to say so when suddenly Rob looked at her and smiled.

'Let's work it out.'

'I'm sorry?'

'You visiting Aidan. We can work it out. I still have some

holidays to take before the end of the year and there's no point in me carrying them over to next year if I'm hoping to leave early in the year.'

'Are you serious? You'll take time off so that I can go?'

'I'm a reasonable man, Linda. If you feel you need to go away for a bit, then I'll do what I can to support that. Talk to Aidan and we can agree on a time. To be honest, work has been really busy and I feel exhausted, so a break would be nice.'

Linda didn't know how to react. She was thrilled that he'd agreed to her going but on the other hand, the fact that he considered being at home was a break both annoyed and worried her in equal measure.

'So go on then,' he continued. 'Go and ring Aidan and tell him you're going to visit. I'll check my dates in work tomorrow and we can take it from there. I'm quite looking forward to this, actually. I want to start putting some distance between me and the job and my golf swing could do with some practice.'

Linda leaned over and kissed her husband lightly on the lips before scurrying out of the room and up the stairs. Sitting on her bed, she put her head in her hands and tried to gather her thoughts. What a mess. How could she ever tell Rob about the book now? He'd already told his boss he wanted to leave so what was she to do? She knew she should have said something weeks ago when it had become clear that she wasn't going to be able to finish it. Why was her life so bloody complicated?

But on the plus side, it looked like this break was really going to happen and suddenly the thought of getting away seemed even more enticing. She needed some time to think. She deserved it. And maybe not being in the house surrounded by the problems would be a positive thing. With a bit of distance, it was always easier to make decisions. And seeing her old friend would be a bonus. She'd met Aidan at a creative writing course fifteen years before and they'd just clicked. When he'd moved to Spain with his partner, she'd been devastated but she'd also known it was the right thing for him. He had no ties and living by the sea was something he'd always dreamed of. He needed his creative space, he'd said. *To create my masterpieces, dahling.* A picture of his ever-tanned face popped into her mind and she smiled. She pulled her mobile out of her jeans pocket and dialled.

'*Hola, cariño! Cómo estás?*'

Linda's heart leaped at the sound of her friend's voice. 'Go on, you show off,' she said, giggling. 'I bet they're the only words you know.'

'I'll have you know my Spanish is *fluido. Es perfecto!*'

'Okay, okay. I believe you. Now, how the hell are you? I haven't spoken to you in ages. How's James?'

'James is wonderful, as always. And I'm fabulous. Everything is going great. Come over and visit. I feel like a broken record saying that to you. But you're never going to, are you?'

'Well, actually…'

'Stoppit! Don't tell me you're coming over! Are you? You're not. Are you really? Tell me. Stop keeping me guessing!'

Linda laughed. 'I'd tell you if you let me get a word in.'

'Sorry, sorry, go on.'

'I was actually ringing to ask you if you'd mind if I came over for a bit. Not too long – maybe a few days or something.'

'Mind! Would I mind? Darling, I've been trying to get you here for five years. Why would I mind? *James!* He almost blew her ear off as he shouted for his husband. 'James! Linda's coming over. She's coming to visit at last.'

Aidan's excitement was palpable and Linda was delighted. She hoped that Rob would get time off work soon because now that she'd decided to go, she couldn't wait.

'So tell me all the details,' said Aidan. 'When, where, how … ? And what made you decide to come at last. I'm thrilled, of course, but curious too. Is everything okay with you? You haven't had a fight with Rob or anything, have you? I mean you shouldn't run away, if that's what it is. You need to sort things out befo—'

'Relax, Aidan.' Linda was exhausted just listening to him. 'Rob and I are fine. He's going to look after things here while I'm gone. And as to why I'm coming over now – I'll save that for a nice cool glass of sangria and a table full of tapas.'

'Deal. So when are you arriving?'

'I haven't booked flights yet but I'm hoping it will be in the next few weeks. I'll let you know.'

'Great stuff. Well, you'll fly into Murcia airport and once we know the details, we'll pick you up there. It's just a fifteen-minute ride home.'

'Listen, Aidan. I don't want to intrude, so I can book a hotel. Just send me the names of the closest ones to you.'

'You'll do no such thing. I've been trying to get you here for so long, do you think I'm going to allow you to stay anywhere else but with us? We'll have your room ready and I'm not taking no for an answer. There's plenty of room.'

'Thanks, but I thought you lived in a one-bedroom apartment? Or am I imagining things?'

There was a silence before he spoke again and for a second Linda thought they'd been cut off. 'We moved, actually. To a bigger place.'

'Oh really? It just shows how much I've kept in touch. So there are two bedrooms then?'

'Well, let's just say we have a lot more space than before. So it's no trouble at all.'

'Okay, if you're sure then. It will be much nicer than staying on my own in a hotel. I'm really looking forward to it now.'

'And we are too. It will be great to catch up properly again and I can't wait to show you around.'

'Great. I'll be in touch as soon as I have dates.'

'Give my love to Rob, won't you? And tell him we'll look after you here.'

'Bye, Aidan. See you soon.'

'*Adiós, amigo. Te veo pronto.*' And he was gone.

She threw her phone onto the bed and lay back on the comfy feather duvet. It was only eight o'clock but it wouldn't be difficult to fall asleep there. They'd recently done the room up and the soft creams and purples were very relaxing. Despite Rob's reluctance to do much around the house, he was a perfectionist and liked everything to look neat and tidy. He hated mess and so other than a

Precious Amber Rituals candle and matching scented sticks placed carefully on the dressing table, the room was free from clutter. Of course it wouldn't be so neat if Linda didn't pick up Rob's boxers and towel from the floor every morning and carefully make up the bed. She'd sourced the headboard and lockers from an antique shop and had painted them cream to fit in with the décor, and the heavy purple velvet curtains added a touch of decadence.

The sound of a bed creaking from the room next door reminded her that she'd hardly spoken to Ben since he'd got home from school. Both children had eaten their dinner at speed and retreated to their bedrooms. She could tell from the low murmuring coming from Shauna's room that she was on the phone so she decided to pop in to have a chat with Ben. She knocked softy on the door but walked in before there was an answer. Small for his age, he looked child-like lying on the bed, a fluffy blanket covering his legs, his face glued to the pages of a book. He didn't even look up when she stepped inside.

'Hiya, love. Are you okay?'

'Yep.'

'What are you reading?'

'*A Dance with Dragons.*'

'I thought you were reading *Game of Thrones.*' She sat down at the end of his bed, hoping for at least a few civil words.

'Same series.'

'Any good?'

He shrugged his shoulders, still not looking up, and she suddenly felt a surge of rage. She reached over and grabbed the book from his hands.

'Mum! What are you doing?'

At last some eye contact. 'Ben, I was talking to you. You could have at least put your book down for two minutes to talk back to me. Honestly, sometimes I feel like you don't live in the real world at all.'

He grabbed the book back out of her hand. 'Reading is good, Mum. What if I was out drinking or running wild around the streets? I'm not doing anyone any harm.'

'That's true,' she said, gently, aware that it was the most he'd said to her in weeks. 'And I love that you read so much. But a little bit of wild never hurt anyone.'

'Well, it's not me. I'm happy with my books.'

A surge of love washed over her at his innocent face. He really was a good boy. He was good academically and he never caused her a bit of trouble. And yet he worried her every day. His hermitic behaviour wasn't normal for a boy his age and she sometimes wished he'd go off with some friends and get into a bit of mischief.

'So is that all?' It was clear he wasn't up for chit-chat.

'Tell me about school,' she said, in an effort to draw him out.

'Nothing to tell.'

'Did you have a good day?'

'Same as ever.' He was back looking at his book.

She shifted further onto the bed to catch his eye again. 'Why don't you make some plans for this weekend. I haven't heard you talk about Cian or Leo in ages. What are they up to these days?'

He shrugged.

'Why don't you see if they'd like to come over on Saturday. You could all walk down to the village and get a burger or something.'

'Maybe.'

Linda sighed and stood up. It was clear she wasn't going to get much more out of him at the moment. But at least he hadn't balked at having the boys over at the weekend. Cian and Leo had been Ben's best friends since their first day at primary school. They'd done everything together and had been a tight little group. But since they'd started secondary school last September and gone to different schools, it seemed they'd drifted apart. Linda wasn't sure Ben had any friends at all in school and that worried her. But people had reassured her that the first year could be challenging for everyone. The hours were longer and the work harder. Between school hours and homework, there wasn't much time for anything else. 'He'll adjust,' her mother had said. 'It will just take time.' She hoped so. Because looking at him from the bedroom door, his head tilted towards his book, he looked so young. So vulnerable. She wanted to sweep him up in her arms and hug him like she used to when he was little. But at thirteen, he didn't do hugs anymore and that made her sad.

She stepped out of the room with a sigh and closed the door. The sound of laughter coming from Shauna's room startled her and she wondered if she had somebody in there with her. But she was probably just on the phone as usual. It felt like she was losing her two children. One didn't communicate with her at all and the other spoke to her like she was a piece of dirt on her shoe. She'd always prided herself on being a good mother. She'd brought her children up well – or so she'd thought. So where had it all gone wrong?

Her head was pounding as she headed back downstairs, all earlier excitement about her trip to Spain dimmed. She'd been mad to think she could get away on her own for a while. How could she leave her dysfunctional family? How would they get by without her? But then Ger's words resonated in her head. *You've got to fasten your own seatbelt before you attend to the children. Because if you're not safe, then the children won't survive.* And maybe she was right. She had to recharge her own batteries so that she'd have the energy to cope with all that life threw at her. A little bubble of excitement began to rise again and she realised that's what she needed. She needed to feel alive. To feel that zest for life again.

Rob was sitting in his armchair reading the newspaper when she burst into the sitting room. No doubt the dinner things would be still sitting on the table, as always, waiting for her to do her wifely duties. But it didn't bother her tonight. Because tonight she was making plans to reclaim Linda Costa. She was going to start by taking better care of herself. She'd been shocked when she'd looked at herself properly in the mirror. She'd really let herself go. But there was no reason she couldn't make herself beautiful again. She still had those big eyes that Rob had always called her 'pools of darkness' and a good hair product could sort out her frizz. And a trip to the Mac counter could sort her out with some new make-up so she could begin to feel confident again. Then she was going to head off in search of that bubbly, happy girl who she was sure still lived inside her.

'I'm going.'

'What?' Rob glanced at her over the top of his paper.

'Just as you suggested. I'm heading over to see Aidan.'

'That's great, love.' He resumed his reading.

'Rob, you're not listening to me. I'm actually going. I'm going to go over to Spain alone to finish my book and to take some time out.' She walked over and pulled the paper out of his hands and threw it on the coffee table.

'Jeez. Take it easy, love. What has you so fired up?'

'I feel you're not taking me seriously. Did you hear me? I'm going. I've already been on the phone to Aidan and he's delighted so all that's left is to fix the dates. Preferably in the next week or two.'

Now she had his attention. 'That soon? What's the hurry?'

'God, Rob. Have you not been listening to a word I said? I need a break and it can't come soon enough. Now, are you going to support me like you said you would? Are you going to arrange time off work to look after things here?'

He looked as though he was about to object when suddenly a smile crept across his face. 'Sure, love. We'll work something out.' And he was back reading his paper.

He didn't think she'd do it. He was just humouring her – making the big gesture of offering to hold the fort but all the time believing she wouldn't go through with it. She was raging with herself for thinking he was sincere, but she wasn't going to back down now. She was going to make sure it happened. As she walked into the kitchen to the post-dinner mess, her phone beeped in her pocket. It was Aidan.

Hurry over, Linda. I can't wait to see you. We're going to have the best time.

And there was a picture of a sunset over the beach. Her heart leaped at the thought of it and she decided right there and then that nothing was going to stop her. Not the looming deadline for her book. Not her ailing dad or her troublesome kids. And certainly not her husband. Because this was his time to step up and allow her to blossom. To find herself, as Ger would say. As she scraped the remains of the dinner into the bin and loaded the dishwasher, she was aware of the bubbles of excitement in her stomach. Something told her that the coming months would change her life for ever. One way or the other.

Chapter 4

'Morning, Rob. I hear you're leaving us.'

'News travels fast around here, doesn't it,' said Rob, forcing a smile. Jim Quinn was dangerous. He always had his ear to the ground and knew everything that was going on in Delahunty Insurance. Except he didn't always have his facts right.

'You know what this place is like,' laughed Jim. 'The walls have ears.'

Rob strode quickly to his office and closed the door behind him before he could be drawn into the conversation. Shit! What the hell was he doing? He'd gotten carried away with the whole notion of changing his life. Getting out of the humdrum of nine to five and starting something afresh. He'd be fifty next year and he wanted it to be the start of a whole new chapter in his life. Since Linda had gotten her huge advance she'd been at him to reduce his hours in work or give it up altogether and although he'd balked at the idea at first, he'd warmed to it eventually. But the problem was that Linda thought giving up his job would mean him spending a lot more time at home. And that wasn't part of his plan at all. The thought of hanging around the house all day filled him with dread. He'd be bored to tears. He needed to be out in the workforce earning money. Being a man. And if he was to try and get a business off the ground, he'd need to invest time into it and that would mean being out of the house a lot – setting up meetings, schmoozing with people who could help him and generally working more hours than he was at present. It wouldn't matter if the money didn't roll in straight away, because with the remainder of the mortgage paid off from Linda's advance, the pressure was off. But now as the word had gotten out that he was leaving, he was having second thoughts.

He opened the Brooker file in front of him but his thoughts were a million miles from settling a claim for a burglary. Up until last year, life had been great. He, Linda and the kids had a proper set-up – one to be envied. He had a good, pensionable job while Linda was at home looking after all that domestic stuff. Yes, she'd aspired to being a published author, but she'd managed to fit her writing in between the house stuff. It had been the perfect arrangement. But ever since the book deal, things had changed. She now moaned relentlessly about housework and the kids and claimed they should share the chores at home. He'd never heard anything so ridiculous. He wasn't there, for God's sake. He left for work at seven thirty every morning and wasn't home until at least six thirty in the evening. She was at home and other than a bit of writing when things were quiet, she had all the time in the day to do other stuff. There was no comparison between their jobs. Yes, she'd earned a huge advance for the writing and he was delighted to have that as a backup for them, but it couldn't be compared to a long, hard day of work five days a week.

He was startled suddenly by a knock, followed by his office door opening. Tanya, one of his colleagues, stood there with a file in her hands.

'Rob, I answered your phone earlier when I was passing by. It was Margaret Lester to say she's running a bit late today. She said she'd be here around ten. Give her a buzz if it's a problem.'

'That's fine, Tanya. Thanks for answering the call.' Rob often dreamed of releasing Tanya's raven hair from the many clips that secured it into a neat bun at the back of her head and watching while she shook it all out. He'd then remove those black-rimmed glasses, and with her startling green eyes she'd invite him to touch her. He'd peel her clothes off slowly and bury his head in her ample breasts. It was a scene he lived out in his head almost every day and one that invaded his dreams. They often worked together on projects and they made a very good team.

'Rob?' She was hovering at the door, obviously waiting for a response to a question he hadn't heard.

'Sorry, what was that?'

'I was just saying did you want to catch up on the Morton file later. Come to my office around twelve if you're free.'

'Yep, that suits me. I have no other appointments today.'

He watched through his window as she tottered on her kitten heels back to her own office, before giving himself a mental shake. He would never go there. The fantasies he harboured in his head would remain there because he'd never cheat on his wife. And besides, despite his inappropriate thoughts, he respected Tanya. She was smart and hard-working, and they often spent their lunchbreaks chatting about all sorts of stuff. It was good to have somebody who was interested in his views and who wanted to spend time with him. He was sure that she would have liked more from him if he wasn't married. She'd never said as much but it was there in the way she looked at him and how she acted. Nothing had ever happened between them and never would, but it did his ego good to know that he was still desirable.

He sighed as his thoughts returned to his wife. Things had just become so monotonous between him and Linda. She used to be so vibrant. So up for a laugh. Their sex life had been great and they were never short on ideas in the bedroom. They used to like to keep things fresh and interesting and never, ever boring. He smiled to himself as he remembered how they'd pull themselves apart, drenched in sweat but happy and sated. They'd sleep like babies afterwards and would always wake up in great form, feeling like the luckiest people on earth.

Nowadays sex was routine. If Linda wasn't too tired to partake, they'd just go through the motions, neither feeling particularly satisfied afterwards. The thing was, he still lusted after his wife. He wanted more than anything for them to get back what they had before. But he was only human and if things didn't change soon, he wasn't sure what was going to happen. He'd given the impression to Linda that he was on board with her plan of a little trip away, but nothing could be further from the truth. He hated the idea and he was hoping that by him being nice and accommodating about it, she'd change her mind. He really didn't want her to go, for several reasons. Firstly, he really didn't fancy having to run things at home on his own. Dealing with tedious stuff like housework and looking after the kids wasn't for him. But the main thing was he was afraid that Linda going away would just serve to broaden the already growing gap between them. He was scared.

A ping from his computer jolted him out of his reverie and he sat up straight, running his hand through his thick mop of black hair. He really shouldn't allow himself to think the worst. Things were good for the most part with him and Linda and there was no point thinking otherwise. He just needed to find a way to get them back on track. To remind them of how things used to be before life got in the way. Linda had said that she wanted to get away to recharge her batteries but maybe that was another way of saying she was bored. Bored with her routine and bored with him. He put his head in his hands and tried to think of a solution. Maybe if he spiced things up a bit – was a bit more spontaneous like he used to be – then she'd appreciate him more.

Buoyed up with the idea, he felt a flutter of excitement. Their bedroom lives could certainly do with some improvement so maybe that's where he'd start. He could feel himself being turned on as he pictured Linda naked – confidently sprawled across the bed, waiting for him to please her. Lately she'd insisted on having the lights off, claiming she'd put on weight and would hate it if he tried to look at her body. But he'd soon put an end to that. He'd reassure her she was beautiful and help her to relax.

'Margaret Lester is here,' came a voice from reception through his phone. 'Should I send her in?'

'Please do. Thanks.'

As he cleared some of the rubbish from his desk, he saw Tanya coming out of her office to go to the kitchen. Her slow, sexy walk suggested she knew he was watching. And it was as though she was putting on a show for him as she bent down to pick something up off the floor. The picture of Linda quickly faded from his mind, replaced with one of Tanya lying on his bed. Those breasts. That soft white skin. He was sure she wore those low-cut tops on purpose just to tantalise him. And it certainly worked. He sighed and forced himself to pull the Lester file from his drawer and concentrate on the meeting ahead. Once that was finished, and he'd spoken with Tanya, he'd make his excuses and slip off home. If things went well, he should finally be able to stop having inappropriate thoughts of other women and Linda would forget her silly idea of heading off to Spain without him.

Rob's excitement grew as he turned the corner into the little housing estate where he lived. Linda would be surprised to see him. It was only one thirty and he'd managed to sort things out in work so that he could have the rest of the day off. He'd stopped off at their favourite deli in the village and had picked up some quiche and salad and some of the breads Linda liked. Ben and Shauna would be at school, so they'd have the house to themselves. It was the perfect opportunity for them to spend some quality time together and for him to show his wife how much she meant to him.

Her little black Volkswagen Golf sat in the driveway, reassuring him of her presence, and he pulled his Audi in beside it. Loosening his tie and opening the top button of his tailored shirt, he swept his hand through his hair before opening the front door. An overwhelming smell of garlic greeted him and he followed the clattering sound of pots into the kitchen.

'Hi, love,' he said, taking in the chaotic scene. 'You look busy.'

Linda spun around to face him. 'I'm always busy. And what are you doing home anyway? It's only lunchtime.'

'I came to surprise you. I've taken the rest of the day off.'

'Oh,' said Linda, turning back to resume her task of stirring multiple pots on the hob. 'Nice.'

'You don't sound very happy about it. Why don't you leave all that and come and sit down? I'll make us a nice cup of tea and we can chat.'

'Rob, I really don't have time to chat.' She nodded towards her laptop, which was open on the kitchen counter. 'I'm trying to get some writing done in between chopping vegetables and stirring pots. Can't you see I'm up to my eyes?'

He went over to her and leaned against the kitchen counter. 'What's all this anyway?' he said. 'It looks like you're feeding an army. Why don't you forget about dinner? I've brought home some stuff from the deli in the village. We can have that instead.'

'Oh well that's lovely. If you'd told me that a couple of hours ago, I could have concentrated on writing this book instead of spending all this time cooking. But I've already been to the shops, prepared the chicken and the vegetables, made the sauce, before remembering that Shauna is completely veggie now and won't touch a chicken and pasta bake. So I have another dinner on the go for her, which I'm sure she'll turn her nose up to and I just can't—'

'Linda, Linda. You've got to calm down. How can you let a little thing like dinner get to you so much? You'd want to come to work with me and see what real pressure is.' He had the words out of his mouth before he realised what he'd said but it was too late to save himself. She spun around to face him, eyes glistening with anger and her mouth trembled as she spoke.

'How dare you, Roberto Costa. How bloody dare you. Just because you go out to your high-flying, poncey job in a suit and tie and talk shite all day to gullible customers doesn't make you any better than me. You sit on your arse at your desk for most of the day when I'm at home juggling a million things and getting no appreciation for it.'

'Linda please. I—'

'No, Rob. It's not on. This is why I feel like I'm at the end of my tether. Do you realise what my day consists of?'

'Of course I—'

'Well, let me tell you.' She paused for a breath, but he knew it was no use intervening. He'd have to let the storm run its course.

'I get up in the morning,' she continued, 'with a million things on my to-do list. I empty the dishwasher, clean up after breakfast, hoover, dust, clean the toilets and that's even before I get my own breakfast. Then I need to plan the dinner, and more often than not, that requires a trip to the supermarket to stock up on food. And while the dinner is on, bearing in mind it wasn't made by the fairies, I sort out the washing I put on earlier, iron the dry clothes and put on another load. So when I finally have time to take a breath, and bear in mind we're into the afternoon at this stage, then, and only then, I might have a chance to sit at my desk and do some writing.'

Rob was about to say something, but she wasn't finished yet.

'And then when I finally get the chance to settle down to my writing job, the kids are home from school and the chaos begins again.'

He could see she was trying not to cry but she was shaking and her lip was quivering. He looked at her with her chestnut hair piled up on top of her head, her dark eyes glistening with tears, and he couldn't have loved her more.

'Come on,' he said, gently taking a ladle from her hands and placing it on the kitchen counter. 'Come and sit down. I'm sorry for saying what I said. It was insensitive. I know you work hard and I probably take you for granted a lot of the time.'

That seemed to pacify her slightly. She switched the cooker off and allowed him to lead her to the kitchen table. Sitting down, she put her head in her hands, elbows leaning on the table, and rocked back and forth slowly. This worried Rob slightly and he wasn't sure how to handle her behaviour.

'Linda love, look at me.'

She raised her head slowly, but began rubbing her temples.

'How come you're feeling this way now? What's changed in the last few years? I thought you were happy. I thought you enjoyed being at home. What's got you so frustrated with everything?'

'That's just it, Rob,' she said, finally sitting upright in the chair. 'I haven't been happy for a long time. You just haven't noticed.'

Rob's blood ran cold. Was she about to say that she wanted to leave him? Surely not. Surely whatever was wrong could be fixed easily enough. They loved each other, didn't they? Till death do us part. She reached over and took his hand.

'It's not your fault. Well, not really. You're out all day so you don't see how hard it is for me.'

'But the kids are older now. More self-sufficient. Surely your life is easier now.'

'Having teenagers makes the baby years seem like a doddle. Did you know that Ben seems to have some sort of social anxiety? I can't get him to go out with his friends or even to have them over. And Shauna is another story. She's heading down a road we don't want her to go and I don't know what to do about it.'

Rob smiled. 'They'll be fine, love. It's just the usual teenage stuff. I wouldn't worry about it.'

'You see,' she said, her lip beginning to quiver again, and he feared a repeat of her earlier breakdown, 'that's your answer to everything. "I wouldn't worry about it." But somebody has to worry. Somebody has to do something about it. I've been down to the school more times than I can count about Shauna's behaviour. Did you know that?'

'Well, I knew you had to speak to her year head on a couple of occasions, but I didn't—'

'More than a couple, Rob. And did you even know she'd turned vegetarian, making my life twice as difficult? Honestly, if you think running a household and rearing a family while trying to fit in a day job is easy, why don't you try it for a bit.'

'Why don't we make love?'

Her mouth opened but no words came out.

'Come on, Linda. Let's go upstairs right now and make love. While it's just the two of us – no kids, no distractions, just you and me.'

'I … I can't believe you're asking me to do that when we're in the middle of an argument.' She was mad, but he could see a flicker of something in her eyes that encouraged him to continue.

'Remember when we were younger and we used to have blazing rows? Remember how we made up afterwards? Didn't you always say that the best part of our arguments was the making up?'

Her face softened then and a smile formed on her lips. 'They were good times. When we were young and free and had the whole world at our feet.'

'Well then, let's pretend. Let's pretend nobody else exists and it's just the two of us.' He stood up and held out his hand. 'I love you, Linda. And I want you to be happy. Let's be spontaneous like we used to be. Come on, live a little.'

To his relief she stood up and took his hand and allowed him to lead her up to the bedroom. Maybe this would be the start of something new for them. Maybe when he was running his own business there'd be more afternoons like this when they could reconnect and bring back some of the old magic. He certainly hoped so.

Afterwards they lay side by side, each looking up to the ceiling, lost in thought. It hadn't been the explosion he'd hoped for and he was left feeling a little bit empty. He glanced sideways at Linda and by the look on her face, he guessed she was feeling the same way too.

'Rob,' she said, not looking at him.

'Yes?'

'I still need to get away.'

Something felt different. Wrong. And tears pricked his eyes.

'It won't be for long,' she continued. 'But it's something I need to do.'

He reached over and took her hand in his. Squeezing it tightly, he nodded his head in resignation. It would make or break them, he was sure of it. But it had to be done.

Chapter 5

'I think it's fabulous, love. You go off and have a good time. You deserve it.'

Linda smiled at her mum's reaction to the news that she was heading off to Spain for a couple of weeks. Alice Bell was a young woman trapped in the body of a seventy-eight-year-old and given half the chance, she'd be on that plane with her daughter.

'Thanks, Mum,' said Linda, perching the phone on her shoulder while she tried to get through the mound of ironing that seemed to multiply overnight. 'I feel guilty about it but I think it's the right thing to do.'

'Of course it is. And why would you feel guilty? Aren't you entitled to some time away?'

Linda sighed.

'And don't start thinking like you're abandoning them,' continued her mother. 'You do a lot for that family of yours and now it's their time to give back.'

She smiled at her mother's perception. 'I suppose you're right. And anyway, I've booked the flights now. I go a week from today and to be honest, it can't come soon enough.'

'Good girl. Now, I'd offer to go over to the house and help while you're gone but between golf and bridge and looking after your daddy, I don't think I'll have the time.'

'Don't worry, Mum. I don't expect you to come over. It will do Rob and the kids good to have to fend for themselves for a while. Maybe they'll start appreciating how much I do for them.' She hung a sixth shirt belonging to Rob on a hanger and wondered if he ever gave any serious thought to how clean, ironed shirts were always hanging in his wardrobe.

'That's true,' said her mum. 'And Shauna should be chipping in more. She's sixteen years old. She should be well able to cook a dinner at the very least.'

'Oh, she's capable alright. But there's always an excuse not to help out. She doesn't want to break her nails. Her hair will get smelly if she cooks and she's not due to wash it. She has her period. Honestly, that girl could dodge an elephant if it was running at her. Her latest excuse not to help out in the kitchen is that she's a veggie now and it offends her to touch meat!'

'Well, let her make vegetarian meals. Use your head, darling. Don't let her get away with it. It won't bode well for when she's older and living out of home. I love that girl to bits but she has a lot to learn.'

Her mother had a point. Linda had been helping with chores at home from about the age of four and she grew up appreciating how much needed to be done in a house. And she had also gained valuable skills like cooking and managing a budget from an early age. She'd really have to do something about Shauna's behaviour before it was too late.

'Are you still there, love?' There was concern in her mother's voice. 'I didn't mean to criticise. It's just that after her recent drunken episode and from what you've told me about her attitude towards you, I worry, that's all.'

'I know you do, Mum. And so do I. It's just Shauna and I seem to clash over everything. Maybe me going away will be a good thing for her. Maybe Rob will be able to handle her better. She's a real daddy's girl and wouldn't want him to think badly of her.'

'You see? It's the right thing to do all around. Get yourself off and forget about home for a while. Get that book written and enjoy some you-time. I've a good mind to join you myself.'

Linda stifled a giggle. 'Maybe you could fly out for a few days after I get settled. I'm sure Aidan wouldn't mind.'

'Ah I'd love to. But what would I do with your daddy? He wouldn't cope on his own.'

'Send him over to Rob and the kids,' giggled Linda, imagining her husband's reaction to looking after his grumpy father-in-law. 'Since he thinks running a house is a doddle, it would give him something to do.'

Her mum laughed out loud. 'Tempting though it is, I think I'll leave this trip to you. It wouldn't be worth the fall-out if I told your daddy I was escaping off to Spain without him.'

Linda decided to say no more on the subject, just in case her mother decided to rock up to Spain with her dad in tow. 'I have to go, Mum. The kids are off early today and I have a mountain of things to get done before they come home. I'll try to get over to you before I head off next week.'

'Take care, love, and we'll chat soon.'

Linda set her mobile phone down on the kitchen counter and rubbed her neck. She knew she shouldn't talk on the phone while ironing because she always ended up with a crick in her neck. But it made a menial job so much easier when she could chat while doing it. Delighted with having got through such a huge pile of clothes, she folded up the ironing board and unplugged the iron.

Just then, the front door slammed and Linda sighed. The precious few morning hours seemed to have slipped away from her and it was already lunchtime. School finished at one on Fridays and although she hated to admit it, it was her least favourite day of the week. It's not that she didn't like having the kids around. They didn't bother her much, for the most part. But it was impossible to get any writing done between doors slamming, TV blaring and a constant stream of traffic in and out of the kitchen. Ben could often be found standing staring into the fridge, moaning that 'there's no food in this house', while Shauna could be heard making retching sounds at the sight of anything that didn't either grow on a tree or come from the ground. After Linda's first book was published, Rob had promised that they'd build an office at the back of the house for her but it had never happened. So she mostly perched at the kitchen table with her laptop, which was fine when the house was quiet but when everyone was home, it put her right in the middle of all the activity.

The sound of a bedroom door slamming shut told her it was Shauna who'd come home. Ben would at least come in and say hello, whereas her daughter wouldn't bother unless she wanted something. Suddenly thoughts of clear blue skies and sandy beaches flooded her mind and she knew she was doing the right thing by getting away. Let Rob live her life for a while. Maybe she'd even make a few appointments and stick them on the calendar. Shauna needed to have blood tests to check her iron levels, which had been very low earlier in the year, and Ben was due an orthodontist appointment. Her husband needed to see what she had to juggle on a day-to-day basis. There was no point in making it all too easy for him. A smile crossed her lips as she headed upstairs with a basket of clothes to give to Shauna. She was going to enjoy hearing about the chaos from afar.

'Shauna.' She knocked on her daughter's bedroom door but there was no sound from inside. 'I have your washing here, love. I'll just leave it outside.'

Shauna's low iron meant she got very tired and would often take a nap when she got in from school. Linda didn't want to disturb her because while she was asleep, there were no dramas. But something was niggling at her as she walked back downstairs. It had gone very quiet very quickly. There were usually plenty of bangs and crashes to be heard from Shauna's room before she got to the point of a nap.

So, whether from motherly instincts or just curiosity, Linda turned around and headed back up the stairs. Her heart began to beat faster as she put her hand on the door handle and pushed it open.

'Mum!'

Linda's eyes opened wide when she saw her daughter scrambling to sit up with Craig Boland sprawled half way across her.

'Jesus Christ, Shauna. What's going on here?'

They both sat up looking dishevelled and guilty and Linda didn't know whether to laugh or cry.

'We weren't doing anything wrong, Mum. We were just kissing so what's the problem?'

It was true. Or at least Linda hoped so. They were both fully clothed and it looked like they were just having a snog. Although if she hadn't come in … But she had, and she was going to let them know she wasn't standing for that sort of behaviour.

'Craig, I think you should head off home now. Tell your mum I'll see her for tennis someday next week.' Mentioning his mother was a threat and he knew it. Craig Boland was a harmless enough kid but she didn't want Shauna getting into anything serious with a boy. Although she hated to admit it, she was probably more worried about Shauna's bad influence on him than the other way around. The boy grabbed his jacked and scuttled off without saying a word and Linda braced herself for her daughter's wrath.

'For fuck's sake, Mum. What did you go and do that for?'

'Language, Shauna. And don't you dare speak to me like that. I won't have you bringing boys up to your bedroom. Who knows what would have happened if I hadn't walked in.'

'Oh chill, for God's sake. We were only kissing. What's the harm in that? Did you never kiss a boy when you were my age?'

'What I did at your age is no concern of yours. And I'm not saying there's anything wrong with a bit of kissing but there's a time and a place. And the right place isn't up in your bedroom alone. There are too many temptations up here.'

Shauna lay her head back on the pillow and put her hands over her ears. 'Please don't do the birds and the bees talk again. I couldn't stand it.'

'I think we've covered the birds and the bees previously,' said Linda, smiling at her daughter, 'but it would be nice to have a chat. A heart-to-heart just like we used to.'

'Can we do it another time? I have a splitting headache.'

Linda relented. 'Okay. Now, are you coming down for something to eat? Dinner will be late tonight because Dad has a meeting but there's nice fresh bread there if you want a sandwich.'

'I'm alright. I'm going to take a nap.' That was the end of the conversation. Shauna rolled onto her side and stuck her earphones in her ears. How easily she could dismiss her mother. How easily Linda allowed her to.

Ben was coming in the door when she came back downstairs and, unlike Shauna, she didn't have to persuade him to eat. He muttered a hello and went straight to the fridge. She watched him stand there for about three minutes glaring into the packed shelves before closing it and muttering, 'There's never anything to eat in this house.' He grabbed a packet of crisps from the treat drawer before retreating upstairs.

At that point, Linda would usually lecture him about healthy eating. She'd offer to make him a sandwich to have with his crisps and would warn him off playing his video game until he'd finished his homework. But she didn't have the energy today. If he wanted to eat rubbish and play the Xbox for the rest of the evening in his room, she wasn't going to argue. At least with both children upstairs, she could take advantage of the peace and quiet. She took her laptop from the dresser drawer and sat down at the kitchen table.

She scrolled through her documents and clicked on the one entitled *Book 2 – Will Never Happen*. She smiled to herself remembering Ger's reaction when she'd seen it one day. Linda had let her read a section to see if it flowed well and when she noticed the name, she tutted and shook her head. 'Linda, for God's sake,' she'd said, rolling her eyes. 'What have I told you about positivity. You get back what you put out into the universe. And you're setting yourself up to fail. Now you need to change that to *Book 2 – Bestseller*. Linda had meekly complied but as soon as Ger had left, she promptly deleted what she'd written and changed the title back to her negative one. She was all about realism.

Reading back the small amount she'd written, Linda quickly realised how out of touch she was with the book. The problem was consistency. She needed to get her bum on the seat and stay there until the words flowed out of her like a waterfall. At the moment, it was more like a blocked tap with drips here and there. The word count showed her she'd just passed ten thousand, which was a long way from the hundred thousand words that her publisher would expect. She had a mountain to climb and she wondered if she'd ever get there. Spain was her last hope and if that didn't work, she could forget it.

For the next hour she tried to concentrate, but pictures of Shauna and Craig kept flooding her mind. She'd really want to keep an eye on that pair. If they were bold enough to lie on Shauna's bed kissing while she was in the house, what would they do if they had the house to themselves? A cold chill ran down her spine. Shauna was sixteen years old, for God's sake. She was way too young for any of that funny business. She'd have to warn Rob. He'd lose his mind if he was to walk in on them like she had today. Suddenly, a smile crossed her lips at the thought. Although she'd still worry, it would be up to Rob to deal with things at home while she was away.

She tried to drag her mind back to the screen in front of her but too many thoughts were whirring around in her head. Eventually she realised she was just wasting her time, so with a sigh she snapped her laptop shut. There was no point trying to drag the words out when they wouldn't co-operate. And besides, she had a lot to organise before she left for her trip. It would definitely do her some good to take herself out of the equation at home for a while and concentrate on herself. A bubble of excitement rose again in her stomach. She had some packing to do.

Chapter 6

'So there are two containers of bolognese in the freezer – one normal meat one and a smaller veggie one. I've frozen some of that stew from yesterday and there's a huge bean curry in the pot that should do you for a couple of days.'

It was Friday afternoon and Linda was about to leave for her trip to Spain. 'Oh, and there's some cooked chicken in the fridge if any of you want to add it to the curry. And I got that ham that—'

'Linda, Linda. It's fine. We'll be fine, won't we, kids?'

'Yeah, go on, Mum,' said Shauna, giving her a friendly push. 'We have it all under control.'

This both pleased and worried Linda in equal measure. 'And what about you, Ben? Will you be okay while I'm gone?'

'Yes, Mum.' He didn't look at her and she could tell he was close to tears. Guilt threatened to rise up and strangle her but she wouldn't allow it to. She'd come this far and she was going to go, no matter what.

'Come on,' said Rob, ushering her from the kitchen. 'I want to get you to the airport as soon as possible so I don't get stuck in rush-hour traffic on the way home.'

Linda went to each of her children and hugged them tightly before walking out the door and into the car. She waved as the car pulled away from the house and it was only then she allowed herself to cry. She couldn't help it. Big fat tears formed in the corner of her eyes and spilled down her cheeks as she rummaged in her bag for a tissue.

'Don't cry, love,' said Rob, reaching over to touch her leg while keeping one hand firmly on the wheel. 'You need this, remember? You need to get off and recharge those batteries. And as you said yourself, you haven't a hope of finishing that book while you're at home. So look on it as a work outing. A necessity.'

She squeezed his hand in response, but something had changed. Something felt different. It was as though she was going off to make some big decisions and she wondered if her life would ever be the same again. She loved her husband. And she probably always would. But the big question on her mind was whether or not she was still *in* love with him. They had a good life but the truth was, she just wasn't happy. She hadn't been for a long time.

She glanced sideways at him as he expertly negotiated the traffic to bring them smoothly onto the M50 heading to the airport. He was such a lovely man. Handsome too, with his sallow skin and deep brown eyes. She'd fancied him like crazy when they'd worked together all those years ago. She couldn't believe her luck when he'd asked her out and then when things had progressed, she'd felt like the luckiest girl in the world. And he'd been good to her. He'd given her the two most precious things in her life, for starters. Her children, although they tested her patience, were her world and no matter what, her main priority would be to make sure they were happy.

She lay her head back on the headrest and closed her eyes. It was the day that Rob had come home from work early three weeks before that had changed everything. He'd been so lovely, coming home to surprise her and bringing lunch with him. His intentions had been good. They always were. But for some reason it had confirmed to her that there was a disconnect between them that she didn't know how to fix. And when he'd suggested they make love, she'd thought that maybe that would help things. A bit of spontaneity, just like the old days. But that's when it had all fallen apart. He'd wanted to look at her but she wanted to hide under the covers. It had all felt so awkward. So staged. As though they were playing parts in a movie and just had to get on with it. Afterwards she'd felt empty and as she'd glanced over at her husband lying beside her, she'd mourned the loss of the wonderful, exciting love affair they'd had for so many years.

'Here we are, love. You were dozing off there.'

'Gosh, so I was,' she said, realising they'd already pulled up outside Terminal One. 'So I suppose this is it.'

'Come on, I'll get your bags,' said Rob, hopping deftly from the car and opening the boot.

She followed him to the kerb where he carefully placed her

case and they stood looking at each other for a few seconds. It was strange saying goodbye to her husband as they were so rarely apart. Stepping forward, she placed her head on his chest and wrapped her arms around his waist.

'I love you, Rob. You know that, don't you?'

'Of course I do,' he said, squeezing her tightly. 'And I love you too. You'd think you were going off for a year, with all the fuss. Go and make the two weeks count. Write your book and have some fun. Then come back to us rested and happy and we can start making plans for the future.'

She nodded and kissed him softly on the lips before heading into the terminal building. How could she tell him that she wasn't sure she could see a future anymore? She'd probably been thinking that way for a while but had refused to dwell on it. But since that fateful day three weeks ago, she'd thought of nothing else. It was all such a mess. She didn't want to break up her lovely family but she just didn't know if she wanted to spend the rest of her life with Rob. Her head was a mess.

She sailed through security and even had time to sit and relax for a while. She bought herself a cup of tea and a scone and took her beloved Kindle from her bag. In years gone by, she'd have crammed a number of books into her suitcase for a holiday but now she loved that she could download as many as she liked on the Kindle. She selected a few and they appeared on her home page within seconds. She was going to enjoy having the time to read in peace and, glancing at her watch, she decided she'd have ten minutes to get started on the first one.

The time flew by and thanks to Ryanair's 'on time' pledge, she was up in the air within an hour. She ordered a glass of wine and it was only then that she finally began to relax. She was going to try, as much as possible, to leave her problems back in Ireland and concentrate on herself for a while. She couldn't wait to see Aidan and to find out what his life was like over there. The thought of the sea and sunshine filled her with excitement and almost made her forget her troubles. By the time she was finishing her second glass of wine, they'd started their descent to Murcia airport and she felt like a teenager about to embark on her first holiday away without her family.

Despite her protests earlier, they'd taken her lovely red cabin suitcase off her to put into the hold. She'd hoped to keep it with her to aid a quick exit once she got to the airport. She hated all the waiting around and fighting for a place closest to the carousel where people elbowed each other out of the way while they waited anxiously for the first glimpse of their luggage. Twenty minutes later, she was one of those people. A young couple tried to skip in front of her by shoving their brat of a kid under her arm, but she wasn't having any of it. That same kid had run up and down the aisle of the plane for almost the whole journey. He'd been pretending to be a plane by stretching out his arms and making engine noises with his lips, and despite most of the passengers tilting their heads in an 'ah look how cute' way, she just thought he was annoying. She had a chance to get her own back now, so she manoeuvred her body to block his view and didn't even feel guilty when he began to cry.

The moving carousel was having a hypnotising effect on her and she feared she'd fall asleep standing up. Damn that second glass of wine and damn the fact that she was so out of practice at drinking that even a sniff of alcohol could get her drunk. Still, it wasn't an altogether unpleasant experience and once she was safely tucked into Aidan's car and on her way, she'd be fine. Unfortunately, her suitcase was one of the last to appear, meaning she had to make way for demon child and his parents to grab theirs first. But she was determined that nothing, no matter how annoying, was going to bring her down. She was in Spain. Alone. Away from all the stresses of home and she was going to make the most of it.

The long wait for her luggage had somewhat sobered her up and by the time she walked through the arrivals gate, she was almost back to herself. It didn't take her long to pick out her friend's glowing face and she rushed to embrace him.

'I can't believe you're here,' he squealed, oblivious to the stares of people around. 'We have so much to talk about. This is going to be fabulous.'

Linda moved back and held him at arm's length to have a better look. 'Jesus, this Spanish life suits you. Would you look at the colour of you. And your hair is practically white.'

'Would you stop. Look at the state of me. I fell asleep on the sofa and jumped up when I saw the time. You're lucky I'm dressed at all.'

She linked him companionably and as they left the building and the warm air wafted over her, she felt inexplicably calm. This would be the place where she'd sort her life out. She was sure of it. And she had two whole blissful weeks to do it.

'So where's James tonight?' she said, fastening her seatbelt as Aidan sped out of the airport like a man on a mission. 'I thought he'd be here with you.'

'He's at home preparing some tapas for us. We guessed you'd be hungry but it's a bit late for a big meal.'

She could feel the wine sloshing around in her stomach and she wasn't sure if she'd be able to eat anything, but by the time the car pulled up at the gate, she was ravenous.

'Here we are,' said Aidan, leaning out the window to punch in a code. 'Home sweet home.'

Linda's eyes almost popped out of her head when she saw the beautiful villa, with its own private pool and grounds. 'This is amazing, Aidan. I can't believe you live in such a swanky place. Is it divided into apartments inside?'

'Em, not exactly.'

'It's never one place,' she said, her mouth gaping open. 'You're not telling me you and James live here alone. Just the two of you.'

'I'm afraid so.' His cheeks reddened as she stared at him. 'Not what you were expecting then?'

The car came to a stop and she didn't have time to answer him as James appeared at the door to welcome her. She stepped out and again felt the heat embracing her tired body. She went straight to James and hugged him tightly.

'Welcome to Spain, Linda. You're going to love it here so much that you won't want to go home.'

He didn't know how close to the truth he was but she smiled and hugged him back. 'This place, though. It's unbelievable. I thought when you said you'd moved to somewhere more spacious that you meant an apartment with an extra bedroom. But wow!'

'Come on,' said Aidan, appearing at her side with her suitcase. 'Let's get you inside and we can show you around.'

It was like a palace. The white marble floors inside lent a cool contrast to the boiling temperature and the modern décor filled the place with light. Everywhere seemed to be white, with little splashes of colour, and Linda felt as though she'd just walked into the pages of *Vogue Living*. James led the way into the equally white kitchen, where he'd set the table with an array of delicious-looking treats.

'Let's eat,' he said, indicating for her to sit down on one of the white leather chairs. 'We can show you around afterwards. Will you have red or white?'

Linda hesitated for a moment, remembering how the earlier wine had made her feel. Still, out here she had no responsibilities. No alarm clock waking her up in the morning. Nobody to be accountable to except herself. So no reason to stay sober.

'White please,' she said, holding out her glass. 'And make it a large one. We have a lot to talk about. Starting with how the hell does a struggling writer afford a place like this?'

'We're just looking after it for a friend,' said Aidan. 'He's overseas at the moment so he didn't want to leave it empty.'

Linda shook her head in wonder. 'Amazing. He's some friend to hand over this place. How long will you have it for?'

'We're not sure,' said James. 'Now, let's have a toast to us all. The Three Musketeers. Here's to a fun-filled, fabulous couple of weeks.'

They laughed as they clinked glasses but a look between Aidan and James hadn't gone unnoticed by Linda. They were being very coy about their home. Avoiding questions and looking shifty. Well, they were only on their first glass. Give it another two or three and she'd find out what was going on. Because there was no way they could afford a place like this on salaries like theirs, and she had her doubts about the friend story. So either they were secret millionaires or they'd come by the money through ill-gotten gains. She hoped it was the former, because the other was too shocking to contemplate. But one thing was for sure, she'd get to the bottom of it. Just like Detective Fiona Regan in her novel, she was good at sniffing out the truth.

Chapter 7

Linda sat close to the pool trying not to retch as she sipped a glass of water. Her over-sized sunglasses hid the black circles beneath her eyes as she huddled under the shade of a tree. The burning sun was threatening to split her head in two and she winced at the pain. It was a far cry from how she pictured herself when she'd thought of her time in Spain. She'd imagined her bikini-clad body turning golden beneath the glistening sun as she sipped sangria from a glass decorated with colourful umbrellas. Still, it was only day one. There'd be plenty of time for the Spanish experience once she'd settled in.

Aidan and James had been the perfect hosts the previous evening and had given her the most wonderful welcome. James was a chef, and a very good one too, and it had showed in the food. He'd made her close her eyes while she tasted the delicious bite-sized portions and she'd been amazed at how her taste buds had exploded with the flavours. But then of course it was necessary to clear the pallet with some wine between tastings, hence the rotten hangover today.

They'd both left before she even woke, and Aidan had written a note to say he was meeting his publisher and would be back for lunch. A glance at her phone told her it was just gone twelve so hopefully she'd be over the worst before he got back. Her stomach was beginning to make hunger noises, which was a good sign, compared to the 'threatening to vomit' noises it was making earlier. She might even be able to manage some leftover tapas soon enough.

The late September sun was still strong enough to cause serious damage, so she sat up and slathered herself with sun cream before venturing out from under the tree. Once she'd found the optimum position, she lay back and began to relax. She envied Aidan's dedication to his writing. Although if she was half as talented as he was, she might be a bit more enthusiastic. He wrote children's books. Wonderful stories of magical worlds with fairies and goblins that could draw children in with the very first sentence. And he illustrated too. He'd even won an award for a book he'd both written and illustrated a couple of years back.

Just then her phone rang, startling her, but she smiled when she saw Ger's name flashing up on the screen. 'Hi, Ger.'

'Hello, you. So you've done it. I honestly didn't think you would.'

'I wasn't sure myself,' said Linda, shifting her bum to a more comfortable position on the sun lounger. 'But you were right.'

'About?'

'About needing to get away. As soon as I realised that, I knew I'd have to do it. For my sanity.'

'Go on then. Tell me all about it. I'm so jealous of you over there in the sun. It's lashing rain over here.'

'It's amazing, Ger. You'd want to see the house. It's like something out of a magazine.'

Ger whistled. 'I thought you said they lived in an apartment.'

'I did. And I thought so too. But it's a mansion. They said they're looking after it for a friend but I'm not sure. It sounds a bit fishy to me.'

'What do you mean?' said Ger. 'Why would they lie? Do you think they own it?'

Linda thought for a moment. 'I don't know. It's just how they are when I ask them about it. They give each other that look.'

'What look?'

'You know the one where your eyes close slightly and your head tilts. It's like they're trying to decide what or how much to tell me.'

Ger giggled. 'You're gas, Linda. You'd know you were a writer. Always looking for a story. I reckon you're imagining the look. They're probably embarrassed because they're getting it rent-free or something. They wouldn't want you to think they're free-loaders.'

'Maybe,' said Linda, but she wasn't convinced.

'And anyway,' continued Ger, 'didn't you say that neither of them had a big salary? So how could they afford something like that?'

'Exactly.'

'Okay. I'm lost. I'm not sure where you're going with this but forget about the house for the moment. Tell me about Spain. What's it like over there? What are you up to?'

They spent a pleasant twenty minutes chatting and by the time they'd finished, Linda was feeling a whole lot better and was looking forward to some lunch. It was almost one o'clock so maybe she'd go in and get something ready for when Aidan got home. She'd hate him to think she was waiting for him to make her something to eat. And anyway, the sun was getting way too hot. She'd come back out in the late afternoon when it was cooler and maybe get stuck into her book. She reached down underneath the sun lounger where she'd left her Kindle and checked to see if it needed to be charged. Switching it on, she waited until the screen filled with her newly downloaded book. Nadia Bernio. Now there was a woman she envied.

Her first book had been published over a year ago and had been hugely successful. It was branded as 'racy fiction'. Something along the lines of *Fifty Shades* but with more of a story to it. Despite her determination to hate it, Linda had thoroughly enjoyed the book. It had relatable characters and the sex scenes, although fairly graphic, were tastefully written and certainly made her heart race. It had sold millions of copies all over the world, as had her second one, which Linda had loved also. She'd just published her third, which was the one on Linda's Kindle, and she couldn't wait to get stuck in.

Leaving everything else outside ready for her return later, she gathered up her phone and Kindle, for fear they'd overheat in the sun, and headed in. The cool floor tiles were a joy to her burning feet and she almost felt cold from the air-conditioning. Ten minutes later she had the table set for two and had made a big bowl of fresh salad. She'd found a baguette on the granite counter, which Aidan must have bought fresh earlier, so she sliced that up and placed it in a bread basket. Last night's leftovers were covered in the fridge so she wouldn't take those out until Aidan was home.

She began to wander around downstairs while she waited and again was blown away by the beautiful décor. Although, she thought with a smile, it would never survive a visit from a child. There'd be no way their friend would have lent them this place if they'd had children. She ran her hand across the soft velvet lime green cushions which were a stark contrast to the bleached white sofa, and sunk her toes into the silver grey shaggy rug. She thought about her furnishings back home and wondered how she could ever be happy with such drab, old-fashioned stuff again.

Thinking of home jolted her back to reality and she wondered how they were getting on. She imagined they'd have all slept in since she wasn't there to drag them out of the bed.

'Hellooooo. Linda? I'm home.'

The sound of Aidan's voice echoed into the kitchen and she went to the hall to greet him.

'You were up and out early,' she said, kissing him on the cheek. 'How did the meeting go?'

'Not too bad. Let's grab some lunch and I can tell you about it. I'm starving.'

'Is this okay?' she said, pointing to the spread on the table. 'If you'd rather something else, I can—'

'Linda, it's great. Thanks for doing this.' He eyed up the wine on the table. 'Although I think I might have a cup of tea with it. I'm not sure I could handle another sip of wine.'

'Exactly what I was thinking,' said Linda, taking the wine off the table and putting water in the kettle for tea. 'I'm surprised you have any left, actually.'

Aidan laughed as he plonked himself down in a chair and proceeded to load salad onto his plate. 'The well never runs dry in this house.'

'And speaking of which,' said Linda, seeing an opportunity to quiz him about things. 'How long will your friend be away?'

'What friend?'

'The one who owns this house. When have you to give it back to him?'

He avoided looking her in the eye. 'Probably not for a while yet. He's gone off to America and could be gone until after Christmas.'

'Well, that's lucky for you, isn't it? It's good of him to trust you with such a gorgeous place. Especially since the interior is so white. It must be a nightmare keeping it clean.'

'It's not so bad with just the two of us here. But enough about me. Have you spoken to Rob today yet? How is he surviving without you?'

She felt a little pang of guilt at the fact she hadn't even checked in with him yet. 'I thought I'd wait until later to ring. I don't want him thinking I'm checking up on him.'

'And what you were saying last night,' said Aidan, adding some more tapas to his plate. 'Did you really mean it?'

Oh God. She couldn't remember half of what was said last night.

She remembered telling them that she was fed up at home. She'd told them that she was having trouble writing her book and that nobody at home seemed to realise that she had a job to do outside of cooking, cleaning and being everything to everyone. She hoped she hadn't said more than that because she wasn't ready to face how she was feeling about Rob.

'Linda?' Aidan was staring at her, waiting for a response, but she didn't know what to tell him. 'Come on, Linda,' he said, standing up to make the tea. 'You can talk to me. I'm worried about you. What you said last night – I don't know if it was the drink talking or if it's really how you feel.'

'Aidan, I can't remember what I told you but I'm guessing it was a load of rubbish. I had way too much to drink.'

Aidan nodded as he placed the cups on the table and sat back down. 'We all did. But you seemed very certain.'

'Oh God,' she said, rubbing her temples. 'About what? Just tell me what I said.'

'You said that you didn't love Rob anymore,' he said, watching her carefully. 'You said that your marriage was done and that you were here to figure out how to move forward.'

Hearing Aidan say those words was startling. Had she really said that? Had she actually said that she didn't love her husband and that she was leaving him? She must have been even drunker than she thought because she couldn't remember that conversation at all.

'It was such a shock, you know,' continued Aidan. 'I really thought you and Rob had the perfect marriage. What happened, Linda? What's happened to make you fall out of love with him?'

'I haven't. I mean, nothing's happened.' She tried desperately to gather her thoughts. 'It must have been the drink talking last night because my marriage is still alive and well. I don't know what made me say something like that.'

Aidan raised an eyebrow. 'Sometimes alcohol brings out the truth.'

'Well, not on this occasion,' she said, defiantly. 'We might be having one or two problems but I still love Rob. We have a great marriage and two wonderful children. Our lives are good so why would I want that to change?'

'The lady doth protest too much.'

'Aidan, seriously. I'd tell you if it was true.' But would she? Would she tell her friend when she hadn't even admitted it properly to herself? Maybe Aidan was right in saying that alcohol brings out the truth. Her head was a mess and she really wasn't sure how she felt. Was it enough to love someone if she felt unhappy every day? Or was Rob only part of the overall picture that was making her feel so fed up? She sighed and shook her head as Aidan waited patiently.

'I'm not lying to you, Aidan,' she said, her voice wobbling. 'But I haven't really figured out how I feel yet. I'm not happy at the moment but that's because of a combination of things – not just Rob. It's Rob and the kids and the house and this bloody book. Everything has been getting on top of me these last few months and that's why I felt I needed to get away.'

She went on to tell him about her mini breakdown a few weeks before when she had almost hopped on a plane to get away. She spoke about the problems she was having with Shauna and how she worried about Ben. He listened carefully without interrupting until she finally sat back in her chair, drained from her outpouring.

'Do you know what I think?' he said, reaching his hand across the table to take hers. 'I think you've had an exhaustion breakdown. Plain and simple. You have so much going on that I'm exhausted even thinking about it. This break is going to be the best thing that ever happened to you. It will give you time to figure out a few things. Some distance between you and the family will be a good thing. It will help you decide what you really want. And hopefully get your marriage back on track.'

Linda squeezed his hand. 'You're right. A bit of perspective will be a good thing. And I'm sure Rob and I will work things out. Maybe two weeks of running things at home will make him realise how much I actually do.'

'Exactly. You see? Things are looking up already.'

'I'm sick of talking about myself,' said Linda, shoving her plate away and sitting back in the chair. 'I want to hear about your meeting this morning. Things must be going well for you if they're meeting you on a Saturday. Have they offered you a new book deal?'

They spent another hour chatting about the book business and Aidan's current project, illustrating a poetry book for children. They spoke about Linda's book, or the lack of it, and Aidan promised to help her to move forward with it.

'When you get settled in after a day or two, you should take advantage of the peace and quiet during the day,' he said. 'Set yourself a word count every day and I can read it as you go along, if you like. We can discuss it, like a book club, in the evenings.'

It was exactly what she needed. Somebody to take her seriously. Someone who was interested in her work. Who treated her like a professional. At home she was just 'Mum'. Her lack of recognition as an author in her own home didn't give her much inspiration to keep going. But over here, she felt inspired. Maybe she would get that book written after all. Maybe all was not lost.

Aidan insisted on cleaning up and ushered her back outside to take advantage of the late afternoon sun. She lay back on the sun lounger and felt at peace. As she picked up her Kindle to get stuck into her Nadia Bernio novel, one thing kept going around and around in her head. If they were just looking after the house for this mysterious friend, why were there so many framed pictures of Aidan and James all around the house? Something wasn't adding up and she was going to make it her mission to find out what.

Chapter 8

'I can't eat this,' said Shauna, pushing her plate away from her. 'It's gross.'

'A bit of respect please, Shauna,' said Rob, shocked at his daughter's insolence. 'I've spent all afternoon making dinner so you'll eat it and be grateful.'

'Dad, I'm a vegetarian. You can't give me pasta with chicken in it.'

'I forgot about your little fad,' he said. 'Here, give it over to me and I'll take the chicken out of it.'

'Eeeww! Are you serious? The chicken was in the sauce. Being a veggie is not just picking the meat out of things. And it's not a fad.'

Rob sighed. 'Okay, you win. Make yourself a sandwich or something.'

It was only Sunday, two days since Linda had left, and he was already finding the whole house husband thing tiresome. It wasn't rocket science. It wasn't that he couldn't manage. But it was so draining to have to constantly keep check on the kids and be at their beck and call.

'I'm not really hungry, Dad, so I'm heading out for a while.' Shauna stood up, shoving her plate further into the centre of the table, and headed for the door.

'Hang on there, Missy,' said Rob, glancing at the clock on the wall. 'It's six o'clock and it's a school night. Where are you off to?'

'Just out.'

'Shauna Costa! You're sixteen years old. Not twenty-six. You'll tell me where you're going or you're not stepping outside that door.'

She looked as though she was going to bite back but then had second thoughts. 'Emily's,' she said, not looking at her dad. 'I won't be late.'

'Be back here by nine o'clock. I want you both in bed at a reasonable time tonight and up bright and early in the morning for school.'

Shauna rolled her eyes but said no more before slamming the front door behind her. Rob winced as the house seemed to reverberate from the force and he wondered when had his little girl become so disrespectful. He turned to Ben, who'd been very quiet during the confrontation, and saw he was engrossed in his phone.

'Ben. You know the rule about phones at the dinner table. Put it away now please.'

'But we've finished dinner.'

'Yes, but we're still at the table. I thought you and I could have a chat, just the two of us.'

Ben looked at him suspiciously. 'About what?'

'I don't know. How's school?'

'Fine.'

'Have you made many new friends in secondary school?'

'Some.'

'How come you don't have them over here?'

Ben shrugged.

'You know you can invite your friends over any time.'

'I know.'

It was torture trying to get any information from him. 'Any plans for this evening?'

Another shrug. 'Homework maybe.'

Rob sighed. 'Okay, off you go. Although why you leave homework until last thing on Sunday evening is beyond me.'

His son scurried off, leaving Rob sitting at the table alone. Sighing, he stood up to clear away the things and he wondered if he'd been wrong to agree to his wife going away for such a long time. Two weeks hadn't seemed like much when she'd spoken about it but now as the days spread out in front of him, it seemed like an eternity. Every inch of the kitchen worktops was strewn with pots and pans and dirty dishes, and he felt himself getting angry as he tried to jam it all into the dishwasher. Why should the kids get off scot-free? He'd made them a lovely dinner and where was the gratitude? They were off doing their own thing and he was left to clean up. A thought struck him suddenly and he leaned back on the counter and laughed out loud. God, he was turning into his wife! How many times had he heard Linda say that? How many times had he listened to her and rolled his eyes when she moaned about being left to clean up after making a dinner? How often had he told her to stop nagging?

By the time he'd finished cleaning up, it was after seven and he wondered what Linda was doing. It was after eight in Spain so they probably wouldn't even have had dinner yet. Just like his Sicilian family, they dined very late over there because it was so warm earlier in the day. Suddenly he longed to hear Linda's voice, so he grabbed his phone and went into the sitting room to give her a call. He made himself comfortable on the beige corduroy sofa and noted how untidy the room was. He made a mental note to get the kids to do a tidy-up before they went to bed.

'Hi, love', he said, smiling at the sound of her chirpy voice. 'How are you getting on?'

'Hi, Rob. Just hold on a sec.' There was a shuffling sound and he could hear voices in the background. 'Now, that's better.'

'Where are you? Are you not at the house?'

'Of course I'm at the house.' There was a sharp tone in her voice and then it softened. 'Where else would I be?'

'I thought maybe you'd gone out for dinner. Anyway, how are things with you? How are you getting on?'

'Good,' she said. 'It's lovely over here. Aidan and James are out a lot of the time during the day so I have time to myself.'

'That's great. So are you getting lots of writing done?'

'A fair bit. It's so peaceful and quiet. It makes me wonder how I ever got that first book written at home.'

'I know what you mean. It's not exactly a calm environment here, is it?'

She immediately sounded alarmed. 'Why? What's happened? Are the kids okay?'

'Linda, Linda. Everything is fine. It's just hard to get work done while the kids are around. I tried to go through a file earlier for a meeting I have next week and I had interruption after interruption from them looking for me to provide the answer to all life's problems.'

She laughed loudly. 'I'm so happy you've seen that side of things. It's hard being at home, isn't it?'

'Well, I wouldn't exactly say it's hard. It's not rocket science or anything. I just think they might be taking advantage of the fact that I'm new to this house husband thing. I bet they're not as sassy with you.'

'I think you'll find they are. And what do you mean you have a meeting next week? I thought you'd taken the two weeks off.'

'I have,' he said, kicking himself for mentioning the meeting. 'It's just an important client that we've been finding hard to pin down. The meeting has been arranged for next week and I really have to go. It will just be a few hours while the kids are at school.'

There was a silence and he could tell she wasn't overly pleased but what could he do? It was his job. His career. He was taking as much time as he could but certain things had to be done.

'Listen, I should probably go shortly,' she said, and again, he was sure he could hear muffled voices in the background. 'I've just slipped away from the table to chat to you but we're just about to have dinner. Any plans for the next few days?'

'Nothing much except I'm going to meet Dan Rahilly for a game of golf in the morning when the kids are at school. And don't worry, I'll have everything organised and I'll be home before them.'

'Tomorrow morning?'

'Yes. I didn't play today because I promised you I'd be here for the kids. So I thought I'd sneak a game in while they're gone tomorrow.'

'But Ben has an orthodontic appointment.'

'What? When?'

'Tomorrow at 11.30. I wrote it on the calendar. You'll need to pick him up from school at around eleven and then drop him back afterwards.'

Rob's heart dropped. 'I didn't know about that. I can't cancel out on Dan tomorrow. We've been trying to organise a game for ages and it's all booked now. We'll have to reschedule Ben's appointment.'

'We can't do that,' said Linda, and she sounded adamant. 'We've had that appointment for ages and if we cancel, it could be weeks before he gets another one. You'll just have to reschedule your golf.'

'Can't he go on his own? Surely he's old enough.' He could hear the desperation in his own voice, but he *was* desperate. He'd been looking forward to the game for the last week and after spending the weekend in with the kids, he really needed some head space.

'Rob! For God's sake. He's thirteen. No! He cannot go on his own. You'll just have to do what I do every day. Suck it up.'

'Well there's no need for …'

'Listen, I have to go,' she said, not giving him a chance to reply. 'Aidan is calling me and I don't want to be rude. I'll chat to you again tomorrow. Bye.'

The call ended and he stared at the phone in shock. It was like he was living somebody else's life. When had Linda ever been so forceful? Shit! He'd better cancel the golf now because if he didn't bring Ben to the appointment, Linda would be on the warpath. This wasn't how he'd hoped to start the week.

Still, he wanted to show her he could cope. He needed for her to come home and see that things weren't as complicated as she made them out to be. If she came home in two weeks and the house was falling apart, all the sacrifices they'd made to get her away to Spain wouldn't have been worth it. Because he wanted them to work. He really did. He loved his wife more than anything else in the world and he longed to get back what they had once had. That spark. That heart-stopping moment when they'd look at each other. He longed for the passion and the excitement of their youth and he was going to do whatever he could to make it happen. So if that meant not playing golf for a couple of weeks or putting up with his daughter's insolence, so be it.

Right. He'd get himself organised so that he could sit down and at least watch the golf on telly later on. He felt a renewed vigour, realising the reason he was doing this. He'd show Linda he wasn't just the guy who brought home the money. He'd show her he could be just as involved as she was with the family and the home. How difficult could it be really? Linda's reaction to things lately had been way over the top but he was going to try to be the guy she wanted him to be.

Hauling himself up off the sofa, he went upstairs to check on Ben. He tapped gently on the door and at the same time pushed it open. His heart was filled with love when he saw his son sitting on the bed, his school books spread out in front of him. Ben looked up, his pen poised mid-air.

'Hi, son. Are you doing homework?'

'Yep.'

'Your room is a bit of a state, though. How about giving it a bit of a clean. That bin badly needs to be emptied.' He pointed at the bin that was overflowing with scrunched-up pages and shook his head at the mess.

'Dad, I'll do it later. I have loads of study to do first.'

'I'll leave you to it, so. And just to remind you that you have an appointment with the orthodontist in the morning. I'll pick you up from school at eleven.'

'Cool.'

Ben's head bent back to his books, so Rob left him to it and closed the door quietly behind him. He was a good boy. Linda had been worried about his lack of socialising with the other boys in his new school but Rob liked that he didn't want to go out much. It was enough that they had to worry about Shauna and, besides, Ben was only thirteen. Practically still a baby.

He went downstairs and grabbed a black refuse sack from under the sink. He'd empty the bins upstairs but after that, it was up to the kids to do their rooms. He had enough to do. Ben didn't even look up when he went back into the room and emptied the contents of the overflowing bin into the sack. He did Shauna's room next and her bin was even worse. The room stank of God only knows what, so he flung open the window to let some air in. Their bin was next and then the one in the bathroom, before he headed back downstairs with a full load. Although he was tempted to shove the whole lot into the normal rubbish bin, he knew he had to sort out the recycling, so he began the painstaking job of trawling through the contents of the bag. But he was pleased with the results ten minutes later, having lightened the normal rubbish load by taking out the shampoo bottles and the toilet-roll inserts.

He emptied the last few things from the bag onto the floor and suddenly his heart began to beat quickly. He couldn't believe what he was seeing. It had been a long time, but there was no mistaking the distinctive box. It was a pregnancy test. He didn't know how long he stood there staring at it, but he was in shock. Shauna was only sixteen. Why the hell would she be doing a pregnancy test? She didn't even have a boyfriend. Or none that he was aware of anyway. He eventually picked the box up from the floor and saw that it was open. Slowly he removed the stick from inside. He was almost afraid to look. But he forced himself to. Even with all the instructions Linda had left, nothing had prepared him for this!

Chapter 9

Linda wasn't sure why she'd lied to Rob. It just seemed like the right thing to do. It's not that she felt guilty for enjoying herself. Well, not really. But it was just that she wanted him to think of her trip as a working holiday. Not the party holiday that it was turning into. Aidan and James had invited some of their friends over for drinks and nibbles and it was promising to be a great night. She was loving not having any responsibilities. It brought her right back to a time when life was simple and all she had to worry about was what she'd wear for her next night out. She knew she should be getting stuck into her writing, but it was only Sunday. She'd only been in Spain for two days and there'd be plenty of time for work over the next two weeks.

She left her phone on her bed and went back out to join the party. The guests were a mixture of James' co-workers from the restaurant and some of Aidan's creative friends. They seemed like a lovely bunch and she already felt as though she'd known them for a long time. They were easy to chat to and she was being treated like the guest of honour. It felt really good. She felt special. It was a long time since she'd felt that way and she was going to enjoy it while it lasted.

'Well?' said Aidan, as she slipped back into her chair beside him. 'How is everything at home?'

She took a long sip of her cool white wine.

Aidan raised an eyebrow. 'That bad, is it?'

She laughed. 'Not at all. They're all fine actually.'

'You mean he's running the house like a dream and wonders how you ever got yourself into such a flap about something so simple?'

'Ha! Not quite.' She looked around to see if anybody else could hear but they were all engrossed in their own conversations. 'But he may be just realising that running a house isn't all plain sailing.'

'Linda Costa! What have you done? I know by that mischievous face that you're up to something.'

'You know me too well,' she said, taking another, longer sip. The wine was delicious and so easy to drink. 'I may have organised some appointments just to keep him on his toes.'

'Go on.' Aidan moved in closer and lowered his voice, as though they were plotting a crime.

'I made an orthodontist appointment for Ben last week. It's for tomorrow morning.'

'And what's so bad about that? Don't you bring the kids to appointments all the time.'

Linda felt a slight pang of guilt. 'Yes, but I only made it after I checked Rob's diary and saw that he'd organised to play golf.'

'Oh you're such a bad girl,' laughed Aidan. 'But I love it. What did he say?'

'He was raging. He'd given up his golf today so he could spend the day at home and had planned to go tomorrow while the kids were at school.'

'Maybe he'll still go. He could cancel the orthodontist easily enough, couldn't he?'

'He could. But I told him that it would be impossible to get another appointment and we'd waited ages for that one.'

Aidan shook his head. 'Remind me to never cross you.'

'I do feel a little guilty about it now,' said Linda, biting the edge of her lip. 'It's not like me to be so manipulative. But I made that appointment one day last week after we'd had a row. It seemed like a good idea at the time.'

'There's no harm done,' said Aidan gently. 'Rob can play golf any time. Now forget about what's going on back home and let's have a great night. More wine?'

She held out her glass willingly and sat back to take in the scene. The warm air wrapped itself around her and there was just the hint of a breeze. She closed her eyes and took a deep breath. The buzz of chatter and the scent of flowers filled her head; and she felt as though she hadn't been this happy in ages.

'A penny for them.'

She looked up, startled, to see one of Aidan's guests had pulled his chair over to her side and was smiling as he looked right into her eyes.

'Sorry, I was in another world.'

'I noticed,' he said, smiling, and his bright blue eyes sparkled like the ocean.

She'd never quite seen anybody like him before. He was Indian and Spanish all rolled into one but his blue eyes looked as though they didn't belong on his tanned face. He was gorgeous and she'd noticed him from the moment he'd walked in earlier.

'Kabir,' he said, reaching out his hand to shake hers. 'I don't think we've been properly introduced.'

She took his hand and her insides flipped as he pulled her slightly towards him and kissed her on both cheeks. 'Linda,' she said, blushing, despite her attempts to act cool. 'So how do you know Aidan and James?'

'My parents own the restaurant where James works. They own a few around La Zenia but they're getting old so I'm overseeing things for them.'

'Cool.' Jesus, she sounded like one of her kids.

'So, Linda. James tells me you're an author. That's a pretty *cool* job.'

He emphasised the word 'cool' and Linda couldn't figure out whether or not he was mocking her. But his smile was kind and he seemed like he was genuinely interested to find out more. 'I'm not sure I'd classify myself as an author. Well, not yet anyway. But I'm trying my best.'

'But didn't I hear you have a book published?' he said, leaning an elbow on the back of his chair. 'Surely that means you are absolutely and completely an author.'

She laughed at that. 'Well, I suppose I am. It's just that I'm having trouble writing my second one and I feel like the first one was just a fluke.'

'You're way too modest, Linda. If I had a talent like that I'd be shouting it from the rooftops. But writing wouldn't be my forte. Actually, I don't have a creative bone in my body. I'm in awe of Aidan and all his artistic friends.'

She was enjoying chatting to him and with every sip of wine she was relaxing more and more. He was good company, as were all of the guests, but he'd made that special effort to start up a conversation with her and she was grateful to him for that. She was out of practice with the whole social scene and had felt a little awkward at the start of the evening. But it was turning out to be one of the best nights she'd had in ages and she didn't want it to end. She couldn't believe it when she looked at her phone a little later and saw it was past eleven and some of the guests looked as though they were about to leave.

'Stop hogging our guest of honour, Kabir,' said Aidan from across the table. 'Linda, come over here and meet Jenna and Frank. They're heading off shortly.'

Linda immediately shoved her chair back and stood up. She was reluctant to leave her conversation with Kabir, but she didn't want anybody to think she was rude. But the wine suddenly made her legs buckle and she had to steady herself by holding onto the table.

'Whoaa!' said Kabir, jumping up and putting a big strong hand on her arm. 'Are you okay?'

She was mortified. 'Yes, yes, I'm fine. I just got my heel caught in the gravel.'

He held onto her arm a fraction longer than was necessary before she walked across to meet Aidan's friends. They were a lovely couple. Frank, an acclaimed artist who had his work displayed in galleries all over Spain, and Jenna, a writer of children's books, one of which Aidan had illustrated. The story of how they'd met Aidan was interesting, but Linda couldn't stop thinking about Kabir. How he'd reached out to steady her. His hand on her arm. It was as though he'd burned a hole in it because she could still feel the tingle of his touch. She hadn't felt this way in a very long time, and it was both exciting and wonderful.

'It was lovely to meet you, Linda,' said Jenna, kissing her on both cheeks. 'I hope we'll see you again before you head home.'

Home. The word seemed to snap her back to reality. What was she doing, lusting after another man? You'd swear she was eighteen and single. Honestly, she needed to get herself together. She was in Spain for two reasons – to get a break from the stresses of home life and to get her book written. That was it. She wasn't there to flirt with men or to have inappropriate thoughts. Whatever the outcome between her and Rob, he definitely didn't deserve for her to be disloyal.

It was beginning to get nippy and her sleeveless jumpsuit was only paper thin. It looked as though some of the guests weren't ready to leave yet so she'd grab a cardigan and come back out to chat some more. It was almost cooler inside where the air-conditioning was on full blast and she shivered as she walked through the living room into her bedroom. Grabbing a little white cardigan from her unpacked suitcase, she wrapped it around her shoulders and did up the top button to hold it in place. A quick retouch of her lipstick and a brush through her hair and she was ready to go back out.

'We meet again,' came a voice from the kitchen, making her jump as she headed towards the garden. It was Kabir. 'Sorry, I didn't mean to startle you.' He walked over towards her and her heart began to thump like crazy. She hadn't realised how tall he was. How muscular. 'I just came in for more ice. Are you okay?'

'I'm … I'm fine. I just came in to get something to keep me warm.' Shit. That sounded suggestive. His raised eyebrow was accompanied by a smile and she laughed despite herself.

'If I wasn't such a gentleman, I'd offer to keep you warm myself.' She opened her mouth to say something but nothing came out. Luckily Kabir continued. 'I'm just joking, by the way. I wouldn't dream of seducing a married woman. That is, of course, unless she wanted me to.'

She wanted him to. She really did. But she knew it was wrong and it wasn't going to happen. When he looked as though he was waiting for a reply, she wagged a finger at him. 'My mother used to warn me about boys like you, Kabir. *Run a mile, Linda*, she used to say. And mothers are always right.'

He laughed out loud and shook his head. 'I suppose they are. Why don't we head back out to the others then? Before I do something I regret.'

She wanted to stay where she was but she nodded and led the way back outside. With only a few people left, the evening was almost over and Linda chatted to each of the remaining guests before they left. Kabir was the last to leave and he hugged Aidan and James tightly before turning to her.

'Goodnight, Linda.' He took her hand and again leaned in to kiss her on the cheek but she moved awkwardly and their lips brushed together. It was only a slight touch, but Linda felt something stirring inside her that she hadn't felt in a very long time. He allowed his hand to linger on hers for longer than necessary before pulling it away and looking deeply into her eyes. 'I hope we get to meet again soon.'

She was lost for words but nodded and waved as he walked away. It was as though their goodbye had lasted for ages and she was sure Aidan and James would ask her about it, but neither seemed to have noticed anything amiss.

'What a great night,' said James, kissing Aidan on the lips before beginning the clean-up. 'Did you enjoy it, Linda?'

She nodded as she gathered some of the glasses to bring inside. 'It was really lovely. Thanks so much to you two for organising it. I'm only here two days and I already feel at home.'

'That's great,' said Aidan, shoving the patio door open with his shoulder. 'You and Kabir seemed to be getting along really well.'

So he *had* noticed. 'Yes, he's really nice. We had a good chat.'

Aidan nodded as he loaded the dishwasher. 'He's fabulous. I can't understand how he isn't taken. He must be the most eligible bachelor in Spain at this stage. Have you seen those eyes?'

A picture of them was ingrained in her mind. 'I can't say I noticed.'

'Come on, Linda. You'd have to be a stone not to notice how gorgeous he is.'

'Well, I suppose he is. If you like that sort of thing.'

James giggled. 'What sort of thing?'

'You know. Dark and handsome with muscles and—'

'And gorgeous eyes?' Aidan raised an eyebrow and burst out laughing.

'Linda, it's okay. Just because you're married doesn't mean you can't look at the menu. Kabir is gorgeous. And just because you noticed that doesn't mean you've done anything wrong.'

'Okay,' she relented. 'He *is* spectacular! I've never seen anyone like him before. Oh God, those eyes, those muscles. And did you smell him?'

Aidan nodded. 'He always smells divine, doesn't he, James?'

'He does,' said James, wiping down the pristine counters with a disinfectant spray. 'But just be careful.'

Both Aidan and Linda looked at him in surprise and he was quick to clarify.

'I just mean be careful you don't fall for him. I know you and Rob are going to sort things out and I don't want things to get complicated for you.'

'That's very sweet of you, James,' said Linda, touched by his concern. 'But I'm here to escape the complications of my life, not add to them, so you have no worries there. And on that note, I think I'll head to bed and get some sleep. I'm hoping to be able to do some writing tomorrow. I've had plenty of relaxation over the weekend so it's about time I got stuck in.'

'Night, love,' said Aidan, hugging her tightly. 'I'm here all day tomorrow and planning on doing some writing too. I'll be in my office upstairs if you need me but I'm sure we'll grab breakfast or lunch together at some stage.'

'Definitely.' She turned to give James a hug too.

'I'm on the early shift so I'll be gone before you wake up,' he said. 'But I'll be home early and I'll bring something for dinner.'

'In my next life, I'm marrying a chef,' said Linda, as she headed into her bedroom. 'Night night.'

She closed the door behind her and went into the little en-suite bathroom. She was exhausted so she quickly took off her make-up and brushed her teeth. Minutes later she was snuggled up in bed as sleep almost immediately overtook her. But it wasn't a restful sleep. She dreamed about her family and about their lives back in Ireland. In her dream she was rushing around, juggling her job as a mother with her career as a writer. The kids were being lazy and not helping out and the only bright part of her day was when her husband came home from work. She met him at the door and he swept her into his arms. They kissed passionately and she knew everything was going to be alright. Together they could conquer the world. But there was just one problem. In her dream, her husband wasn't Rob. It was the beautiful blue-eyed man she'd met earlier. She was married to Kabir.

Chapter 10

Linda couldn't concentrate on her writing. It was a beautiful day so after she'd had breakfast with Aidan, she'd taken her laptop down to the garden and positioned herself under the shade of a tree. It was a far cry from the kitchen table back home and she breathed in the fresh air gratefully. But despite the beautiful setting, the words just wouldn't come. Her head was too full of what was happening in the real world to allow her to slide into her imaginary one.

Kabir Smith. The man had infiltrated her brain and she couldn't stop thinking about him. That face. That body. That beautiful mixed-up accent. Apparently he was of mixed heritage. His mother was half Indian and half Spanish and his father half Spanish and half English. It was an eclectic mix and it had produced a stunning specimen of humanity.

Linda stuck her glasses on top of her head and rubbed her eyes. This book was going nowhere. She really needed to forget about Kabir and just concentrate on what she had come here to do. She'd probably never see him again anyway. There'd be no reason for her to. But it was startling how that thought upset her. Oh God, she needed a good kick up the arse. Thinking about another man like that when she had a perfectly good one at home. She wondered how Rob had gotten on with Ben at the orthodontist. The appointment should be well over by now. She thought about ringing but then decided against it. Too much procrastination wouldn't get her book written so she'd wait until later when the kids would be home from school and she could chat to them all then.

'I thought this might help you concentrate,' said Aidan, arriving beside her and placing a frothy cappuccino on the ground at her feet. He sat down on the grass and folded his arms over his knees. 'How's it going anyway?'

'Not great, to be honest. It's hard to concentrate.'

'I know. The first time I saw Kabir I could think of nothing else.'

'Wh-what do you mean? I'm not … I mean I wasn't …' Jesus, had she been thinking out loud? Was it that obvious?

'Relax, Linda. I'm only joking. It will probably take you a few days to settle in to your book. It's very different writing outdoors and with the heat of the sun. But once you get used to it, I bet the words will fly onto the page.'

'I hope so,' she said, relieved the conversation had turned from Kabir. 'Because if this book doesn't start taking shape soon, I may forget about it. And that's going to cause a whole lot of problems at home.'

She'd told Aidan about her dilemma, but he was quick to reassure her.

'Linda, you can do it. I know you can. Once the words start flowing, there'll be no stopping you. I can't tell you how many times I've lost inspiration over the years. But it comes back, and when it does, it's always better than ever.'

'Maybe,' she said, not convinced. 'How's your own book coming along? I'd love to have a look at it at some stage.'

Aidan shook his head. 'You know what I'm like. I hate showing anybody until it's finished. But it's all going well. I'm very happy with where I'm at.'

'So this place,' she said, changing the subject. 'How will you ever be able to leave it? And where will you and James live when your friend comes home?'

'*I'm not sure* is the answer to both questions. But we don't have to think about it for a while yet.' He stood up and Linda couldn't help thinking, once again, that he was avoiding the question. She still wasn't convinced about this friend lending them the house. It just didn't add up.

'Hmmmm.'

'What does that mean?' said Aidan, but he looked nervous.

'I'm just thinking that maybe you'd won the lotto and bought this place yourself. But you want to remain anonymous so nobody can know about the house.' She watched his face for a flicker of anything, but he just rolled his eyes.

'If only. Listen, if I'd won the lotto, I'd be shouting it from the rooftops. There'd be none of this anonymous stuff. I'd want to treat all my friends and I definitely wouldn't be trying to hide it.'

'Are you sure about that?'

'You're a scream, Linda. I'm very sure. You have some imagination. And you should be using it for your book rather than wasting it on my boring life.'

'Fair enough,' she said, laughing. 'Now scram. If we keep chatting, it will be lunchtime and there'll be no work done. I'll come in and make us something to eat in an hour or two.'

She tried but failed to write even a single word for the next hour. It was soul-destroying to sit in front of a blank screen and have no inspiration whatsoever. Every now and then she'd have an idea and would poise her fingers, ready to fill the page. But with so many thoughts competing for space in her head, her idea would disappear before it reached her fingertips. She glanced at her phone which she'd put on silent so as not to distract her and saw that she'd a missed call from Rob. He was probably just reporting on Ben's appointment, so she'd catch up with him later. She was also surprised to see that it was almost one thirty. There was no point in trying to get stuck into work now when it was almost time for lunch.

Back inside, she plugged her laptop in to the mains and went to see what was in the fridge. Aidan and James were very minimal with their shopping so she wasn't banking on finding a whole lot.

James seemed to plan dinners for the week so they just shopped for what was needed. Shopping for a family was completely different. Back at home she'd find herself in the shops most days because the amount of food they all got through was ridiculous. And the waste! She couldn't stand the fact that someone would open a pan of bread and not close it properly so it would end up in the bin because it was all dried out.

She closed the fridge again and her eye was drawn to the Kindle she'd left on the counter. Although she hated to admit it, *Blood Room* by Nadia Bernio was fast becoming one of her favourites. A lot of critics and reviewers had slammed it, saying it was like a 'How To' of sex, rather than a good story. But it had pulled Linda in and already half way through, she couldn't wait to read what happened next. She was just about to sit down on a kitchen chair and read a bit more, when Aidan appeared again.

'Come on, we're going out.'

'Where to?' she said. 'I thought we were just going to have lunch here.'

He shook his head and grabbed his phone and keys from the table. 'That was the plan initially, but James rang to say he'd slow-roasted some beef for the special today and we were to go down and have some.'

Her mouth watered at the thought of it. 'That sounds delicious. Just give me a second to make myself presentable.'

Five minutes later, they were walking down the street towards the beach and Linda could already smell the sea air. 'It's very quiet around here, isn't it?' she said, noting that they seemed to be the only ones on the street. 'I would have thought there'd be a lot more tourists around.'

'There are plenty of them alright,' said Aidan, turning to cross the road. 'It's just gone a bit quieter since the kids went back to school. But one of the nights I'll bring you to a place that's never quiet.'

Linda quickened her pace to keep up with him. 'Where's that?'

'A place called Paddy's Point. It's always difficult to get a seat there – even in winter. They have live music every night and their food is delicious.'

'I look forward to that,' she said, as Aidan came to a stop outside a restaurant.

'Here we are. Welcome to James' place. Well, not exactly his, but you know what I mean.'

Linda could feel her mouth watering as a delicious smell of cooking wafted from inside. She couldn't wait to test the food out. They opted for a table outside where they could watch the world go by and as soon as they'd ordered their beef and a bottle of house white, Aidan disappeared inside to find James. The restaurant had a nice atmosphere and was already almost full of customers. It was an international menu and Linda loved the fact that she could have chunky chips with her beef.

'Your wine, *Señora*. Would you like me to pour?'

'Yes, thank you.' She turned around, holding her glass aloft, and almost fell off her chair.

'Kabir! What are you doing here?'

He sat down on Aidan's chair and proceeded to pour the wine into both glasses. 'This is where I work.'

'But I thought … didn't you say … ?' God, her tongue was tied in a knot and she couldn't get the words out.

'I work between restaurants, yes. But I'm here most afternoons because it's the busiest one. I like to be hands-on and help out with service when we've a full house.'

'I see.' She couldn't think of a single coherent thing to say. Her insides were doing somersaults and the woody scent of his cologne was doing all sorts of things to her head.

'So what have you been doing since I saw you last?' he said, sitting back into the chair. 'Have you been getting up to any mischief?'

'What do you mean? It was only last night that you—' She stopped herself suddenly when she saw the twinkle in his eye and realised he was joking with her. She began to relax then and enjoy the banter.

'I'm not sure what mischief there is to get up to over here,' she said. 'It seems like a quiet enough place to me.'

He leaned forward in a conspiratorial way and lowered his voice. 'You'd be surprised what mischief you can find if you look for it. But *only* if you're looking.'

She could feel his minty breath on her cheek and her eyes watered from his closeness. She wasn't sure how to respond to that but luckily Aidan arrived back at the table and the moment was broken.

'Kabir! How are you? I've just been in to see James. That beef looks delicious. Are you going to join us?'

He stood up immediately to let Aidan sit down. 'No, I'm afraid not. It's a full house for lunch so I'll keep going. But I had an idea.'

'Go on,' said Aidan, sitting down and taking a sip of his wine.

'Why don't I take you all out this evening on Dad's boat. We can bring some food and head off to one of the nicer beaches down the coast for a picnic. I'm sure Linda would like to see some of what La Zenia has to offer.'

'That sounds fabulous,' said Linda. She loved boats but they never got the chance to go on any because Rob got seasick. 'What do you think, Aidan?'

'I can't this evening, unfortunately. James and I have a dinner to go to. It's been arranged for ages so we really can't cancel. How about some other evening this week?'

'Tonight's the only night that will work, I'm afraid,' said Kabir, glancing quickly at Linda. 'My dad has hired the boat out from tomorrow, so we won't have access to it after that. Not to worry.'

'Linda, why don't you go anyway? I was feeling guilty about us leaving you alone tonight so that's the perfect solution.'

'I … I don't know.' Just her and Kabir on a boat together. Alone. Sipping champagne and eating strawberries. Surrounded by the sea and nothing to hear but the caw of seagulls and the gentle lapping of the water against the boat. She realised suddenly they were both looking at her and blushed furiously. 'I mean, there's no point in taking the boat out for just me. I'm sure you have better things to be doing.'

'There's nothing I'd rather do,' said Kabir, his eyes boring into hers. 'Come on. It will be great fun.'

'Yes, go on, Linda. You'll have a great time. The boat is fabulous and it's a chance to see a bit more of the area.'

She nodded. 'Okay. Thanks, Kabir. That would be lovely.'

'Great. I'll come and pick you up at six. Bring something warm because it can get chilly out there.' He was walking away as he spoke, and Linda couldn't help wondering if he was afraid she'd change her mind.

The lunches arrived minutes later and James had been right about the beef. It was mouth-wateringly delicious and she devoured every bit of it. They chatted amicably throughout the meal but Linda's mind was on only one thing. She was in a foreign country thousands of miles away from her husband and she was about to go out with another man. Was he just being polite or was it more than that? He'd definitely been flirting with her earlier. They'd had a moment, just before Aidan had come back and it was as though Kabir had wanted her to know what he was thinking. And was tonight the only night the boat was free? It seemed too much of a coincidence. Was Kabir trying to get her alone? Only time would tell. But she was a married woman and she took her vows seriously. If Kabir tried anything, she'd make sure to tell him where he stood.

But as she and Aidan walked back to the villa, she couldn't get thoughts of Kabir out of her head. She longed to run her fingers through that tousled, black hair. To place butterfly kisses on the laughter lines around his eyes. To feel his strong arms around her and his lips on hers. God, she'd only been here three days and she was already being tested in ways she'd never dreamed of. Linda knew, despite everything, that she was a strong woman and would be able to resist any temptation that was presented to her. But the big question was, did she want to?

Chapter 11

'So no dramas then?' Linda was speaking to Rob on the phone but she was anxious to get away so she could start getting ready for her evening out with Kabir. 'How did Ben get on at the orthodontist?'

'We're all good here,' said Rob, but he sounded tired. 'Ben was in and out of the orthodontist in less than five minutes.'

She felt a little sheepish. His whole day of golf cancelled for a five-minute check-up. Although that was the story of her life, so she shouldn't allow herself to feel too guilty.

'You never can tell with these appointments,' she said. 'You were lucky. I've often been stuck in there for hours.'

'I suppose.'

There was an awkward silence and Linda used it as her

opportunity to end the conversation. 'I'd better go, Rob. I've left my laptop open outside and want to get back to writing while it's flowing.'

'Okay, love. Take care. I'll chat to you tomorrow.'

She threw her phone down on the bed and lay her head back on the soft feather pillows. She felt frustrated by how they were with each other. They seemed to have lost the ability to have a normal conversation and instead everything felt wooden and stilted. But her frustration soon turned to sadness. They'd been so good together once. Would they ever get that back again? Or had things just gone too far. She sat up suddenly and rubbed her eyes to force back the tears that were threatening to fall. She didn't have time to think about her problems with Rob now. Kabir was due to collect her in an hour and she hadn't even begun to get ready.

Twenty minutes later she was out of the shower, her hair pinned safely on top of her head. She'd washed it yesterday so there was no need to do it again. Her hair was wiry and thick and took ages to dry so she only washed it once or twice a week. Wrapping her light, cotton robe around her, she went to her suitcase to see what she was going to wear. Having gone through every single thing, she decided she had nothing suitable. But suitable for what? A date? An evening with a friend? Too sexy or exposed and Kabir might get the wrong idea. Too covered up and she'd look like her frumpy aunt. She sat down on the bed and shook her head. Back in Ireland when she'd been packing, she never would have imagined she'd be in this situation. What she needed was advice. Somebody to tell her what to do. And she knew just the person.

'Hi, Ger. Just thought I'd give you a quick call.'

'Linda! Great to hear from you. Are you having a great time over there? What have you been up to? Is it fabulous?'

Linda laughed at the sound of her friend's enthusiastic voice. 'It's great. Listen, I don't have a lot of time but I need your advice.' She told her about meeting Kabir and how they'd clicked straight away. And then about their planned evening.

'A date?' Ger sounded shocked. 'You're going out on a *date* with him?'

'Not exactly,' said Linda, embarrassed by her friend's reaction. 'He's just taking me out to show me around.'

'On a boat?'

'Yes. His dad's boat.'

'Just the two of you?'

'Well, yes but …'

'It sounds pretty much like a date to me.'

Linda had thought Ger would understand but she was beginning to regret having told her at all. 'Ger, I didn't ring for you to tell me off, I just wanted your advice on what to wear.'

'Linda, Linda. I'm not telling you off at all. I'm just surprised, that's all. But I think you're right to take opportunities like this and see what happens. You said you've been feeling invisible for the last few years. So, if seeing this guy helps you find yourself, well then that's a good thing.'

'When you say *seeing him*,' said Linda, trying to choose her words carefully, 'do you mean just going out and having fun, or something else?'

'You're an adult, Linda. Just follow your heart. You'll know what the right thing is to do.'

Tears pricked Linda's eyes at her friend's wise words. 'Thanks, Ger. And the clothes?'

'White jeans, a cotton t-shirt and a warm cardigan. Not too dressy but your legs always look good in white jeans. And I demand a phone call tomorrow with a report on how it went.'

'Definitely,' said Linda, before saying her goodbyes and ending the call.

She only had half an hour left now before Kabir was due so she got to work immediately on her make-up. Not too much but enough to hide the wrinkles that seemed to multiply every day. Just as she was putting the finishing touches to her face but still in her robe, she heard voices out in the living room, and she hoped that Kabir hadn't arrived early. She'd planned to be ready before he arrived and casually sitting on the sofa reading her book. She opened the door a slit to listen. Thankfully it was just Aidan on the phone to somebody, but curiosity got the better of her when she heard her name mentioned.

'No, don't come over here. I don't want Linda quizzing you.' Aidan was pacing up and down the room and his voice sounded agitated. 'She's already been asking questions about the house. She's very smart and it's only a matter of time before she begins to figure things out.'

Linda was alarmed. Figure what out? She knew there was something fishy about the house but she was still none the wiser having listened to Aidan's conversation. There was a long pause where the person on the other end must have been talking, followed by a series of yeses from Aidan. Then the call was finished. She shut the door quietly and went back to getting ready. She really wanted to know what was going on but she could hardly ask Aidan. What would she say? I was listening to you on the phone and I was wondering what you were talking about? She'd just have to bide her time and try to figure it out. She hoped that Aidan hadn't gotten himself into any sort of trouble. That call definitely sounded dodgy and if he had come in to a lot of money recently – enough to be able to buy the villa – Linda prayed that he hadn't been doing anything illegal. But her sleuth work would have to wait for another day because Kabir would be here any minute now.

When he arrived a little while later, Linda was doing what she'd planned and was sitting casually on the sofa with her legs up, reading her book. Of course she wasn't really reading it at all. She was nervously checking her phone and just waiting for the doorbell to ring. She didn't stand up until after Kabir walked into the room, feigning surprise at his arrival.

'We did say six, didn't we?' said Kabir, walking over to greet her.

Linda allowed him to kiss her on both cheeks. 'Yes, we did. Sorry. I've been reading and forgot the time. That's what happens when you find a good book.'

'Linda Costa. Are you telling fibs?' James was looking at her with amusement and then turned to Kabir. 'She's been in that room of hers getting ready for the last hour. I thought she'd fallen asleep.'

She was mortified. 'That's not true, James. I was on the phone and I—'

'He's just winding you up, Linda.' Kabir was smiling at James, who seemed to think the situation was hilarious. 'You look beautiful, by the way.'

'Thank you,' said Linda, shooting James a stern look. 'Should we just get going then?'

'After you,' said Kabir, indicating for her to walk in front of him. He touched her back gently and she felt the heat of his hand boring into her. 'I hope you have a strong stomach because the sea is a bit choppy this evening.'

Aidan came out of his room to say goodbye and he and James stood at the door to wave them off. As they sped away in Kabir's Grand Cherokee jeep, it made her giggle to see them both standing there like proud parents. She wondered what they were thinking. Did they sense the chemistry between her and Kabir? Or did they assume it was nothing more than an innocent evening out? Although how could she expect them to know what was going on when she didn't even know herself?

It wasn't long before they were out on the open sea in the boat. And it was more than just a boat. It was a luxury yacht and Linda's eyes had almost popped out of her head when she saw it.

'Your dad really owns this?' she'd said in amazement. 'It's unbelievable. I thought when you'd said a boat, that I'd be handed a set of oars and we'd be rowing out to sea.'

He laughed at that and expertly got the engine going, guiding them out beyond the crashing waves. He looked content at the helm. Masterful. And Linda couldn't stop staring at him in admiration.

'Do you want to have a go?' he said, indicating the wheel. 'I'll show you what to do.'

She didn't hesitate and found herself holding the wheel with Kabir at her back, his arms stretched around her, helping her turn it. A picture came to her mind of the scene in *Ghost* where Patrick Swayze was behind Demi Moore as she worked on her pottery wheel. It was one of the most sensual movie scenes ever and she could almost hear 'Unchained Melody' playing as she thought about it.

'Watch out!' Kabir's warning snapped her back to reality just in time to turn the boat away from some rocks. 'That was a close one.'

'Maybe I'll leave the steering to you,' she said, suddenly feeling uncomfortable with their closeness. 'I'll just sit back and enjoy the view.'

She was exhausted but exhilarated by the time they moored the boat further down the coast, and when they stepped off to find a nice spot to sit down for a while, Linda was surprised at the array of food Kabir had brought. He'd thoughtfully packed everything, from fruit and salads to sliced meats, cheese and olives. They found a gorgeous little alcove at the back of the beach that was shaded from the wind, so they laid a blanket on the sand and sat down.

It felt very intimate but strangely comfortable. She didn't feel ill at ease once and there were never any gaps in the conversation. She told him about her life at home, being careful not to say there were problems between her and Rob. She didn't want it to look like she was opening the gate for something to happen.

'Your husband,' said Kabir, adjusting himself to a more comfortable position on the blanket. 'I hope he appreciates you.'

'Of course,' said Linda, a little too quickly. 'He's a good man.'

Kabir nodded slowly. 'And a very lucky one.'

He held her gaze for what seemed like an eternity and it was as though those blue eyes were boring into her soul. The tension between them was palpable and for a few seconds, she thought he was going to kiss her. She held her breath.

'We should probably pack up and head back before it gets dark.' Kabir began to clear up the remainder of the food and the moment was broken.

It was almost eleven when he pulled the jeep into the grounds of the villa. They'd had a drink in a beach bar when they'd come off the boat and the time had flown by. She felt sorry that the evening was over but, in a strange way, she was also relieved. Despite how she felt, she hadn't allowed anything to happen. She'd stayed loyal to her husband and had resisted temptation. Kabir hopped out of the jeep to walk her to the door.

'If it were my place, I'd ask you in for a drink,' she said, rooting in her bag for the keys. 'But sadly, it's not.'

Kabir shook his head. 'I've already kept you out late enough. You should go and get your beauty sleep and wake up refreshed and ready to write that book tomorrow.'

'I live in hope. Thanks for a lovely evening.'

They stood for a moment in silence and that's when Linda knew. She saw it in his eyes. He wanted her. His look spoke a thousand words and her insides melted under his gaze.

'Night, Linda.' He moved forward and let his lips linger on her cheek. Just one cheek. None of the polite air kisses on both sides but one long, lingering, merest touch on her right cheek. He touched her hands as he kissed her, and she felt a bolt of lightning run through her fingertips. He pulled away then and waited while she fumbled at the lock on the front door. She eventually opened it and turned to him, but he was already walking away. She waved as he drove off, before stepping inside and closing the door firmly behind her.

All was quiet, and as Aidan and James weren't ones to stay out late, she assumed they were in bed. Kicking off her shoes, she quietly padded to the bedroom, noting how her legs felt like jelly beneath her. What an evening it had been. As she sat at the dressing table to take off her make-up, she relived every moment of it. She wondered what Kabir was thinking. What was he hoping for? That moment between them back on the beach – she definitely hadn't imagined it. It had seemed like he was going to kiss her and then thought better of it. What would she have done? How would she have reacted? Even though nothing had happened, she felt suddenly overwhelmed with guilt. Because she had no doubt. If in that moment, Kabir had tried to kiss her, she would most certainly have kissed him back.

Chapter 12

'Dad, can I have money for my lunch?' said Shauna, appearing in the kitchen with her jacket on, ready to walk out the door. 'And can you hurry or I'll be late.'

Rob looked at his daughter and shook his head. 'Shauna, sit down and have some breakfast. You can't go running out the door with nothing in your stomach.'

'Seriously, Dad. I don't have time for this. Can you please just give me the money?'

'Bye, Dad,' said Ben, brushing past his sister on his way out. Now there was an easy child. He'd been up early, had his lunch made and was sitting eating Weetabix when Rob had come downstairs.

'Bye, son. Have a good day.'

'*Dad*. I need the money *now*!' Shauna's voice was bordering on shouting and Rob didn't like it one bit.

'I'll tell you what, young lady. You sit down and have some breakfast and then I'll drive you to school after so you won't be late.'

She looked as though she was about to punch him. 'I told you I'm not hungry and I'm meeting somebody along the way, so I don't want a lift.'

'Who are you meeting?' He felt like he didn't know much about his daughter's friends and he wanted to learn more. 'Do I know her?'

'Him. It's Craig. Now, can we have the father–daughter chat later because I really don't have time right now.'

Rob sighed. 'Okay, okay. But you don't need money for your lunch. Look, I made it for you. Not a piece of meat in sight.'

He held out a lunchbox but she turned and headed for the door. 'No, thanks. Mum always gives me money for lunch on Tuesdays.'

'But I—'

'Have to go, Dad. I'll just use the emergency money Mum gave me. You can replenish it later. See ya.'

Rob was left staring at the back of the door, the freshly prepared lunch in his hands. He'd been proud of his work that morning. He'd gone to a lot of trouble to prepare little salad sandwiches and had put together a few bits he knew Shauna liked. He'd thought she'd be delighted. So much for that. It felt like he didn't know his daughter at all.

Sitting down on a kitchen stool, he drummed his fingers on the counter and tried to get his thoughts together. Finding that pregnancy test on Sunday had been a shock. Thank God it was negative at least, but that didn't get away from the fact that his sixteen-year-old daughter must be having sex. Was it with this Craig lad, he wondered? He'd have to do some digging and find out more.

Ever since he'd found that bloody test, he'd wanted to tell Linda about it. He'd wanted to ask her what they should do. Should they sit Shauna down and try and talk to her reasonably? Should they demand for her to tell them who the boy was and go and see his parents? After all, Shauna was underage, and Rob was guessing the boy probably was too. But he hadn't mentioned it to Linda at all. He'd toyed with the idea, of course. The selfish part of him realised that if he told her, she'd probably be on the first plane home. And he really wanted her to come home. This sort of stuff wasn't his forte and he needed her to be the one to make decisions. But then he'd realised that he'd just look like he couldn't cope. And all the sacrifices he'd made would amount to nothing. Linda would be home in less than two weeks and they could talk about it then.

He went to the kettle and flicked on the switch. Placing a teaspoon of coffee in a mug, he waited for the water to boil. He could never think properly until he'd had his first coffee of the day. He added a dash of milk and a half teaspoon of sugar to the boiling drink and sat back down at the kitchen counter. Now what would Linda do in this situation? He needed to channel his wife and think as she would think. And then he had it.

His coffee was too hot to drink yet anyway so he left it to cool and headed upstairs. Feeling slightly nervous about what he might find, he opened the door to his daughter's room. The place was a mess with clothes strewn everywhere and schoolbooks and notes piled up in the corner. There were empty crisp packets on the floor and the remnants of a pizza on a plate on the locker. He went to open the window again but then thought better of it. He didn't want Shauna to know he'd been searching her room so he'd better leave things as he found them. But where was he going to start? With a sigh, he began with the drawers beneath her bed.

He felt slightly uncomfortable rummaging through her underwear, and he wondered if he was breaking some sort of law of privacy. But he was doing it for her own good. He wasn't even sure what he might find but he was hoping that having a look around her room would give him an insight into what was going on with her. Ten minutes later he'd found nothing of interest and decided to give up. He could feel his mood darkening as he went back downstairs and although the kitchen looked like a bomb had hit it, he wasn't in the humour for housework at that moment. What he needed was to get back to doing some real work. In his own job, he was powerful. He was knowledgeable and in charge. He always knew what to do and how to do it. He really needed to feel like that again because he felt he was losing control at home and he didn't like it one bit.

He toyed with the idea of getting a few files sent over to him from his job but he needed to get away from the house for a while. So although he was casually dressed in jeans and a polo top, he decided to head over there himself and he could bring some stuff home with him to work on. His mood lifted a little as he sat behind the wheel heading towards Delahunty Insurance. He felt like himself again, doing what he knew best.

Tanya, who was talking to a colleague when he arrived, raised an eyebrow as he slipped into his office and she followed him in to find out more. 'What are you doing here, Rob? I thought we wouldn't be seeing you for a couple of weeks.'

'That was the plan,' he said, rummaging through a filing cabinet. 'But I don't want things piling up for when I get back so I'm going to bring some stuff home and keep up to date.'

She hovered at the door for a moment and looked as though she was going to say something but then changed her mind and walked back out towards her own office. Rob tried not to look at her retreating back. He had way too much stuff going on in his head to add Tanya into the mix. Although she did look particularly sexy in that short black skirt that clung to her beautifully. He gave himself a mental shake and continued to gather the things he needed.

Twenty minutes later, he was about to leave when Tanya came back in and shut the door behind her. She stood with her back up against the door, her breasts heaving as she breathed heavily. Rob froze on the spot. He didn't know what to say. How to react. It seemed like she was waiting for him to make a move and he could feel that familiar stirring down below.

'I need to be quick,' she said, walking towards him. 'Jim Quinn has been watching me.'

'Wh-what do you mean?' The mention of his colleague's name threw him.

She moved even closer and he could feel the sweat beginning to form on the back of his neck. 'Jim Quinn. He's been in here looking up your files. I caught him yesterday. He was photocopying pages and I think he was contacting some of your clients.'

'Oh.'

'I just thought I'd warn you because I know how hard you've worked on some of those files. Jim is a sneaky one. He'll wade in and take credit for your work, if he gets the chance.' She looked around nervously, as if expecting Jim Quinn to be standing behind her.

'Well, thanks for the warning,' said Rob, his head spinning. He wasn't sure whether he was relieved or disappointed that Tanya hadn't been about to make advances on him. 'I'll make sure to lock the cabinets this time.'

'No problem,' she said, heading back to the door. 'You're a hard worker, Rob. An asset to this company.'

She hovered again, the door half open.

'Was there anything else, Tanya? Because I'm going to finish up here and head home.'

'It's just that I heard you might be leaving. I thought you would have mentioned it to me before the gossips got a hold of it.'

'I'm sorry, Tanya. I didn't think the news would travel quite so fast. And nothing has been finalised yet, so I'll keep you updated.'

'Well, I really hope you don't go. It just wouldn't be the same around here without you.'

She left before he could reply and he stood for a moment, contemplating the last few minutes. He was an asset, she'd said. It wouldn't be the same here without him. God, he really did love this place. Was he crazy to contemplate leaving?

He gathered his stuff, locked his filing cabinets and headed out. Tanya was at the photocopier and he gave her a wink and a nod of thanks and then shot Jim Quinn a dirty look as he passed him at the water dispenser. He was back on the road in minutes with his head full of a number of things. Bloody Jim Quinn. Rob had always known he was trouble. Talk about sneaky! But then his thoughts wandered to Tanya and what had happened back in the office. It seemed silly now, but for that moment when she'd closed the door and stood with her back against it, his mind had allowed him to believe she was looking for something of a sexual nature. He'd been convinced of it. And how would he have reacted if she'd tried it on with him? Would he have pushed her away, displaying his wedding ring and telling her he was taken? He pictured her full breasts pushing out of her low-cut top and wondered would he have been strong enough. He hoped so, but he was only human.

By the time he got home, he was consumed with guilt. Thoughts of Tanya were filling his head and making him aroused when he really should be thinking of his wife. If only things were better between him and Linda. He missed being close to her, and not only from a sexual point of view. There just seemed to be a distance between them that he wasn't sure how to fix. He had a sudden urge to hear her voice so he threw his files on the kitchen counter and dialled her number. She answered straight away.

'Hi, Linda. How's it going?'

'Good, good. And you?'

'All fine here too. How's the writing going?'

'Not bad. I'll get there eventually. How are the kids?'

'They're fine.' He hesitated for a moment and then asked, 'Do you know a Craig?'

'Craig Boland? Yes, that's the guy Shauna is seeing.'

Rob was astounded. 'She's going out with this guy? How did I not know this?'

'Well, they're not exactly going out,' said Linda. 'They're just seeing each other.'

'Same difference.'

'Well, apparently it's not. The kids just "see" each other these days until they make it official. Then when it's official, they can say they're going out.'

Rob shook his head. 'Well, that's a load of rubbish. They're either together or not. And how long has this been going on?'

'Why? Has something happened?' She sounded anxious and he felt guilty for worrying her.

'No, nothing. It's just she mentioned she was walking to school with him and I'd never heard of him before.'

'Oh. That's okay then. I thought you were going to tell me something terrible. Just keep an eye on her, will you? She hasn't been on her best behaviour recently.'

'I'm beginning to sense that,' he said, remembering their exchange that morning. 'But it's nothing I can't handle. What are you up to today?'

'Writing. As usual. Actually, I'd better go because I don't want to lose the flow. I'm in the middle of a scene.'

'You always seem to be in a rush.' There was accusation in his voice.

'I'm sorry,' she said. 'But I'm finding this book difficult to write so when I have the flow, I have to go with it.'

He was going to argue with her but decided against it. 'Okay, Linda. Chat later.'

She ended the call without a further goodbye and he was left feeling lonely and frustrated. He hated how their conversations seemed to just consist of a necessary exchange of pleasantries and information about the kids. And he didn't really get any sense from Linda that she appreciated all he was doing. After all, he'd taken two weeks of his precious holidays to run things at home while she swanned off to Spain. Not many husbands would be so generous and accommodating. Maybe he should tell her about Shauna and the pregnancy test. She'd soon realise where she needed to be.

With a sigh he sat down at the dining table and spread his files out in front of him. He had plenty to keep him going for a while. At least getting stuck into his own work would take his mind off other things. Before long he was immersed in clients' cases and his mood began to lift. He'd collect some more files over the coming days and that way, he'd be able to keep himself right up to date.

His phone pinged then and he was pleasantly surprised to see it was Linda. Until he read the text. *Don't forget Shauna's appointment for blood tests in the morning. She needs to fast for 12 hours. And just to remind you to ring the plumber about that radiator in our bedroom. Lx.* Unbelievable. She didn't have time to chat to him but she could take the time to send a text full of demands. Fuelled by anger, he stood up and paced up and down the room. Sometimes he wished Linda had never got that book deal. Things had been good between them before she started getting notions about herself. He sat back down and put his head in his hands. He pictured his wife lying on a lounger, enjoying the tropical sun, her body gleaming with suntan oil. As he became aroused, he was alarmed to find that the picture of Linda in his head was replaced by one of Tanya. But who could blame him? He'd seen more of Tanya lately than his own wife. And then a thought struck him. If he was on holidays and still working, he shouldn't have to go into the office to collect files. He should have them brought to him. Maybe tomorrow he'd give Tanya a ring and see if she might drop some over for him. He knew it was a dangerous move and with the way he was feeling, he didn't know if he could trust himself. But he'd played safe all his life so maybe now it was time for a change.

Chapter 13

Linda was in heaven. She'd never seen so many fabulous shoe shops under one roof before. Zenia Boulevard was a shopping centre just a twenty-minute walk from Aidan's place and he hadn't been lying when he'd told her it was even better than Dundrum Town Centre in Dublin. It housed a lot of the big English high-street shops such as H&M and Primark but it was the little Spanish shops that Linda was interested in. She'd never understood why people on holidays went on a shopping spree to Zara or New Look when they could do that back home. She wanted to look at stuff in shops she'd never heard of. To buy things that nobody back home would have. She'd already picked up a divine pair of nude sandals and was in the process of buying a gorgeous pair of knee-high black boots.

She'd been working on her book since early that morning but

had only managed to write a few hundred words. Monday night's outing was playing on her mind, making it difficult to concentrate. She must have relived the night a hundred times in her mind since then. She'd analysed every last detail, from what Kabir had packed for them to eat to how it felt when his hand had brushed her skin. And the truth was, it had felt good. Delicious, even. She used to feel that way about Rob but it was a long time since he'd had that sort of effect on her.

It was two days since the boat trip and she hadn't heard anything from Kabir. It was stupid of her to be bothered, really. He didn't owe her anything and she wasn't looking for anything. But she'd thought he'd at least have rung or texted to say he'd enjoyed the evening. She'd sat out in the garden for most of the day yesterday either writing or reading and had checked her phone every few minutes in case she'd missed a call. She was quite shocked at how disappointed she was that he hadn't made contact.

She paid for her second purchase and headed towards a little coffee shop she'd spotted on her way in. As she walked, she tried to focus on her husband. She wanted to feel passionately about him just like she used to. But their last conversation yesterday had left her feeling flat. They'd just said what they had to say and nothing more. She hadn't felt any affection from him and if she was honest, she hadn't given him any either. Linda thrived on affection and had always got it in bucketloads from her husband. But not lately. He was a great provider and always made sure she and the children had everything they needed but in recent times he failed to see that Linda needed his love and affection more than anything.

At the coffee shop, she sat down at a table and gratefully dropped her bags at her side. The waiter came to her immediately and she ordered a cappuccino and a croissant. Yesterday was the second time she'd lied to Rob in as many days. Well, she hadn't lied to him exactly – she'd just been a bit liberal with the truth. He hadn't asked her if she'd been out, so she hadn't told him. It was one of those things that would have sounded far worse than it was. Her going out alone with a gorgeous, single man wouldn't exactly fill Rob with faith in her. And although nothing had happened, it had happened in her head a hundred times over. Oh God, she was losing the plot!

Her coffee and croissant arrived and just as she was about to take her first sip, she heard a voice she recognised. The animated tones and the speed with which the words were coming out left her in no doubt that it was Aidan. She looked around, ready to say hello and laugh at the coincidence of bumping into him, only to see there was a large trellis with flowers all over it blocking her view. She managed to peep through one of the gaps and confirm it was him, sitting with a man she didn't recognise. They had some documents in front of them so she guessed it was a business meeting. She'd leave them to it because Aidan probably wouldn't thank her for interrupting them.

She checked to see if anyone was watching her watching them, and when she was sure nobody was paying any attention, she continued spying on them, straining her ears to hear what was being said. The other man was younger than Aidan, probably around early thirties, and spoke with a broken English accent. His rugged features and wild hair made him look a little crazy and it was obvious he was agitated. Linda tried to focus to hear what they were saying.

'So when will I get that money?' said Aidan, pointing to a page in front of them. 'I was waiting way too long last time.'

The other man ran his hand through his long hair. 'That was an error. I'll make sure the money is in your account by the end of next week at the latest.'

Aidan nodded. 'Good. Because that house has eaten into my funds and I need to get some more cash in quickly.'

Linda gasped. She knew it. The house wasn't on loan to them from a friend. They'd actually bought it themselves. It was unbelievable. How could they afford such luxury? And even more importantly, why were they lying about it? They were speaking in low tones so she adjusted her position to hear better.

'Relax,' said the rugged guy. 'It's all in hand. And the next batch of stuff is due in from Asia next week so the money should start rolling in then.'

That seemed to satisfy Aidan. 'Okay. Just keep me in the loop. And as I said before, I have a friend staying with me at the moment and I don't want her to know anything. Not yet, anyway. I'm sure she'll find out eventually but let's keep it quiet for now.'

'Okay, boss. Whatever you say.'

Linda sat back, her heart thumping like crazy. She couldn't believe what she'd heard. Actually, she didn't know what it all meant but it didn't sound good. What the hell had Aidan gotten himself into? And this stuff coming from Asia – was it drugs? Jesus! She hoped not but it certainly sounded that way. Her head was in a spin and her coffee and croissant sat in front of her untouched. But she had no appetite. She just wanted to get away from there without Aidan seeing her and have a think about what she'd heard. So, throwing ten euros on the table, she grabbed her bags and skulked off, keeping her head down until she was way out of sight.

She'd completely lost interest in shopping so she decided to head back home. She hadn't bothered with sun cream earlier because it had been dull but now the sun was beating down on the back of her neck as she walked and she knew she'd have to get home quickly if she didn't want to be scorched. She hurried along the street, her head full of the conversation she'd just heard.

None of it made sense. Aidan was such a nice guy who always did and said the right things. That's what had drawn them to each other all those years ago at the writing course. He'd been so generous and kind, encouraging her and all the others with their work, praising their efforts even though his own was far superior. She'd been drawn to his upbeat personality and his sense of fun. But never, ever would she have imagined he'd be involved in something sinister. There must be another explanation. But what?

She let herself into the house and almost cried with relief when the cool air hit her. Her top was wet with sweat and her tongue was stuck to the roof of her mouth. She went to the sink and downed two glasses of water in quick succession. Leaning back on the kitchen counter to sip her third glass, her eyes scanned the room. It was a beautiful modern building with some classic touches here and there. The ornate cornices over the doors were at odds with the minimalistic décor and yet it worked really well. Linda reckoned the place must have cost Aidan well over a million euros.

The front door opened suddenly, causing Linda to almost jump out of her skin. '*Hola. Estoy en casa.*'

It was James, full of the joys of life as usual. He was a breath of fresh air and Linda could see why Aidan loved him so much.

'Hi, James. I thought you were working today.'

'I was,' he said, throwing his backpack on the floor beside the sofa and flopping down on it. 'I was up and gone while you were still only half way through your sleep. My shift is over for the day, thank God.'

She went over to join him. 'So what's with the Spanish speaking. I didn't think you knew the language.'

He laughed. 'I don't. Well, I didn't. Aidan and I have been taking night classes. You can't live over here without knowing the basics at least. We were total beginners when we started but we know slightly more than nothing now!'

'Well, it sounded good to me. A proper accent and everything.'

'Why thank you,' said James, blushing. 'So what have you been up to today? Work or pleasure?'

'A bit of both. I did a small bit of writing and then went to the Zenia Boulevard for a bit of retail therapy.' She wasn't about to tell him that she had seen Aidan or what she'd heard.

'Fabulous. Did you buy anything nice?'

'See for yourself,' she said, reaching down to grab her bags from where she'd left them beside the sofa. 'I'm in love with all the shoes over here.'

He examined the purchases and gave a low whistle. 'I like your style, Linda. You should come shopping with me and Aidan. We could do with giving our wardrobes a boost for the winter months.'

She saw an opportunity to find out some information. 'But aren't you and Aidan saving to buy a place of your own? Aidan always said he didn't want to rent for ever.'

'That's true.' Not a flicker of anything. 'But we also have to live. You can find some lovely clothes at great prices over here.'

She nodded. 'I noticed that. Maybe we'll go out over the weekend. Right, I'm going to change and get back to my writing for a while. What are you up to for the afternoon?'

'Sleep,' he said, rubbing his eyes. 'If I don't get a couple of hours' shut-eye now, I won't even last until dinner before I fall asleep. And I promised Aidan I'd make his favourite fish pie later.'

'Yum,' said Linda, her stomach rumbling. She remembered the untouched coffee and croissant and suddenly felt ravenous. 'Where is Aidan, by the way? Did he say he was meeting somebody today? He seems to always be out and about meeting publishers and the likes.'

James shook his head. 'No meetings today. He went to the library to do some writing. He likes to go there a few days a week. He says it inspires him. Now I'm going to get some sleep before I collapse. We can chat later.'

Linda watched him head into his bedroom and wondered how much he knew. Did he actually know Aidan had bought the house? Had they bought it together? Did he know where the money came from? Or was this something Aidan was doing without his knowledge? So many questions. Linda was curious by nature and she was determined to get to the bottom of the mystery before she had to go home.

She couldn't wait until dinner before eating so she made herself a cheese and ham sandwich and sat down at the kitchen counter. In her youth she'd have been outside, doused with baby oil and wearing a G-string. She wouldn't have let a moment of the sun escape her until she was tanned over almost every inch of her body. She smiled at the memories of her younger years. When she'd go on a two-week sun holiday, she'd allow herself to burn for the first few days, knowing that it would peel or maybe even blister, before eventually turning a golden shade of brown. Back in Ireland, she'd get some oohs and aahs for a week or so until her skin would become patchy and eventually go back to her normal milky white. How could she have thought that a week or two of being glowing and tanned could be worth the pain and suffering? These days she wouldn't step outside before applying factor 50 and would spend most of her time in the shade.

Glancing at the clock, she knew she should really try to get some writing done before dinner, but she just couldn't face it. It was becoming more and more difficult to drag the words out of herself and the more she thought about it, the more she avoided it. It was getting late anyway so she made the decision to just relax and read until dinner. She wondered what they were doing at home. It was strange being able to relax when she was so used to being pulled in every direction. It had taken her a couple of days to accept her state of tranquillity, but she was loving it now and didn't want it to end. But thankfully she didn't have to think about that for a while so, grabbing her Kindle, she put her plate and cup into the dishwasher and went to relax on the sofa.

She lay back and savoured the feel of the cool leather before opening *Blood Room* where she'd left it the previous day. It was a particular juicy bit and she wanted to savour it. But just as it was getting interesting, her phone began to ring in her handbag, which she'd left beside the sofa. She grabbed it and began to root for the phone. If it was Rob again, she'd let it go to voicemail and call him back later. She really wasn't in the mood for speaking to him. But when she saw the display, she answered without hesitation.

'Hi, Linda,' said Kabir, his voice low and husky. 'I hope I'm not disturbing you.'

'Not at all,' she said, her book already forgotten. She'd felt a little guilty when they'd exchanged phone numbers on Monday night but now she was very glad they'd done so.

'I was just wondering,' he said slowly. 'Could I take you out again tonight for a drink? Nothing fancy. Just a pub and a pint.'

She laughed at that. 'I like the sound of that, but can I have wine instead?'

'*Sí*, Linda. You can have whatever your heart desires.'

A little bit of her melted at his accent. Today he sounded particularly Spanish and she wondered did his accent change depending on who he'd been spending time with.

'So eight o'clock?' He was still talking. 'I'll pick you up from your place.'

'I … well, yes. I suppose that's fine.' She didn't stop to think about what Aidan would say about her having another night out with Kabir. Or what Rob would think if he knew. Because if she allowed herself to think too much about it, she wouldn't go. And right at that moment, she couldn't think of anyone else she'd rather be with.

Chapter 14

'So where's this place we're going to?' said Linda, as she and Kabir sped out of town in his jeep. 'I hope it's somewhere casual because I'm not dressed for anywhere fancy.'

'Don't worry.' He glanced sideways at her. 'You look beautiful and you'll love where I'm taking you.'

She didn't really care where they were going. She just liked being with him, so she sat back in her seat and relaxed. He was so easy to talk to. So ready to listen. He was interested in hearing all about her and seemed to understand how complicated her life was. They chatted amicably as he drove, and she was surprised how comfortable she felt.

'Right, here we are,' he said, turning the jeep off the road and in through the gates of a little house. It was one of the prettiest houses she'd ever seen and although it was small, it was beautifully kept. The walls were painted a pale salmon colour and the most beautiful blooming pink flowers crept up along the front of the house and over the door.

'Who lives here? Are we just picking someone up or are we staying?'

'Come on,' he said, hopping out of the jeep and rushing around to open her door. 'You can meet them when we call. You're going to love them.'

Something didn't feel quite right but Linda went along with it anyway. He ushered her up to the front door and banged three times with the little brass knocker. It looked at first as though there was nobody home, but when Kabir knocked again, there was a sign of movement inside. Suddenly the door was swung open and there stood an elderly man and woman, both beaming from ear to ear.

'*Mijo*,' said the woman, reaching her arms out and placing her two palms on Kabir's face. She kissed him on both cheeks and then turned her attention to Linda. 'And who is this beautiful lady?'

'This is Linda, Mama.' He stepped aside so that the woman could get a better look. 'Linda, this is my mother, Sofia and my father, Nicolas.'

Linda was rooted to the spot. He'd brought her to see his parents? Seriously? They'd known each other a few days and Kabir knew she was married. What on earth was he thinking? But she didn't want to be rude. They seemed like nice people and it wasn't their fault that their son was being an idiot.

'Lovely to meet you,' said Linda, accepting Sofia's kisses on her cheeks and shaking hands with the quieter Nicolas.

'Come, come.' Sofia beckoned them to follow her into the house and as they did so, Linda managed to whisper to Kabir.

'What the hell, Kabir? Why are you bringing me here?'

'I'm sorry,' he whispered back. 'They've just been going on and on at me about never meeting any of my girlfriends.'

Linda gasped. 'Kabir, I'm not—'

'I know you're not my girlfriend! But can you please just give my mother the pleasure of thinking you are? Just for one night.'

She was about to object until she saw the look of panic on Kabir's face.

'Please,' he said, squeezing her hand. 'Just do this one thing for me. I know I should have asked you beforehand, but I chickened out. Please, Linda. What harm could it do?'

'I suppose.' She was less than enthusiastic but Kabir was right. What harm could it do?

Sofia had prepared a feast for them and Linda's eyes almost popped out of her head when she saw the spread on the table. There were bowls of seafood paella, plates of Spanish omelette, salads, breads, cheese and crackers … the list went on and on.

'So what do you work at?' said Nicolas, as they passed dishes around the table to share. It was the first time he'd spoken since they'd arrived.

Linda tried to chew the enormous mouthful of omelette she'd stuffed into her gob before answering. 'I'm a writer. I work from home so that I can spend more time with …' She was about to say 'the children' and then thought better of it. Whatever game they were playing, it probably didn't involve her having children.

'With?' She'd been hoping he wouldn't pick up on her unfinished sentence.

'With my imagination.' What a save! 'I can think better at home where it's quiet rather than in a busy office.'

'So how long have you two been together?' said Sofia, cutting herself a piece of crusty bread.

'Mama, what did I tell you about questions? It's no wonder I never bring anybody home.'

'Kabir. Don't speak to your mother that way.' Nicolas looked angry. 'We brought you up better than that.'

'Sorry,' said Kabir, his head bent like a bold child. 'But I don't want Linda to feel uncomfortable.'

'It's fine, honestly,' said Linda, not wanting to end up in the middle of an argument. 'We haven't been together long, have we, Kabir?' She diverted the question to him and he shifted in his chair.

'Em, no. Not long at all. But it feels like we've known each other for ever.'

God, he was really going for it. Linda felt like she was in some sort of weird dream and for a moment thought about making her excuses to leave. But suddenly something about the situation, in all its absurdity, made her giggle and she had to cough to disguise it.

'Are you okay, Linda?' Sofia poured her a glass of water. 'Here, take a sip of this.'

She gratefully accepted the drink, using the time to compose herself. She glanced at Kabir and was glad to see how uncomfortable he looked. It had been wrong of him to put her in this situation. Had that been his game all along? Get to know her so that he could bring her here to keep his parents happy? But now that she was here, she may as well go along with it. She could ask Kabir later what the hell he'd been thinking.

'Linda?' Sofia sounded concerned and she realised all eyes were on her, waiting to see if she'd survived the choking incident.

'Sorry. Yes, I'm fine. Just something went down the wrong way.'

'That'll be Sofia's spices,' said Nicolas, nodding his head knowingly. 'I keep telling her to go easy on them, but will she listen to me? No. She tells me: *What do you know about cooking, Nicolas? You've never prepared a meal in your life.*'

Sofia was quick to respond. 'Well, it's true, isn't it? I cook, you eat. That's how it's been for the last fifty-two years.'

'Yes, fifty-two years of too spicy food. It's a wonder I don't have an ulcer by now.'

'Nicolas, if I wasn't here to feed you and look after all of your—'

'Mama! Can we not argue in front of our guest please? Linda doesn't want to hear it.'

'I'm sorry, Linda,' said Sofia, looking ashamed. 'Where are my manners?'

Linda waved her hand to dismiss the other woman's apology. 'Don't worry. You remind me of my own parents, actually.'

'Kabir tells us you're from Ireland. Are your parents over there?'

'Yes, they're in Dublin. And I don't live too far away.' She realised she'd made a mistake when she saw the look on Sofia's face.

'Ireland? You live in Ireland?' The woman looked as though she was about to cry. 'I just assumed you'd moved over here.'

'Mama, I told you Linda just came over here recently. She still considers Ireland as home, don't you, Linda?'

'Well, yes. I came here to write my book. I'm just not sure how long I'll be staying yet.' It was the best she could do. If only Kabir had warned her, she might have been able to make up something more convincing.

'I see,' said Nicolas, nodding. 'But now that we have you here, we won't let you go, will we, Sofia?'

'Absolutely not.'

Linda felt alarmed and found herself looking around to see if there was a way to escape. She imagined them imprisoning her and not allowing her to leave the house. What the hell was she doing? She was in a house with complete strangers who seemed to think she was about to join their family and live happily ever after with them. The whole thing was completely absurd.

Kabir seemed to sense her discomfort and told his parents that Linda had been writing a lot late at night and was exhausted. They wouldn't be staying much longer, he said, much to Linda's relief. They chatted some more about general stuff until eventually Kabir stood up and said they'd have to go. Sofia immediately jumped up and began wrapping up leftovers in tin foil and Linda walked out of there with a few days' worth of supplies.

'Bloody hell, Kabir,' she said, as they got into the car. 'I can't believe you put me in that position.'

'I'm sorry, Linda. But just let's get out of here and then we can chat.'

Nicolas and Sofia stood at the door waving continuously and Linda waved back until they were no longer in sight. 'So? I think you owe me an explanation.'

Kabir sighed. 'I'm really sorry about that. Honestly, I am. I hadn't planned it or anything but my parents are old and are always going on about me settling down and finding a nice woman.'

'So you recruited me to act as that woman?'

'God no. Please don't think that. I dropped in to see them last night and Mum was driving me mad, asking if there was anybody special in my life. She never stops. She keeps telling me I should be married at this stage and asking why I'm not trying to find somebody to settle down with.'

Linda wondered the same thing too. Kabir was gorgeous. He was a decent, hard-working guy with his own house, a great income and he had charm in bucketfuls. Yet he was still single at thirty-eight. Maybe he had some dark secret that was getting in the way of him settling down. Or maybe it was her writer's brain looking for a good story!

'You have to believe me, Linda. It was just spur of the moment. I told them about meeting you at James and Aidan's and they immediately jumped to conclusions.'

'And you didn't correct them?'

'No.' He looked embarrassed and she almost felt sorry for him. 'They said they were delighted I'd found somebody special and Mum immediately started making plans for tea tonight.'

Linda tried to stifle a giggle.

'What's so funny?' said Kabir, looking confused.

'I'm sorry, Kabir, but that accent!'

'What's wrong with my accent?'

'There's nothing wrong but I can't believe how you've gone from an almost perfect English accent with a hint of Spanish, to an almost perfect Indian one.'

He laughed at that. 'It's when I see my mother. Everybody comments on it. I suddenly become a little Indian boy. It's bizarre.'

Kabir had grown up in Spain but had gone to college in England. He'd stayed with his English grandparents, which was where he'd developed his perfect English accent. But the lure of the sunshine had brought him back to Spain in his twenties, where his accent had become mixed from spending so much time with his parents.

'So, am I forgiven for earlier then?' said Kabir, interrupting Linda's thoughts. 'I honestly didn't mean to make you uncomfortable.'

'It's quite funny really,' said Linda, remembering how excited Sofia had been to see her son with someone. 'Have you never brought anyone home before?'

He shook his head. 'I've never been with anyone long enough to want to take them home. It's just how it is. At least meeting you might keep them off my back for a while.'

'As long as I don't have to do it again.'

'I promise,' said Kabir, stopping the jeep on the street. 'And just to make it up to you, I'm taking you for a very large glass of wine.'

'In an actual pub this time?'

He laughed as he hopped out and came around to her side of the jeep to open her door. 'Definitely in a pub. No more surprises.'

The rest of the evening was very pleasant and Linda enjoyed Kabir's company. They chatted about a lot of different things, including Linda's family, and she surprised herself by how much she opened up to him. She told him about the circumstances that had led to her coming to Spain and she even told him a little about how she was feeling about Rob. She felt a little disloyal speaking about her husband, but Kabir was a good listener and it was good for somebody to understand.

By the time he dropped her home, she felt exhausted and he made fun of the fact that her head had kept falling to her chest as she dozed off in the jeep. She denied it, of course, but it was all in jest. He walked her to the door and as he turned to face her, he took her hand.

'If circumstances were different,' he said, looking into her eyes, 'I'd want to be with you.'

The words hung in the air for a moment and Linda could feel her heart beating faster and faster. She wasn't sure how to respond but the truth was, she felt the same. Kabir was pretty much the perfect man and when she was with him, she was relaxed and happy. He took a step towards her and his face was just inches from hers. She closed her eyes. Although she knew it was wrong, she couldn't resist him. She wanted to taste the sweetness of his kiss and run her hands through his luscious hair. She needed to feel like a woman again. Like she was special. And Kabir made her feel that way.

What she didn't expect was for Kabir to put his arms around her and pull her close to him. He buried his face in her hair and squeezed her tightly. She'd been sure he was going in for the kiss and she felt disappointed that it hadn't happened.

'Thanks for tonight,' he said, pulling away from her. 'And I'm sorry again for tricking you like that.'

She shook her head. 'It was a bit weird but weirdly enjoyable. Your parents are lovely. I hope you find a woman someday that you can bring home for real.'

He shrugged. 'Night, Linda. I'm sure I'll see you again soon.'

Stepping inside, she closed the door quietly and kicked off her shoes. As she headed into her bedroom, something James had said the other night kept ringing in her head. He'd warned her not to fall for Kabir. And she'd been adamant that she wouldn't. But as she well knew, life has a habit of throwing curveballs and she hated to admit it, but it seemed that she was falling for the beautiful man who'd come into her life and added some excitement – just when she'd needed it most.

Chapter 15

Linda had woken up feeling very anxious. She hadn't slept well, with thoughts of both Rob and Kabir whirring around in her mind. It was coming close to the end of her first week in Spain and although she'd managed to get some writing done, her head was even more messed up than it had been before she'd come over.

If she was living in the moment, life was good. She loved the Spanish sunshine and relaxed way of life and she was having a great time getting to know Kabir. But she was also aware that that wasn't real life. Her time over here would be over at the end of the following week and her Spanish dream would be a distant memory.

But what if it wasn't? What if she made the decision to completely change her life? What if she moved over here, just like Aidan had done, and started afresh? She could check out schools and bring the children over. They'd soon get used to living in Spain and although there'd be teething problems, they could all settle into a fabulous new way of life. And she'd have Kabir. That was if he wanted her. Would it really be possible to make such a bold move and turn her life upside down?

Then there was Rob. Despite her doubts, was she really ready to leave everything they had behind? They'd been married for such a long time and had gone through so much together. And how would the children feel if they split up? She knew she couldn't live her life unhappily just to please her children. It wouldn't be fair on them in the long run. But she definitely needed to consider them and how their parents splitting up would affect them. On the other hand, if she thought her marriage was over, maybe moving to Spain wouldn't be a bad idea. If she stayed in Ireland, would she always feel the need to try and fix things? Or even worse, to accept her unhappiness and stay in a dead relationship?

It was almost noon and Linda hadn't even had breakfast yet. She had no appetite and her head was pounding. There was no chance she'd get any writing done while she had so much on her mind so she made herself a cup of coffee and brought it to the sofa. She was alone in the house and the silence was making her nervous. It was giving her too much time to think. Too much space to worry about where her life was going.

She sat down and took a long sip of her coffee, allowing the smooth drink to coat her tongue and warm her insides. She began to feel a little calmer. She would look at her situation sensibly and figure out the best course of action. She had to be realistic. All of a sudden she had a desperate need to talk to her children.

She hadn't spoken to them much since she'd left, mainly because they'd either been elsewhere when she'd talked to Rob or reluctant to come to the phone because they'd been watching telly or playing Xbox. But it was Thursday and they were off school so maybe now would be a good time to catch them. It drove her mad that the kids seemed to have a day or half day off almost every week. How was a parent who worked supposed to account for that? Suddenly she wanted to see their faces, so she picked up her phone, selected WhatsApp video call and dialled Ben's number.

'Hi, Mum.' His gorgeous face appeared in front of her and she could feel tears prick her eyes.

'Hi, Ben. How are you? What are you up to?'

'Just in my room reading. How is Spain?'

'It's lovely. But I miss all of you. How is school? Any news?'

'School is okay. Cian and Leo are coming over for a sleepover tonight since we have no school tomorrow.'

Linda almost fell off the sofa in shock. 'Cian and Leo? Really? I didn't think you were friends with them anymore.'

'I never said we weren't friends, Mum. I just haven't seen as much of them since secondary school. Dad said we can get pizza and watch a movie.'

'That's brilliant, love. It'll be great for you to catch up with them and see how they're getting on in their new school.'

'Yeah.'

Linda could see he'd had enough. He was a boy of few words and even that short conversation had been more than she'd gotten out of him in weeks. 'I'll let you go, so,' she said. 'Tell Daddy I'll give him a ring in a while. I'm going to try Shauna now. Enjoy your night and I'll talk to you tomorrow.'

She ended the call and sat back on the sofa. Fair play to Rob. She wondered what he'd done to get Ben to agree to a sleepover. He hadn't had one of those in the last year. Still, however it had come about, it was good news. Ben needed to see his friends and not spend all his time alone in his room. It would be good for him.

She opened her WhatsApp again and dialled Shauna's number. But the phone rang and rang until the call ended. She dialled again and after a few rings, Shauna's bedraggled face appeared on the screen.

'Mum. What the fuck?'

'Shauna Costa. Mind your language. What's wrong with you?' She looked like death, with mascara running down her pale face and her hair standing up all over the place.

'I've just woken up. Actually, you've just woken me up.'

'Sorry about that, love, but it's after twelve. I thought you'd be well up by now.'

'Why should I be?' Shauna lay back on her pillow and held the phone in the air so she could see her mother. 'I was out last night and there's no school today.'

'Out? What do you mean out? Out where?'

'Relax, Mum. Just over in Jenny's. And her mum was there, in case you think we were up to something.'

'I wasn't suggesting that. But I do want to make sure you're behaving, after what happened the other week.'

'Jeez! Are you going to hold that over me for the rest of my life? I made one mistake. I should never have touched that vodka but there's not one person my age who hasn't tried alcohol at some stage. I was just unlucky to have been caught.'

Linda hated how Shauna normalised it. It had been such a big deal for her to see her sixteen-year-old in a drunken state, but Shauna had barely apologised for it.

'So how is Dad getting on?' said Linda, trying to prolong the conversation and get as much info out of her daughter as possible. 'Is he managing okay without me?'

Shauna shrugged. 'Not much to manage really, is there?'

Linda bit her tongue. Obviously Rob's attitude towards the running of the house had rubbed off on their daughter.

Linda probed further. 'So what's it like having Dad at home instead of me?'

'To be honest, he's driving me crazy.'

Linda couldn't help feeling smug. 'Why? What has he done?'

'Just the way he goes on,' said Shauna, scrunching up her nose in the same manner she did when Linda told her to clean her room. 'He keeps making me lunch for school even though I tell him I don't want it. These little salad sandwiches all cut into quarters. And grapes and strawberries and that sort of shit.'

'I won't tell you again, Shauna. Stop that language. We didn't bring you up to speak like that.'

'Sorry.' She didn't look a bit sorry. 'And he wants us to sit together for dinner every day. *Like a proper family*, he says. He even fills a beaker full of juice for me. Honestly, I haven't brought a beaker of juice to school since I was about six!'

'Well, don't be too hard on him,' said Linda. 'He's trying his best.' But Linda was astounded at how hard he was actually trying. It had been years since she'd made a lunch for the kids. They usually helped themselves and she even turned a blind eye to the fact that they took crisps and chocolate more often than healthy food. And there was Rob making proper packed lunches and getting them all together for dinner. She knew she should be delighted how well he was doing but a little piece of her was disappointed. She wanted him to fail. To realise it was all too much for him and have a newfound respect for her when she got home.

'So is that all, Mum? Can I go back to sleep now? I'm meeting Craig later so I'll need to get some shut-eye beforehand.'

Linda gave up and let Shauna go. She'd wanted to ask her why she'd need to get sleep before meeting Craig. But she knew that would have led to another argument and she'd had enough of those.

Seeing both her children's faces made her feel more connected with home. She'd love to be there later to see Ben with his friends. She'd been so worried about him lately that it would be lovely to see him laughing and having fun. She'd even felt a pang when she spoke to Shauna. Despite all her daughter's faults, Linda missed her and would love nothing better than to give her a hug and tell her she loved her. She sat back on the sofa and closed her eyes. She pictured Rob and willed herself to miss him too. But all she felt was an emptiness.

Maybe what she needed was to see his face. To see those gorgeous brown eyes and help her remember why she fell in love with him. Without further thought, she dialled his number.

After a few rings, she was presented with a picture of his ear and a muffled hello. 'Look at the phone, Rob,' she said, giggling. 'Turn it around.'

'I can't hear you. What did you say?' He looked at the phone and realisation seemed to dawn. 'Linda! It's you. I couldn't hear you there for a second. Why are you doing this face thing?'

'I just wanted to see you. I thought you'd be pleased.'

'I am, I am. It's just you know how I hate these things.'

'I do,' she said. 'But it's worth it to see each other, isn't it?'

He ran his hands through his hair and sighed. 'Linda, your voice is all out of sync. Can we not just do a normal call?'

She was about to object and then wasn't bothered. 'Okay. Hang up and I'll ring you back.'

'That's better,' he said, brightly, as he answered a normal voice call. 'Now I can concentrate on what you're saying.'

There was no point arguing about it. 'I spoke to the children,' she said. 'They said you're managing things well there.'

'I'm doing my best. But it's not exactly rocket science, is it?'

Her hand tightened around the phone and she could feel anger beginning to bubble. 'No it's not. But sometimes it can be a hell of a lot harder.'

'Well, everything is running smoothly so you don't need to worry. Ben is having his friends over tonight and I'm going to order pizza for them as a treat.'

'So he was telling me. How did you get him to agree to that?'

'I had a chat with him. Told him he needed to spend less time alone and more time with his friends. I suggested the sleepover and with the promise of pizza and Ben and Jerry's, it was a no-brainer for him.'

Linda resented the fact that she'd tried everything to get Ben to have his friends over, to no avail, but as soon as his dad mentioned it, it was a done deal.

'I know you've tried, love,' continued Rob. 'But sometimes you just need a firm hand. No molly-coddling – just tell him how it is. I think he appreciated being spoken to like an adult.'

'But I always speak to him like that.' She was actually sulking now. 'And he always says he'll have the boys over sometime, but it never happens.'

'Well, it's happening tonight,' Rob said, victoriously. 'He'll have a great time and will soon realise what he's been missing. Sleepovers are the best part of being a kid.'

She had to agree with him there. Her sleepovers had been legendary when she was younger. She'd been very popular at school and all the girls used to vie for her attention. Ger was her best friend, of course, and was always invited, but she'd often had a few more too. Her parents had been very accommodating and with her being an only child, they'd always encouraged her to bring friends over.

'Linda, are you there?'

'Sorry, yes. I was just thinking about my sleepovers when I was younger. Yes, Ben will have a great time with his friends. I'm glad you got through to him.'

'Me too,' he said, and then there was a pause. 'I miss you, Linda.' Her heart softened at the sound of his whispered voice. 'And,' he continued, 'I miss you in our bed every night. I know you've been overwhelmed with stuff but I want our physical relationship to get back on track. I want us to bring back the excitement.'

'What do you mean?'

'Come on, Linda. You know exactly what I mean. We used to have so much fun in the bedroom. Isn't it time we got some of that back again?'

'And you think that will fix everything, do you? A romp in the bedroom and all our problems will be solved?' She was incredulous. He just didn't seem to get it.

'Well, it's a start. And I was thinking. Maybe your mum could come and look after the kids at some stage and we could both go and visit Aidan. It would be nice for the two of us to get away.'

Her heart began to pound at the thought of her two lives colliding, but she answered calmly. 'Maybe.'

'I know you haven't been happy lately, Linda.' His voice had changed to a more serious tone. 'But I want to change all that. I want you to be happy and I want to be the one to make it happen.'

Tears welled up in her eyes. He really knew how to play with her emotions. She was up and down like a yoyo! 'Thanks, Rob. I really do appreciate that.'

'No problem. Now go and write that book. I want to get some work done before the house descends into bedlam later. I took a few files from work so I'm juggling home and work at the moment.'

'Just like I do.' It was barely a whisper.

'Yes, love. Just like you do. I'll chat to you later.'

She threw the phone down beside her and rubbed her temples. Instead of making her feel better about things, that call had only served to confuse her more. But she'd learned two things. The first was that she still loved her husband. The sound of his voice had made her long to feel his arms around her. To bury her head in his chest and feel happy and secure just like she used to. But the second thing wasn't so good. Much as she loved Rob and cared for him, she wasn't sure that was enough. She wanted so much more and was beginning to doubt if he was the one who was going to make her happy for the rest of her life.

Chapter 16

Rob sat back in his armchair, an array of newspapers in front of him on the coffee table. He couldn't remember when he'd last taken time to read the paper cover to cover. He'd been out to the shops early to buy some breakfast rolls for Ben and his friends and he'd picked up the papers then. He took a sip of his coffee and felt smugly satisfied at the sound of Ben and his friends laughing upstairs. Linda had been saying for weeks that she'd been worried about their son. About the fact that he was turning into a recluse and not wanting to see his friends. But all it had taken was a bit of encouragement to make him see what he was missing out on.

His mind wandered to the call he'd had with Linda the previous day. He was really beginning to miss her. It seemed strange that she was in a foreign country without him, living a life he wasn't part of. His idea for them both to go back there together was inspired. It would be something for them to focus on. If they got some time away together, maybe they could get that spark back. He knew it was still there, lingering beneath the surface, but they just needed to find it again.

He had to admit, running a house wasn't as easy as he'd thought. He'd always pictured Linda having loads of time to herself at home. He could never understand why she'd moan about her workload when she had all day to potter around. But he was beginning to see a different side to things. It wasn't just the chores in the house that had to be handled – it was also the children. He hadn't imagined that there'd be so much to think about. As far as he'd been concerned, they went off to school early in the morning and Linda didn't have to worry about them again until they came home in the evening. But now he could see that wasn't the case.

Rob tried to concentrate on his newspaper but the noise from upstairs was beginning to give him a headache. He was glad that Ben was spending time with his friends but he'd had enough at this stage. He'd give them another hour and then he'd drive the boys home. He couldn't wait to report back to Linda about how well it had gone. They'd ordered pizza and watched a movie and had gone to Ben's room then for the rest of the night. Rob had woken once or twice to the sound of loud giggles coming from their room, but other than that, it had all gone smoothly.

A few minutes later, Rob was about to go up and tell the boys to quieten down, when suddenly there was a yell from upstairs.

'Dad! Daaaaaaaad!'

Rob dropped his paper and dashed upstairs. He burst into the room and the stench hit him like a slap in the face. Cian was sitting on the edge of the bed bent over a pool of vomit. It seemed that everything from this morning's breakfast to last night's pizza had emerged from his stomach and Rob was almost sick himself at the sight.

'What's happened?' he said, looking at the other two boys, who were holding their noses, a look of disgust on their faces.

'We ... we were just fooling around,' said Ben, trying not to look at Cian, who was still retching. 'And then Cian said he didn't feel well.'

'Okay. Ben, go and grab some stuff from the kitchen. Towels and cloths and a plastic bag. Leo, go and help him.'

The boys scurried off and Rob reluctantly went to Cian and sat beside him. 'You'll be okay,' he said, patting the boy awkwardly on the back. 'You probably just ate too much.'

Cian nodded but Rob could see he was shaking. He really didn't look well. His face was a greenish shade of white and his hair was stuck to his forehead with sweat. So much for a relaxing morning reading the newspapers. The boys came back then, and Rob handed Cian a towel while he proceeded to clean up the mess. It was disgusting. The smell was vile and although he tried to get on with things, it was hard not to analyse the contents of the vomit.

'I think we should get your mum to come and collect you,' said Rob, having visions of Cian being sick on the lovely grey upholstery of his car. 'I'll give her a ring when I'm finished cleaning this up.'

Cian nodded through his tears and Rob felt sorry for him. They'd had such a good night that it was a pity it had to end this way. He felt responsible. Maybe he'd fed them too much. He'd wanted to please them so had bought a selection of chocolate and ice-cream for them to have after their pizza and the breakfast rolls he'd bought earlier were huge.

'Ben, will you go and get the anti-bacterial spray from—' Rob froze. As he looked around, a torrent of liquid sprayed from Ben's mouth and Leo had to duck to avoid being hit. It was like something from *The Exorcist* and he just wanted to run away.

'Jesus,' said Ben, holding onto the wall to steady himself. 'I feel awful.'

Rob tried to think quickly. 'Okay, okay. I think you boys must have got some food poisoning or something. Leo, are you okay?'

'I think so,' he said, looking shocked. 'Can I go home now, Mr Costa?'

'Go downstairs,' said Rob, decisively, 'and ring your mum. Tell her to come and collect you. I'll explain it to her when she gets here. She'll have to keep an eye on you in case you get sick too.'

'My head hurts, Mr Costa.' It was Cian, who'd lain back on the bed and looked like death. 'I want to go home.'

'Yes, yes, I think that's for the best. I'll go ring your mum now. Ben, are you okay?'

Ben nodded. 'I feel a bit better now. Sorry about the desk.'

Rob looked over to see that Ben's vomiting had been so ferocious it had sprayed all over his desk, covering books and pens and anything else that was there. 'Not to worry. We'll sort it out. Let's just get the boys collected and then we can go about cleaning up. Open that window for starters and let in some fresh air.'

'What's going on in here?' came a voice from the bedroom door. 'It smells like rotting flesh.'

'Shauna, can you make yourself useful and come and help please?'

'Eeew,' said Shauna, backing away as she realised what was happening. 'There's no chance. And I'd check the vodka if I were you, Dad.'

She was gone before Rob could respond and his head swung around to look at his son. 'Ben?'

Ben was sitting on the floor with his head in his hands. He didn't look at Rob.

'Ben Costa! Do you have something to tell me?' Rob wanted Ben to say Shauna was ridiculous. That she was just being mean and vindictive. But he didn't say a word and Rob's blood ran cold.

'Please tell me you didn't touch any alcohol,' he said, his mind in turmoil. 'You wouldn't, Ben, would you?'

Ben looked up slowly, tears pouring down his face. 'I didn't want to, Dad. I'm sorry.'

'Oh Jesus Christ.' Things were going from bad to worse. 'What did you drink? Where did you get it from?'

Cian suddenly sat up again and Rob managed to get a towel to him just in time to catch another stream of vomit. 'I want to go home,' he cried again.

'Right,' said Rob, more decisively than he felt. 'I'm going to ring your mum now and get you home. We can talk about the alcohol thing when everyone is better. But just tell me what you drank and how much.'

Ben pointed to his wardrobe and Rob went and opened the door. There was a litre bottle of vodka half empty so he took it out and examined it.

'Did you take this from downstairs? Was this in our drinks cabinet?'

'Yes,' said Ben. 'I'm sorry.'

'Is that it then? You all had this between you? Nothing else?'

Ben nodded. 'I won't do it again, Dad. I swear. I didn't even like it.'

'We'll deal with that later.' He walked out of the room, his thoughts in a whirl. He might have expected that of Shauna, but not Ben. Ben was thirteen years old, for God's sake. He was a good boy. He was never in trouble in school and never caused them a moment's grief. God, he hoped it wasn't the start of it.

It was an hour and a half later before Rob sat back down on the sofa, his newspapers where he'd left them, his coffee barely touched on the table. He was exhausted. He'd managed to get the room cleaned eventually, bed clothes in the wash and a load of Ben's books and stationery bagged and in the bin. He'd had to go and speak to both Leo and Cian's mums who'd come to collect them, and he could tell by their reaction that they wouldn't be letting their precious children over for a sleepover again. It was a disaster.

'Is it okay if I go over to Craig's house now?' said Shauna, appearing at the sitting room door. 'I've unloaded the dishwasher and cleaned the kitchen.'

Rob was astounded. 'Thanks, love. And yes, that's fine. Just be back for dinner around four.'

'I'll be back well before that. I'm just going for an hour or two.' She hesitated a moment. 'Are you okay, Dad?'

'I'm fine,' said Rob, shocked that his daughter even asked. 'It's been a trying morning, though.'

'I know. But you did a great job. Right, I'm off. See you later.'

It was strange how the tables had turned. His thirteen-year-old, model child was in bed sleeping off a hangover, while his troublesome daughter was helping out in the house and being particularly nice. How was he going to explain that one to Linda?

Half an hour later he was beginning to relax again. He'd checked on Ben and he was sleeping soundly, and all was quiet in the house. Just then, he noticed a police car driving up the road. As they lived in a small cul-de-sac, Rob was curious to see which house they were going to. He went to the window and peeped through the wooden blinds. The car went to the top of the road, turned around and slowed down just outside. Maybe they were going to the next-door-neighbours. But Rob had an uneasy feeling. He knew before they even got out of the car that they were coming to him. The two policemen came up the driveway and knocked on the door. His blood ran cold for the second time that day.

'Mr Costa?' said one of them, as Rob opened the door. 'Can we come in please?'

'Y-yes. Of course. Come in.' He held open the door, terrified about what he was about to be told. 'Is everything okay? Is there something wrong?'

'Don't be alarmed,' said the second cop. 'Everyone is okay, but we just need to ask you a few questions.'

What had Shauna done now? It must be Shauna, because although Ben's behaviour had been less than perfect, he'd been at home for the last couple of days. Rob didn't know how much more he could take. He led the policemen into the living room and indicated for them to sit down.

'So what can I do for you, officers?'

'We just need some clarity on something,' said one, flicking through his notebook. 'And hopefully we can sort this out here instead of going to the station.'

'I'll help you in whatever way I can,' said Rob, prickles of sweat forming on his forehead.

'Okay,' said the other guy. 'I'm going to read you something and I want you to tell me what it means.'

Rob began to sweat profusely. 'Go on.'

He cleared his throat before reading from his notebook, glancing at Rob as he did so. 'Mr Costa, are these your words? *Job done. I've buried the body. What now?*'

Chapter 17

'Oh my God,' said Linda, barely believing what she was hearing. 'What happened then?'

'Well, they didn't take me down to the station, thankfully. They were satisfied when I got Ben down and he produced his phone.'

'But what was it all about? Why would he do something like that?' Linda was exhausted after a busy week and was planning a relaxing night in with her book. When Rob had rung, she'd thought it was just to check in as usual, so she was shocked at what she was hearing.

'Apparently it was something they'd seen on a prank show. They'd picked random numbers and had sent a variety of silly texts. Unfortunately, one of Ben's was more sinister than silly and had caused a chain reaction.'

'Jesus. What was he thinking? So he texted a random number saying, *Job done. I've buried the body. What now?* I can't believe he did that.'

'But it gets worse,' said Rob. He sounded stressed and Linda almost felt sorry for him. 'Somebody replied to ask where.'

'What? I hope he didn't answer.'

'He did. He said, *In the waste ground behind Liffey Valley.* The number he'd randomly picked was an elderly man in Cork, who thought it was his duty to inform the guards.'

'Christ almighty. So the police took it seriously? They thought that Ben had actually buried a body?' It was the most bizarre thing Linda had ever heard.

'Not quite,' said Rob. 'They traced the phone and because Ben's phone is registered to me, they thought it was me.'

'What a palaver. I might have believed that of Shauna, but not Ben.'

'There's more.'

'Go on,' said Linda, her head ready to explode from all the information. 'It couldn't be worse, surely.'

'Well, I think I know the reason why Ben's judgement wasn't the best.'

Linda felt nervous. 'Do I want to know?'

'Probably not,' said Rob. 'But I have to tell you. Ben and his friends got their hands on a bottle of vodka last night and were probably drunk when they were texting.' He went on to tell her about the earlier dramas of the vomiting and having to explain everything to the mothers.

'So how is he now?' said Linda, trying but failing to picture her baby son drunk. 'Was he sick all day?'

'No. He slept for three or four hours after the police left and was hungry when he woke up. He had some toast and was fine after.'

'You should ring the other mothers,' said Linda, suddenly remembering Cian and Leo. She was sure Rob wouldn't have thought of that. 'Just to show a bit of concern.'

'I'm a step ahead of you there. I rang them both earlier and apologised for what had happened. I made sure they knew that the boys hadn't gone out and that they'd gone straight to bed after their pizza and movie.'

Linda was impressed. 'That's good. I hope they realise that all three boys were to blame and not try and pin this on Ben. It's so out of character for him to behave that way.'

'I know. I had a long chat with him this evening and he's mortified. He said that it was Leo's idea to take the vodka. He said he didn't want to drink any but he felt under pressure to. I told him I'd let him know tomorrow what his punishment is.'

'Poor kid.'

Rob's tone changed suddenly. 'He's not a poor kid at all, Linda. He did the crime, so he should do the time. It wasn't as though the boys held him down and poured it into his mouth.'

'I know that,' said Linda, thinking of Ben's little innocent face. 'But don't you think he's been punished enough?'

'No. I. Do. Not.' Linda winced as Rob almost shouted the words. 'If you'd had to go through a day like this, you wouldn't be so forgiving. It was a nightmare, Linda. And this mollycoddling of yours is not going to do him any good.'

'I don't mollycoddle him.'

'For God's sake, Linda. Of course you do. You tip-toe around the kids and let them get away with murder. They need a firm hand and that's what they're getting from me for these two weeks.'

'A firm hand, eh?' Linda's blood was boiling. 'Funny how the only time Ben has had an incident like this was while I was away and you were applying your *firm hand!*'

'That's hardly fair,' said Rob, raising his voice again. 'At least I was prepared to do something to get him out of the rut of spending all his time in his bedroom alone. What have you done about it?'

'I've tried. And it's hardly fair that you're blaming me for the kids' bad behaviour. I've been trying to tell you for months about what's going on with them but you're usually either in work or too tired to listen. I've wanted us to tackle things together. Like a normal couple. But you seem to think that the running of the house and managing of kids is my department and not something you should worry about.'

'Well, I'm managing it now. And I think I'm doing a pretty good job.'

'You are joking, aren't you?' said Linda through tears of rage. 'The house is in chaos. The kids are in chaos.'

'Well, maybe it's because their mother abandoned them so that she could have a holiday away in Spain!'

'How dare you, Rob. How bloody dare you. We discussed this. It was agreed. And I'm not having a *holiday*, as you put it. I'm taking time out because I've been so stressed and I'm also using the time to finish my book. The book that's given us more money than you earn in a year!'

'There's no need to bring money into it,' said Rob, a warning in his voice. 'Or this conversation could go down a road we don't want it to.'

'What do you mean by that?' Linda's hand shook from the tight grip she had on the phone. She was raging at what her husband was saying.

'I mean that if we're going to talk about money, why don't we talk about the fact that I was the sole earner for years. The fact that I was the one who worked hard and brought home the money while you sat at home all day.'

'Oh yes. I sat at home and did nothing. The children reared themselves. And there was a little band of fairies that lived under the stairs that came out at night and ironed all your shirts, did the shopping, made the dinner, cleaned the house …'

'Look, Linda. I think we're getting way off track here. I'm sorry if I upset you. That wasn't my intention.'

She was a little thrown by his apology, but she still felt mad at how he'd spoken to her. 'Well, have you any more surprises for me? Any other dramas other than my thirteen-year-old son drinking vodka and having the police believe he's murdered somebody?'

There was silence on the other end of the phone.

'Well?'

'I suppose I may as well tell you.' Rob spoke slowly and Linda felt suddenly alarmed. Again.

'What is it?'

'It's just Shauna. I found ...'

He didn't finish the sentence and Linda was getting impatient. 'You found what, Rob?'

'I ... I found out she's seeing a guy.'

'Oh, for God's sake,' said Linda, rolling her eyes. 'We had this discussion already. Craig Boland. You have a short memory.'

'Of course. Sorry, my brain is mush at the moment. Yes, we did speak about him. She seems to be seeing a lot of him.'

'I know.' Linda sighed. From what she saw in the bedroom the previous week, it seemed like they could be seeing quite a lot of each other. Literally. It was something they'd have to deal with but one thing at a time.

'Actually, speak of the devil. I hear Shauna coming in now. I'm going to go and chat to her before she disappears up to her room.'

'Okay,' said Linda, glad the conversation had come to an end. 'Talk to you tomorrow.' She put the phone down. She felt drained. It was exhausting arguing with her husband. She rarely got the upper hand and usually came out of it feeling frustrated.

Lying her head back on the sofa, she closed her eyes and tried to control the thoughts that were whirring around inside. She'd been glad when Aidan and James had said they were going out. They'd asked her if she'd like to go with them but she'd declined, preferring to spend the evening alone. Today marked the end of her first week in Spain and she'd had very little time to herself since she'd arrived. She wasn't complaining. It had been a wonderful week. But she also needed time to think. To do some soul-searching and figure out how she was going to proceed with her life.

She felt uneasy after that conversation with Rob. Part of her was glad to hear he'd had a tough day but she didn't want it to be at Ben's expense. The poor kid. It really wasn't like him to get into trouble like that and she wondered was it some sort of rebellion against her going away. She could feel that old guilt beginning to resurface and managed to push it away before it consumed her. Ben was a teenage boy and naturally curious about things. He was just experimenting. Pushing the boundaries. How many times had she wished he'd be a little more naughty? He was always such a good boy and Linda had felt that he needed to sometimes break out of that mould. Well, he'd certainly done that now.

She glanced at her phone and saw it was almost nine o'clock. The argument with Rob was playing on her mind and she knew she should sort it out. At home, she always made a point not to go to bed on an argument. Her mother had always taught her that. But she just wished Rob felt the same. It was always her who'd go to him and try and sort things out. He'd just be happy to go to bed and forget about it. The next day, he'd continue as though nothing had happened whereas she'd have lain awake all night and things would seem even worse the next day.

Suddenly, she knew what she needed to do. Sitting up, she grabbed her phone from the coffee table and punched in a number. She didn't want to feel this way. She was lonely and confused and her head was pounding from trying to sort everything out. She waited as the phone rang and just when she thought it wasn't going to be answered, there was a click, and a low husky voice whispered in her ear.

'*Hola, cariño*. How are you?'

The words made Linda melt and she sank back into the sofa to listen to his voice. 'Hi, Kabir, I'm good thanks. I … I wondered if you'd like to meet?'

'Yes, of course I would. I thought you didn't want to see me after the other night. Bringing you to my parents was unforgiveable.'

'Don't worry about that,' she said, hugging the phone to her. 'You can make it up to me tomorrow.'

'Tomorrow?'

'Yes.' She suddenly felt brave. This was what she needed. She was sick of pleasing everyone else and leaving herself last. She wasn't going to overthink this one and she was going to go with her gut.

'Linda? What's happening tomorrow?'

'I'll tell you what's going to happen, Kabir. Tomorrow I'm going to come over to your apartment and you and I are going to spend some quality time together.' She knew the following days could change the course of her life for ever but she was willing to take that chance.

Chapter 18

'I just want you to be careful, that's all,' said Aidan, as he and Linda sat at the kitchen counter sipping cappuccinos. 'Kabir is a lovely guy but you have a lot to lose.'

Linda nodded. 'I know. But I've spent my whole adult life being careful. Being considerate of others and putting everyone before myself. I just want to be me again. To do what I want to do and not what I'm told I *should* do.'

'And this is what you want, is it?' Aidan looked stressed as he ran his hand through his cropped blond hair. 'What you really want?'

'I don't know,' conceded Linda with a sigh. 'I honestly don't know. Yesterday I was sure. After the argument with Rob, I just wanted to go out there and forget I had a husband.'

'And now?'

'As I said, I just don't know anymore. I'm not as angry today.'

Aidan reached over and touched her hand. 'You should never do things in anger. If you're just doing this to hurt Rob, don't do it. You'll just end up hurting yourself.' Linda nodded quietly and Aidan continued. 'But if it's something you really want to do. If it's something you've thought about and you've weighed up the consequences, well then do it.'

Linda's head was spinning. It was the day after her proposal to Kabir and she was beginning to get cold feet. It had been so unlike her to make a suggestion like that. To just ring some man up and tell him she wanted an invitation to his house. God, she'd been so forward. So pushy. But Kabir hadn't minded one bit. He'd been only too glad to go along with her plan and had agreed to make her dinner at his apartment at 6 p.m. Aidan was going to drop her there and the getting home part she'd figure out later. If she did go home.

'The thing is,' she said to Aidan, 'it's just a meal. It doesn't have to be more than two people sharing some food and having a good chat.'

Aidan looked at her, his eyebrows raised. 'Seriously? Do you honestly believe that?'

'Why not, Aidan? We haven't even kissed properly yet. Why does having a meal together at his place mean we have to end up in bed? Why can't we just have a nice time and keep all our clothes on?'

'And is that what you want? To keep all your clothes on?'

Linda thought for a moment. She pictured them finishing their meal and Kabir taking her hand. He'd lead her to his bedroom where he'd slowly and carefully peel away each item of clothing from her body. He'd run his fingers over every curve before burying his face in her breasts. His hands would find her soft flesh below and stroke her until she cried out for more. He'd—

'Linda?'

'Oh God. Yes. No. I mean, I don't know. Oh, Aidan. I'm really attracted to Kabir. And if I'm brutally honest, I'd love to be intimate with him. But I just don't know if I'm ready to throw everything I have with Rob away. Tell me what to do.'

Aidan's voice softened. 'I can't tell you what to do, Linda, except follow your heart. But think ahead. If Kabir is going to be just one night of lust, never to be repeated again, is it worth losing everything for? Could you live with the guilt, even if you didn't tell Rob? But then again, if you and Kabir have a real connection, could it be something more? Is there a chance for you two? I'm afraid it's down to you to figure all that out.'

Linda nodded. 'I know. I suppose I'll just leave it in the lap of the gods. I'll go over to Kabir's as planned and see what happens. I won't drink too much so I can stay level-headed. And anyway, Kabir is good company. I'm looking forward to spending time with him.'

Aidan didn't look convinced but he didn't say any more. Just then the front door opened and James came in. He'd been working since early that morning and had finished his shift for the day. He came over to join Aidan and Linda at the counter.

'Grab me a cup of coffee, Aidan love, will you? I'm shattered.'

Aidan did as he was asked and James turned to Linda. 'I hear you're going over to Kabir's tonight.'

Linda was surprised he knew. 'Who told you? And yes, I'm going over for dinner.'

More raised eyebrows. 'Hmmmm.'

'And what's that supposed to mean?'

'I just worry about you,' said James, not looking at her. 'What if dinner leads to something else. Are you prepared for that?'

'Listen, James. I don't want to be rude, but I've just had all this off Aidan. Can we not talk about it anymore?'

'Okay, okay.' James held his hands up in resignation. 'I'm just thinking of you and about your relationship with Rob. Don't throw it away for a moment of madness. Because that's what it would be. Madness.'

'I thought you liked Kabir.'

'I do like him,' said James slowly. 'But I also know him and I'm not sure he's the right man for you.'

'Jesus, we're not getting married or anything. I'm going for dinner with him, for God's sake. I think you both just need to back off.'

'I'm sorry, Linda. I just care about you.'

'Me too,' said Aidan, placing James' coffee in front of him. 'We both just want the best for you.'

'I know,' said Linda with a sigh. 'And I'm sorry too. But let me just do what I think is best and whatever happens, it's on my head. Now Aidan, are you still okay to bring me in an hour? I've got to go and get ready now.'

Aidan nodded as he slipped in beside James, planting a kiss on his cheek. 'Of course. I'm ready when you are.'

'Come in, Linda. Welcome to my little home.' Kabir greeted her with a kiss on both cheeks and stood aside to allow her into the apartment.

'Thanks, Kabir. It's beautiful.' And it was. Linda was surprised that a single man would have such good taste. She'd expected a bachelor pad – tones of brown and beige, a centrepiece of a massive telly and a few beanbags on the floor for comfort. But instead it was beautifully decorated in soft tones of peach and cream. The suite was a deep shade of orange, punctuated with cream cushions and there were even fresh flowers in a vase on the coffee table.

'Come and sit at the table,' he said, leading her over to the kitchen. 'Dinner is just about ready, so I'll serve up straight away. I hope you're hungry.'

'Starving.' She wasn't a bit hungry. The butterflies in her stomach had taken over and she didn't think there'd be room for any food.

She watched as he expertly juggled pots and pans until he returned with two full-to-the-brim plates of delicious-looking food. She was impressed. Again, she'd assumed it would be some pasta or a salad of some sort but it looked like Kabir had gone to a lot of trouble.

'And in case you think I've gone to a lot of trouble,' he said, watching as her eyes lit up. 'It's the slow roasted beef from the restaurant. James had it on the menu again today so I asked him to put aside two portions for us.'

So that's how James had known about their date. 'It looks amazing, Kabir. I had it in the restaurant earlier in the week and I've never tasted anything like it.'

'I know.' His eyes twinkled. 'I remembered.'

She was touched by his thoughtfulness.

'But,' he continued, 'the vegetables are all my own work. Just in case you think I'm completely helpless.'

Linda laughed and felt happy to be in his company. She pushed the food around her plate as they chatted, cutting small pieces and taking ages to chew. She didn't want to appear rude but the anticipation of what the night might have in store was playing havoc with her stomach. Kabir looked gorgeous in a pale blue shirt with the top few buttons open. His hair flopped over his forehead and he smelled of a mix of cooking oil and musky cologne. She was finding it difficult to concentrate on the conversation and it wasn't long before he noticed she was distracted.

'Do you not like it?' he said, looking worried. 'I can get you something else if you like. Here, let me take it away.'

She grabbed his hand as he leaned over to take the plate and, once again, it was as though a bolt of electricity had shot through her. 'No, it's fine. Honestly. I just don't have a huge appetite over here. With the heat and everything.'

She was still holding onto his hand and he wasn't in a hurry to take it away. Their eyes met and she could tell that he knew. He knew what she was thinking, and she was pretty sure he was thinking it too. He eventually sat back down, and they continued to eat in silence until she couldn't take the tension any longer.

'Kabir, what's this?'

'What do you mean?'

'This. I mean us.'

'Just two people enjoying each other's company.' He wasn't making it easy.

'But do you see it as—'

'Shit. The churros.' He jumped up from his chair and dashed to the oven where smoke was beginning to bellow out. 'I forgot I put them in there to heat up and now they're ruined.'

He took out the cremated churros and threw them on the kitchen counter. 'And I have a lovely chocolate sauce to go with them too. Damn!'

'Don't worry about it,' said Linda, anxious to get back to their unfinished conversation. 'I probably wouldn't have had room for it anyway.'

'God, I'm sorry. I'm such an idiot. I can put something else together. Maybe I can chop up a few things to dip in the chocolate. Yes, that's what I'll do.' He took out a punnet of strawberries from the fridge.

'Kabir. Please. I won't eat dessert. Just come back and finish your dinner. Honestly, it's fine.'

'Are you sure? Because it won't take me long to whip up something.'

'A cup of coffee is perfect. I don't want anything else.'

He nodded and sat back down, the spoiled dessert clearly playing on his mind. 'Everything was so perfect and now I've gone and ruined it.'

'It's still perfect, Kabir.' She reached over and took his hand. 'I don't need dessert to enjoy myself. I'm having a lovely time.'

He squeezed her hand. 'Me too. I love being with you.'

'Same here,' said Linda, her heartbeat quickening. They were only inches apart, hands touching, and she could almost taste his breath.

'Come on,' he said, keeping hold of her hand as he stood up. 'Let's go over to the sofa where it's more comfortable.'

She was happy to oblige, although her legs almost buckled beneath her. She couldn't even blame the wine because she'd hardly touched a drop. She was clearly nervous but she knew now that it was what she wanted. She could deal with the consequences later but right now, she wanted Kabir.

They sank down into the soft suede cushions but just as soon as they were there, Kabir jumped up again. 'I'll just get us those coffees and bring them over.'

Linda was about to object but then she realised that he must be nervous too. For some reason she'd thought she was the only one. That Kabir was well used to situations like this. But it seemed he felt awkward too and it made her want him just a little bit more. She waited patiently until he came back with two steaming cups and laid them on the coffee table in front of them.

'Milk, no sugar? Is that right?'

'That's perfect,' she said, reaching over to take a sip. 'You have a good memory for details.'

'Only for things I want to remember. So tell me some more about your life in Ireland. Do you have brothers or sisters? And what about hobbies?'

She was thrown by the questions. She'd thought they were done talking but obviously not. They drank their coffees and chatted about trivial things. Just like Linda, Kabir was an only child. She learned that he loved to paint with watercolours, although he admitted he wasn't very good, and had been a keen motorcycle racer when he was younger.

As they chatted, they sank further into the sofa until their thighs were pressed up against each other. The sexual tension was huge between them and Linda hadn't felt so turned on in a very long time. Kabir's body felt warm beside hers and before long, his words were just a whirr floating in the ether, and her mouth was dry with anticipation. Finally, she couldn't supress her urges any longer. She moved her face closer to his and he stopped talking. They looked into each other's eyes and she could see he had tears in his. It was a moment of wonder. Of tenderness. And she felt as though she was floating on air. She closed her eyes as their lips met and a million fireworks exploded in her head. It was just as she'd imagined. Soft and gentle. He tasted of red wine and coffee and she felt as though she could live in his kiss for ever.

But all too soon a ping from his phone distracted him and he pulled away. The magic was broken, and Linda felt as though she'd been dropped on the floor from a height.

'I'm sorry. I just need to check this.' He grabbed his phone from the coffee table and tapped it to check the text. He shook his head as he read it. 'Trouble in one of the restaurants. I'm sorry but I'm going to have to head over there.'

'What? Now?' Linda couldn't believe it.

'Yes, I'm afraid so.' He was already up, slipping his shoes back on and bringing the coffee cups over to the sink. 'That's what happens when you're the boss.'

'But you've been drinking. You can't drive.' She was desperate now.

'I'm going to call a taxi. And one for you too.' He was punching numbers into his phone. 'They're usually very quick.'

He wasn't wrong. Both taxis arrived within minutes and he walked her to hers, kissing her lightly on the cheek before she got in. 'Sorry again,' he said. 'Maybe we can do this another night.'

'Sure,' she said, feeling deflated. 'Call me.'

As the taxi drove away from the apartment, her thoughts were running riot in her brain. She recalled that moment when she and Kabir had kissed. When the world had stopped, and they were the only two people in it. She desperately tried to remember a time when it had been like that with Rob. It had been a while. She tried to make herself think of her husband and feel the way she used to, but right in that moment, Kabir was the one she wanted. The question was, did he want her? Was the phone call really an inconvenience or just an excuse for him to get out of a situation with her? She remembered the warning James had given her earlier. And it wasn't the first time he'd warned her. Was there more to it than she'd initially thought? Was James just being a friend or did he know something?

By the time the taxi pulled up outside the villa, she was exhausted. She paid the driver and let herself in. She was glad the place was quiet so she wouldn't have to answer questions about the night.

She slipped off her shoes and quietly padded into her room. Sitting on the edge of her bed, she tried to gather her thoughts. She felt empty. Disappointed. It wasn't how she'd anticipated the night ending. However, as thoughts of Rob continued to crowd her mind, she wondered if tonight was really a disaster or was it a blessing in disguise.

Chapter 19

The water lapped over Linda's feet as she walked along the beach. It seemed the fine weather had brought families out in their hordes to enjoy the last days of the summer sun. Aidan said that it had been a scorching July and August, with temperatures up to 38 degrees, but although it was still lovely, the October sunshine was a lot more manageable. She smiled at two young children, probably about five or six, who were squealing in delight as they poured water from buckets into a hollow they'd made in the sand. Memories of past holidays filled her mind suddenly and she was transported back in time. Shauna and Ben had loved the beach and their holidays had mainly consisted of building sandcastles and swimming in the sea. Life had been so much simpler back then.

As she reached the cliffs at the end of the beach, she checked her phone. It was still early so maybe she'd stroll up to the path and do the cliff walk before heading home for breakfast. She loved walking early in the morning. It always invigorated her and put her in better form. But the truth was, she'd barely slept the previous night. After the fiasco in Kabir's apartment, she'd been left feeling peculiar. Disappointed and relieved at the same time. She couldn't quite get her head around it.

She turned away from the water to head up to the path and suddenly felt very lonely. Everywhere she looked she could see families. There was laughter and chatter as Sunday picnics were devoured and sandcastles made. Linda wondered if she'd ever get that family feeling back again. Would she, Rob and the children ever have another holiday together? Would they ever spend any more time together as a family at all? It was a bleak thought and she felt very scared about the future.

Her feet were aching from her new flip-flops so she decided to sit for a while before walking any further. She plonked herself down on a low wall at the back of the beach so that she could have a good view of everything. She wondered how everyone at home was. What were they all doing for their Sunday? A cloud of homesickness descended on her suddenly and she needed to feel connected with home again. Checking the time, she realised her mum and dad would probably be at mass so she wouldn't get them on the phone. Her kids would most likely be still in bed and she still wasn't ready to speak to Rob following their argument on Friday. There was only one other person she wanted to speak to so she took her phone out of her pocket and dialled the number.

'Hi, Ger. How are things?'

'Linda. I've been dying to ring you all morning, but I didn't want to *disturb* you.'

She emphasised the word 'disturb' and Linda balked at the insinuation. 'You wouldn't have been disturbing me at all. I'm out walking on the beach.'

'Oh really? Alone?'

'Yes, alone.' Linda was beginning to regret having rung her friend the previous day to tell her about her date with Kabir. 'And in case you're wondering, I've been alone since coming home from Kabir's house last night at around ten.'

'Oh.' Ger actually sounded disappointed. 'So what happened?'

'Oh God, Ger. I'm a terrible person.' Linda felt tears well up in her eyes. 'Honestly, I don't know what's come over me lately. But it's just not like me.'

'Back up there for a minute,' said Ger, concern in her voice. 'Firstly, you're not a terrible person. And secondly, why do you think you are? What happened last night?'

'Nothing at all. Well, except for a kiss.'

'A *kiss*? That's not nothing! Come on, I want details.'

Linda spent the next ten minutes filling Ger in on the events of the previous night. She told her everything, from what they had for dinner to how Kabir's lips had tasted. She wanted to say it all out loud. To make it feel real. Because sometimes it seemed like she was in the middle of some sort of weird dream and she was going to wake up any moment.

'So how do you feel about Kabir now?' said Ger, when Linda had finally finished. 'Are you falling in love with him?'

Linda winced at those words. 'Don't be ridiculous, Ger.'

'Why is it ridiculous? People fall in love all the time. And you said he was pretty perfect.'

'He is. Well, I thought he was. Oh I don't know. He is gorgeous, but love is a very big word.'

'And what about Rob?' Ger's voice was quiet. 'Where does he fit into all this? Or does he fit in at all?'

Linda sighed. 'I don't know. And that's the honest truth. Last night I wanted something to happen with me and Kabir. I really wanted it. I wanted him to take me into his bed and make mad passionate love to me.'

Ger gasped, but Linda continued before she could say anything.

'But then when I came back home, I kept thinking about Rob.'

'Surely that's a good sign,' said Ger. 'If you're beginning to miss him, maybe a bit of distance was all you needed to bring back those old feelings.'

'But that's just it, Ger. At the moment, I miss the idea of what we used to have. I miss the passion and the excitement. But if the truth be known, I'm not sure I actually miss him.'

'It sounds to me like you have a lot to think about so. It won't be long until you're home and you'll have to start making decisions.'

'I know. Just five days left. Part of me wants to go back to my old life. The safe, easy option. But the more I think about it, I honestly don't know if I can.'

'Because your feelings are stronger for Kabir than for Rob?'

Linda thought for a moment. 'I really don't know, Ger. Right now it feels that way but I'd be giving up so much if I left Rob.'

'I don't envy you,' said Ger. 'That's a lot of emotion to have to deal with.'

'Also,' continued Linda, 'I'm consumed with guilt. How can I go back to Rob, even if I wanted to, and pretend all this didn't happen? How could I go on as normal after I had this … this *thing* with Kabir?'

'I think,' said Ger, speaking very slowly, 'you'll have to tell Rob. Be upfront with him. Tell him you met someone else. At the moment, there isn't much to tell. You met someone, you fancied him, there was a bit of a kiss but you didn't take things any further. If nothing else happens, you and Rob should be able to work things out. That's if you want to.'

'And if something more happens between now and then?'

'Well, then you'll have to be honest about that too. Secrets and lies will tear you apart anyway so it's better to be up front. If you and Kabir take things further, then maybe the decision will be taken out of your hands. Rob might not want to take you back.'

It was a stark reality and Linda hadn't thought of it that way before. She'd always thought she was in control. She'd always imagined that she'd be the one to decide their fate but maybe Ger was right. Why did her life have to be so bloody complicated?

'I saw Rob yesterday, actually.' Ger's words cut into Linda's thoughts. 'He seemed pretty down.'

'Where did you see him? What did he say?'

'I dropped over with a veggie casserole,' said Ger. 'I know you wanted him to cope on his own but I'd cooked way too much for myself and I thought he and the kids would use it.'

'That was good of you. What time was this?'

'Yesterday evening. Around eight. Apparently your mother had dropped a lasagne in earlier in the day. They won't go hungry anyway.'

Linda couldn't help wondering whether, if she was the one at home alone, anyone would drop food in to her. Probably not.

'He said your mum was in rotten form,' continued Ger. 'She'd had a fight with your dad and Rob said he thought she was looking to stay.'

Linda giggled at that. 'Oh God, could you imagine? My mum staying with Rob and the kids. She'd drive them all insane!'

'I think if she'd moved in, Rob would have moved out. But she went off home after she'd cleaned the kitchen and washed the floors. And apparently, you've only rung her once since you left.'

Linda felt guilty. That seemed to be the story of her life now. 'I've been avoiding her, to be honest. She knows me too well. When I rang her the other day, I found myself telling her things I didn't want to. She has a way of extracting information from me!'

Ger laughed. 'God, I love your mum.'

'I do too,' said Linda, 'but I really don't want her to know about Kabir. I just couldn't hack a lecture from her about loyalty and marriage and how to stand by my vows.'

'I know what you mean,' said Ger. 'But give her a ring. You'll be glad of her support in the end. And on that note, I have to go. I have a million and one things to do. I'll give you a buzz tomorrow to see how you are.'

Linda didn't feel like walking anymore so, sticking her phone into her pocket, she headed home. Aidan didn't know how lucky he was being just a ten-minute walk from the beach. She'd love to live by the sea. It was so calming and relaxing. Where she lived was lovely and she had great neighbours, but there was noise and traffic and a constant sense that people were in a hurry. Here life was a lot slower. People took their time and everyone seemed to be chilled out. Maybe that was just because she was on holiday. Maybe it would be different if she was going out to work every day. But from her experience, La Zenia was a little piece of paradise and she could quite happily see herself living there.

All was quiet as she let herself into the villa. James had the day off and Aidan had said he wasn't working either, so they'd planned a rare lie-in. She didn't want to wake them, so, taking off her shoes, she went to the kitchen to prepare herself some breakfast. The walk had lifted her spirits a little and she felt inspired to get stuck into her writing. When her egg had boiled and her toast was ready, she poured a cup of tea for herself and sat down at the kitchen counter. But just as she was about to take her first bite, the doorbell rang. She froze for a minute. They rarely got visitors at the villa so the only person she could think of that might be calling was Kabir. She looked down at her crumpled t-shirt and shorts and saw there was still sand between her toes. She knew her hair was a mess from the wind and she hadn't even bothered to put make-up on. Shit! The doorbell rang again, and she knew she'd have to answer it before Aidan and James were woken by the racket.

Reluctantly she got up, trying to tame her hair with one hand while flattening the creases out of her t-shirt with the other. Taking a deep breath, she swung open the door, ready to make her apologies to Kabir for her appearance. But it wasn't Kabir. Her mouth fell open.

'Mum! What on earth are you doing here?'

'I've left him, Linda. I've left your dad. I just can't take it anymore.'

'Wh-what are you talking about? You can't have left Dad. Don't be so ridiculous.'

'I can and I have,' she said defiantly. 'Your daddy is a grumpy, unappreciative idiot and I can't be with him one minute longer. So am I going to remain standing here or are you going to invite me in?'

'Of course,' said Linda, still in shock. 'Come in and sit down.'

She moved the large suitcase to just inside the front door and led the way to the sofa. She couldn't get her head around the fact that her mother was there. In Spain. It was as though she had two lives running parallel and now one was spilling into the other. It felt weird.

'A cup of tea would be nice too,' said her mother, breaking into her thoughts. 'That rubbish they serve on the plane is like dishwater. I have some Lyons teabags in my case, if you have none here.'

'Mum, the tea can wait. I want to know what's going on. How did you even find your way here?'

'I got the address from Rob. And unless you want me to collapse from tea withdrawals, I suggest the tea *can't* wait.'

'Hold on. So Rob knew you were coming?' Linda was still trying to get her head around it all. 'You told him but you didn't tell me?'

'Of course he didn't know, Linda. I brought him over a lasagne yesterday and I asked him for the address. I said I wanted to send something to you. He never guessed I was sending myself!'

Linda couldn't help a giggle. 'Oh, Mum. It is good to see you but what about Dad? Did you even tell him you were coming over?'

'Of course not. We got mass last night instead of this morning so he'll only realise I'm missing when his dinner doesn't materialise in front of him.'

'You have to ring him, Mum. He'll be worried sick.'

'Worried sick my arse.'

'Mum!'

'I'm sorry, darling, but it's about time that man learned that I'm his wife, not his slave. I just can't live with his demands one minute longer.'

Linda's head was spinning. 'And are you planning to stay for one night? Or two? Or how long will it take for you to teach him a lesson?' She eyed her mother's case suspiciously and concluded that there was a hell of a lot more in there than was required for just a night or two.

'For as long as it takes. It was a brainwave I had yesterday morning when your daddy practically threw his eggs back at me because they weren't runny enough. I thought to myself: *If Linda can come to Spain to sort her life out, well then maybe it would work for me too.*'

Linda sighed. 'I'll make us that cup of tea now.'

'Thanks, love. You're a life-saver.'

As she stood waiting for the kettle to boil, Linda cast a glance at her mother. She looked way younger than her seventy-eight years. It was funny. Linda had never really thought of her as a woman with needs. She saw her as a wife and mother. That was her role in life. But wasn't that what Linda was striving so hard to get away from herself? The labels. The kettle clicked and snapped her out of her reverie. She'd come to Spain to relax. To get away from the stresses and strains of life. But there was just no getting away from the drama that seemed to follow her everywhere. As she poured the water into the cups, she wondered what could possibly happen next.

Chapter 20

Rob was finding it hard to concentrate. The argument he'd had with Linda on Friday was weighing heavily on his mind. They'd said some horrible things to each other and it had left him feeling angry and frustrated. If she was at home, they'd have sorted it out by now. They'd have talked it through and things would have gone back to normal. They were good like that. They never went to bed on an argument and it had kept their relationship working well all these years. But with Linda being away, things were different. It wasn't the same trying to sort things out over the phone. As a result, he hadn't spoken to her since. That was three whole days. They'd had a few texts back and forth but neither of them had actually picked the phone up to have a conversation.

He tried to focus on the file in front of him, but it was no good. He was exhausted from tossing and turning all night and if he didn't do something to energise himself, he'd soon be asleep at the table. Maybe a run was what he needed to blow off the cobwebs. It was funny, he was never this tired when he went to work every day. Even though he worked hard and the days were long in the office, he always had energy when he came home. But this thing of getting up early to make lunches for the kids, making sure they ate breakfast and doing the housework while they were at school wasn't for him. And add to that the shopping, the cooking and the worry about what the kids were up to. It never ended and there never seemed to be enough hours in the day to get everything done. And the truth was, he just couldn't keep on top of it all. God, he was beginning to sound like his wife!

He went upstairs and changed into a tracksuit before warming up for his run. He wasn't as fit as he used to be, and he'd like to change that. He used to love running and swimming and barely a day went by when he didn't do something energetic. But these days he'd become lazy about his fitness and it was beginning to show in the little paunch that was peeping over the top of his trousers. He'd always had a good physique, but he was aware that he was speeding towards fifty and his body wasn't as co-operative as it used to be.

As he pounded the streets, he thought about Linda and wondered why she just didn't seem attracted to him anymore. He was a decent-looking guy and Linda had always enjoyed the fact that he got a lot of attention from other women. 'Remember you're taken,' she used to say, in a possessive way. And he'd enjoyed the fact that she was jealous. But not anymore. Sex with him seemed to be the last thing on her list these days. He was at a loss to know what to do. Their relationship seemed to be breaking down and he felt it was out of his control.

Sweat poured down his face as he ran faster and faster. His lungs felt as though they were about to burst but he wasn't going to stop. He felt angry at Linda. She'd shown absolutely no appreciation for what he was doing. He'd literally stopped his whole life so that he could step into her shoes. And all so that she could go sailing off to Spain without a worry in the world. He'd had the hardest day on Friday and all she'd done was blame him for not having control. The house was in chaos, she'd said. She'd even had the cheek to bring money into the conversation, insinuating that she was the chief earner. She really knew how to push his buttons. He'd supported his family for over twenty years and just because she'd got one payment for her books, albeit a large one, she felt she had the right to belittle his patriarchal role.

He knew he'd have to stop soon or he'd collapse. He hadn't set out to run so fast but his anger had spurred him on. He'd already done a complete circuit of the village and thought about doing a second one but he knew he shouldn't push himself too hard. Slowing down a little, he headed back in the direction of home and his breath began to return to normal. He let himself in and immediately went to the kitchen to pour himself a large glass of water. Ever since the big snow earlier in the year, something had happened to the water supply and the tap water had never been the same. So although he favoured the bottled stuff, he gladly downed two glasses from the tap in quick succession.

Glancing at the clock, he was glad to see it was only 11.30 a.m. He'd have at least another four hours of peace before the kids descended on him again. He was planning to just stick something handy into the oven for their dinner, so he was relatively free until later. He'd do another bit of paperwork and then maybe he'd put his feet up and binge-watch *Breaking Bad*. He'd started the series on Netflix about six months before and had never gotten back to it, so it seemed like now was the perfect opportunity. He felt quite pleased with himself as he headed upstairs to the shower. This was more like it. A peaceful house and him with his feet up watching telly. He might even stick a pizza in the oven for himself.

The powerful jets of water from the shower massaged his aching body and he stood for a long time, trying to channel more positive thoughts. The run had dampened his anger and he felt readier to speak to Linda and to try and sort things out. When he finally stepped out onto the fluffy shower mat, he felt completely calm. He'd take a few hours to himself and then he'd give her a ring.

After towelling himself dry, he glanced in the mirror and was shocked to see his face was red as a beetroot and little beads of sweat were beginning to form again on his forehead. Only last year he'd been running 10K a few times a week and now a measly twenty-minute run had left him half dead. It made him even more determined than ever to get himself fit again. He took some small scissors from the bathroom cabinet and began to tackle his nose hair. He always blamed his hairiness on his Sicilian blood and although he benefited with a fabulous head of thick hair, it was the stuff that grew from his nose and ears and various other places that he objected to.

Just then, as he had the scissors positioned up his left nostril, the doorbell rang. He froze for a moment, trying to think who it could be. He wasn't expecting anyone so it was probably just one of those charity collectors. He hated answering the door to them. He was always polite but sometimes they were very insistent. He'd had this guy once who, when Rob said he didn't want to sign up for five or ten euros a week to give a poor child his sight back, had glanced into the house and shaken his head. Rob had been furious and had immediately rung the charity to complain. It turned out it had been a bogus caller and Rob had been very glad he hadn't been sucked in.

The bell went again and Rob began to think he should answer it. It could be a delivery and if he didn't answer they'd leave one of those notes to say it had to be collected from the depot. He quickly grabbed Linda's towelling dressing gown from the back of the door and ran down the stairs. He winced at the pain in his body but continued until he got to the front door. He swung it open, expecting the postman, but his insides did a flip when he saw who it was.

'Hi, Rob. Is this a bad time?' Tanya from the office stood there, files in hand, and Rob froze on the spot.

'I ... no. It's just ... I wasn't expecting you.'

'Obviously,' she said, with a wry smile, looking him up and down. 'We spoke on Thursday and you said you had enough work to last you over the weekend and I said I'd bring some files over on Monday. The ones we've been working on together.'

'Oh yes, yes. Sorry, I'd completely forgotten.' And he had. He'd phoned Tanya at a weak moment, when he'd been feeling lonely and sexually frustrated. He'd savoured the idea of her coming to his house while he was alone and he'd dreamed of what might happen. But the reality was that he had no intention of cheating on his wife, no matter how bad thing were between them.

'If it's a bad time, I can just leave these with you and talk you through some stuff on the phone later?'

'No, not at all. Where are my manners? Come in.' She'd come over especially so he wasn't going to turn her away. He held the door open and she stepped inside. It was weird seeing her there. So out of context. He felt uneasy and unsure how to behave as he led the way into the dining room where he'd been working. 'I've just been for a run so you'll have to excuse the sweatiness. I'm a bit out of practice.'

'You shouldn't overdo it,' she said, placing her files down beside the ones he'd been working on. 'Ease yourself in gently.'

He nodded. 'I do push myself a lot but that's how I am.'

'I gathered. And are you really sure you want to load more work on yourself? I can manage this stuff on my own. Don't you want to take a break from it?'

He idly flipped through one of the new files. 'I definitely don't want to take a break. It's the only thing keeping me sane at the moment.'

Tanya raised an eyebrow. 'Being at home not all it's cracked up to be?'

'It's probably harder than any job I've done,' he grinned. 'But don't tell Linda I said that.'

She laughed. 'Well, how about making me a tea? We can go over these files and I'll get out of your way after that.'

'I think I can manage that. Take a seat and I'll be back in a flash.' Rob left the kitchen door open a slit and as he waited for the kettle to boil, he glanced out at Tanya. She was dressed in her usual office uniform of a tight black pencil skirt and a silky blouse. It seemed that she'd taken extra care today. Her hair looked freshly blow-dried and she had a full face of make-up on. Usually she just wore a touch of bronzer on her face or didn't bother with make-up at all. Her blouse seemed extra tight too, and it looked as though her breasts might fall out of it as she pored over the files. Rob wondered had she made a special effort for him. Was she there for more than the files? He hoped not because tempting as though it might be, he wasn't going to allow himself to go there.

When the water boiled, he made a pot of tea and, suddenly becoming conscious of wearing only a dressing gown, he realised he should go up and change. 'I'm just letting the tea brew,' he shouted to Tanya as he headed for the stairs. 'I'll be back in a … ouch, ouch, ouch …' He was forced to drape himself over the banister as his leg began to cramp. It was agonising. It felt as though somebody had tied something very tight around his left leg and it was getting tighter and tighter.

'Rob? What is it?' Tanya jumped up from her chair and came out to the hall to see what was going on.

He was stamping his foot on the floor to try and ease the pain but it wasn't working. 'Cramp in my leg.' He could barely get the words out.

'Here,' said Tanya, kneeling down on the floor. 'Sit down there and I'll sort it out for you.'

He was in too much pain to argue so he fell back onto the bottom stair and allowed Tanya to take his leg and massage it. He remembered a conversation he'd had with her one day when he'd learned that she was a trained masseuse, so she obviously knew what she was doing. Slowly but surely the pain began to ease, and it was only then that Rob became aware of his situation. Tanya, the woman who regularly invaded his dreams, was kneeling in front of him working her magic on his leg. He was suddenly aware of his nakedness beneath the robe and he could feel himself being turned on as her hands kneaded his calf. He closed his eyes for a moment and allowed himself to relax. He imagined her hand moving slowly up his leg towards his—

'Dad, I've just come back to collect— What the fuck …?'

It was Shauna and she didn't look happy. Her mouth gaped open and the scene seemed to be frozen in time.

'Shauna, what are you doing home? And it's not what it looks like. It's just … a cramp. I have a cramp.' Rob stood up, wrapping the belt of the dressing gown tighter around his waist. 'Tanya was just sorting me out.'

'I bet she was,' said the teenager, shaking her head. 'And a cramp? Is that the best you could come up with? I wasn't fucking born yesterday.'

'I swear,' said Rob, beginning to panic. 'We were just doing some work and my leg started cramping up.'

'It's true,' said Tanya, standing up and reaching for her handbag. 'Your dad went for a run and his legs aren't accustomed to—'

'And you can shut the fuck up,' spat Shauna. 'I'm talking to my dad.'

'Shauna! You apologise to Tanya now. I'm not having you speak to her like that. Or anyone, for that matter. You need to control your language.'

Shauna's face was stony. 'I think it's you who needs to control yourself, Dad. You're disgusting.'

Before he had time to reply, she turned around and left, slamming the front door behind her.

'I'd better go,' said Tanya, looking flustered.

Rob nodded. 'I think you'd better. I'll walk you out.'

'I'm sorry about all that,' she said, as she stepped outside. 'I feel responsible.'

'There's no need, Tanya. Don't worry. It'll be fine.'

But as he headed back inside, he wondered would it be. Would it really be fine? As if things weren't bad enough between him and Linda, now Shauna was going to run to her and tell her he was having an affair or something. And Linda might just believe her. What a mess. What a bloody, sorry mess!

Chapter 21

'If you like I can take you to our local shopping centre today,' said Aidan, placing a plate of bacon and eggs in front of Linda's mother. 'It's fabulous. It's better than the Dundrum Town Centre and Liffey Valley put together.'

'That sounds great,' she said, digging into her breakfast. 'You're so good, Aidan. How am I ever going to thank you?'

Linda rolled her eyes as she sipped her coffee. Aidan and James had woken up with the commotion the previous morning and Linda had been mortified that her mother was there, together with enough luggage for a week. But they'd welcomed her fondly, assuring her that there was plenty of room and she could stay as long as she wanted. They'd listened to her woes about how her husband treated her and they'd oohed and aahed at her stories, which only encouraged her even more.

'What about you, Linda?'

'Sorry, what?' She'd tuned out of the conversation and now Aidan was looking at her, waiting for an answer.

'Are you going to come with us? Alice and I are going to go shopping after breakfast. James is working all day but I'm going to take a day off.'

'No, you two head off. I'll take advantage of the quiet house and get some writing done.'

'Honestly, darling,' said Alice, shaking her head at her daughter. 'You need to give yourself a break. I know you came here to write but you also came to shed yourself of some of the stress you were carrying back home.'

Linda didn't have the heart to tell her that a shopping day with her would probably just add to the stress. She loved her mum, she really did. And they got on really well. But that was when she had her in small doses. And she could think of nothing worse than a day trawling through the shops, with Alice telling her that she should stop wearing black and that she was getting too old to be wearing skirts above the knees.

'Linda?'

'Sorry, Mum. I was miles away. And I have been taking time out. But I'm also aware that I just have a few days left here and still a lot of the book to write.'

Alice nodded knowingly. 'Well, I did hear something about a

certain young man who's been keeping you occupied. Exactly when were you going to tell me about him?'

Linda glared at Aidan, who promptly stood up, his face flushed. 'I'll leave you two ladies to chat while I go and get ready.'

'Well?' said Alice, her eyebrows raised. 'James was telling me that you've been seeing somebody over here. Is that right?'

'I haven't been *seeing* him in the way you mean. Kabir is good company. We get on. End of story.' She wondered why James would have told her mother about Kabir. Unless it was just a slip of the tongue.

'Listen, love. I'm not judging you. We're in the same boat, you and me. So if some sexy Spanish man showed an interest in jumping *my* bones, I'd definitely be willing to give it a try.'

'Jesus Christ, Mum.' Linda had never heard her mother speaking that way. 'Firstly, nobody has jumped my bones and secondly, I can't believe you said that. You wouldn't do that to Dad. I know you wouldn't.'

'I would, you know. Just because I'm in my seventies doesn't mean I don't have needs. Your daddy's idea of love-making is—'

'STOP!! Mum, that's too much information. I don't want to hear about what you and Dad get up to. That's gross.'

'Why, dear? Just because we're old? Old people have working bits too, you know.'

'Oh God. Just shut up, will you?' Linda wanted to melt into the ground.

'Don't speak to me like that, Linda. I've brought you up better than that.'

'I'm sorry, but seriously. What's come over you? You're beginning to sound like a randy teenager.'

Alice dropped her head and Linda could see there were tears in her eyes.

'Mum, don't. I didn't mean to upset you but I'm just shocked, that's all. All this talk about you not wanting to be with Dad anymore is just messing with my head. I always knew he was difficult to live with but you leaving him? That's just crazy. Have you even rung him yet? For all we know, he might have reported you as missing and half the country could be out looking for you.'

'Calm down, love, will you? Of course I've rung him. I just gave him a few hours yesterday to stew and I called him last night. I'd left him a note too, so it's not as if he was dragging that stub of a leg out around the streets looking for me.'

Linda was lost for words. It was as though her mother was having a mid-life crisis at the age of seventy-eight. She felt a little bit sorry for her, but she was also angry. Her mother knew how important these two weeks were to her. She'd wanted to get away from the stresses of home and now her last few days were going to be spoiled by having to deal with someone else's problems too.

'So tell me about this man,' said Alice, her voice softer. 'What's been happening?'

Linda clammed up. It wasn't a conversation she wanted to have with her mother. It really wasn't a conversation she should be having at all. But on the other hand, maybe it would be good to talk about it. Although her mum was getting on in years, she was wise and perceptive and usually had good advice to give.

'Linda?'

She hesitated for a moment more before deciding to tell all. 'Kabir is lovely, Mum. He works with James and I met him here the night after I arrived. We clicked straight away. He's just easy to be with, you know?'

'Not complicated.' Her mother understood.

'Exactly,' said Linda. 'There are no complications. No expectations. We just chat about everything and worry about nothing.'

'And you haven't done anything yet?'

'Of course I haven't.' Linda was quick to respond. 'And I don't intend to.'

'Are you sure about that? Because when you say his name, your whole tone changes and your eyes light up. I'm your mother, Linda. I can tell when somebody has affected you.'

Was she really that transparent? 'I told you. He's just good company.'

'I'm not buying that.'

Linda sighed and sat back in her chair with her hands over her face.

'Come on, love. Tell me what's going on. I know things have been difficult for you at home recently and nobody would blame you for straying.'

'I haven't strayed,' said Linda, taking a piece of kitchen towel from the roll on the table and dabbing at the corner of her eyes. 'Well, not exactly. But ...'

'But?'

'I've thought about it.' There, she'd said it. And suddenly it all felt too real. 'I really like him, Mum. When I'm with him, I feel like

I used to when I was in my twenties. Before marriage and children. Before I lost myself.'

'And can you see a future with him?'

She thought for a moment. 'I don't know. Sometimes I think I can but then I think of Rob and the children and I don't want to throw all that away.'

'Well, for starters, you'll never throw away the children. They're yours for keeps and no matter what, they'll always be your children and you'll love them until the end of time. But Rob ... now, he might be a different story. How are you feeling about him? Do you still love him?'

'I ... I don't know. Sometimes.'

'I know that feeling,' said Alice, sagely. 'You've got a lot of thinking to do, Linda. Just be careful. Don't rush into anything and don't do anything you might regret later.'

Linda nodded. 'I know. It's a mess, isn't it?'

'It's only a mess if you allow it to be. Don't let the situation control you. You're the boss of yourself so take control. Make your decisions but know the consequences at the same time. Follow your heart but make sure your head gets a say too.'

'Thanks, Mum.' Suddenly Linda was grateful to have her mother there. She was wise and talked a lot of sense. She'd burst into her life the previous day and had brought a sense of reality and a reminder of home and for that, Linda had been angry. But it probably wasn't a bad thing. She needed to be reminded of her life back home and how much she had to lose.

'And on that note,' said Alice, standing up and beginning to clear the dishes from the table, 'I'd better go and get ready. A bit of shopping with Aidan will take my mind off things and stop me worrying about how your daddy is getting on without me.'

Linda felt guilty for making the conversation about her when clearly her mother had problems too. 'So you're worried about him then? I thought you didn't care.'

'Well, of course I care, Linda. You don't spend most of your life with somebody and suddenly not care. But he's still an ungrateful old codger and needs to be taught a lesson.'

'I see,' said Linda, smiling to herself. It seemed like her mother was just throwing her toys out of the pram. Nothing more serious than that. After she'd licked her wounds for a few days, she'd be back home and things would be as they should be. Linda couldn't help wishing things were as simple for her.

A little while later, when her mum and Aidan had left, Linda settled down to do some writing. If she was honest, Spain hadn't given her the inspiration she'd thought it would. She'd imagined writing out in the sunshine every day and the words flowing from her head onto the page. Somehow she'd thought that being in Spain would cure her of her writer's block. But instead, she found herself daydreaming when she was supposed to be writing and her progress to date was negligible. And considering her deadline was looming, she was having doubts that she'd ever get it finished on time. Sometimes she thought that maybe she'd picked the wrong genre. Crime was difficult. It was hard to think up storylines that she'd no experience of and to make them sound authentic. She'd heard somebody say once that real life can be stranger than fiction and she was beginning to understand that now. Maybe after this book, if she ever managed to finish it, she should write a novel about ordinary people with ordinary lives. Ordinary can be fascinating and compelling. Look at Maeve Binchy and how she wrote her stories around a cast of normal people and they were always wonderful and interesting. But she'd have to write this one first and then she could start thinking of what to do next.

Two hours later, her word count had gone down by a thousand as she'd spent her time deleting rather than moving forward. She was honestly sick of it. She was so far away from where she needed to be, it seemed like an impossible task. And now with her mother here, she was going to have even less time to move things along. She could feel the panic rising in her stomach but, closing her laptop, she gave herself a mental shake. She wasn't going to let the fear of failure win.

Putting the book out of her mind, she sat back and thought about the next few days. Things would be different now that her mum was here. Even though Linda had told her about Kabir, she'd still feel awkward going out to see him. She didn't want it to look as though she was being flippant about her marriage or uncaring about Rob's feelings. She needed to think it through now and decide what she was going to do.

It was three days since her argument with Rob and although she was angry about the things he'd said, she was also a little bit scared. She was used to pushing him away and he'd always come back. She'd tell him she didn't want to go to the cinema and he'd bring her for a meal or a drink. She'd claim she was too tired when he looked for sex and he'd just cuddle her instead. She'd argue with him and he'd never hold it against her and would always be happy to forget about their disagreement. He was good like that. But in the last three days, he hadn't made one attempt to ring her. And even the texts back and forth were few and far between and each one instigated by her. Maybe he'd had enough. And she didn't like the feeling of not being in control of the situation. It was time to ring him.

Her heart began to beat faster with every ring of the phone. Rob always had his phone on him and rarely missed a call so it seemed like he was ignoring her. What if he'd decided he liked his life without her in it? What if the decision was taken completely out of her hands? Surely that would be a simpler solution. She wouldn't be the one ending things. But was it really what she wanted? She still wasn't sure.

'Hi, Linda.'

She was overwhelmed with relief at the sound of his voice and she had to gulp in a breath before she spoke to him.

'Linda? Are you okay?'

'Yes, I'm fine. I was just swallowing a mouthful of tea. How are you?'

'I'm good. What about you?'

'I've been better.'

There was silence on the other end of the phone and Linda thought for a moment he'd hung up. 'Rob, are you still there?'

'Yes,' he said, his voice barely a whisper. 'I can explain.'

Now she was really confused. 'Explain what? What are you talking about?'

'What are *you* talking about?'

'Rob, what's happened? What do you need to explain?'

There was another pause before he spoke. 'I broke your favourite vase. You know the Waterford Crystal one? I knocked it over when I was dusting.'

'Oh thank God,' said Linda, relieved that there wasn't another drama. 'You gave me a fright there.'

'Thank God for what? That I broke the vase?'

She giggled. 'No. Thank God that you weren't going to tell me another story about one of the kids drinking or being arrested or something worse.'

'No, no. Nothing like that. Just a broken vase. I thought maybe Shauna had told you.'

'I haven't spoken to her in a few days but never mind the vase, I'm impressed that you were dusting in the first place.'

He laughed at that and the tension was broken. 'I miss you, Linda. I can't wait until you come home.'

'I miss you too.' She'd said it as a reflex, but she was surprised to realise it was a little bit true. She didn't know what was going to happen with Kabir or where it might lead, but Rob had always been such a huge part of her life and at that moment she missed him. 'Oh and you'll never guess what,' she said, beginning to enjoy the chat. 'Mum is here.'

'She's what? I don't believe it.'

'Yep. She rocked up yesterday with a suitcase, declaring that she'd left my dad.'

'No way.' He couldn't have sounded more shocked. 'She's actually left your dad? She was just here yesterday with a lasagne. Actually, now that I think of it, she was very keen to get your address. Oh God, if I'd known, I never would have given it to her.'

'Don't worry,' said Linda. 'I'd rather she was here where I can keep an eye on her. I've rung Dad and he's angry but he's also worried. I actually felt a bit sorry for him.'

'I'll call over and check on him tomorrow. I'll talk to him and see if there's anything I can do. How long is she staying there?'

Linda thought of the large suitcase. 'I honestly don't know. Aidan and James have really taken a liking to her and she thinks she's very trendy hanging out with a gay couple.'

Rob laughed out loud. 'Your mum is hilarious.'

'She has her moments,' said Linda, laughing too. 'But listen, I'd better let you go. I want to start dinner before the others come home or else they'll be thinking I'm always waiting to be served. They've been very good to me.'

'It sounds like it,' said Rob. 'I'll chat to you again tomorrow. Bye, love.'

Linda ended the call and felt her spirits rise. That was the best conversation she'd had with Rob in ages. It had felt easy – just like it used to. She felt closer to him than she had in a long time and it was a great feeling. Her thoughts flitted to Kabir and she wondered if she'd made a mistake getting involved with him. It had made things very complicated. Guilt overwhelmed her suddenly, but she pushed it aside. She couldn't allow herself to wallow.

She went into the kitchen and opened the fridge to see if there was anything she could cook for dinner. There were plenty of eggs and potatoes so she'd make a Spanish omelette and they could have it with salad. She sang to herself as she prepared the food and it occurred to her that she hadn't done that in a long time. She was beginning to feel like herself again. For the first time in ages, she felt like everything was going to be okay.

Chapter 22

'This is delicious, Linda,' said James, as they all sat around the table eating the dinner Linda had prepared. 'I'd have you on my team in the kitchen any day.'

Linda blushed at the compliment. 'Thanks, James. It's far from the fabulous meals you make but I'm glad you're enjoying it.'

'You should have come with us today,' said Alice, loading her fork with food. 'That shopping centre is amazing. I bought so much that I think I'll need another case to bring my stuff home.'

Linda seized the opportunity to question her mother again. 'And when do you think that might be, Mum? Have you booked anything yet?'

'No. And I'm not in a hurry to either.'

'But don't you think Dad has learned his lesson by now? I'm sure he's really missing you.'

'Missing having a servant, more like.'

Linda tried again. 'It's hardly fair on Aidan and James though, Mum, is it? They weren't banking on two of us coming to stay.'

'The boys don't mind, do you?' She looked from one to the other. 'They've said I can stay as long as I like.'

'Of course you can,' said Aidan, staring lovingly at Alice. '*Mi casa es tu casa.*'

Alice batted her eyelashes in response. 'I don't know what that means but it sounds lovely.'

'You two,' said Linda, who couldn't help giggling, 'are like two starry-eyed lovers. Should we be getting worried?'

'I wish,' said Alice, taking a slice of bread from the basket. 'Now if I was thirty years younger …'

'And if he wasn't gay,' said James, joining in with the banter. 'But I'm afraid he's taken anyway so you have no chance.'

Linda had never imagined that spending time with her mother could be so much fun. Back home, she saw her a couple of times a week but usually her dad was there, and he had a habit of bringing the mood down. It was nice to see her in a different environment. Linda could already see the change in her from when she'd arrived the previous day. She'd been stressed and upset but now she was relaxed and enjoying herself.

'So how can you two boys afford a house like this?' said Alice, changing the subject. 'I assume you own it yourselves? Or are you just renting?'

Linda balked at her mum's direct question but maybe she'd be able to get more information out of them than Linda could.

'I wish we did own it,' said Aidan, running his finger around the rim of his wine glass. 'A friend of ours owns it actually. He's just letting us stay here while he's abroad.'

Alice looked impressed. 'Wow! Now there's a great friend to have. Imagine trusting somebody with a house like this. No offence to you two, of course.'

'None taken,' said Aidan, smiling. 'And yes, he's been very generous. We pay him rent, but he doesn't charge much. We're very lucky.'

'You certainly are.' But Alice wasn't finished quizzing them yet. 'So where has he gone, this friend of yours?'

'Australia,' said Aidan, dipping some bread into the sauce on his plate.

Linda had been listening intently. 'I thought you said he had gone to America.'

'No,' said James, a little too quickly. 'We said he'd gone to Australia. He'll be there for another few months at least.'

'I see,' she said, nodding slowly. 'I must have misheard.' But she knew she'd heard perfectly well. Aidan had definitely said their friend had gone to America. That must mean that James knew about the house too. That he was in on whatever dodgy thing Aidan had gotten himself into. Linda had thought that maybe James was as clueless as she'd been about the ownership of the house, but obviously not. She was dying to find out more but she didn't want to make them suspicious. Luckily Alice wasn't so coy and was happy to ask all the questions Linda was afraid to ask.

'So where will you go when your friend comes back?' said Alice, looking from one to the other. 'I can't imagine you'll be able to afford to rent anything like this again.'

Aidan shook his head. 'No, probably not. But we should be able to find somewhere reasonable enough. Property isn't too expensive here and as long as I'm with James, I couldn't care less where I live.'

Alice beamed. 'You two are so cute. But you'd want to think about getting your foot on the property ladder. Renting is just dead money. Even if you start small. Buy your own one-bed apartment and in a few years, you might be able to sell up and buy a two- or even a three-bed. You have to start somewhere.'

Linda watched their reactions but neither of them flinched.

'We'll bear that in mind,' said James, smiling at Alice. 'But thankfully we don't have to worry yet. Now, are we all finished here and I'll make us some tea? I brought home a lovely *tarta de santiago* from the restaurant and wait until you taste it. It will blow your minds.'

'Oh God,' said Linda, her mouth watering. 'Is that the almond one that we had the other day? I'd sell my soul for a piece of that. It's delicious.'

'Almond cake was your daddy's favourite too,' said Alice, looking into the distance. '*King of desserts* he always said when he saw it on a menu.'

'For God's sake, Mum. You're speaking about Dad as though he was dead.'

'I am not,' she said, defensively. 'The old grump is alive and well. Or at least he was when I spoke to him an hour ago.'

'I didn't know you were speaking to him today,' said Linda. 'How is he coping without you?'

'Oh he's well able to cope. He just likes moaning about it. He was in a very bad mood and just wanted me to tell him I'd be home on the next plane.'

'And I'm guessing you didn't agree?' Linda already knew the answer but she lived in hope.

'Of course I didn't, Linda. And until he starts recognising how he's been treating me, I'm going nowhere. If I go home now, nothing will have changed. Everything will be back to just the way it was last week, and the week before and the week before that.'

Linda's heart sank. Much as she was enjoying being with her mother, she didn't want her to stay for a few more days. That's all that Linda had left of her Spanish adventure and she wanted to be able to make the most of it without worrying about what her mother was up to. Just then, a knock on the door startled them all and Aidan got up to answer it. For a moment, Linda imagined seeing her dad standing there, his clothes unwashed and creased and his face forlorn. She held her breath just in case. But it wasn't him.

'Kabir. Come on in. We're just having dinner and there's plenty.'

Linda looked up, alarmed. Much as she wanted to see Kabir, she didn't want it to be under the watchful eye of her mother.

'Thanks for the offer,' he said, stepping inside and glancing over at Linda, 'but I'm not staying. I was just passing and thought I'd drop in to see if Linda wanted to go out tonight.'

'Not tonight,' said Linda, 'but thanks.' She tried to explain by way of sign language, nodding towards her mother and rolling her eyes. 'I'll give you a ring later.'

Kabir looked disappointed. 'I just wanted to make up for the other night. I felt bad having to run off on you like that.'

'There's no need. Honestly.' She was beginning to feel a bit uncomfortable having the conversation with an audience listening to every word and she just wished Kabir had rung her instead.

'And what's stopping you from going out tonight?' said Alice suddenly, looking towards Linda as she stood up. 'And since nobody else is bothering, I may as well do the introductions. I'm Linda's mum. I guess you're Kabir, Linda's … friend.'

Kabir flushed a deep shade of crimson. 'Yes, I'm Kabir. Nice to meet you Mrs … ?'

'Alice,' she said, holding out her hand for Kabir to shake. 'Linda has told me all about you.'

'She has?' He looked towards Linda, his face clouded with worry.

Linda stood up and walked towards them. 'Yes, I've told her how welcoming you've been and how you've been showing me around La Zenia.'

'You're not what I expected,' said Alice, looking Kabir up and down. 'Handsome, aren't you?'

Linda was mortified and Kabir's face seemed to be turning redder by the minute. 'Mum, stop trying to embarrass him and go back to your dinner. Come on, Kabir. I'll walk you out.'

'It was nice to meet you, Alice,' said Kabir, looking relieved to be escaping. He waved at James and Aidan and stepped outside. 'Well, that was awkward.'

'I know!' giggled Linda. 'Sorry about that. My mum doesn't have any filter. She just says what she thinks.'

'So I noticed. You never said your mum was coming over here.'

Linda walked with him towards his car. 'That's because I didn't know. She turned up unexpectedly yesterday, suitcase in tow, and declared she's left my dad.'

'No way! Has she really?'

'For now anyway,' said Linda. 'He's not an easy man to live with so I can't say I blame her. But I also know she loves him, regardless of all his faults, so I reckon it will all blow over in a few days.'

Kabir smiled then and his whole face lit up. 'Well, I guess now we're even. You've met my parents and I've met your mum.'

'I hadn't thought of it like that,' said Linda, smiling as realisation dawned. 'So now I don't feel so guilty about my mum's loose tongue. You probably deserved it.'

'I suppose I did.'

They both stood in silence for a few seconds until Kabir spoke again. 'So what have you told your mum? I mean, about us.'

'What is there to tell really, Kabir? I just told her the truth.'

'About everything?' He looked worried.

'If you're talking about the kiss, well then no. I didn't tell her about that.'

'Thank God.'

'Oh, cheers for that,' said Linda, feeling a bit hurt. 'You really know how to make a girl feel good.'

'I'm sorry. I didn't mean it to come out like that. It's just that you're married, and I don't want your mother to think badly of me. Of us.'

Linda shook her head. 'My mum is a little bit crazy but she's got a good head on her shoulders. She knows the situation. I didn't say anything about the kiss but she knows that I like you.'

'She does?' He looked at her intently. 'You do?'

It was Linda's turn to blush. 'Well, isn't it obvious? I really do like you, Kabir, but I also have a lot to lose if this goes any further.'

'I like you too,' he said, taking her hand and squeezing it. 'But I respect your situation and I won't push you.'

She felt it again. That bolt of electricity from the touch of his hand. It was like he was breathing new life into her and it made her crave more. 'So what were you thinking about for tonight?' She couldn't resist.

'I was just thinking I'd take you for a drink. There's a nice cocktail bar down near Paddy's Point so maybe I could come and collect you and we could walk there. It will give us time to chat.'

'That sounds good to me,' she said, already imagining them strolling down the street hand in hand. 'Will we say about nine? It's already seven so I'll need time to shower and change.'

'That's perfect. I'll pick you up then.' He leaned over and kissed her briefly on the lips. Just a whisper of a kiss but it almost made Linda go weak at the knees. He released her hand then and hopped into his jeep.

'Bye,' she said, waving as he spun the jeep around on the gravel. She watched until he disappeared, and she closed her eyes to relive the kiss.

When she was with Kabir, it was as though nothing else and nobody else mattered. She was able to push all thoughts of home aside and just live in the moment. But when she was alone, guilt overwhelmed her as she remembered that she was a married woman with a family waiting for her back in Ireland. She wished she could keep up with her own thought process because it was beginning to exhaust her.

Nobody even heard her come back in. All three were chatting animatedly and laughing at the same time. She was tempted to just slip into her room unnoticed, but she knew that would only arouse suspicion. Especially from her mother. So she re-joined them at the table and waited for the flood of questions.

'Well?' said her mother, raising her eyebrows. 'Are you going out?'

'I am.'

'What time?'

'He's coming here at nine.'

'And where are you going?'

'Just to some cocktail bar. We're going to walk there.'

'I see,' said Alice, nodding her head slowly. 'And are you going to go back to his place after?'

'For God's sake, Mum. What sort of a question is that?'

'I think it's a reasonable one,' said James. 'Weren't you there the other night?'

Linda glared at him. 'Kabir invited me for dinner. Yes. And I left straight after because he had an emergency or something with one of the restaurants.'

'Oh is that what he was talking about?' said Alice. 'When he said he wanted to make up for the other night?'

'I suppose so,' said Linda, wishing they'd just change the subject. And why was James sticking his nose in? Surely he'd know that Linda wouldn't want to share all that information with her mother. And that was the second time he'd done it.

'Just remember what I said, love. And be careful.'

'Oh God, can everybody just shut up about me seeing Kabir. He's a nice man. We get on well. Nothing has happened and it's not going to. It's just two people enjoying each other's company. I'm a married woman and I'm planning to keep it that way so please everybody just BUTT OUT!'

There was a moment's silence before Alice spoke. 'Linda, there's really no need for that. We're all just looking out for you.'

Linda was shaking. 'I know, Mum. But why can't I just have a nice time without everyone making it into something it's not? I really don't need that.'

'I'm sorry, Linda.' James reached out and put his hand over hers.

'Me too,' said Aidan, coming to give her a hug. 'It really is none of our business so we should just let you get on with things.'

'I'm sorry too,' said Linda. 'I shouldn't have shouted like that but there are a lot of things going on in my head at the moment and sometimes I feel as though it might burst.'

'We understand, love,' said her mother. 'Why don't you go and have a nice long shower and clear your head. Go and have a good time tonight. In another few days you'll be home and everything will be back to normal.'

Linda nodded and headed into her bedroom to get organised. She'd be home and everything would be back to normal, her mother had said. But would it? She wasn't even sure what was normal anymore.

Chapter 23

Linda was in the middle of blow-drying her hair when the doorbell rang. 'Shit!' she muttered to herself, glancing at the clock. It was only 8.40 and Kabir wasn't due until nine but the chances were it was him. Aidan and James had gone out for a walk and her mother was having a rest in her room, so she'd have to answer the door herself. She switched off the dryer and headed out.

'Kabir. You're early. I wasn't expecting you for a while yet.'

'Sorry about that,' he said, stepping inside as she held open the door. 'It's a bit of a habit of mine. I hate being late so I always end up being way too early. Would you like me to wait out in the car?'

She shook her head and indicated for him to take a seat on the sofa. 'Not at all. I'll just be about ten minutes.'

'Take your time. There's no hurry.'

'Okay. I'll make you a coffee while you wait.' She quickly boiled the kettle and made him an instant before heading back into her room. As she finished blow-drying her hair, she noted how quickly the greys seemed to be appearing. She'd just got her colour in two weeks before and already there was a sprinkling of silver along her roots. In the last few years she'd also become conscious of the fine lines that were appearing around her face. Laughter lines, her mother called them, but Linda knew that there hadn't been much of that of late. She hated getting older. Although she had another few years until she'd be fifty, she was already dreading the big milestone.

When she'd finished, she sprayed her hair with the shine product she'd bought in Sephora during her shopping spree the other day and applied another coat of her favourite nude lipstick. Not too bad at all, she thought, checking herself out in the mirror. She rooted in her bag for her Lady Million perfume and gave herself a liberal spray before heading back out to Kabir.

'You look nice, love,' said her mother, from her place beside Kabir on the sofa.

Linda quickly took in the scene. Her mother was wearing lipstick – and that only happened on very rare occasions. She also had her best cardigan and walking shoes on. Surely that couldn't mean what she was thinking it meant. Her mother wouldn't do that, would she?

'Kabir has very kindly asked me to join you both,' she said, smiling at Linda. 'Isn't that nice of him?'

Linda shot Kabir a glance and he mouthed a sorry. 'But it's a long walk, Mum. Wouldn't you prefer to relax tonight? You were saying earlier that you were exhausted.'

'That was before I had my forty winks. I'm fresh as a daisy now.'

'And we're going to a cocktail bar. You hate cocktails.'

'I'm sure they serve other stuff too,' she said. 'And anyone would think you didn't want me to go, the way you're going on.'

'I'm sure Linda didn't mean it that way,' said Kabir, standing up and holding out his hand to help Alice. 'And if you get too tired, we can always get a taxi back.'

Linda rolled her eyes. Although she was enjoying having her mother around, she really didn't want her playing piggy in the middle with her and Kabir all night. And what had come over Kabir, asking her to join them? Linda couldn't figure him out. Although he was showing all the signs of being interested in her, it seemed that he was keeping her at arm's length at the same time. It just didn't make sense.

'Come on then,' said Alice, linking Kabir as they walked outside. 'I won't have either of you saying the aul' one is slowing you down.'

It was an intriguing walk, to say the least. Kabir pointed out places of interest along the way while Alice talked incessantly about everything from her husband's stub of a leg to homelessness in Ireland. All Linda's thoughts of walking hand in hand with Kabir had dissipated as her mother continued to link him. And in a weird turn of events, it was Linda who felt like the piggy in the middle.

'Here we are,' said Kabir, stopping outside a very modern-looking cocktail bar. 'Let's go in. I could murder a mojito.'

Browns Bar was even more impressive on the inside. There was a long bar area running along one side with rows of stools and behind it was an impressive array of colourful bottles on brightly lit shelves. A little further down, there were people dining, and despite having already eaten, Linda's mouth watered at the sight of the delicious-looking food. Kabir noticed her eyeing up a burger as a waiter passed.

'We could get a table if you'd like to eat?' he said. 'They do the best burgers in La Zenia.'

Linda shook her head. 'I couldn't tonight. Not after the dinner I had. But maybe another night.'

'That's a bit presumptuous, isn't it?' said Alice, ushering them towards three free stools. 'Maybe Kabir has other plans for the week.'

'I didn't mean … I wasn't presuming …'

Kabir laughed as they sat down. 'I know, I know. It was just a throwaway comment. But we should definitely come here to eat before you leave. You'll love it.'

'Yes, that would be lovely,' said Linda, giving her mother a death stare. 'But I'll have to see how the week goes. I still have a mountain of writing to get through, so I'll have to give that priority.'

'Three mojitos,' said Alice, catching the eye of a young bartender. 'On the rocks.'

'Mum! What are you doing? You and cocktails don't mix well, remember? Let me order a nice glass of wine for you.'

'No, love. That was a long time ago and it was that coconutty one. Kabir says this one is basically mint and lime and there's barely any alcohol in it at all.'

'Well, I didn't exactly say—'

'Don't worry, Kabir love. Linda is just being an alarmist. I wouldn't drink it if I thought it would do me any harm.'

Linda sighed. The next hour was spent drinking mojitos – two for her and about five for her mum and Kabir. Kabir seemed to be able to handle them well whereas her mother was almost falling off the stool by eleven o'clock. She'd actually plonked herself on the stool in between the two of them and had been hogging the conversation all night. And to make things worse, Kabir was hanging on her every word, looking at her with stars in his eyes. What was it about her mother that attracted people to her? She seemed to mesmerise everyone she met with her charm and her stories. Tonight was certainly turning into a bit of a nightmare and Linda couldn't help wishing she'd stuck to her original plan of a cup of tea and an early night.

'Maybe we should call a taxi now?' suggested Kabir, nodding towards Alice, who had just decided that it would be a good idea to sing 'The Fields of Athenry'. 'I can drop you two home and go on home myself. I'll have to pick the jeep up tomorrow.'

'*Low lie in fields, of Athenry, where once I heard a young fleabag cry ...*'

'Oh Jesus. Mum, it's time to go home. Come on. We can wait outside for the taxi.'

'But I don't want to go yet. *Our love is song the wings, we had dreams of on the sing ...*'

'Let's go, Alice,' said Kabir, looking concerned. 'I don't think they allow singing in here.'

'Ah they're just a bunch of Spanish snobs. They wouldn't know culture if it jumped up and hit them on the nose … *By lone and pins an all, I watched a hunger ca-aa-aalling, Michael they have taken you away …*'

Linda was beginning to panic. The bar staff were all watching in disbelief and customers were whispering and pointing. All she needed now was for her mother to vomit, to top off one of the worst nights of her life. It had been the same story five years before when they'd gone to a fancy bar in town to celebrate her mum and dad's anniversary. Her mum had insisted on drinking cocktails, thought it would be funny to sing television theme tunes in an Elmo voice and eventually vomited all over the table. Linda had wanted the ground to open up and swallow her and she was beginning to feel the same now.

'What are we going to do?' whispered Kabir to Linda, keeping one hand on Alice to steady her as she rocked back and forth. 'She's in a right state. I don't even know if a taxi will take her.'

'Oh God. I hadn't thought of that. Maybe I should give Aidan a ring. I'm sure he'd come and get us.'

'*Sure she'll wait in hold in Bray, for her lovin' Bounty Bay …*'

Linda grabbed her phone from her bag. 'Aidan, can you do me a huge favour …'

Twenty minutes later they were in Aidan's car heading home. They'd eventually gotten Alice out of the bar by Linda feigning illness and even in her drunken state, her motherly instincts had kicked in.

'Are you okay, love?' said Alice, pushing Linda's hair lovingly behind her ears. 'You've probably just drunk too much. You'll be okay in the morning.'

Linda nodded. She didn't trust herself to say anything. Thankfully Browns Bar wasn't far from home and minutes later they were helping Alice out of the car and into the house. Kabir couldn't get away quickly enough and Linda couldn't blame him. Aidan said he'd drop him home, so as soon as they got Alice inside, Kabir kissed Linda briefly on the cheek and headed back out to the car. There was nothing like a drunken mother to kill a bit of romance. Linda was mortified at her mother's behaviour and made a mental note to ring Kabir to apologise the next day.

'Make me a cup of tea, love, will you?' said Alice, plonking down heavily on the sofa. 'All that singing has made me dry as a desert.'

'The only thing I'm giving you, Mum, is a large glass of water and a helping hand into bed.' Linda just wanted to go to bed herself and forget about the disastrous night.

'Don't be ridiculous, love. I can't go to bed without my cup of tea. I can make it myself if you're still not feeling well. You really shouldn't drink cocktails if you can't handle them.'

Linda couldn't believe her ears. 'I've had two cocktails, Mum. Just two cocktails. Whereas you and Kabir were knocking them back like they were going out of fashion.'

Alice sighed and stood up, heading for the kitchen. Linda followed her and watched as she filled the kettle and got a cup ready with a teabag. She loaded the dishwasher with the few cups and plates that were scattered on the counter and wiped down the surfaces with a cloth.

'You've sobered up pretty quickly,' said Linda, confused at the change in her mother's demeanour. 'Only five minutes ago you were drunk as a skunk.'

'Not me, love. I'm completely fine.'

'But how could you be? You've been drinking all night.'

Alice remained silent as she waited for the kettle to boil and when she eventually poured the water into her cup, she turned to face Linda. 'I had two cocktails, Linda. Well, two alcoholic ones. I told the bartender after that to make mine alcohol free.'

Linda was astounded. 'I don't understand. What about the singing. And the swaying on your stool. Kabir and I were nervous wrecks in case you'd fall off.'

'Come and sit down, love,' said Alice, taking her tea back over to the sofa. 'I think we need to have a little chat.'

'What's going on, Mum?' Linda felt suddenly nervous. Maybe her mother was going to announce that there was something wrong with her. That she had cancer or something and that she was fulfilling some sort of bucket list. Oh God, now Linda really did feel sick as she sat down and waited to hear what her mother had to say.

'Kabir is gorgeous,' she began, speaking slowly as she sipped her tea. 'He's handsome and intelligent. He has a good job and owns his own apartment. He looks after his mother, loves children and even does some charity work at a local homeless shelter.'

Linda felt confused. She was still waiting for the *I have cancer* statement and when it wasn't forthcoming, she realised she might have been assuming too much. She really didn't know where her mother was going with all this, but she listened as Alice continued.

'He's a bachelor and from what I can see, probably one of the most eligible ones in the area. Let's face it. He's a catch and he's going to make some woman very happy.'

So there it was. Rob had never been Alice's favourite person. She'd never really wanted them to get married in the first place because she'd worried about his ideas of a traditional family. Her own career in recruitment had been ended by her husband's demands that she stay at home, and she hadn't wanted that for Linda. She'd warned Linda to keep her own identity and not let Rob force his beliefs on her, so when Linda had chosen to give up her job to be a stay-at-home mum, Alice had been furious. But Rob had proven himself to be a good husband and father over the years and Alice had certainly warmed to him. But there'd always been that little niggling doubt in her head and she hadn't kept it a secret from Linda. Now it looked as though Alice had found the perfect son-in-law. Kabir was the type of man that she'd always wanted for her daughter and she was going to try and push Linda into giving him a chance.

'Are you listening to me, Linda? I'm not saying all this for the good of my health.'

'I know, Mum. Kabir is gorgeous and fabulous and rich and perfect. And you think he'd make me very happy.'

'*You?* He won't make *you* happy.'

'What do you mean?' said Linda, trying to keep up. 'But you just said—'

'Linda, love, I said he'd make *somebody* happy. And that somebody is certainly not you.'

'Oh.' Linda wasn't sure what to say to that.

'You're missing my whole point,' said Alice, finishing off the last drop of her tea and placing the cup on the coffee table. 'I can see how much Kabir has going for him and how you'd be attracted to him. It would be hard not to be.'

'And?'

'I think you're feeling vulnerable, love. You're missing something in your life, and you think Kabir is going to give it to you. You and Rob are just going through a rough patch and I'm scared you'll regret it if you throw your marriage away.'

'But I'm not going to just throw my marriage away. I haven't been happy for a while and I haven't decided what I'm going to do about it, but I don't plan to just throw everything away.'

'What you don't seem to understand, Linda, is that it may be out of your hands. You might think that you can have a fling over here and then go back to your life at home. You might think that you can weigh up the pros and cons of each relationship – test the waters, so to speak – and then make your decision. But as soon as Rob hears about what you've done, he may not want to remain married to you anymore.'

It was the second time she'd heard those words and the stark reality of her situation was like a slap to the face. She sat back into the sofa, trying to get things straight in her head.

'What I'm trying to say,' continued Alice, 'is that you'd want to be completely sure of Kabir before you do anything you'll regret. Because as far as I see it, once you've done something, there's no going back.'

'Even if Rob doesn't find out?' She knew she was grasping at straws, but she didn't feel ready to make any decisions yet.

Alice nodded. 'Even if Rob doesn't find out. It will eat you up inside. You'll always worry that somebody will find out and tell him and even aside from that, the guilt you'll carry around will destroy you.'

Linda pondered on that for a moment. 'How can you be sure, Mum? What makes you such an authority on all this?'

'Because it happened to me.'

Linda was alarmed. 'What do you mean? Were you unfaithful to Dad?'

'It was years ago. A weekend away in Nice with the girls. It happened just once and I regretted it immediately.'

'Oh my God! You actually cheated on Dad? So what happened? What did he say?'

'I never told him. It was a once-off. A bad decision and I swore it would never happen again so I decided he'd be better off not knowing. And it was definitely the best decision for him anyway. It would have killed him.'

'And for you?'

'It's been the bane of my life ever since. There isn't a day that I don't think about the lies and deceit. I should never have done it. I know that. But I've certainly been punished for it. The guilt is horrible, and I know I only have myself to blame.'

Linda couldn't believe what she was hearing. 'So is that why you put up with him? With his grumpiness and his demands?'

'Partly,' she said, wiping a tear from her eye. 'But mostly because I love him. I always have. He's my life, Linda, and even though he's a cantankerous old codger, he loves me and I love the bones of him.'

'Tell me why you love him so much, Mum.'

Alice looked surprised. 'What do you mean?'

'You said you love the bones of him,' said Linda, watching her mother carefully. 'You said yourself he's grumpy and cantankerous. So what is it about him you love so much?'

Alice thought for a moment before replying. 'He wasn't always like that, you know. When I met him, he was the most kind-hearted, patient, loving man I'd ever met. He was handsome and passionate and had a gentleness that I found really endearing.'

'But that was a long time ago, Mum. Is it the memories of how he used to be that keeps you loving him? Are you in love with the past?'

'Are you asking that for me or for yourself, Linda? Are you worried that you're more in love with what you and Rob used to have rather than what you have now?'

Her mother was so perceptive. 'I don't know … no … I'm not sure …'

'Well, to answer your question,' said Alice slowly. 'I love him because I know that all those wonderful qualities are still a part of him. We've had a long love affair, your daddy and me. Almost sixty years now. Things have changed over the years and I'm not saying it's all been a bed of roses, but ours is a deep love and I couldn't imagine life without him.'

Linda's eyes welled up with tears at her mother's beautiful words.

'And,' continued Alice, 'we still have our moments, you know. Usually when there's nobody else around and often in the bedroom.' She winked and Linda burst out laughing.

'Too much information, Mum. So I take it you haven't really left him then?'

'Just for a break. I could never leave your daddy for good. And besides, I felt I had a mission over here. I was worried about you. I read between the lines when you phoned me and I guessed you were about to get into something you might regret. The way you're feeling now – that's how I felt all those years ago. You're so like me, love.'

'And tonight?' said Linda, her head spinning. 'What was that all about?'

'Something told me that tonight could be the night. So I just thought I'd chaperone you two.'

'But the singing and the swaying. If you weren't drunk, you're the best actress I've ever seen.'

'Sure don't I always love a sing-song? You don't have to be drunk to start one.'

Just at that moment, Aidan arrived back and raised his eyebrows when he saw the two women sitting together. 'Feeling better now, Alice?'

'Yes, thank you. And I'm sorry we had to drag you out. I'll make it up to you.'

'No need,' he said, heading towards his bedroom. 'I'm off to bed so I'll see you two in the morning.'

'I think I'll head too,' said Alice, standing up. 'It's been a very tiring night.'

Linda stood up too and enveloped her in a hug.

'What's that for, love?'

'Just for being you. Fantastic, wonderful, caring you.'

Alice flushed with pleasure. 'You're pretty fabulous yourself, Linda. Now go and have a think about what I've said. You have a long life ahead of you, please God, and you want to make sure it's a good one.'

Linda watched her mother's tiny frame walk away and felt a surge of love. So Alice had actually come over to Spain to try and save her daughter, and not, as she'd claimed, to leave her husband. She'd sensed that Linda was about to make the biggest mistake of her life and she was there to stop her. Linda was lucky to have her mum in her life. So many of her friends' parents had passed away and she felt privileged to still have both of hers. But the question was, would Linda take her mother's advice? That, she thought wearily, remained to be seen.

Chapter 24

Rob's heart felt heavy as he pushed the shopping trolley through the aisles of Supervalu. It was early Tuesday morning, the day after Shauna had walked in on him and Tanya, and he'd been worried sick ever since. Shauna had refused to speak to him. To let him explain. She'd just taken a sandwich to her room when she'd come home from school and hadn't emerged except to get a glass of water. Rob had tried to reason with her. To at least get her to listen to his side. But she'd point-blank refused, stating that she couldn't bear to even look at him. He'd been tempted to pull out the *I'm your father, give me some respect* card but the truth was, he'd been feeling way too guilty.

He looked at the piece of paper in his hands and scratched his head. He really hadn't a clue what an aubergine looked like before it was cooked so he'd have to use the process of elimination. He'd been thinking of ways to get through to Shauna and had come up with the idea of food. In Sicilian tradition, food was a very important part of life and was used to express emotion. A simple bowl of pasta was like a hug after a busy day and home-made pizza meant happiness. A baked ziti or potato casserole brought to a house at a time of bereavement showed sympathy and a cheeseboard with cured meats was pure joy. So Rob had decided to make a vegetarian lasagne and he hoped she'd be impressed by the effort he'd gone to. Being in transition year, she seemed to have a lot of time off and he'd noticed from the school calendar that she had a three-hour lunch break today. As she usually came home for long lunches, he was planning on having the meal ready so they could talk while it was just the two of them.

Half an hour later, he was home. He'd opted for a ready-prepared bag of vegetables along with some dried lasagne sheets and jars of both white and red Dolmio sauce. A little part of him felt he was cheating by going for the easy way out, but it was the thought that counted. As a child, he'd watched his mother make pasta. It seemed like the most simple and natural thing in the world. She never would have dreamed of using the dried stuff, claiming it had no flavour and was too processed, and God forbid she'd use a jar of sauce. He'd often quoted his mother to Linda and it had never gone down too well. He understood why now.

A little while later, as the lasagne baked in the oven, he went about setting the dining room table nicely with table-cloth and napkins; he even took a pretty yellow chrysanthemum from the window box outside and placed it in a narrow vase in the centre. He was aware of the fact that Shauna would be suspicious of his actions, but he didn't even care. He was desperate. If he could just get his daughter onside. Speak to her like an adult and explain that things had been a bit rocky between him and her mum. If he could convince her that what she'd seen the previous day was completely innocent, he might have some chance of her not speaking to Linda about it. He'd toyed with the idea of telling Linda himself. Getting in first, so to speak. But he knew the situation had looked bad and with the way things were between them, he wasn't sure Linda would understand. Or worse still, she might not believe him.

A glance at his watch told him it was 12.45 so it wouldn't be long before Shana was home. He went to remove the tin foil from the lasagne and add an extra sprinkling of cheese. He'd surprised himself at how much he'd learned about the kids since Linda had left. He now knew that the cheesier the better for Shauna, she didn't like mashed potatoes and preferred basmati rice to long-grain. He knew Ben detested sweetcorn and that baked beans made him sick. How had he never known these things before? Was it because he'd been so detached from the family? He'd always prided himself on being there for them but was it the case that he'd just appeared for dinner when it was put on the table? And just expected that his washing and ironing would be done and back in his wardrobe when he needed it? Had he really been such an idiot?

The lasagne was almost ready so he popped a garlic baguette in beside it to heat up. The smell was delicious, but he wasn't sure if he had an appetite. At least not until Shauna agreed not to say anything to Linda. Rob hated that he had to defend his actions when nothing had happened. He hated that he was trying to keep it from Linda. But the truth was that it had looked bad. He'd gone over and over it in his head the previous night and he really couldn't blame Shauna for jumping to conclusions.

Just as he was lifting the lasagne out of the oven a few minutes later, he heard the front door opening. Great timing. He stuck two plates in to heat while the lasagne was resting and waited for Shauna to appear. But the sound of her bedroom door slamming told him she wasn't in the mood for chatting, so he'd just have to go and get her. He sighed as he went upstairs. He was really beginning to see what Linda had been talking about for the last year. Rob had always seen Shauna as his little girl. He'd never seen her darker side and had refused to believe Linda when she'd tried to tell him that their daughter was out of control. He was almost nervous now to go and speak to her.

'Shauna,' he said, opening her bedroom door. 'I've made some—'

'For God's sake, Dad. You can't just barge into my room like that. I could have been getting changed or anything.'

'You're just lying on your bed, Shauna. Don't be so dramatic.'

'That's not the point. I'm sixteen years old, not six. The days are gone where you could just open the door to my room. This is my private space and I shouldn't have to worry about people coming in uninvited.'

Rob was beginning to get angry. 'I'm not just people, Shauna. I'm your father. It's different for me.'

'Is it really?' she said, sitting up, her eyes flaming. 'So you think it would be okay if you came into my room and I was standing here naked?'

'Of course not,' said Rob, shocked at the insinuation. 'But you've just arrived home from school. I followed you straight up.'

'Forget it, Dad. You'll never understand.'

'Well, why don't you make me? Make me understand what's going on in your life, Shauna. We used to be so close, you and me. We never talk anymore.'

'Yeah, well that's because I'm not a little girl anymore. I don't believe in fairy tales and I certainly can't be palmed off with lies.'

There it was. The underlying accusation. She was glaring at him with hatred and it made him almost recoil.

'Close the door on your way out, will you?' she said, lying back down and sticking her earphones in her ears.

Rob was torn between wanting to slap her and hug her. She was really being very difficult but at the end of the day, she was just defending her mother. In her eyes, Rob had betrayed Linda and Shauna wasn't letting him away with it. But he was determined to explain to her. To get her onside. He hadn't spent all morning preparing for this just to throw it all away. He walked towards her and pulled an earphone from her left ear.

'For fuck's sake, Dad!'

'Shauna, I've had enough of this foul mouth of yours. You've got to stop all this bad language. It's disgusting.'

'Whatever.' She tried to put her earphone back in but Rob's hand stopped her.

'I've made lunch for us. Come on down and we can have a chat.'

'I'm not hungry.'

'It's your favourite. Vegetarian lasagne. Extra cheesy. And I've even done some garlic bread.'

'Still not hungry.'

'Shauna,' he said, exasperated. 'Just do as I say, please. Come down and at least have the courtesy to eat something after I spent all morning making it.'

She looked as though she was about to object again but changed her mind. With a sigh, she threw her earphones on the bed and swung her legs around onto the floor. Standing up, she pushed past Rob and headed downstairs. As he followed, he wondered where it had all gone wrong. Where was the little girl who loved to sit on her daddy's knee and wanted to be a fairy when she grew up?

He ushered her into the dining room and went to get the food from the kitchen. When he came back with the plates, he was at least glad to see she was sitting quietly and her face had softened a little.

'Why all the fancy schmancy stuff?' she said, nodding towards the beautifully decorated table. 'Are we expecting somebody else?'

'Nobody else,' said Rob, placing a plate in front of her. 'Just the two of us. I just thought it would be nice. We can relax and have a chat.'

'Ahhh!' Shauna nodded knowingly. 'You want to make sure I know that yesterday was completely innocent and that you genuinely had a cramp in your leg.'

'It's not just that. I wanted to chat to you to see what's going on in your life. I want us to be close again, just like we used to be.' He eyed her carefully. 'And now that you mention it, I actually did have a cramp yesterday. I know what it looked like but I swear to you, that's all it was.'

'Tell that to somebody who cares.' She stuffed a mouthful of lasagne into her mouth and the fact she didn't spit it out again made Rob feel proud.

'But you obviously do care, love. You haven't spoken to me since yesterday and look at how you're behaving.'

'I always behave like this.'

'No you don't, Shauna. At least not with me. Maybe you and your mum clash and you show her your harsher side, but I've always known you to be loving and kind.'

This seemed to throw her because her expression changed and she almost looked as though she might cry. Rob used the opportunity to continue.

'I know sixteen is a difficult age, love. But you need to know you can always talk to me. You can tell me anything. I won't judge you. I just want you to be happy. Happy and safe.'

Suddenly her face turned dark again. 'Why are we talking about me? I thought this conversation was so that you could convince me that the slut that was here yesterday isn't your fancy woman.'

Rob was exasperated. 'Shauna, there's really no need for that. And you know she's not.'

'How do I know? From what I saw yesterday, I'd say the chances are very high that she is.'

'We're just going around in circles here,' said Rob, rubbing his forehead. 'Have you said anything to your mum yet?'

'Ah, so that's what this is about. Speak nicely to me and I might not tell Mum. All that talk about you thinking I'm loving and kind and you wanting me to be happy. It's all to butter me up so I won't say anything.'

'No! That's not what this is. Yes, it's true. I'd like you not to say anything to your mum. But those other things I said – I meant every one of them.'

'If it was all so innocent, why are you afraid of me saying anything to Mum?'

'Because she'll jump to conclusions, just like you did. Because she'll be upset. And because I'm not sure she loves me enough anymore to believe me.'

Shauna stopped eating and looked at him. 'Wh-what do you mean?'

Rob sighed. He hadn't meant to say that but the words had just spilled out. 'Look, Shauna. Your mum and I have been having problems lately. Nothing major but just a few small hiccups. One of the reasons she went away was to get a break from everything – including me.'

'But I thought she went to write her book?' Shauna actually looked as though she might cry, and Rob felt sorry for her.

'That too. But it was a combination of things. I probably haven't been doing my bit around here and I've always expected her to do the lion's share of the housework. I haven't really appreciated that she also has a job to do and it all just got on top of her.'

'Are you two getting a divorce?'

'Absolutely not,' said Rob. 'It's not going to come to that, but we do have some stuff to sort out.'

Shauna nodded and when she spoke, her voice was barely a whisper. 'I won't say anything. I don't want you to split up.'

Rob's body sagged with relief. 'Thanks, love. I wouldn't ask unless it was important. And I swear to you, nothing happened with me and Tanya. It really was a cramp.'

She nodded and Rob didn't know whether she believed him or not. But the main thing was that she wasn't going to say anything to Linda so he could rest easy about that. But there was another thing he needed to talk to her about and now seemed like the perfect opportunity.

'Shauna, so tell me about you and Craig.'

The question seemed to take her by surprise. 'What about me and Craig?'

'I'm just curious. Are you close? Is it a long-term thing or just a passing phase?'

'Well, I'm not getting married,' she laughed, 'if that's what you're asking. Seriously, Dad. We're just seeing each other, not committing for the rest of our lives.'

He nodded. 'But what does *seeing* each other entail?'

'What do you mean?'

He had to tread carefully because he could see the dark shadow moving across her face again. 'I mean, do you just go for walks? Hold hands? Kiss?'

She shook her head but he could see a flicker of a smile. 'God, you're so embarrassing, Dad. Me and Craig – well, we're just getting to know each other.'

'And?'

'And yes, we've had a kiss and cuddle.' She blushed and looked down at the table. 'I really don't want to talk to you about this, Dad. Can we change the subject?'

'Are you having sex with him?' He hadn't meant to blurt it out like that. It had just come out at speed before he'd had the chance to censor it.

Shauna's head shot up and she glared at him. 'Bloody hell, Dad! I'm sixteen. Of course I'm not having sex. How can you ask me a question like that?'

'Come on, Shauna. Stop playing the innocent. I know.'

'You know?' She actually looked confused. 'You know what?'

'I know about what you've been getting up to.'

'Well, can you please tell me,' she said, her voice beginning to shake with anger, 'because I haven't a clue what you're talking about.'

He'd have to say it now that he'd started so he just came out with it. 'The pregnancy test. I found it in your bin.'

Her face went from red to white. 'Wh-what?'

'I saw it with my own eyes, Shauna. When I was emptying the bins. There's no point denying it.'

'It's not ... I mean I didn't ... It's not mine.

'Honestly, Shauna. Do you think I'm stupid? You're sixteen years old, for God's sake. You shouldn't even be thinking about sex, let alone having it. What on earth's got into you?'

'What's got into *me*? You can't talk. You and this ... this slut of yours.'

'How dare you speak to me like that,' said Rob, shaking with anger. 'Just who do you think you are? Honestly, if I'd ever spoken to my parents—'

'Blah blah blah ... It's always the same thing, isn't it? You were the perfect son and I'm the daughter from hell. Well, I'm sorry I'm such a disappointment.'

'Don't turn this around on me, young lady. I know what you're doing here and I'm not falling for it. We're talking about you and what you've been up to. Now can you please tell me what the hell is going on with you?'

'As if you really care what's actually going on with me, Dad.'

'Of course I care, Shauna. I'm just worried. You're way too young to be having sex.'

'I'm not staying here to listen to this rubbish,' said Shauna, standing up suddenly. She was actually crying, and Rob felt he was losing control of the situation. 'You have a very low opinion of me, Dad. All this lovey-dovey talk and fancy lunch was for one reason only and that was to shut me up. Now I know what you really think of me, I might not keep your dirty little secret any longer.'

'Shauna! Don't be like—'

'Don't be like what, Dad?' She glared at him. 'The disappointing daughter? The let-down of the family? Well, maybe you'd all be better off without me.'

'Shauna, wait. We should talk—'

She'd slammed the door before he'd finished. He could hear her hurrying up the stairs and a creak of her bed told him that there'd be no more talking to her for now. How had it all gone so wrong? He thought he'd been handling things so well but it seemed now he'd gone and ruined everything. Maybe he should just ring Linda and come clean. He'd tell her everything – about the pregnancy test and about Shauna jumping to conclusions about him and Tanya. At least then they could tackle their daughter together and find out what the hell was going on with her. With a heavy heart, he picked up the phone.

Chapter 25

'Hi, Rob,' said Linda, sitting back in her chair outside. She'd been writing for the past few hours and was making progress for once, but she'd been just about to take a break when the phone rang. 'I wasn't expecting to hear from you until later.'

'I like to mix things up a bit,' he said, and she could almost picture the twinkle in his eye. The twinkle she loved.

'I miss you, Rob.' It took her by surprise, but she realised that this time, she really meant it. She suddenly wanted her old life back again. She'd spent the last ten days fantasising about a better life. A more exciting life. But the chat with her mother the previous night had made her think a lot about things and she realised that Kabir had just been a distraction. A glimpse into her youth. She'd wanted to feel young and free again but what she really needed was stability and love. And Rob offered her both of those things in abundance.

'I miss you too, love. I really need you back here. There are things I just can't manage on my own.'

'Like what?' Alarm bells began to ring in her head. 'Is everything okay?'

'Things could be better,' he said, his voice weary. 'You've no idea what's been going on here.'

'God, what is it? Are the children okay?'

'Relax, Linda. It's nothing like that. Well, not exactly. It's just things aren't running as smoothly here as I'd like.'

'Are they not? I thought you had everything under control there.' There was accusation in her voice and she knew it. They'd started the conversation on such lovely terms and she didn't want to change the mood, but he'd given her such a lecture the previous week about the right way to manage things at home that she couldn't help making a point.

'Honestly?' he said quietly. 'I hate to admit it, but I may have lost control.'

'Oh Jesus, what did you do?'

'It's not what I did, Linda. It's what I haven't been able to do.'

'Go on.' She was getting anxious and wished he would just get to the point.

'It's Shauna. She's out of control. I thought I could handle it. Handle her. But I just can't seem to do anything right. Everything I say is wrong, everything I do is wrong. When I try to talk to her about it, she opens her foul mouth and a torrent of abuse spurts out. Even when I try to be nice – try to see her point of view – she acts as though I'm the devil out to ruin her life. I swear, Linda, she's insolent and rude and …' He paused for a moment. 'Are you laughing? Linda? Are you serious?'

'Oh Rob,' she said, her eyes welling up with tears of laughter again. 'This is exactly what I've been telling you these last few months. Don't you remember? I've said all those things to you about Shauna and you refused to believe them.'

'Well, I know you said she was being difficult, but this is on a different level altogether.'

'Really? Do you think? Bad language, insolence, rudeness, not listening to reason, drinking … Do I need to go on? I've been trying to talk to you about this for ages. Trying to get us to have a united front and show her that she can't behave like that. But you've refused to listen. Shauna's always been your little girl and you just didn't want to hear it.'

He sighed heavily. 'I suppose you're right. But she's never been like this with me before. Every time you told me something about her behaviour, I could never see it. She was always nice to me. How could I have missed something like that?'

'Maybe because you were never there,' said Linda quietly. 'Maybe physically you were, but not emotionally. You always left the kids to me. Just like you did with the house.'

'I know, Linda. I've been thinking about that a lot these last ten days. I'm beginning to see the amount of work you've had to do over the years.'

Linda's shoulders sagged with relief.

'Are you still there, Linda?'

'Yes, I am. You have no idea how much I needed to hear that. I hope it means that things are going to change at home. That I'll get more support.'

'Absolutely. I can't wait until you get home and we can talk about things. I feel like we have so much to discuss. So many plans to make. Our future is looking bright, love. I can feel it.'

She hugged the phone closer to her. For the first time in a long time Rob's words were making her feel happy. She was excited to go back and see what the future held. But there was still a little cloud hanging over her head. Kabir. He'd already rung twice that morning, but she hadn't answered. And after her mother's warning the previous night, she felt worried. If she told Rob that she'd been seeing Kabir and that they'd kissed, it could be the end for them. Rob was certainly not going to take it well and Linda worried that he might not be able to forgive her. But on the other hand, if she kept it to herself, would the secret eat her up for the rest of her life? Just like it had done with her mother?

'… going out partying and having a wild time.' Rob was still talking and Linda was jolted out of her reverie when she realised he'd mentioned something about partying. She was confused for a moment. Had he been talking to Aidan or James? What did he know?

'Linda?'

'Sorry, what was that?'

'I was saying that now that your mother is there, she's probably put a stop to you going out partying and having a wild time.'

'But I haven't been. I mean, I wasn't—'

'Linda, Linda! I'm joking. I know you're not there to party. But I know that you're a night owl and Alice is a lark. Does she have you tucked up in bed with a hot chocolate by ten o'clock?'

Linda laughed at that. 'She tries to but I'm having none of it. You know me – I can't sleep before midnight.'

'So what do you do with your evenings then? I mean, if you don't go out, what do you do with your time?'

She wondered for a moment if he suspected something but she dismissed the thought as quickly as it had come into her head. She'd given him absolutely no reason to be suspicious, so she needed to stop being paranoid. 'Sometimes we go out to eat. And other times we just sit in and chat. The time seems to fly over here.'

'When you're having fun,' said Rob, his voice quiet.

'It is fun being here, Rob. It's lovely to spend time with Aidan and James. But really there's no place like home and I can't wait to see you all in a few days.'

'I'm so glad you said that, Linda.' He sounded relieved. 'We can't wait to see you too. Now tell me more about what it's like having your mother there. Is she driving you mad?'

'Actually no. She's been great. We've had some nice chats and she's helped me see things through different eyes.'

'Really? Like what?'

'It's hard to explain. She's just helped me put things in perspective. I'll tell you more when I'm home. But for now, I want us to have a think about what we're going to do about Shauna. Any ideas?'

Rob sighed. 'I really don't know, Linda. I'm at a loss. She has such a potty mouth. I honestly can't believe some of the words that come out of it. I'd never really heard her swear before and now it seems she never stops.'

'And I can't believe you've never heard her before. She really does play Daddy's Girl around you, doesn't she?'

'She used to, but not anymore. She's shown me her true colours these last few days.'

'So was it anything in particular that she's said or done that has you worried or is it just how she's behaving generally?'

Rob's silence sent alarm bells ringing in Linda's head. 'Rob? What is it?'

'Did you know that she and Craig were having sex?'

'WHAT?' Linda almost fell off the chair. Of all the things she thought he was going to say, she hadn't expected *that*. 'What do you mean? How do you know?'

'I found a pregnancy test.'

'What? Where?'

'I was emptying the bins in the bedrooms,' he said, 'and I just came across the box. I was terrified to look inside, Linda. Honestly, I held my breath for ages before looking.'

'And?' Linda was holding her own breath in anticipation.

'Negative,' he said quickly. 'Thank God. But the fact remains that Shauna did the test, which means she must have had sex. At least once. Honestly, Linda. I'm so mad at her. She knows better. We didn't bring her up to—'

'Rob, let's just take a step back and look at this calmly.'

'Calmly? Are you serious, Linda? Shauna is sixteen years old. What are we going to do? This is just not on. And why are you so casual about it? I thought you would have been—'

'It's mine.' Linda's voice was barely a whisper.

'What's yours?'

'The pregnancy test. It's mine. I did one before I left for Spain.'

'What? But why would you? I don't understand.'

'To check to see if I was pregnant, obviously.' She knew she was being smart but she wasn't sure how to handle the situation.

'But you're on the pill. And we're always really careful. Oh God, have you stopped taking it? Did you want to get pregnant?'

'Of course I haven't stopped taking it, Rob, and I can categorically tell you I do *not* want to get pregnant. But nothing is completely safe and accidents do happen. I was late and I've been so hormonal these last few weeks that I thought maybe, just maybe, I could be pregnant.'

'Oh my God,' was all that Rob could say. 'I can't believe you actually thought you were pregnant. And what if you had been? What then?'

Linda sighed. 'I honestly don't know, Rob. I know that babies are a blessing but at this stage of our lives? I'm not sure I would have coped very well.'

'It would have been a big upheaval alright,' said Rob, concern in his voice. 'But we don't have to worry about that now. It hasn't happened, and we'll just have to make sure it doesn't happen any other time. I think our baby-rearing days are over.'

'I agree. So what did you say to Shauna?'

'Oh God. I wish you'd told me about the test, Linda. No wonder Shauna was so upset when I said it to her.'

'So what did you say?'

'I just asked her if she was having sex with Craig. I told her I found the test.'

'Ouch. That was pretty up-front. Did she go ballistic?'

'Yep. I feel so bad now. She was really upset. Crying actually.'

'Wow. I can't remember the last time I saw Shauna cry. She must have been mad as hell with you.'

'She was,' said Rob, his voice trembling. 'She went up to her room and slammed the door. She said some awful things. Worrying things. I should probably go and check on her now. But what am I going to say? Do I tell her the test was yours?'

'Don't say anything for the moment,' said Linda, trying to think quickly. 'Just check she's okay and I'll ring her later. I'll explain about the test and how it was an easy mistake for you to make. I'll convince her to forgive you.'

'No,' said Rob, panic in his voice. 'Don't ring her. Let me tell her.'

Linda was puzzled. 'Why should I not ring her? It will be better coming from me. She probably won't want to talk to you now anyway.'

'Everything is such a mess, Linda. I'm an idiot.'

'No you're not,' she said, feeling sorry for her husband. 'It was an easy mistake to make. Look, don't worry about it. I'll give you a ring once I've spoken to her and you can apologise to her then. Now I should go and get some work done here. I'll talk to you later.'

Linda snapped her laptop shut. She didn't feel like writing

anymore. There was more drama in her own life than there was in her novel. Massaging her temples, she realised she felt exhausted from everything. Exhausted and stressed. A sudden ping from her phone startled her out of her reverie and she glanced at the screen. *Hope you're okay. I've been ringing you but no answer. Call me. Kabir x.*

She really didn't want to speak to him so she gathered up her things and went inside. Both James and Aidan were out and her mother had gone shopping again, so the house was quiet. She made herself a cup of tea, took her Kindle and headed into the bedroom. She'd immerse herself in *Blood Room* and try to forget about everything else.

As she settled down to read, she found she couldn't concentrate. She was worried sick. What had she been thinking when she'd said that the test was hers? She'd just blurted it out. It had broken her heart to hear Rob lamenting the loss of his little girl's innocence. He'd sounded so crestfallen that she'd wanted to give him some hope. And despite the fact that she and Shauna hadn't been seeing eye to eye, her instinct had been to protect her reputation. Even from Rob. She'd have to have a chat with Shauna first, but she'd eventually have to tell Rob that he'd been right all along. The pregnancy test he'd found wasn't actually hers so there was no other explanation for it. Although it broke her heart, she knew that they'd have to face up to the fact that their sixteen-year-old daughter was having sex.

Chapter 26

Linda opened her eyes and tried to remember where she was. Her head was awhirl with thoughts and she found it hard to focus. It was as though she'd been drinking but she was quite sure she hadn't had a drink at all. She sat up in the bed and rubbed her eyes. As she looked at the clock and saw it was after 4 p.m., the events of earlier began to come back to her. The conversation with Rob. His revelations about Shauna. Her lies. Oh God! But maybe she could use this as an opportunity to talk to her daughter properly. Woman to woman. She wouldn't argue with her but instead she'd be calm and allow Shauna to speak. She'd tell her she understood and let her know she was there for her. She might even be able to finally break down the barrier that had been growing between them of late.

Swinging her legs out of the bed, she sat for a moment, willing her body to co-operate. She felt as though she'd run a marathon. The mind was a strange thing. All her thoughts and emotions were weighing heavily and were having an impact on her physical being. Although all the eating out and rich foods weren't helping either. She made a mental note to get herself back on track as soon as she was home. She'd get Ger to do some yoga sessions with her and maybe she'd even go out running with Rob. They used to do that in years gone by. Before the kids. Back when they used to make time for each other and do things together.

She ran her hands down over her t-shirt and shorts to smooth out the crinkles that had formed while she was sleeping and checked her face in the mirror. Up until a few years ago, she used to pride herself on looking younger than her years. But the face she saw looking back at her now told a very different story. Her eyes were bloodshot and the skin beneath them was dark and sagging. Her previously smooth forehead had formed worry lines and even her hair seemed to be sprouting more greys than usual.

As she was about to head out to the kitchen to make herself some lunch, she heard the front door opening. Aidan had said he'd be back around lunchtime so maybe they could have something to eat together and have a chat. She hadn't spoken to him much these last few days. She'd been so consumed with her own problems that she hadn't really given much thought to her friend.

As she opened the door to go out to him, she heard his voice, and he didn't sound happy. She paused, leaving the door open a slit so that she could hear what was going on. As she peeped through the opening, she saw Aidan flop down onto the sofa, his phone to his ear, and he looked stressed.

'But what's the delay?' he said. 'I don't understand and to be honest, I'm getting a bit sick of it.'

Linda wished she could hear the response, but she waited and watched as Aidan reacted to whatever was being said by the person on the other end.

'I know, I know. But you said that last week. Are you going to get onto the Asian guys and try to put a push on? Because we need to strike while the iron is hot. No stuff means no money.'

Linda put her hand over her mouth to stop her gasping out loud. She looked at Aidan's beautiful face and wondered if he could really be involved in something seedy. His soft features had a sincerity about them, and she was having trouble imagining him involved in a drugs ring or something worse.

'You know I always deliver on time. Those guys need to start appreciating that or something is going to give.'

There was a long pause and a lot of nodding and head-shaking by Aidan as Linda strained to try and make out the conversation.

'Bottom line,' he said, and there was a warning in his voice. 'If they don't come up with the goods very soon, I'll have no hesitation in getting rid of her. I can kill her off and that will be the end of it.'

Linda gasped out loud this time and fell against the door in shock. The door swung open as she tumbled onto the floor, banging her head against the leg of a lamp table as she fell.

'Sorry, I have to go,' said Aidan into the phone, before throwing it on the sofa and rushing to Linda's side. 'Linda! What happened? Are you okay?'

Linda sat up slowly, rubbing her head. 'I … I'm fine. I must have tripped coming out of the bedroom.'

Aidan knelt down beside her. 'Don't get up yet. Did you bang your head? You might have concussion. I should probably call an ambulance.'

'Don't!' said Linda, panicking. 'I'm perfectly fine. Just let me lean on you and I'll get up.'

'I didn't even realise you were in the house,' he said, helping her into a standing position. 'I thought you were still outside writing.'

Her legs felt wobbly as she walked towards the sofa to sit down. 'I had enough of writing for one day so I came in a couple of hours ago. I was exhausted so went for a bit of a siesta.'

'Look at you, going all Spanish on us. So were you asleep up until now?'

Linda guessed that Aidan would be worrying she'd overheard the conversation. And she couldn't blame him. She wasn't sure if she was more dazed from the bang to the head or from the threats she'd heard coming from his mouth.

'Yes,' she said. 'I've just woken up.'

'Well, you just stay there and I'll make us a cup of tea. Are you sure you don't need to go to the hospital? Or at least see a doctor?'

'I'm fine, Aidan, honestly. It was more a shock than anything. I'd say I'll have a bump on my head but nothing more than that.'

She watched as he rushed off to make the tea. Aidan O'Brien, children's author and illustrator. Kind, generous, loving and an all-round decent guy. He didn't fit the profile of a drug lord. Or a killer, for that matter. Although how would she know, to be fair? Maybe he was one of those people that she read about in books that had a secret life. Nice guy by day, killer by night. Oh God, she was really letting her imagination run riot. But the fact remained, she was worried about him. Maybe he'd gotten into something that he couldn't get out of. Maybe he'd bought the house and then owed so much money that he was desperate to get it from somewhere. It was going to be a difficult conversation to have but she'd have to talk to him.

'Here we go,' said Aidan, arriving back with two cups on a tray, together with a plate of delicious-looking cakes. 'James brought these home from the restaurant last night so I thought it would be rude not to eat them.'

'Thanks, Aidan.' Linda took a cup and sipped the tea slowly. 'So tell me. How are things with you? I feel like I've been the centre of all our conversations lately and I haven't really asked much about you.'

'Well, compared to yours, my life is dull and boring.'

'I doubt that,' said Linda, thinking back to the conversation she'd overheard. 'You're living the dream out here in Spain – writing and illustrating your children's books, married to a gorgeous man and look at this place. You've been given the opportunity to stay in a fabulous house that you never would have been able to afford on your salary.'

She let the words hang in the air for a moment, but he didn't even flinch, so she continued. 'So who were you raising your voice to on the phone just then?'

His head shot up at that. 'What do you mean? When?'

'Just now, before I fell over. I was coming out of my room and it sounded like you were arguing with somebody.'

'Oh, just a few minutes ago? That was James. And we weren't really arguing. We were just having a friendly dispute about dinner. He wanted to bring something home from the restaurant but I want us to go out.'

It was definitely a lie but she wasn't sure how to get him to open up to her. 'It sounded pretty heated to me.'

'Two gay, food-obsessed guys clashing over what to eat,' he said, a twinkle in his eye. 'It's always going to get heated.'

'Hmmmm.' She didn't want to push it.

'And speaking of heated romances, how are things between you and Kabir?'

'There is no me and Kabir,' she said, annoyed that he'd managed to steer the conversation back to her. 'And there certainly isn't any heated romance.'

'I'm just teasing,' he said, slowly. 'But I'd love to know what you're thinking. I know we chatted when you arrived first about your relationship with Rob but we haven't spoken about it since. Do you feel any better about it? Or has this thing with Kabir clouded your thoughts?'

She was about to say that she didn't have any 'thing' with Kabir and that Aidan should mind his own business, when suddenly her shoulders sagged and she could feel big tears form in the inside edge of her eyes.

'What is it, Linda?' Aidan said, concern in his voice. 'What's wrong?'

'Oh, Aidan, I think I've messed everything up. I'm such an idiot.'

'What are you talking about?'

'Kabir. Rob. It's all such a mess. I've been so stupid and I don't think I can ever make things right again.'

'Oh no, you didn't, did you?'

She was thrown for a moment. 'I didn't what?'

'Sleep with Kabir. You've slept with Kabir, haven't you? I knew you two were getting close, but I didn't think that—'

'No! I didn't sleep with him. But I wanted to.'

Aidan sat back on the sofa and laughed. 'You're such a little drama queen, aren't you? Nobody could ever blame you for a thought that's in your head. You thought about it, but didn't act on it. I think everyone is guilty of thoughts like that now and again.'

'But you don't understand,' she said, her voice breaking. 'We got very close when I went over to his place. And I think it would have happened except for the fact that he was called away.'

'But it didn't, Linda. Nothing happened, so I don't know what you're worrying about.'

'I wouldn't say nothing.'

'Oh?' He sat forward again, waiting for her to continue.

'He kissed me. We kissed.' Saying it out loud and seeing her friend's face made her feel like the worst human being ever. Poor Rob. He didn't deserve that.

'You did?' said Aidan, his eyes opening wide. 'Tell me more.'

She told him about the date at Kabir's house and how she'd wanted something to happen. She told him about the kiss and how it had made her feel. She'd wanted more and if Kabir hadn't had to leave, she was in no doubt that it would have happened. It felt good to talk to somebody about it but it still didn't change the facts.

'And do you want to pursue it? This thing with Kabir.'

Linda took a moment before shaking her head. 'No.'

'Do I sense a hesitation?'

'If you'd asked me that question a couple of days ago, the answer may have been different. But I've done a lot of thinking and I know now for sure that I love Rob. Mum made me realise that I'd wanted things to be like they were in our youth. I was hankering after the days when we were young and free and life was simple. But the reality is, we'll never get those days back again. Things are different. We have a family. Responsibilities. Things have evolved and so has our relationship.'

'So Rob's the one then?' said Aidan, beaming. 'I knew you two could work things out.'

Linda nodded. 'Rob is my future and I want to be with him. I want to get our lives back on track and forget all of this ever happened.'

'Well, thanks a lot,' said Aidan, pretending to look hurt. 'I thought you've enjoyed spending time with us.'

'You know what I mean, you idiot. Of course I've loved spending time with you. I'm talking about Kabir and what I've done. I want to wipe it from my memory and move forward with my life.'

'I don't know much about these things,' said Aidan, watching her carefully, 'but I think maybe what's happened over here will turn out to be very significant for you. Maybe rather than wiping it from your memory, you should embrace it. It was an experience you had, and it made you realise what's important in your life.'

She nodded slowly, trying to take it all in. 'You're very clever, you know. And you're also very lucky to be in such a strong relationship.'

Aidan's eyes lit up. 'I know. James is fabulous. I adore him. And I don't like to brag, but I think he adores me too.'

'Of course he does,' laughed Linda. 'You two are perfect for each other.'

At that moment her phone rang and she pulled it out of her pocket, she saw it was Rob. She rejected the call because she was enjoying her chat with Aidan too much. She could call him back in a while. But then it rang again and once more she rejected it. She'd explain to Rob later that she was in the middle of something when he rang. But when it rang for the third time, alarm bells went off in Linda's head, so she answered it immediately.

'Hi, Rob. What's up?'

'Linda! Thank God I got you. I think we have a problem.'

Chapter 27

'What is it, Rob?' She sat forward on the sofa, alarmed at his tone of voice. Aidan had left the room to give her some privacy, so she was alone.

'It's Shauna.'

'Oh God, what's happened? Is she okay?'

'She's gone.'

'What do you mean she's gone. Gone where?'

'I don't know,' he said with a sigh. 'After our argument earlier, I thought it was best to just leave her be. Let the dust settle. You said you were going to ring her later so I figured I could talk to her again after that.'

'But I told you to check on her to make sure she was okay. She's probably just gone to Craig's or something. She'll want you to be worried. To suffer.'

'I think it's a lot more serious than that, Linda.'

Linda's blood ran cold. 'Why? How?'

'She left a note.'

'Saying what?' She was beginning to panic. Sixteen was a very vulnerable age and Shauna was very unpredictable.

'I went up to the bedroom just to make sure she'd gone back to school. I hadn't heard her go out so I thought she might try and take the afternoon off. That's when I saw the note lying on her bed. Here, I'll read it to you,' he said. 'It says, *Dad, I'm going. Don't look for me. From your slutty daughter.*'

'Jesus, Rob. I don't like the sound of that. You must have really made her feel like crap.'

'She was the one doing most of the talking, to be honest. She wouldn't let me get a word in. But I keep thinking about the last thing she said.'

'What was it?' Linda's heart was thumping out of her chest.

Rob hesitated.

'Rob?'

'She said we'd be better off without her.'

'Oh Jesus! Have you tried ringing her?'

'Of course I have. About a hundred times. Her voicemail cuts in straight away when I dial her number and she's posted nothing online, according to Ben.'

'Her friends, then. We'll have to ring her friends and see if they know where she is. And Craig, of course. She could just be hiding out at his place.'

'I've already done that. I have Emily and Laura's numbers here so I tried them both and got Craig's number from Emily. None of them have spoken to Shauna today. Apparently, she didn't go back to school for afternoon classes and nobody has seen her since morning.'

Linda tried to get her thoughts together. 'So what do we do now? Should we go to the police or something?'

'I don't think they'd take us seriously, Linda. I was sitting here having lunch with her earlier today. She'd probably need to be gone more than twenty-four hours for them to even consider looking into it.'

'But we can't just do nothing,' said Linda, tears beginning to pour down her face. 'What if she does something … something awful? We need to find her, Rob. We need to get her home.'

'I know, love.' His voice was soft. Comforting. 'I'll do whatever I can from this end. I'll drive around and see what I can find out. Do you know any of her other friends? Or anyone else we haven't thought about? Either phone numbers or addresses.'

'I have a few addresses in my phone I can send you. But get Ben to help. He can look at her social media and contact people on her friends list. He's good at that sort of thing. Get him to find out if anyone at all has heard from her or maybe he can even get her on social media himself.' She was suddenly filled with energy and was pacing up and down the room.

'Good idea,' said Rob. 'He's here now so I'll tell him what you said. Hang on.'

Linda paced while Rob recounted the conversation to their son. She was filled with fear. There were always horrible stories on the news about children going missing and never being found. Or even worse. She often watched their parents giving interviews, distraught with grief, and always thought to herself: *There but for the grace of God go I.* And now she was one of those parents. Would she be on the news in days to come, pleading for her daughter to come home? Or even worse, pleading for the person who hurt her daughter to be found. Oh God, she couldn't bear thinking about it. Her head began to spin and suddenly her legs buckled beneath her. She just managed to get to the sofa before her body collapsed in a heap, and she landed half on the sofa, half on the floor.

'What the hell … Linda. LINDA!' Her eyes began to focus and she could see her mum kneeling over her. She was supporting Linda's head in her hands and her voice was shrill and panicky. 'Are you okay, Linda? What happened?'

'I'm … I'm okay, Mum.' She pulled herself up onto the sofa and leaned her head back on a cushion. 'I just felt a little weak. Oh God, Rob. The phone.' She pointed to the phone, which had fallen to the floor, and Alice picked it up.

'I've got it, love. Hello, Rob? It's Alice. Linda's just had a bit of a turn.'

Linda took the chance to get her breathing back to normal while her mother spoke to Rob. She could see concern grow in her face as

Rob relayed the story to her and suddenly Linda was glad her mum was there with her.

'Right,' said Alice, ending the call and taking charge. 'Firstly, are you feeling okay?'

'I'm fine, Mum. It was just the shock.'

Alice nodded. 'Okay, then. Stay where you are. I don't want you fainting on me again. But can you pull up any addresses or numbers you have for Shauna's friends on your phone and send them to Rob. He's going to go out now in the car and see what he can find out.'

For once, Linda was glad to have her mother bossing her around. 'Yes, I have a few addresses but I'm not sure she even sees these girls anymore. I don't know much about the new friends she's made in secondary school. She keeps telling me I don't need to know them. That she's not a little girl anymore.'

'Well, send him what you have and let's put our thinking caps on and see if there's anyone else she'd go to see or anywhere she might go.'

'What about the hospitals,' said Linda, her voice shaking with fear. 'Should we try those?'

Alice looked shocked at the suggestion. 'I don't think so, love. I don't think there's any need. Not at this stage anyway.'

Linda nodded, glad her suggestion had been shot down. 'There. I've sent those few addresses to Rob so he can head out and start looking. But I feel so helpless here. I want to do something. Actually, let me try her number again.'

She dialled her daughter's number but just like Rob had said,

Shauna's voicemail clicked in straight away. It wasn't like Shauna to switch her phone off. It would be more her style to just reject any calls she didn't want to take, whereas switching off altogether meant she had no means of communication at all. It just didn't sit right with Linda and her anxiety began to build again.

'Alice, you're home,' said Aidan, coming back into the room. 'I suppose you bought up half the— What's wrong?' He stopped dead when he saw the look on their faces.

'It's Shauna,' said Linda, wiping tears from her eyes. 'She's gone missing.'

'Oh Jesus, no. Is that why Rob was ringing? How long has she been gone? What can we do?'

With the help of Alice, Linda told Aidan what had transpired that afternoon and a little bit of background about Shauna's recent behaviour. It sounded bad when she said it out loud. It sounded like Shauna was unstable and volatile and God only knew what she might do if she was feeling upset.

'Linda had a little turn when she was talking to Rob,' said Alice. 'I came in just in time. I think it was the shock that made her dizzy.'

Aidan looked at Linda. 'Did you faint? Maybe it's something to do with the bump you got to the head. I told you we should have brought you to the hospital.'

'What bump on the head?' Alice looked from one to the other.

'It's nothing to worry about, Mum. I just tripped earlier and bumped my head. No big deal.'

'It's a big deal,' said Alice, 'if it's caused you to faint. Maybe you have concussion. I think we should get you to the—'

'I'm not going to the hospital, Mum. Not while Shauna is missing. And I'm perfectly fine, so let's deal with one drama at a time.'

'Okay,' relented Alice. 'But you make sure to tell us if you're feeling weak again. You might need to get checked out whether you like it or not.'

Linda nodded as tears pricked her eyes. 'I don't know what to do, Mum. Tell me what to do. I feel so helpless. What if this is Shauna testing us? Trying to tell us something. She might be thinking we're not looking for her. And how is that going to make her feel?'

'Linda, Linda. Stop overthinking things. We're going to do all we can to find her. And if she's missing for much longer, we'll get the police involved. They'll be able to trace her phone and things like that. But I suspect she'll arrive home soon. She'll breeze in and act like nothing's happened. You wait and see.'

'Your mum is right,' said Aidan, rubbing Linda's shoulder. 'It's only been a few hours so she's probably just sulking somewhere. It will be okay.'

'What about Dad?' said Linda, suddenly. 'She could be gone over to him. Mum, give him a ring now.'

Alice took her phone out of her bag immediately. 'You could be right, actually. For whatever reason, he and Shauna seem to have a good relationship.'

Linda waited with bated breath while Alice dialled the number. Her mother was right. Her daughter and her dad had a strange sort of bond. They were an unlikely pair, but they got on so well together. Shauna was the only one who could get him out of a bad mood and he was the only one who could make her laugh. Please God she'd be there and they could all stop worrying.

Unfortunately she wasn't. Alice shook her head as she put her phone down on the coffee table. 'He hasn't seen or heard from her but I made him promise to ring me if she turns up.'

'And do you think he's telling the truth?' said Linda, hopefully. 'Maybe she's hiding out there and has persuaded him not to tell us.'

'He's telling the truth alright. Because he got excited at the thought of her going over to visit. He said he'd get her to pick up a few things in the shops and maybe she could make a bit of dinner for the two of them.'

Linda shook her head. 'Unbelievable. Is that really all he cared about? Was he not worried about her? About what might have happened to her?'

'I actually didn't tell him the full story, Linda. I just said she wasn't home and we thought she might have gone over to him. I didn't want to give him a fright or upset him. It wouldn't do for him to have a heart attack while I'm over here.'

'Good thinking. You really do love him, don't you, Mum?'

Alice looked quizzically at her daughter. 'Of course I do. I love him to pieces. He's a difficult man but he's my man and I'd die if anything happened to him.'

'That's lovely,' said Aidan, who'd been listening to the exchange. 'I hope James and I are as happy as you two when we get old.'

'Hey, less of the old, if you don't mind. I'm in my prime, I'll have you know. Age is only a number and—'

'Can we just get back to Shauna please,' said Linda, trying to get them to focus. 'I'm going to give Rob a ring back and see if there's any news.' She dialled the number and he answered immediately.

'Hi, Linda. No news here yet. I'm in the car with Ben. We've just been to a couple of her old friends' houses but no luck.'

'Shit. I was just thinking. Have you given her any money lately?'

'No. Nothing.'

'I gave her some emergency money before I left so she has that. Although that won't get her very far.'

'She spent that,' said Rob. 'So as far as we know, she had nothing. Unless …'

'What?' Linda's heart was beating like crazy.

'Hang on. I'm just going to pull in for a minute to check something.'

There was silence for a few moments and Linda couldn't bear it. 'What is it, Rob? What's happening?'

'It's my credit card. It's gone. It was definitely here this morning because I used it to pay for shopping. And I know I put it back in afterwards because I noted how the leather was worn in the card holder.'

'Oh no.' Things were just getting worse and worse. 'That's not good news. If she has your card, she can afford to go anywhere. Do anything.'

'Linda,' said Rob, his voice more upbeat. 'It's great news. I'll ring the bank now and get them to check if there's been any activity. If we know where she's used the card, well then we might be able to find her.'

'Oh. I hadn't thought of that. Okay, I'll let you go and you can give them a call. Ring me the minute you hear anything.'

'Will do,' said Rob.

Just at that moment, there was a knock on the door. 'I'll go,' said Aidan. 'It's probably James. He's always forgetting his key.'

Linda continued chatting to her mother while Aidan went to answer the door, and she almost jumped out of her skin when he shouted at the top of his voice.

'LINDA!'

She looked up and couldn't believe her eyes. Standing up, she felt her legs might buckle beneath her again. Shock and relief flooded her body as tears poured down her face.

'Mum!' said Shauna, running to her and wrapping her arms around her. 'Dad thinks I'm a slut. Please say you don't hate me too.'

Chapter 28

Rob couldn't settle to anything. He'd dropped Ben to school earlier because it was raining and had come home to go through some files. But despite having spent the last hour poring over one of his customer's accounts, nothing he'd read had actually reached his brain. His emotions were all over the place and he didn't know what to think. Ever since Linda's call the previous night, he'd been both relieved and worried sick at the same time.

He still couldn't believe Shauna had actually gone to the airport by herself, booked a flight and then travelled alone to Spain. He knew lots of adults who hated travelling alone. They worried about getting lost and negotiating all the steps through the airport like security and boarding. But Shauna, a sixteen-year-old girl, had managed to do all that having never done anything like it before. He couldn't believe it when Linda had rung to tell him. If circumstances were different, he'd be feeling really proud of her right now.

Relief had flooded through him when he'd got the call. For a few terrifying hours, he'd imagined all sorts of awful things. He'd worried that Shauna might manage to disappear altogether or worse still, that she'd come to some harm. And it would have been all his fault. His fault for wrongly accusing her of something and his fault for not having the decency to apologise to her.

He was grateful she was safe and sound with her mother now but he was still worried about what she might say about him and Tanya. He'd been thrilled when she'd promised to keep it to herself at first. It had been a little bit of emotional blackmail on his part, telling her about their marriage troubles, but it had worked beautifully. That was until he'd stuffed it all up by accusing her of having sex. He shook his head at the memory of the confrontation. He really could have handled things much better. He glanced at the clock on the wall and willed his phone to ring. Linda had been planning on having a good chat with Shauna and she'd promised to let him know what transpired. He was anxious to know what his daughter had said and whether or not she'd mentioned Tanya. Either way, it was out of his control now, so he'd just have to wait and hope.

He'd gone over that scene with Tanya again and again in his head and the more he thought about it, the more convinced he was that Tanya had wanted something to happen between them. They'd both flirted with each other for years and it had always been innocent but lately there was more of an edge to the flirting. He could see something in her eyes. Something that said she wanted him. And the way she'd massaged his leg. It had been so sensual. Not like one of those sports massages you got when you went to a physio. She'd deliberately moved her hands up higher and higher on his leg, kneading the flesh with her fingers until he'd felt himself go hard. She'd known exactly what she was doing. He was sure of it. But he had to take some of the blame. He hadn't exactly discouraged her. If Shauna hadn't come home when she had, God only knows what would have happened next.

The thought of that scared him. He was a hot-blooded man, after all. If something was handed to him on a plate, he'd find it hard to resist. And the way he'd been feeling of late, there's a chance that he might have given in to Tanya's advances, if she'd made any. He'd like to think that he'd have resisted. That he'd have told her he was married and he wouldn't do anything like that. But if he was honest, he'd thought about making love to Tanya for a very long time and if the opportunity had arisen, maybe he'd have taken it. And that would have been the end of his marriage to Linda.

He stood up and went to the utility room to check on the washing machine. It was the second load of colours he'd put in that morning and he still had to do the whites. You'd think there was a family of eight living in the house with the amount of washing he seemed to do every day. He was beginning to suspect that the kids were throwing clean clothes into the laundry baskets because they were too lazy to put them up into their rooms. There was still ten minutes left on the cycle, so he'd make himself a cup of coffee.

As he waited for the kettle to boil, his thoughts turned to Linda again and whether or not Shauna had told her about Tanya. Had she made her believe that he was having an affair? He was dying for Linda to ring, but at the same time he was terrified. If Shauna had told Linda what she saw, it would be difficult to claim complete innocence. Because although he hadn't actually done anything wrong, he'd wanted to. And if he was going to be honest with his wife, he'd have to tell her that.

He took his coffee over to the counter and sat on a stool to think. How was he going to handle this whole sorry mess? What was he going to do? Think, Rob, think. He closed his eyes and leaned his elbows onto the counter with his chin in his hands. There must be a way to sort everything out without anybody getting hurt. It was such a mess. And the Tanya situation was only a small part of it. The main issue was the fact that Linda wasn't happy and as a result their marriage was failing. He needed to find a way to show his wife that he still loved her and that they could be as happy as they used to be.

And then it came to him. He didn't know why he hadn't thought of it before. The one thing that had come out of all this was that he realised he couldn't live without Linda. He'd always known that he loved her but being without her had made him realise just how much. And now, faced with the prospect of losing her, he was distraught. So why was he sitting at home moping? Why wasn't he going out there to claim the love of his life? Linda had been so fed up with her lot, so bored with the humdrum of everyday life, that she had to get away. So, if he had any chance of winning her back, he had to be the man that she needed. He had to make a big gesture – one that was sure to remind her why she married him in the first place. With renewed energy and a surge of excitement, he grabbed his laptop and began to Google flights. And then his mobile rang.

'Hello?'

'Mr Costa?'

'Yes. Who's this?' The number had come up as unknown.

'This is Ben's school here. There's been an accident.'

The Accident and Emergency Department of Tallaght hospital was jam packed as Rob helped Ben to a seat. Once he had him settled, he stood in the queue to check in. A quick scan of the room told him that they could be there for a very long time and he couldn't help wondering if he was being punished for something. It had been a hell of a couple of weeks and there seemed to be no let-up with the drama.

Ben had tripped while doing the Beep Test in school and had fallen badly on his foot. It had immediately swelled, and he'd been in a lot of pain, hence the phone call to take him to hospital. It didn't look like it was broken, because he could still move it, but the PE teacher reckoned it was soft tissue damage and would need to be checked out in hospital, just in case. This was the fourth or fifth time Ben had to be brought to A&E in the last few years and it occurred to Rob that this was the first time he'd brought him. Ben was a clumsy kid and very accident prone, but it had always seemed like the natural thing to let his mother bring him to hospital when he needed to go.

'Is it very sore?' he said, sitting back down beside Ben. 'The receptionist said we'd be called by a triage nurse very soon so maybe we won't be waiting as long as we think.'

'Hopefully not,' said Ben, wincing with the pain. 'It's killing me.'

When Rob had been told that because Ben was only thirteen he could go to the children's A&E, he'd been delighted. He'd been to the other A&E once himself with a cut to his finger and he'd never forget it. It had been the worst night of his life. The nurse had put a drunken man beside him who proceeded to talk incessantly while spit flew in every direction. There'd been a homeless woman just looking for shelter from the cold and although Rob had felt sympathy for her, the stench had been unbearable. Two young guys had come in, obviously high on drugs, and had proceeded to punch the face off each other right in front of him. When the security people pulled them apart they'd sat down on the floor and it looked as though they were going to behave – until an unsuspecting man dribbled his cup of water over one of them while passing, and the young fella had jumped up looking for a fight. It had been like watching an episode of *Love/Hate* except the action had all been happening right in front of him. Rob had feared for his life at that stage and had hoped that he'd never have to set foot in that place again.

But now, as he looked around the room, he wondered whether the children's A&E was much better. Directly in front of them, there was a woman holding a basin for a child of around six. The girl was grey in the face and kept making retching noises. There was a couple beside him with a baby who was screaming his lungs out and on the other side was an overweight kid who'd just stuffed himself with a bag of smelly cheese and onion crisps and was now saying he felt like being sick. Rob closed his eyes and wished he could disappear.

Ten minutes later he was pleasantly surprised when Ben's name was called and they escaped the madness. The nurse was lovely and checked Ben over thoroughly. She agreed with the PE teacher's assessment and didn't think his foot was broken either, but she gave him something for the pain. He needed to have an x-ray anyway so she gave them directions and handed Rob a piece of paper to bring with them.

'Thanks,' said Rob, helping Ben up off the chair. 'Do you think there'll be much of a wait down at x-ray?'

'There shouldn't be,' said the nurse, holding open the door. 'Twenty minutes max, I reckon.'

'Did you hear that, Ben? We could be home in the next hour.'

The nurse laughed. 'Oh, I wouldn't count on it, Mr Costa. When you get back from x-ray there's a wait for the doctor.'

'Really?' Rob's heart sank. 'How long?'

'We don't give out times,' said the nurse, looking amused. 'But you could be looking at eight or ten hours, to be honest.'

Rob almost swallowed his tongue with shock. 'Ten hours? Are you serious?'

She nodded. 'Could be more, could be less. It's hard to say. But we have to put urgent cases first. And it's busy today with ambulances incoming. And of course they have to take priority.'

Rob walked in a daze to the x-ray department. Only hours before, he'd been sitting at home in a quiet house thinking about his wife. He'd been relieved not to have to worry about Shauna and had been grateful that the house would be quiet with just him and Ben for a bit. He longed to be back there now, enjoying the peace and planning for the future.

He knew he was being dramatic – it was only one day out of his life. But time was of the essence at the moment and he needed to make sure he handled things with Linda the right way.

Back in the waiting area following Ben's x-ray, things seemed to have quietened down. The baby who'd been screaming was asleep and the retching child now had colour in her cheeks and didn't look on the verge of vomiting. The pain relief seemed to have worked for Ben and he'd fallen asleep, so Rob closed his eyes and tried to do the same.

But there was too much going on in his head to allow sleep to overtake him. He began to realise what an idiot he'd been over the years. How could he have expected Linda to do so much with the house and with the children while he just did his normal nine to five job? He'd always felt like he should relax after a hard day's work but he never gave a thought to the fact that Linda's work never ended. The nights she'd spent in A&E with Ben while he'd slept. The times she'd stayed up into the early hours when one of the children had a vomiting bug. The stress she'd endured trying to juggle her job, the house and the needs of the children. He was beginning to see it all now and it didn't show him in a very positive light.

'Excuse me, can I just get in there?' The voice broke into his thoughts and he opened his eyes to see a very overweight woman trying to squeeze into the chair beside him. She took over part of his chair too and he moved over as much as he could so as not to have his body squeezed up against hers. She had a boy of around two with her and she sat him on her ample lap.

'He's not well,' she said, pointing to the boy's green-looking face. 'He's been sick all morning.'

'Oh,' said Rob, instinctively pulling his legs back for fear of a torrent spewing forth from the child's mouth. 'The poor thing.'

As luck would have it, he moved just in time as the child began to vomit ferociously on the floor. The stench was unbearable, and Rob tried not to breathe in the rancid air.

'Good boy,' said the mother, patting his back. 'Better out than in.'

Rob turned the other way, trying not to retch himself, until suddenly he felt a weight on his lap and looked around in surprise.

'Here, hold him for a minute, will you? I'll have to go and get something to clean this mess up.'

The child looked at Rob and began to cry as the mother disappeared to look for a nurse. Rob felt like crying too, as he bounced the child up and down, willing him to stop. 'It's okay,' he said. 'She'll be back in a minute.' The louder he cried, the faster Rob bounced him, remembering when his own kids were little and he used to bounce them on his knees.

'I wouldn't do that if I were you,' said the mother, appearing back with a roll of paper towels. 'All the bouncing might make him—'

It was too late. The child opened his mouth and emptied the contents of his stomach all over Rob. It was the most vile thing that had ever happened to him. He never would have imagined that so much could come out of someone so little, but it had exploded like a firework and had managed to cover not only Rob's lap, but his hands and feet too.

'Sorry about that,' said the mother, taking the child and handing Rob the roll of paper towel. 'But you should have known that bouncing a sick child wasn't a good idea.'

Rob wondered was this the universe punishing him. Was it a penance for how he'd behaved, not only in the last week but for the last number of years. Well, if that's what it was, he'd take it. All he cared about now was getting his relationship with Linda back on track and he was going to move heaven and earth to do it.

Chapter 29

'And the child vomited all over him,' said Linda, tears pouring down her face. 'I know I shouldn't laugh but it really is hilarious. Poor Rob.'

'Eeuw!' said Shauna, shaking her head. 'That's disgusting.'

Alice nodded. 'Yes, but it might give him a taste of what it's been like for you over the years, Linda. He's never really gotten much involved in stuff like that, has he?'

'I suppose not. I've had a few dodgy A&E visits with Ben, and Rob has never offered to take over. It's just how he is, Mum. He's not a bad man.'

'I know, love. But still, no harm for him to experience it now.'

'So what's Dad saying about me?' said Shauna, buttering a slice of toast and taking a bite. 'Does he still hate me?'

'Of course he doesn't hate you, love. I keep telling you that.'

'He does. I could see it in his eyes.'

'Maybe I'll leave you two to chat,' said Alice, standing up and taking her cup and plate with her. 'I'll finish this in my room.'

'There's no need, Mum. Honestly.'

'It's okay, love. You and Shauna need to talk. I can catch up with my gorgeous granddaughter later.'

Linda watched her mum leave and turned to Shauna. 'So how are you feeling today, love? How are you really feeling?'

'I'm okay. Just tired. I didn't get much sleep last night.'

'Well, maybe you should go back to bed for a while this morning. Catch up on some sleep and then maybe we'll do something later. But...' She looked at her daughter's troubled face. 'I think we need to have a proper chat first, don't you?'

Shauna nodded.

'It's a lovely morning,' said Linda, standing up, 'so why don't you go outside to the patio and I'll bring us out a fresh cup of tea. Things always seem better out in the sunshine.'

She watched as Shauna headed outside and her heart swelled with love. She looked different. More childlike. Although Linda hated to admit it, she'd probably built up a bit of resentment towards her daughter over the last year because of her behaviour. She'd caused a lot of trouble at home and Linda had stopped looking at her like her little girl. But really, that's all she was. A little girl who was having adulthood thrust upon her before she was ready to face it. Kids were expected to grow up way too soon these days and it made Linda sad to think about it.

Leaning against the kitchen counter waiting for the kettle to boil, Linda could see Shauna sitting back on a garden chair, her eyes closed, face turned to the sun. It was hard to believe she was here in Spain with her. When Aidan had opened that door the previous night and Linda had seen her standing there, she'd been overwhelmed with both shock and relief. But Shauna had been way too upset to talk about things and Linda hadn't forced the issue. All she'd got from her was that she'd taken Rob's credit card, booked a flight and had given the taxi driver the address once she'd arrived at Murcia airport. Linda would never have believed that Shauna would have the courage to do something like that, not to mention an airline allowing a sixteen-year-old to fly alone. But it seemed that, according to Ryanair, a sixteen-year-old was an adult and no questions were asked.

She placed two cups of steaming tea on a tray with a couple of pastries that Aidan had kindly bought earlier and went out to join her daughter. Shauna had cried for ages after she'd arrived the previous night. She just kept saying she was sorry over and over again until Linda finally made the decision that she should go to bed. The poor kid was emotionally drained and Linda feared she'd have some sort of breakdown if she didn't get some sleep. She'd been dying to question her about a number of things but her motherly instincts had told her that she'd get a lot more out of Shauna when she was fresher in the morning.

'Here we go,' said Linda, placing the tray on the glass table. 'Weak and milky, just as you like it.'

'Thanks, Mum.' Shauna took the tea gratefully and cupped her hands around it. 'I'm really sorry, you know. I'm sorry for all the fuss I caused yesterday and for everything. I'm such a loser.'

'Shauna Costa! Don't you ever say that about yourself. You are absolutely *not* a loser or anything like it. You're a teenager who's lost her way a little. But that's why you have parents. To guide you and try to set you on the right path.'

'So you don't hate me, then?'

'Of course I don't.' Linda reached over and took Shauna's hand. 'How could you ever think that?'

'I'd hate me, if I were you or Dad. I've been a nightmare.'

'You have a bit,' giggled Linda, trying to lighten the mood. 'But hopefully we can move on from here and things will get better.'

Shauna looked down into her cup. 'I suppose Dad has told you about why we argued?'

'He did, love.'

'About the test?'

Linda nodded. 'Do you want to talk about it?'

Shauna sipped her tea and looked uncomfortable. Linda sat back and waited. She didn't want her to shut down. It had been a long time since they'd had a proper mother–daughter chat and she wanted to make sure it was a good one.

'I won't judge you,' said Linda, her voice soft. 'If that's what you're worried about. I was young too once, you know. Although you wouldn't think it to look at me now.'

Shauna's head shot up. 'You're gorgeous, Mum. You're almost three times my age and you have better skin and teeth and hair than I have. Seriously, don't you ever look at yourself?'

Linda was shocked. She would never in a million years have imagined her daughter thought of her that way. It was a long time since anybody had said anything like that to her and it took her a moment to take it all in.

'Sometimes,' continued Shauna, 'I wonder if I'm really your daughter.'

'How can you say that, Shauna?' Linda felt hurt. 'Have I ever given you reason to think that?'

'No, it's nothing you've said or done. It's just that you're so ... so nice. I mean, you're kind and generous and always thinking of other people. Whereas I'm selfish. Aren't you always telling me that? I only ever think of myself. And I look like shit.'

For once Linda didn't feel like correcting her daughter's language. 'Shauna, seriously. How can you think like that about yourself? You're beautiful – inside and out. You're just going through a lot of changes at the moment and it's absolutely compulsory for a sixteen-year-old to be selfish. It's in the rule book.'

Shauna laughed at that. 'Well, I wish somebody would give me that rule book because I'm really not sure what I'm doing.'

'God, Shauna. If you'd seen me at your age, you'd have a completely different opinion. I was all over the place. I hated the world and I thought the world hated me. I was on medication for acne and it made me like a she-devil.'

'Really?'

'Oh yes,' said Linda, enjoying the look of shock on Shauna's face. 'There was drinking and smoking and not to mention the way I treated my parents. God love them, I gave them such a hard time.'

'But I bet there were no pregnancy scares,' said Shauna in a quiet voice.

Linda stopped and looked at her daughter. 'Why don't you tell me about it.'

Shauna nodded and took a deep breath. 'I'm not having sex, Mum. I swear.'

'But why the test then?' said Linda, confused. 'Your daddy said he found a used one and it was negative. I think it's safe to say we can rule Ben out and it's certainly not mine, so I'm assuming it was yours?'

'Yes, it was mine.'

There was an awkward silence before Linda spoke again. 'I told your daddy it was mine.'

'What?' Shauna's head shot up. 'Why would you do that? What did he say?'

'It was just instinct, I suppose,' said Linda, remembering the shocking moment when Rob had told her about the test. 'He was so devastated at the thought of you having sex that I suddenly wanted to make everything okay for him. And to protect you too, I suppose.'

'Oh God. So now he thinks the test wasn't mine? I came over here because I couldn't bear the thought of Dad thinking badly of me. He's always treated me like his little girl and I hated that he found the test.'

'We'll have to tell him eventually, love. I can't lie to him about something so important. But why don't you explain to me first? Tell me what it's all about.'

Shauna shifted in her chair and looked as though she was about to cry. 'Me and Craig were on his bed a few weeks ago. We were just kissing. We had all our clothes on and everything, I swear.'

'Go on.' Linda felt uncomfortable hearing this but it was important.

'I … I think Craig got a little bit too turned on and he … you know …'

'He forced himself on you?' Linda couldn't believe what she was hearing.

'No, Mum, no. He wouldn't do that. He just got excited and things happened. You know, down there.' Realisation began to dawn on Linda as Shauna continued. 'He had shorts on and it came through and it went onto my leggings.'

'And you thought that maybe you could get pregnant?'

Shauna nodded and looked ashamed. 'Yes. I Googled it, you know, just to find out. And it said that there was probably no chance, but I wanted to make sure. I was scared.'

'Are you telling me the absolute truth about this, Shauna? Is that what really happened?'

'Yes, Mum. Do you think I want to tell you that? I'd hardly make it up.'

'I know. I'm sorry. It was just a shock, your dad finding that pregnancy test. I've been so worried.'

'I'm sorry, Mum. I really am.'

Linda went and wrapped her arms around her daughter. 'It's okay, love. It's going to be okay. You did nothing wrong. But we are going to have to have a serious talk about you and Craig. If things are hotting up to that extent, we'll have to think about what's going to happen in the future.'

Shauna nodded. 'To be honest, it's kind of put me off him. It was gross.'

Relief flooded through Linda's body and she slumped back on the chair. She suddenly saw Shauna as her little girl again. The little girl who used to sit on her knee and want a cuddle. The little girl who used to come to her crying when some other child was mean to her. No doubt they'd have turbulent times ahead – it came with the teenage territory. But Linda was glad that the little girl who was lost had found her way home.

Just then her mobile rang, startling them both. Linda saw it was Rob so picked it up immediately. 'Hi, Rob. How's it going there?'

'It's a nightmare,' he said, whispering into the phone. 'We've already been here three hours and when I asked a nurse how much longer, she said it could be another six or seven!'

'That's awful,' said Linda, feeling bad for laughing at the situation earlier. 'And how is Ben? Is he in a lot of pain?'

'Ben is fine. The painkillers seem to have worked so he's asleep here beside me.'

'Well, why don't you try and get some rest yourself. Especially if you're going to be there for hours yet.'

'Are you joking, Linda? I'm on high alert here. There are kids everywhere threatening to spew, and with the amount of coughing and sneezing going on, I'd be surprised if I don't end up sick myself.'

Linda stifled a giggle. 'I'll let you go so. I'm here with Shauna and we're having a chat.'

'Is she okay? Did you explain about the test? Tell her I said sorry for assuming it was her and I'll talk to her later.'

'I'll tell her.' She looked at her daughter's anxious face. 'But I think she understands.'

'Your dad says he's sorry,' said Linda, finishing the call and turning to her daughter. 'And he'll chat to you later.'

'It's me who should be sorry. I suppose you'll be telling him the truth about the test as soon as possible?'

'The truth is always best, love. But I'll explain everything to him so there's no need for you to talk to him about it again. It's enough that you've told me. And I'm very proud of you for speaking to me about it.'

Shauna smiled and her whole face lit up. 'Thanks, Mum. And in the meantime, you wouldn't have a bikini I could borrow, would you? This sun looks too good to waste.'

'I do actually,' said Linda, standing up. 'And maybe I'll take the day off and join you. It's been a while since you and I spent quality time together.'

Shauna stood up suddenly and hugged her mum. 'I love you, Mum. You're the best.'

Tears sprang to Linda's eyes. It had been a long time since she'd heard those words from her daughter and it felt wonderful. She'd come to Spain to try and figure out her life. To get her head straight and find out what she wanted. She'd never have thought that her time away would have brought her and Shauna closer together. But she was very grateful that it had. And now she had just two days left in Spain and a lot to sort out. But she had a renewed energy, buoyed up by events of the last twenty-four hours. She was going to talk to Rob. There was no point in her preaching to Shauna about the truth if she wasn't prepared to heed her own advice. And Rob would understand. She'd stopped things with Kabir before they'd gone further. She'd realised in time that it was Rob she wanted. She just hoped, when everything was out in the open, that he'd still want her too.

Chapter 30

'Listen, Linda. You have a chance now to make things good with your family. That's what you want, isn't it?'

Linda nodded. It was late afternoon and she was sitting with Aidan at the kitchen counter. Shauna had gone for a nap and her mum had gone out walking. James was at work so it was just the two of them.

'But I still think you need to sort things out with Kabir,' he continued. 'He's a decent guy and he seems to have fallen for you.'

'I'm really not sure I want a confrontation, Aidan. I think it would be better if I leave things as they are and don't contact him again.'

Aidan shook his head.

'What?' said Linda. 'I barely know the guy. He's hardly going to think that he and I are heading off into the sunset. He knows I have a family. A husband.'

'Yes,' said Aidan, slowly, 'but is he still texting you?'

'Yes, but—'

'And is he still likely to contact you again?'

Linda nodded. 'It seems as though he wants to keep in touch.'

'Well, isn't it better that you go and see him and tell him you made a mistake. That you don't want to hear from him again. Make sure he's out of the picture before you tell Rob anything.'

'And you still think I should tell Rob?'

'I do. If he loves you, which I know he does, he'll understand.'

Linda wasn't so sure. 'But it will hurt him, Aidan. If I tell him that Kabir and I kissed. I'm not sure I could forgive it if he was the one who'd been unfaithful.'

'But you haven't exactly been unfaithful, Linda. It was just a kiss. It could have been so much worse.'

'I think sometimes a kiss is worse,' said Linda, beginning to fret. 'Sex can be just a lust thing, but a kiss is intimate and sensual and usually means something.'

'And did it? Did it mean something?'

Linda thought for a moment. 'I suppose at the time it did. I was caught up in the moment and I'd be lying if I said I didn't enjoy it.'

'Well, maybe keep those details to yourself,' said Aidan. 'You can tell the truth but maybe leave out a couple of things that would only upset him unnecessarily.'

'I think that's a good plan,' said Linda. 'I just hope he'll understand.'

'I'm sure he will. And I'll tell you who will too. Kabir.'

'You're not going to let this go, are you?'

Aidan laughed. 'You know me. I'm like a dog with a bone. So are you going to speak to him, then?'

'I don't know, Aidan. My flight is the day after tomorrow and I have loads to do; I might not get the chance.'

'Just make the time, Linda. I honestly think you'll regret it if you don't.'

Linda suddenly felt angry. 'It's okay for you, Aidan. You and your perfect relationship with James. You've no idea what it's like.'

'We have our ups and downs too, you know. No relationship is perfect.'

'Well, it's a lot more perfect than mine. I'm just doing my best here to try and salvage my marriage and I'm not sure if speaking to Kabir is top of my priority list.'

Aidan nodded. 'I know what you're saying but it will tie up some loose ends for you. And you'll need those texts and phone calls to stop. Otherwise you could be back on track with Rob and next thing he'll find a text from Kabir on your phone. Just speak to him. Tell him you've enjoyed getting to know him but you don't want him to contact you again. And then you'll be free to start repairing your relationship with Rob.'

'I suppose you're right,' said Linda, massaging her temples. Her head felt as though it might burst from tension. She just wanted her life back. Her nice, normal life. It was funny. That was the life she'd run away from and now she just couldn't wait to go back to it.

'And there's no time like the present,' said Aidan, standing up. 'I'll drive you over to his place now, if you like. And if he's there, I'll wait while you speak to him. It will be all finished with then, Linda. And you'll feel a whole lot better.'

Linda sighed as she stood up. 'Okay. Just let me go and freshen up.'

'Don't make yourself look too desirable,' said Aidan, as she walked off to get ready. 'It will break his heart even more.'

She kept her blue jeans on and changed her t-shirt for a baggier one. Aidan was right. She didn't want to look too appealing. Looking at her face in the mirror, she decided against putting on any make-up. She just applied a moisturiser to her dry skin and scooped her hair up onto the top of her head. Slipping her feet into a pair of flip-flops, she was satisfied she'd nailed the right look for a break-up chat. If you could call it that since they were never really together.

Aidan was very wise and was right about a lot of things. He'd been right about her speaking to Kabir. She was dreading the conversation but she was also excited to move on. To speak to her husband and tell him how much she loved him and wanted to get their lives back on track. Having her mum and her daughter there had made her realise the importance of family and how lucky she was to have such a wonderful one. She suddenly wanted to hear Rob's voice again, so she dialled his number.

He was still at the hospital. Six hours later. He wasn't in good form, understandably, and Linda felt sorry for him. She'd never really acknowledged what he'd done for her. The fact that he'd taken the time off work to allow her to go away. She'd been so caught up with her own troubles that she hadn't really considered the fact that he was being very accommodating and considerate. One of the things that had driven her away was his lack of consideration for her position. His ideal that a woman should do the bulk of the work at home and with the children while he earned the money. And yet he was holding the fort at home while she'd escaped to a foreign country. Wasn't that what she'd wanted all along? He deserved some kudos for that, and she was going to tell him how grateful she was as soon as she saw him.

'Are you ready?' said Aidan, as she walked out of the room. 'It should only take us ten minutes if we get out before the evening traffic.'

They sat in the car in silence. Linda thought about what she was going to say to Kabir. She didn't want to come across as a fool, telling him it was over, when really they'd never been together. She should probably just sit him down and explain that it had been lovely, but she was going back to Ireland and she wanted to try to sort things out with her husband. Surely he'd understand. She hoped so. But what if he didn't? What if he got jealous and tried to ruin things between her and Rob? He could easily contact Rob and say whatever he liked. Oh God, she was beginning to panic now, as Aidan turned off the road and up towards Kabir's house. She wasn't sure this had been a good idea after all.

'Here we are,' said Aidan, pulling up outside. 'His jeep is there so he must be home. Go on. I'll keep the engine running so we can make a quick getaway.'

'Aidan, stop!' He was laughing but Linda didn't see the funny side of it.

'I'm just messing with you, Linda. It will be fine. As I said, Kabir is a decent guy. He'll understand. I'll just wait here and play Flappy Dunk on my phone so take as much time as you need.'

'Okay,' she said, getting out of the car. 'Here goes.'

She walked up the cobbled path and took a deep breath before banging on the door with her knuckles. Kabir was in the process of getting an intercom system installed but it wasn't up and running yet. She waited but there was no sign of him. For a moment she contemplated leaving, but what would that achieve? She banged on the door one more time. When there was still no answer, she looked over at Aidan, who gestured at her to try again.

She could see the lights were on inside and she could hear the faint hum of music, so he was obviously there. The music was probably drowning out any other sound, so she knocked again, harder this time. After another couple of minutes, she walked around to the side of the house to the kitchen window. Perhaps he was preparing dinner with his music playing while he cooked. But the blinds were closed and she couldn't see a thing.

As she walked back around to the front of the house and looked over at Aidan's car, she saw that it was empty. And that's when she saw him standing at the front window. The light from inside was shining on his face and Linda could see the horror written all over it. His two hands were on his head, his fingers entwined in his hair.

'Aidan,' she said, calling over to him. 'Aidan, what's wrong?'

When he didn't respond but stayed glued to the spot, his face staring at the window, Linda's heart began to beat faster. 'Aidan. What is it?'

She quickened her step until she reached his side. 'Aidan, did you not hear me ca—'

Just like Aidan, she froze on the spot. The living room curtains were open just a fraction, but it was enough to see what was going on inside. Kabir was lying naked on the sofa but he wasn't alone. On top of him was another man, their bodies moving rhythmically to the music that was playing.

'Oh my God,' said Linda. 'Am I seeing this right? Is that another man?'

When Aidan didn't respond, Linda looked at him again and saw that he was shaking. Surely *she* was the one who should be reacting like that. It was typical of Aidan to overreact when it really had nothing to do with him.

'This is not happening,' said Aidan at last, tears beginning to pour down his face. 'It can't be happening.'

Linda was confused. 'I know it's a shock but why are you so—' And that's when she realised. Her mouth gaped open when she looked in the window again. The other man had changed position and now Linda could see his face clearly. It was a big enough shock to see Kabir with another man but the biggest shock of all was that the other man was James.

Chapter 31

'Come on,' said Linda, worried that Aidan might faint. 'Let's get you home.'

'No!' He shrugged her off and continued to stare as the two men entwined their bodies even further together. 'I want to stay.'

Linda couldn't bear to look, and she really didn't want Aidan looking either. 'I don't think you should be watching, Aidan. Come on home and you can think about what you're going to say to James later.'

All of a sudden, Aidan snapped. He dashed forward and began to bang on the window.

'Bastard. Fuckin' bastard. I hate you, you cow. Bastard. Shithead. Asshole.'

The two men jumped up and Linda diverted her eyes when she saw the two erect penises. She tried to stop Aidan, but he was in full force, slamming at the window with the palm of his hand and shouting obscenities.

'Aidan, please. You're going to hurt yourself.' Linda was afraid that he'd slam his hand through the window and she'd end up bringing him to A&E. 'They're not worth it. He's not worth it.'

But nothing was going to stop him. Linda had never seen him like this before. Usually so gentle and placid, it was as though the scene had unleashed a monster within. The two men were getting dressed at this stage, their faces racked with guilt and worry.

'Come out here, you bastard,' said Aidan, still slamming at the window. 'Come out here and face me, you cowardly piece of shit.'

Linda tried to restrain him again and finally managed to move him away from the window. He was still shouting but at least he wasn't going to injure himself. She could see that James was coming outside and she was afraid that Aidan would attack him. The poor guy was beside himself with grief and Linda couldn't blame him.

'Aidan! Let me explain,' said James, coming out the front door and walking towards them. 'It was just—'

Aidan lurched forward and planted a punch straight onto his face. James fell over and for a heart-stopping second Linda thought he'd knocked him out. But he sat up, looking stunned, bits of gravel stuck to his face. She turned to restrain Aidan from going at him again but realised he was holding his hand under his arm and was bent over in pain.

'And now I've gone and broken my fuckin' hand,' he said, wincing with the pain. 'You're some piece of work, James.'

'It's my fault,' said Kabir, coming out to join the circus. 'He was just helping me out.'

'Oh, is that what they call it these days?' said Aidan, his hand still safely under his arm. 'Just helping out a friend, was he? Helping you to find your arsehole, was he? Did you lose it or something?'

'Aidan, come on, there's no need for that.' James was struggling to his feet while keeping his distance at the same time. 'Let's go home and talk about this like two adults.'

'I don't want to go home and talk about it, James. I want to talk about it here. So tell me, how long has this been going on? How long have you been pretending to be in love with me while all the time fucking your boss?'

Linda winced. It was so out of character for Aidan to speak like that but it was obviously the grief talking. He'd had a terrible shock. And so had she. But Aidan was the one with so much to lose. Although she was surprised at what she'd just seen, it really didn't matter to her. Kabir didn't matter to her. But she was heartbroken for Aidan, and for the moment she needed to concentrate on looking after him.

'It was just a once-off,' said James, walking towards Aidan with his palm out in front of him. 'I swear, I would never cheat on you.'

Aidan began to laugh hysterically. 'You would never cheat? So what was that? Was I just imagining that naked scene? What was that if it wasn't you cheating?'

Kabir stepped forward. 'What he meant was—'

'And you can shut the fuck up,' said Aidan, spitting the words towards Kabir. 'Nobody asked you, you slut.'

'Well? Explain it to me.' Aidan looked at James and Linda didn't know whether to stay or leave. Kabir looked just as uncomfortable and for a moment she thought about suggesting that they both go inside and leave James and Aidan to it. But she quickly realised she needed to stay by her friend's side in case he lost it again. And on top of that, she really didn't want to be anywhere near Kabir.

'I've known Kabir for a long time,' said James, not taking his eyes off Aidan. 'We both have.'

'So?' Aidan wasn't going to make this easy for James, nor should he.

'I've always suspected that he was gay. I was sure of it, actually.'

'I didn't want to admit it,' said Kabir, looking at the ground. 'I hated the fact that I didn't fancy women. I know it sounds stupid, but I didn't want to be different.'

'So what was I then?' said Linda, piping up for the first time. 'A smoke screen? I thought you actually liked me.' She felt a little hurt, despite the fact that she'd been going over there to say goodbye to Kabir for good.

Kabir looked at her. 'I did. I do. I wanted to make it work with us. That's why I brought you home to my parents. I wanted to be normal.'

'So we're not normal now?' said Aidan, glaring at Kabir. 'Gays are an abnormal part of society. Nice.'

'Of course not. But you have to understand, I come from a very strict, Catholic fam—'

'I don't have to understand anything, actually,' said Aidan, his eyes glistening. 'Whatever you do is your own business. But James, how could you do this to me? To us?'

'Aidan, love, please.' He took a step forward, but Aidan held his hand up.

'Tell me why you did it!'

'It was a mistake,' said James, bowing his head. 'A misguided judgement. I thought I could make Kabir come to terms with his sexuality. Help him to realise that he could be himself and not feel bad about it.'

'I see,' said Aidan, slowly. 'I suppose when you put it like that, it makes sense. You were only trying to help somebody out. We're lucky to be confident with who we are so you were just trying to help Kabir be that same confident person.'

'Exactly,' said James, walking towards Aidan. 'I knew you'd understand. And I promise, it will never happen again.'

Linda could see the scene unfolding before it even happened. James looked relieved as he walked towards Aidan. He felt that he'd talked him around and made him understand. Aidan was smiling and although James was taken in, Linda knew what was going on behind the smile. There was no way Aidan was going to forgive his cheating husband. James stood in front of Aidan and held his arms out. He must have been mad to think that they could hug it out. Linda winced in anticipation as Aidan's smile turned stony and he lifted his fist again. This time he smashed it even harder, right into the centre of James' face.

'Come on,' said Aidan to Linda as James fell to the ground for a second time. 'I'm ready to go now.'

Linda walked after him while looking behind to make sure James was still alive. 'Maybe we should just check if he's okay. I'd hate for you to end up in a police cell after all this.'

Aidan opened the door for Linda and hopped in to the car himself. 'I really couldn't care less where I end up. My life is ruined.'

'Don't say that,' said Linda, as they sped away from the scene. 'It's a setback. A big one, I'll admit, but there's nothing that can't be fixed.'

Looking at Aidan's stony face as he drove home, Linda realised that he didn't believe that. At that moment, he felt beaten. Nothing was ever going to fix this for him, and it was like the end of the world. Poor, poor Aidan. Her heart broke for him and she knew that nothing she could do or say would make it better.

All of a sudden, her own situation didn't seem so bad. Kabir was well and truly out of the picture now and she was free to concentrate on Rob. Surely it wouldn't take much to sort things out. She smiled to herself as she imagined that in just a few days she'd be at home, where she belonged, with her husband and children by her side. She couldn't wait.

Chapter 32

Linda sat out in the garden with her laptop open in front of her. She'd tossed and turned all night, falling in and out of stressful dreams, until she'd finally given in and got up at 6 a.m. There hadn't been a sound in the house with everyone still sleeping and Linda had been glad of the peace and quiet. The previous evening had been an eventful one. Finding James and Kabir together had been such a shock and poor Aidan had been inconsolable. James had come home, and he and Aidan had disappeared into their room for a while. Linda had hoped they'd be able to sort it out but James had come out some time later with a suitcase and a tear-stained face. Despite Linda's best efforts, Aidan hadn't wanted to chat but instead retired to his room with a bottle of wine, and he hadn't emerged for the rest of the night.

She forced herself to focus on the screen in front of her. It was time to make some serious decisions. She'd been reluctant to admit it, but she was going to have to face up to it now. It wasn't working. The book she'd been trying so hard to write was never going to happen. She'd tried her very best but the words simply hadn't co-operated. The twenty-two thousand she had written just weren't good enough. She felt as though she'd run a marathon having completed that amount, so there was no way she'd find it in herself to write another seventy-eight thousand.

She felt like a failure. She didn't want to let anybody down but that's just what she was going to do. Her publishers would be expecting another masterpiece on their desks in three weeks' time and Gretta, her agent, was blissfully unaware of the situation. Gretta had put her trust in Linda. She'd told her she had faith in her ability and was leaving her to get on with it. And now she was going to have to tell them all that she couldn't do it.

But her main concern was Rob and his plans to set up his own business. He'd already spoken to his bosses in work about it, but the truth was, he was going to have to stick with his job if Linda had to pay back the advance she'd received for the book that was never going to be written. It was all such a mess, but she knew what she needed to do. Her sanity was worth a lot more than money and if she continued to force herself to write something that wasn't working, then she'd burn herself out or have a nervous breakdown. What she needed to do now was to put aside the writing and concentrate on her family. They were going to be her priority from now on and once she had spoken to Rob about the situation with the book, they could figure out a way to move forward. Together.

Taking a deep breath, she snapped the laptop shut. That was it. She wouldn't go back to it again. Her eyes filled with tears and suddenly, without warning, they were pouring down her face. It took her by surprise. She wasn't sure if it was sadness for not being able to complete the book or relief that she'd finally given herself permission not to. But one thing was for sure. She loved writing. It was an escape for her. She could check out of normal, everyday life and enter a world of made-up characters and lose herself in their stories. She was certain that it wasn't the end of her writing career. When she was ready, she'd get back to it but maybe not crime this time. If she could reinvent herself, she'd love to do something a little lighter or funny. Maybe she'd even follow in the footsteps of the mysterious Nadia Bernio and write something a bit racy. But next time she'd do it in her own time, just like she'd done with her first book.

'I thought I was the one who was supposed to be in tears.'

Linda hadn't heard anybody come up behind her and jumped at the sound of the voice. 'Aidan! I thought you'd be asleep for ages. Why are you up so early?'

'I couldn't sleep,' he said, pulling out a chair to sit down. 'Despite the full bottle of wine I drank in bed.'

'Oh, Aidan, you poor thing. How are you feeling?' His pale face and red eyes told the story and she felt desperately sorry for him.

He shrugged. 'Like I've been hit over the head with a hammer.'

'And James?'

'James has gone to stay with his sister in Murcia for a week. We need time apart. I can't even bear to look at him at the moment.'

Linda's heart broke for her friend. 'And do you think you can work things out? Or is this the end?'

'I don't know,' said Aidan, tapping his fingers anxiously on the table. 'I honestly don't know. My head is telling me to cut all ties with him. He cheated on me and I didn't deserve that. I've only ever been loyal to him.'

'But?'

Aidan sighed. 'But my heart is telling me to take him back. I love him, Linda. I love him so much. And I just can't imagine my life without him.'

For a brief moment, Linda's mind flitted to Rob and their marriage. She suddenly felt lucky. Rob hadn't cheated on her or betrayed her. He was a good man and she really did love him. And despite her mini-breakdown when she felt her life was falling apart, she knew she had everything to be thankful for.

'What about you and Rob?' It was as though he was reading her mind.

'I want to get us back on track again,' she said. 'I'll be home in two days so I think we'll just sit down together and try and work things out. It's not as though he's done anything bad like …' She froze.

'Like cheating, you mean?' Aidan was smiling through his tears.

'I'm so sorry, Aidan. I wasn't thinking.'

'Don't be sorry. I don't want you tip-toeing around me. James cheated and I've just got to deal with it. But good for you, trying to get things back on track with Rob. For what it's worth, I think you two are perfect together.'

She nodded. 'Thanks. I think so too. And I'm going to be honest about me and Kabir, not that there's much to tell. But I want to start off afresh. No secrets.'

'It's the only way,' said Aidan, looking thoughtful. 'But on another note, how's that book coming along?'

'It's not.'

'I'm sure it's better than you think. Are you almost finished?'

She laughed at that but for once she didn't feel stressed about it. 'No, it's far from finished and I've decided that's how it's going to stay.'

'What do you mean?'

'I've just made the decision to put it away and not write it at all. I just can't, Aidan. And I really don't want to. It's stressing me out and I can't concentrate on anything else because the book is on my mind all the time. I know it makes me seem weak but I've got to do what I feel is right.'

'That's a bold decision,' he said, nodding slowly. 'But it shows you as anything but weak. It takes a strong person to admit that something isn't working and move on.'

'Are we still talking about the book here,' said Linda, 'or might you be thinking of you and James?'

Aidan laughed at that. 'I was actually talking about the book but I suppose it applies to us too. But am I strong enough, Linda? Can I live without him, despite what he's done? I honestly don't know.'

'Follow your heart, Aidan. And it shouldn't lead you too far astray.'

'Listen, I'm sick of talking about me. Tell me more about that book. What are you going to say to your publishers? And have you told Rob yet?'

'I'll have to have a think about how to tell the publishers,' said Linda, dreading that conversation. 'They've no idea how I've been struggling with this one and they're expecting a fully completed book in a few weeks' time.'

'Oh God. You're not giving them much notice, are you?'

She shook her head. 'Don't remind me. And I haven't told Rob yet so that's another thing to worry about.'

'And will you keep writing, do you think?'

'Yes, definitely. But at my own pace. I want to reinvent myself. I know I've only done one crime book, but I feel I was immediately pigeon-holed into that genre when really I'd probably prefer to do something else.'

Aidan sat forward and leaned his elbows on the table. 'I'm going to tell you something now and I don't want you to go mad.'

'What?' Linda was intrigued. 'And why would I go mad?'

'Well, I didn't tell you before because I've told absolutely nobody. Well, except James. But I just made a decision not to—'

'Hello, you two,' said Alice, appearing suddenly by their sides. Shauna was with her and they both sat down at the table. 'I thought I'd be first up but even Shauna here was up before me.'

'And I thought teenagers were supposed to sleep until well after noon,' said Aidan, winking at Shauna.

'Not when I'm on holidays,' she said. 'I only stay in bed when I'm at home and there's nothing to do.'

'So this is a holiday now, is it?' Linda raised her eyebrows at her daughter. 'Well, you'd want to enjoy it while you can because I'm booking you onto my flight on Friday.'

'But can't I stay a bit longer, Mum. Pleeeeease?'

'Don't be ridiculous, Shauna. You can't stay here on your own.'

'But Gran is here. I can stay with her.'

'Listen,' said Aidan, standing up. 'I'll leave you three girls to it and I'll catch up with you later.'

'But what about that thing?' said Linda. 'The thing you were going to tell me.'

'It can wait. We'll chat later.'

'Mum, I assumed you were going to come home with me. Have you not booked a flight yet?'

'I haven't booked anything yet,' Alice said. 'It's nice here, you know. Relaxing. And Aidan is very good about me staying. He said there's no rush on me going home.'

'See?' Shauna looked triumphant. 'Me and Gran can stay here for another week and you can go home to Dad and Ben. I can make sure Gran doesn't get herself into any trouble.'

'You, madam, will be coming home with me. Like it or not.' Linda wasn't going to let her daughter manipulate her. 'You, Ben, Dad and I are going to start spending quality time together.'

'But, Mum …'

'But, Mum nothing. That's the end of it, Shauna. This family has been torn apart recently. And it's probably been mostly my fault.'

'Don't be so hard on yourself, love,' said Alice, putting a hand on Linda's arm. 'You've been exhausted. And fed up. Nothing is your fault.'

'No, Mum. I've been so focused on myself these last few months that I've taken my eye off the ball. Our family needs some tender loving care to fix it and I'm going to make sure I'm the one to give it.'

'I'm sorry, Mum,' said Shauna, coming over to hug Linda. 'I'm sorry for all the upset I've caused and for making you so sad.'

Linda hugged her back. 'You could never make me sad, love. I've just been worried, that's all. But everything is going to be okay now. I'm sure of it.'

'I think this calls for a celebration,' said Alice, clapping her hands together. 'How about all three of us head over to the Zenia Boulevard and do a bit of shopping and then we can have lunch. On me.'

'I hope the shopping is on you too, Gran,' said Shauna, smiling. 'Because I have no money.'

They all laughed and Linda sat back to take in the scene. Three generations of women together. She was a very, very lucky woman. She had everything in the world she could wish for and she was going to start to appreciate it. Two days and she'd be back in Ireland and although she'd loved her time in Spain, she couldn't wait to go home.

Chapter 33

'We're going to have to book on another case for this lot,' said Linda, as they walked back to the villa. 'I can't believe you talked me into buying so much, Shauna.'

Shauna stopped walking and looked at her mother. 'Are you kidding me? You were like one of those quick-change acts – in and out of every dressing room trying on the entire contents of each shop we went into. Honestly, Mum, I've never seen anything like it.'

'She's right, Linda love,' said Alice, who was also struggling to carry her bags. 'You were like somebody possessed.'

Linda laughed. 'Was I really that bad? But aren't the clothes here just fabulous? I'm going to throw out everything in my wardrobe when I go home and replace them. I'm sick of dressing all old-fashioned and mummyish.'

'But old people are supposed to dress like that,' said Shauna. 'You need to start accepting your age, Mum.'

Linda pretended to run at her and Shauna ducked in behind her Gran. 'You cheeky thing! I'm still young at heart, and that's what counts.'

'And what about me?' said Alice, looking at Shauna. 'If you think your mum is old, you must think I'm positively ancient.'

Shauna nodded. 'Yep! One foot in the grave.'

'Shauna!' Linda was appalled. 'You can't say things like that.'

'Gran doesn't care, do you, Gran?'

'I'm well used to you, love. And anyway, growing old is mandatory but growing up is optional. And I'm still weighing up my options.'

'You and your sayings,' said Shauna, giggling. 'You're hilarious.'

Linda's heart soared as they crossed over to the street that led back to the villa. Her mum and her daughter had always had a fantastic relationship. Even when Shauna was at her worst and behaving quite badly, her gran always saw the best in her and Shauna adored her. Their day out had been a tonic. She'd spent far more than she could afford, especially now that she wasn't going to have income from her book, but she didn't care. She'd seen her mum in a new light in the last few days. Although they'd always been close, Linda would never have chosen to spend long periods of time with Alice. She loved her, of course, but sometimes small doses of her motherly advice were enough. But the fact they'd opened up to each other about some very personal things had improved their relationship even more and Linda was absolutely loving spending time with her mother now. And Alice herself seemed to be in much better form. A few days away from her grumpy husband had done her the world of good. And then there was Shauna. Her wonderful, complex daughter. She was like a different girl over here. No bad moods, no insolence and no behaving badly. It seemed like Spain had worked its magic on them all and in the process, brought them all closer together.

She lingered a little behind just to watch the two of them as they walked in the gates of the villa. It was a long time since she'd seen Shauna so animated. It could, of course, have been the shopping spree that had put her in a good mood, but Linda suspected she'd be seeing more of her daughter's nicer side in the coming weeks and months. Although it had only been two days since Shauna had arrived, Linda felt closer to her than she ever had before.

'Come on, Mum,' said Shauna, looking behind. 'Get the key out. My hands are breaking from these bags.'

Linda quickened her step and rummaged in her pocket. 'There you go,' she said, opening the door wide for the other two. 'Go and stick that kettle on, Shauna, and we can have a cuppa with those cakes we bought.'

'Someone's outside with Aidan,' said Alice, dropping her bags on the floor. 'I can't see properly. Is it James?'

Linda shaded her eyes from the sun as she tried to focus. At first, she couldn't make out who it was. They were standing chatting animatedly, each with a glass of wine in their hands. Aidan was facing towards them, but she could only see the other man's back.

He looked too tall to be James, so she ruled him out. She panicked for a moment, thinking it might be Kabir, but then she realised that Aidan wouldn't be having a drink out on his patio with the man who'd robbed him of his husband. And then she realised. The unmistakable way his shoulders shook when he laughed. The awkward way he held a glass of wine. And then he turned, and she saw his face. Without further thought, she dropped her bags and ran outside.

'Rob! I can't believe you're here.' She threw herself at him and hugged him tightly. He embraced her too and kissed the top of her head as she leaned on his chest.

'I had to come,' he said. 'I feel like you've been gone for ever.'

'I'll leave you two to it,' said Aidan, winking at Linda. 'Come inside when you're ready and we can talk about dinner.'

'Thanks, Aidan. She smiled as he shooed her mum and daughter back into the house. They'd been hovering at the door and looked uncertain as to whether they should go out or wait a while. She turned to Rob then. 'Is Ben here too?' Linda looked around, expecting her son to hop out from behind a bush.

'No. He didn't want to come. He's still learning how to negotiate those crutches, so Cian's mum said she'd be happy to look after him for a couple of days.'

'Let's sit down.' Her feet were burning from the walk home and she indicated the chairs around the patio table. 'So I guess Cian's mum has forgiven us for what happened to her son at our house.'

Rob nodded. 'She was very good about it. She blamed the kids –

not me. She said it could just as easily have happened in her house so we shouldn't worry. And she also said she'd be locking the drinks cabinet tonight and keeping a very close eye on the boys.'

'Oh God, I never thought we'd be having this conversation about Ben.'

'Me neither,' said Rob. 'You can just never tell with kids, can you? And speaking of which, how's Shauna?'

Linda thought before answering. 'Do you know, she's absolutely fabulous. Honestly, Rob. It's like somebody has turned on a switch and all her goodness has come out. We had a long chat about things. About Craig, about the pregnancy test and about—'

'The pregnancy test? But I thought you said it was yours.'

Linda hadn't meant to tell him quite so soon but it was too late now to backtrack. 'It was Shauna's, Rob. I'm sorry I lied to you.'

'What? Oh my God. So she is having sex? Why did you make me think it was yours? Jesus. She's only sixteen.'

'Relax, Rob. I really am sorry. It wasn't premeditated or anything. It's just when you told me about it, I was shocked. And I wasn't thinking straight. It just felt right to take responsibility for it myself. I know it sounds stupid now, but it was an instinct thing – I was just trying to protect her.'

'Protect her?' Rob didn't look pleased. 'From who? From me? What did you think I was going to do?'

'Oh God, I'm not explaining this very well. It was more about me protecting her from you thinking badly of her. And protecting your idea of her as your little girl. As I said, it was just an instinctive thing. When I heard how upset you were about it, the lie just came out. I was always going to tell you but I just wanted to have a chat with her first. To see if I could get to the bottom of it.'

He shook his head. 'I suppose I understand. Sort of. So what did she have to say about it?'

Linda spent the next ten minutes telling Rob about the conversation she'd had with their daughter. She felt bad that she'd lied to him but at least she was telling him everything now. And she'd lied with good intentions.

'This teenage stuff is doing my head in,' he said. 'And to think I thought we had it hard when they were babies. Compared to this, the baby days were a doddle.'

Linda laughed. 'I know what you mean. But we manage to get through it, don't we? We make a good team, you and me.'

'We certainly do, love. We can face anything once we have each other.'

His words struck a chord with her and she could feel tears welling up in her eyes. He noticed and reached out and took her hand in his. 'With all the drama of the kids, I haven't really taken time to check in with you, Linda. Has the break away done you any good? Are you feeling better about everything? About us?'

She nodded. 'So much better. It's like the time away has given me some clarity. I'm so sorry about the way I behaved, Rob. I just felt the walls closing in on me and I had to get away. I didn't mean to abandon you or the kids or to make you feel bad.'

'Shhhhh.' He put a finger on her lips. 'It's me who should be sorry. I'm sorry for being an asshole and expecting you to do everything at home as well as your own job. For not taking enough of an interest in what was going on with the children. And mostly for not showing you the love you deserved.'

The tears that had been threatening to fall finally spilled down her cheeks and she rummaged in her pocket for a tissue. 'Oh Rob. I've missed you so much. Just two weeks ago, I couldn't wait to get away. And now I can think of nothing nicer than getting back to my life. To you and the kids. I just didn't appreciate how lucky I was.'

'We're both very lucky,' he said. 'I want to make you happy again, Linda. Just tell me what I need to do to make you feel the way you used to.'

'You don't need to do anything, Rob. You just need to continue being you.' She looked at him then with a smile. 'With maybe a little more help around the house.'

'That goes without saying.'

'And to get more involved with the kids.'

'Of course.'

'And maybe a holiday in the Bahamas?'

'Well, now that's pushing it,' he said, laughing. 'Although a holiday might not be a bad idea, depending on what's happening with my job.'

Linda knew it was the right time to tell him. 'About that. I have a confession to make.'

He looked worried. 'What is it?'

'It's about my book. I can't do it, Rob. Honestly, I can't. I just don't have it in me and it's been making me so stressed.'

'But I thought you were nearly there? That you just needed to finish it off?'

She bowed her head. 'I didn't want you or anyone to see me as a failure. I thought I could do it but it's just not working.'

He was silent for a moment and she held her breath until he finally spoke. 'Does that mean that we might have to give back some of the money you got?'

'Probably.'

'And we won't have the cushion of the money there for me to leave and start my own business?'

'I'm so sorry, Rob. I really didn't mean to—'

'Thank God for that.'

She looked at him quizzically. 'What do you mean?'

'Linda, I've been worried sick. I don't want to leave my job. I got carried away with the notion of setting up a business. You were telling me you wanted me to spend more time at home and I thought this would be the perfect solution. But I can't do it. It's just not me. I promise you I'll do better around the house and I'll take more time off work but God, I don't want to work from home like you do. I'd hate it. I just don't know how you do it.'

'So we've both been worried over nothing,' she said, relief flooding through her. 'This day just gets better and better.'

Rob looked relieved too as he sat back in his chair. 'It's a lesson for us, though, isn't it? We should just be honest with each other and save ourselves a lot of heartache.'

Linda nodded and wondered for a moment if it was the right time to tell him about Kabir. There was no doubt in her mind that she'd have to tell him. They could go home then and start afresh, with no secrets and no lies. But as she looked at his face and saw how his eyes were filled with love for her, she thought it could wait a little bit longer. After all, it was nothing, really. A little distraction that had helped her to see what she really wanted. Rob would understand, wouldn't he? She really hoped so.

Chapter 34

'Rob, are you awake?'

He mumbled something, but Linda could tell that if he wasn't asleep, he was very close to it. They'd all gone out for dinner earlier and they'd had a lovely night. Aidan had insisted on paying, saying he knew the manager and it wouldn't cost him much. It had gotten Linda thinking again about where he was getting his money from. She'd forgotten about her suspicions because of everything that had been happening, but she really wanted to get to the bottom of it before she went home the next day. She'd just have to ask him straight out what was going on and this time she'd demand answers.

She looked around at her husband and envied his sleeping form.

Her mind was too busy to allow sleep. She was thrilled he was there and delighted that they'd had such a good, productive chat, but she was still worried about the Kabir situation. She was afraid that if she waited until they got home to Ireland, she wouldn't tell him, and the deception would eat her up inside. Just like it had done with her mother. But in less than twenty-four hours they'd be home so she wouldn't have much opportunity between now and then to explain things to him.

She shook him gently again. 'Rob, I need to talk to you. Can you please wake up?'

Another snort and a mumble and he was snoring again. She cursed the Spanish wine that was so easy to drink, and Rob had clearly had his share of it. She turned over and willed sleep to come. She forced herself to think of other things that weren't so stressful. She tried meditation – something that Ger had shown her a few months before when she'd been having trouble sleeping. She even tried to count sheep, but eventually realised it was a ridiculous concept that surely had never worked for anyone ever. But all thoughts seemed to lead back to Rob and she knew she wouldn't rest until she had the conversation with him. She eventually gave in, sat up and switched on her bedside lamp.

'Rob, wake up.' She shook him gently. 'Rob. I need to talk to you.'

'What's up?' he said, turning over to look at her, his eyes just open a slit.

'I need to tell you something,' she said. 'Can you just sit up and listen please.'

That seemed to wake him up suddenly. 'What's wrong, Linda? What's so urgent?'

'You know what we were saying earlier about there being no secrets in our relationship?'

'Yes,' he said, slowly, sitting up and fixing his pillows behind him. 'I'm not sure I like the sound of this.'

'I think we're in a good place now; don't you?'

He nodded, a puzzled look on his face. 'Of course I do. But why do I feel there's a "but" coming?'

'Well, it's not exactly a "but". We *are* in a good place. But I just want to be honest about my time here. About what's been going on.'

'Oh God, why do I suddenly feel like I need to have a drink in my hand,' he said, sitting up straighter. 'Go on. What is it?'

'It's not really bad or anything,' she said, feeling nervous. 'It's just that I want to be—'

'Honest! I know. You've said. Linda, please get to the point.' He was getting impatient and she knew she'd just have to spit it out.

'I … I met someone while I was here. A guy.'

His mouth gaped open. 'Oh my God! I don't believe it. You've had an affair, haven't you? Is that what you're trying to tell me.'

She shook her head quickly. 'No, no, not at all. It was nothing like that.'

'Well, what was it like then? It must be something serious for you to feel the need to wake me up in the middle of the night to tell me. Who is this guy and why is it a big deal?'

'It really isn't a big deal, Rob. I just wanted to tell you about him.

His name is Kabir and he's a friend of Aidan and James. Actually, I should say he *was* a friend. But that's a story for another day.'

'Just tell me, Linda. Tell me what happened with you and this … this *Kabir*.'

She tried to ignore the fact that he spat out the name and continued with her story. 'I met him the night after I arrived. Aidan and James had a bit of a party to welcome me and he was here. We hit it off. He offered to show me some of the sites and I agreed.'

Rob's face darkened. 'So you've been seeing him?'

'Well, I wouldn't call it that exactly. He's taken me out a few times to—'

'On dates? Just the two of you?'

'Rob, you're not letting me finish. Yes, we went out a few times, but they weren't dates. He was just being friendly.'

'So you didn't have sex with him?'

Linda balked at the question. 'Of course not. What do you take me for? I told you. It was all very innocent.'

'I'm not buying it, Linda,' he said, pushing the covers back and swinging his legs out of the bed. He stood up and began pacing. 'Again, you woke me up in the middle of the night. If it was all so innocent, why would you do that? Why would you not just tell me about him tomorrow or another day?'

'Sit down, Rob. Please. Nothing happened, but …'

He sat down and glared at her. 'But?'

'But there was probably a bit of an attraction there, if I'm honest.' She looked down at her hands, not wanting to see his face.

'On both sides?'

'Yes.'

He sighed heavily. 'So you fancied him, is that what you're trying to tell me? Or is it that you still fancy him? Do you want to be with this guy?'

'No, not at all,' she said quickly. 'He means nothing to me. It's you that I want, Rob. It's always been you.' He went quiet, so Linda continued. 'I just want us to move forward with a clean slate. No more secrets, as you said yourself. Kabir meant nothing. It was just a little mistake and I wanted to be honest about it.'

'So how far did you go?'

'What?' She was thrown by the question.

'How far did you go with him? Kissing? Tongues? Touching? Go on, I need to know.'

'Kabir, I don't think—'

'*Rob*, Linda. My name is *Rob*. And the fact you said you made a mistake means that something must have happened. Go on, tell me. You said you wanted to be honest.'

She bowed her head again.

'Linda, look at me. If you want us to move on with our lives and have a good relationship, you have to tell me the truth. What happened between you and this, this Kabir guy?'

'It was just a kiss.'

'So there we have it,' he said, standing up and pacing again. 'You kissed. I knew I'd get it out of you eventually.'

'I swear, Rob,' she said, standing up and taking his hand. 'That's all it was. It only happened once and I made sure it didn't happen again.'

Rob sat down heavily on the bed and looked as though somebody had hit him. 'So where did this kiss take place?'

Oh God, she hadn't been prepared for that question. Whatever way she worded it, it was going to sound bad.

'Go on then, Linda. You might as well tell me everything now. Where were you when you kissed? In a restaurant? Out for a walk? What?'

'We were in his apartment.'

'Oh, this gets better and better. He brought you to his place. I suppose he wanted to show you his record collection.'

'Rob, don't be angry. It wasn't how it seems.'

'Well, how was it then? You and him at his apartment. What did you expect was going to happen?'

'I … I don't know.'

'Tell me what the kiss was like.'

'Don't be ridiculous, Rob.' She was now regretting telling him about Kabir at all.

'I'm serious. What was it like? Was it slow and sensuous? Or wild and passionate? Did it last for ages? Was it wet? Were there tongues?'

'Rob! Stop it. Please.'

'At least tell me if you wanted more to happen. Did you contemplate, even for one second, sleeping with him?'

Linda took a few seconds to think of a response, but it was a few seconds too long.

'I knew it,' said Rob, glaring at her, his eyes filled with contempt. 'You wanted him. What happened? Did he reject you? Is that why you suddenly realised you loved me? Lover boy decided he didn't want you so you had to settle for second best?'

'You have it all wrong, Rob. It wasn't like that at all. Yes, there was an attraction there. But I never would have acted on it. I love you too much.'

'Well, I don't believe you,' said Rob, standing up and grabbing the clothes he'd worn earlier from the chair at the end of the bed. 'First there was the pregnancy test, then the book and now this. How can I ever believe a word that comes out of your mouth?'

'Please, Rob. Don't do this. You said we could move forward if I told the truth and that's what I've done.'

'It's too late, Linda. If there's one thing I can't stand, it's lies. Actually two things. Lies and cheating. And it seems you've ticked both those boxes.' He finished dressing and headed for the door.

'Rob, please,' she said, following him and taking his arm. 'I don't want to lose you over something so stupid and meaningless. We can work this out.'

He looked at her then and his eyes were stony. 'I'll be on the sofa. Goodnight, Linda.'

He shrugged her hand away and left the room, closing the door firmly behind him. Linda stared at the door in shock. She couldn't believe it had come to this. That she could have possibly thrown her whole marriage away for the sake of spending a bit of time with a man who she thought liked her but who was really only using her. Had she been an idiot to think that she and Rob would laugh about it? That he'd see the funny side and feel like the victor, having won her back in the end? How could she have misjudged the situation so badly?

She wanted to go out after him. She wanted to lie down beside him on the sofa and wrap her arms around him. She wanted him to tell her he forgave her and that he loved her. She wanted everything to be okay. But it wasn't, and she didn't know if it ever would be again. So she did what they do in all the good movies and threw herself onto the bed and wept until she had no tears left.

Chapter 35

Rob sat in the garden looking out into the distance. He hadn't slept well on the hard leather sofa so he was feeling tired and fed up. He'd come all the way over to Spain to surprise Linda. To tell her how much she meant to him and how badly he wanted to make things work between them. But instead, *she'd* ended up surprising *him* by dropping that bombshell about another man. It had been the last thing he'd expected to hear. Of course she'd tried to make light of it by telling him it had meant nothing, but he didn't believe her. A kiss wasn't nothing. She'd actually put her lips on another man's mouth and shared an intimate moment with him. The thought of it made him feel physically ill.

He took a sip of his coffee and closed his eyes as the thick creamy liquid slid down his throat slowly. It was his third one since he'd woken up and he was finding it strangely comforting. Besides the kiss, the thing that bothered him the most was the fact that Linda obviously found this man attractive. She'd had impure thoughts about him and had circumstances been different, maybe she'd have taken things further. He wasn't sure he could ever forgive her for that.

'Hi, Dad. You look deep in thought.'

He hadn't heard Shauna come out and he almost jumped out of his skin. 'Shauna. Come and sit down. How are you?'

'I'm fine,' she said, sitting down on the chair opposite him. 'Why are you out here so early?'

'I was just awake and it looked like such a lovely day that I thought I'd take advantage of it. It won't be long until we're back to the dreary Irish weather.'

'That's true.' She looked at him then with tears in her eyes. 'I'm sorry, Dad. I'm sorry for my behaviour and sorry for how I spoke to you.'

His heart suddenly filled with love for his little girl. 'It's okay, love. I understand. Your mum has filled me in.'

'About everything?'

He nodded. 'I think so.'

'And the pregnancy test?'

'Yep. That too.'

'Oh God, Dad, I can't talk to you about this sort of stuff. But I'm just sorry, okay? I'm sorry for everything.'

He reached out and took her hand. 'It's okay. I'll leave that sort of talk to your mother. I'm glad you feel comfortable enough to open up to her. It's very important.'

'I know. Mum is great.'

He didn't answer and Shauna picked up on it immediately.

'Is there something wrong, Dad? I mean between you and Mum. I saw the duvet on the sofa.'

He instantly regretted not putting that away before he came out. 'It's just a disagreement, love. Nothing to worry about.'

'Was it about me?'

'Of course not. It's just between me and your mum. And as I say, there's nothing to worry about.'

'I hate it when you two fight. What's happened? Mum told me last night that you two had sorted stuff out. That she was feeling much better and was looking forward to going home.'

Rob sighed. He really didn't want to be having this conversation with his daughter. 'Well, maybe then you should talk to your mum again. Get *her* to tell you what happened.'

'Well, maybe I will,' she said, standing up suddenly. 'At least she doesn't treat me like a five-year-old.'

'Shauna, wait, I'm sorry.' He reached out and grabbed her arm. 'I shouldn't have said that. I'm just tired from not sleeping and to be honest, I don't really want to talk about it.'

'Fine,' said Shauna, pulling away from him. 'I won't bother you anymore.'

She stormed off before he could protest again and he watched sadly as she disappeared inside. She'd meant well but he just couldn't discuss his marital relationship with his daughter. It didn't seem right.

Maybe Linda could speak to her on that level, but even through all this talk of pregnancy tests and sex, he always saw Shauna as his little girl and that would never change.

His coffee had gone cold and he was beginning to get hungry so he picked up his cup and headed inside. He found a box of eggs in the fridge and rummaged around for a pan. A fried egg would be nice with some toast and maybe another cup of coffee to keep him from falling asleep. He filled the kettle with water and was just about to crack an egg onto the pan which was heating, when Linda came out of her room. She stopped when she saw Rob in the kitchen and seemed uncertain where to go.

'Morning,' she said, watching him closely. 'Looks like a lovely day.'

'Sure is.'

'Have you been awake long?' She came into the kitchen and stood beside him.

'A while.'

He was aware of her looking at him intently before she spoke again. 'Rob, can we talk now please? I'd like to explain things properly.'

'We're just going around in circles, Linda. We went over this last night more than once. I don't think there's anything left to say.'

'So is that it? We're over? Just like that?' Her voice had turned angry. 'You're willing to throw what we have away over something so stupid?'

He turned to look at her then. 'Make no mistake, Linda. It's you who threw it all away. And you did it the minute you decided to pursue another man.'

'But I didn't … it wasn't like that.'

'Save it for someone who cares, Linda.'

She opened her mouth to say something but no words came out. Instead she turned and headed back quickly to the bedroom. He heard a sob escape her mouth just as she reached the door and she rushed inside, slamming it behind her. His instincts told him to go after her to make sure she was okay. But he resisted. She was the one in the wrong and he wasn't going to go apologising for anything. He'd done nothing wrong.

He tried to put the confrontation out of his mind as he finished making his breakfast, and minutes later he was heading back outside to eat it on the patio. There was something about the fresh air that made everything taste nicer. In a way he envied Aidan and the life he had here. It was so relaxing. Back in Ireland, everyone seemed to be in a hurry all the time and nobody had time for anyone. Whereas here, everything seemed to move at a snail's pace and people were far less stressed.

When he'd finished his meal, he closed his eyes and began to drift off. The sun was beginning to heat up and although it wasn't scorching hot, it was very pleasant, just right for a snooze. Despite his angst, all his worries began to drift away as he entered that wonderful restful state just before sleep. He recalled reading about that state in a book one time. Hypnogogic, it was called. And it was the most wonderful feeling in the world.

'You bloody hypocrite!'

He woke suddenly with a start, to see his mother-in-law hovering over him.

'Typical bloody man. Can't see the wood for the trees. The absolute hypocrisy of it!'

It took him a moment to adjust to the light. 'What's up, Alice? What are you talking about?'

She sat down beside him. 'Linda. That's what I'm talking about.'

'With all due respect, Alice. I don't think it's any of your business.'

'It becomes my business when my sixteen-year-old granddaughter is upset.'

'Shauna?' Rob was now completely confused. 'I thought you were talking about Linda?'

'Look,' said Alice, leaning forward with her elbows on the table. 'Shauna came to me very upset. She'd spoken to her mum, and Linda told her about your argument.'

'And?'

'She feels caught in the middle, Rob. Linda told her about Kabir and what happened. And how you reacted. And then the poor girl came to me and told me about you and this girl in the office. She didn't know whether or not to tell her mum.'

'There's nothing to tell, actually.' But Rob's heart began to beat faster. He'd forgotten about Shauna walking in on him and Tanya and the fact she'd threatened to tell Linda about it.

'It didn't sound like nothing to me.'

'I don't owe you an explanation, Alice. I don't want to fight with you but this is between myself and Linda.'

'So you're going to tell her then, are you?'

'What would be the point? There's really nothing to tell.'

'I'm sure Linda wouldn't see it that way. Honestly, Rob. You gave Linda such a hard time last night and then this little secret pops up. You're a bloody hypocrite. And you need to have a think about that.' She stood up and stormed off, leaving her venom hanging in the air.

Rob sat for a while, trying to get his thoughts straight in his head. Was Alice right? Was he a hypocrite? He'd made Linda feel bad about Kabir when he really hadn't been a saint himself. He hadn't done anything but without a shadow of a doubt, he'd thought about it. He'd lusted after Tanya for a long time. He found her physically attractive and had dreamed of making love to her. Wasn't that exactly what he was punishing Linda for? Yes, there'd been a kiss between her and Kabir, but he'd been more hurt at the fact that she'd wanted him. He dropped his head into his hands and sighed. Alice was right. He was a hypocrite. A bloody, bloody hypocrite. And with both Shauna and Alice knowing about Tanya now, he was going to have to come clean to Linda. What a bloody mess.

He took his cup and plate and headed back inside. There was no sign of Linda so he guessed she must be still in the bedroom. He took a deep breath and knocked on the door gently, before pushing it open. She was lying on the bed facing the ceiling, her face red raw from crying and streaks of last night's mascara down her cheeks. She looked up in surprise when he entered the room.

'I'm here in peace,' he said, holding his hands up and sitting on the edge of the bed. 'And I'm sorry I made you so upset.'

She sat up and wiped her eyes with her sleeve. 'Rob, I'm so sorry about what happened. About Kabir. About everything.'

'I know, Linda. And I haven't been completely blameless either.'

'Please, Rob. Don't blame yourself. It wasn't anything you did. I was just—'

'Linda, I'm not talking about what you did.' Oh God, now that he was about to say it, it suddenly seemed a whole lot worse. 'There was an incident.'

She looked confused. 'What are you talking about?'

He took a deep breath. 'Before I tell you, I just want you to know that it was completely innocent. Nothing happened and nothing was going to happen. I genuinely had a cramp and Shauna just jumped to conclusions.'

'Hang on,' said Linda, swinging her legs out the side of the bed and moving to sit closer to him. 'What's Shauna got to do with anything. What happened?'

He told her about Tanya bringing over the files and how he'd got cramp and then how Shauna had walked in on them. He rolled his eyes a couple of times and even allowed himself a slight giggle, just to show her how innocent the whole thing was. When he'd finished, he waited for Linda to say something, but she just stared at him.

'Linda, you have to believe me. Nothing happened. Please say something.'

'Do you like her?'

That threw him. 'Tanya? Of course I like her. And you like her too, don't you? You know she's my friend and colleague, but I promise you there's nothing more to it.'

'She's very pretty, isn't she?'

'Well, yes, I suppose.' He didn't like where she was going with this.

'And do you ever think of her as anything other than a friend?'

'No! Linda, I swear. Nothing is going on between us.'

She hesitated before speaking again. 'I believe you, Rob, but just be honest. Have you ever thought of her in a lustful way? Have you ever been turned on by her and wondered what it would be like to be with her?'

He hung his head and that gave her his answer.

'So you've been having lustful thoughts about a colleague and you've been found in a compromising position with her and yet you gave me such a hard time about Kabir.' Her voice was getting louder. More hysterical. 'How dare you, Rob. How bloody dare you.'

'That was different,' he said, but he knew he was losing the fight. 'I didn't pursue anything with Tanya.'

'And I didn't pursue anything with Kabir.' She stood up suddenly and headed for the door before turning to look at him. 'Do you know what, Rob? It doesn't really matter anymore. None of it matters. It is what it is.'

'What's that supposed to mean?' he said, beginning to panic as she opened the door. 'You can't just walk away from the conversation because it's uncomfortable.'

'I think the conversation is done. We're just going to end up going around in circles.' And then her voice softened. 'Let's just let things rest for the moment and see what happens. I'm exhausted and don't want to talk anymore.'

She left the room before he had a chance to reply and he flopped his body back onto the bed. At least now everything was out in the open. No more secrets. But had they both damaged their relationship beyond repair? Or was their love strong enough to lead them back to each other again?

Chapter 36

Linda sat on her suitcase but it still wouldn't close. She'd come over with just one small cabin-sized case but was going home with that, plus a large checked-in one that she'd borrowed from Aidan. She hadn't realised she'd bought so much until she'd started taking everything out of the bags. But she was determined to get everything in, so she opened the case again and began moving things around.

'Knock knock.'

She looked up to see Aidan standing at the door. 'Come in, Aidan. Maybe you can make better sense of this packing than I can.'

'Here, let me have a go,' he said, surveying the contents of the case. 'I know what your problem is. You need to roll, not fold. Honestly, you'd think you'd have learned that at your stage of life.'

'And what stage is that?' said Linda, folding her arms. 'You wouldn't be suggesting I'm getting old, would you? Because that wouldn't be very polite.'

'Would I ever?' Aidan pretended to look offended. 'I might think it, but I'd never, ever say it.'

Linda laughed at that and watched as her friend expertly rolled her new purchases and squeezed them into impossible spaces. He'd finished in minutes and they were able to zip up the case easily.

'I'm going to miss you, you know,' she said. 'I can't thank you enough for having me here and for everything you've done.'

'God, I'm going to miss you like crazy too, Linda. It's been fabulous having you here. And especially in the last couple of days since … well, you know.'

Linda nodded. 'What's happening there? Has James been in touch?'

'He has. We've chatted a couple of times.' Aiden lowered his head and Linda could tell he was still shaken up. 'I do love him, you know. Even after what he's done.'

'It's not that easy to just turn your feelings off,' said Linda. 'So are you going to take him back?'

Aidan sighed heavily and looked at her with tears in his eyes. 'I don't think I can, Linda. He's hurt me so badly. My heart is telling me to give him another chance but my head is telling me not to. I think if we got back together, this thing with Kabir would eventually come between us again. As I said, I love him, but I don't think I can ever forgive him.'

'Oh God, Aidan. I'm so sorry. Have you told him this?'

'No. He's staying with his sister for another ten days. Just to give me some space. And then he'll come back and we'll talk. But I don't think he'll be staying. It's the end for us.' He sat down on the end of Linda's bed. 'But on a lighter note, I'm going away too for a few days. I'm going home to Galway tomorrow for a week. Having your mum here has made me think of mine and I haven't seen a lot of her these last few years.'

'Aidan, that's great. I'm sure she'll love having you home.'

He nodded. 'And it will be good for me. A change of scene. A bit of distance will give me some perspective.'

Linda laughed and shook her head.

'What's so funny?'

'I was just thinking,' she said. 'I came over to Spain for that very reason. To put some distance between me and the family and get some perspective. And now you're doing the same in reverse.'

'I hadn't thought of it like that, but I suppose you're right. Although something tells me our stories will have completely different endings.'

'Whatever happens,' said Linda, 'it will be for the best in the long run. And if you want to spend a few nights in Dublin while you're home, there'll always be a bed in my house.'

'I appreciate that but I'm going to dedicate my week to Mammy. She deserves a bit of attention from me and I know I'll feel better for spending time in the house where I grew up. It'll always be my home, no matter where I live.'

The mention of house reminded Linda that she wanted to confront Aidan about the villa. Part of her felt that it was none of her business. She was going home so she should just leave things be. But the other part of her wanted to talk to him about it. To find out what he'd gotten himself into because it was obvious he was hiding something. And he'd been such a good friend to her, maybe there was a way she could help him.

'I'll leave you to finish off here then,' said Aidan, standing up. 'I'll need to go and pack my own stuff now. My flight's first thing in the morning so I won't be long behind you.'

'Aidan, come back for a minute. There's something I want to discuss with you.'

'That sounds serious. What's up?' He sat down and looked at her suspiciously.

'It's about this place. It's yours, isn't it? You own it.' The statement obviously threw him because he opened his mouth to answer but no words came out. 'I heard you,' continued Linda. 'In a coffee shop with somebody. And on the phone.'

'You what? Have you been spying on me or something?'

'Of course not. I just happened to be in a coffee shop in the shopping centre one day when you were at a table with another guy. I heard you talking about stuff. And you mentioned about paying for the house.'

'A right little detective, aren't you?' He was trying to sound jovial, but he looked shaken.

'And then I heard you on the phone when I was in my room the other day. Aidan, please tell me what's going on. I want to help. Whatever you've gotten yourself into, I'll do all I can to get you out of it.'

'Hold on. I thought we were talking about the house.'

'We are. I'm right, though, aren't I? The villa. It's yours?'

'Yes.'

'I knew it! But I meant what I said. I'd love to help if I can.'

'I'm totally confused, Linda. Help with what?'

'I don't know exactly but you've obviously got yourself involved in something to be able to afford a place like this. Is it drugs? You can tell me, Aidan. I won't judge you.'

He burst out laughing and his whole body shook. 'Seriously, Linda? You think I'm involved in drugs?'

'Well, how else can you afford this? I know what you get paid for your children's books and illustrations and you'd be hard pushed to rent somewhere the size of a matchbox.'

'So your natural conclusion is that I'm a drug dealer. Because there's no other way to earn money.' He was clearly amused, but Linda still wanted answers.

'I didn't just jump to that conclusion,' she said, defensively. 'I heard you talk about delivering the goods and when you were on the phone you even spoke about killing someone.' She said the last words in a whisper while looking around to make sure nobody was listening.

'Oh my God,' said Aidan, clamping his hand over his mouth. 'If that's not adding two and two and getting ten, I don't know what is. Linda, you're completely wrong. Yes, I own this house, but I can assure you, it's all above board and my money was earned in an honest way.'

'But how?' She knew it wasn't really any of her business, but she needed to know.

Aidan sighed and looked pensive. 'Okay, Mrs Detective. I was actually going to tell you this yesterday when you were talking about reinventing yourself … You know that book you're reading?'

'*Blood Room*. Yes. But what's that got to do with anything?'

'Who wrote it?'

'Nadia Bernio. Why?'

'And who is this Nadia Bernio?'

'Some woman who keeps herself to herself. Nobody seems to know who she is. I don't know where you're going with this, Aidan.'

'And why do you think she keeps herself to herself and that nobody seems to have found out anything about her?'

'I don't know. I suppose she just doesn't want people to know who she is. Maybe she has a secret she doesn't want to get out. I really don't know what—'

'Or maybe she's really a man.'

'I doubt it. Because everyone says that—' Realisation began to dawn on her. 'Oh my God! You're not saying that—?'

'What's my name, Linda?'

This threw her again. 'Aidan.'

'My full name.'

'Aidan O'Brien.'

'Maybe take a minute and play around with those letters.' He was smiling – enjoying their little game.

She said the name in her mind and tried to see the letters and then she knew. 'Nadia Bernio. Jesus! You're Nadia Bernio. Aidan, are you serious? This is you? You wrote all this stuff? How could I not know? Why are you only telling me this now? I can't take it in!'

Aidan laughed. 'Yep. Guilty as charged. I am the one and only, Nadia Bernio.'

'But you write about fairies and goblins and draw pictures that children love. This Nadia writes very racy stuff. How does that work?'

'I got fed up with the children's stuff. I was working all hours and it wasn't paying me. I didn't mind at first because I enjoyed it, but I just got tired of it.'

'So you reinvented yourself. That's what you were trying to tell me. I never in a million years would have guessed.'

'Well, now you know,' he said. 'And I'm delighted to be able to talk to you about it. I didn't tell anyone about Nadia. I felt it would get out once I started to tell. And it's not that I don't trust you, but it was more that I didn't trust myself. If I told you, I'd want to tell someone else and someone else and soon my anonymity would be ruined.'

'I understand,' said Linda, still in shock that her friend was the mysterious Nadia Bernio. 'You are a brilliant writer, Aidan. Or should I say Nadia. Honestly, it's one of the best-written books I've read. You're a genius.'

He blushed but was clearly delighted by the compliment. 'Thanks, Linda. Coming from such a talented writer, that really means a lot.'

Linda suddenly burst out laughing as realisation dawned yet again. 'So the deliveries you were talking about? I'm guessing they were manuscripts?'

'Yes. I was delivering the manuscripts on time but the publishers were dragging their feet with the payments. We were also getting some merchandise made in China and there was a mix-up with that, so maybe that's what you heard too.'

'It certainly explains a lot of what I heard. I really did jump to conclusions on that one, didn't I?'

'Maybe just a little,' he said, smiling.

'But there's just one more thing,' she continued. 'You spoke about killing some woman off if they didn't come up with the goods?'

'Well, isn't it obvious?' he said, beaming. 'It was a little threat. I was talking about Nadia. If the publishers weren't going to play nicely, I could just kill her off and nobody would ever know.'

'That's hilarious. And to think I was fretting about you getting into drugs and maybe even being involved in a murder!'

'I don't know whether to laugh or cry,' said Aidan. 'But you know now, and I trust you'll keep my little secret?'

'Of course.' She threw her arms around him and hugged him tightly. 'I'm honoured that you told me. You're a great friend, Aidan. And I really hope everything works out for you.'

'And for you too, Linda. Because you deserve to be happy too.'

When Aidan left the room, she finished her packing and sat down on the bed, exhausted. It had been an interesting trip and it wasn't quite over yet. They had an hour before the taxi came to bring them to the airport. She had one more thing left to do.

Chapter 37

'Do you love me, Rob?' He was sitting out in the garden enjoying the last of the sun before they had to go home.

'What sort of a question is that?'

'Just answer it. Do you love me?'

'Of course I do. It's just that we've been—'

'Do you want to be with me?'

'Linda, I don't know where you're going with this. What's it all about?'

'It's simple, Rob. Do you want to be with me?'

'I do. But it's complicated.'

'Life is complicated, Rob. Relationships are complicated. That's the very nature of things. But the way I see it is, if you love me and want to be with me and I love you and want to be with you, well then we've got to give it a shot.'

He pushed his sunglasses up onto the top of his head and looked at her. 'It's just everything that's happened in the last day or two. It's made things feel different. We've both made mistakes and they're not easy ones to forget.'

'You're right,' she said, slowly, considering her words. 'We've both made mistakes and it might take a while to come to terms with them, but can't we do that together?'

'I suppose.'

'Well, don't sound too enthusiastic.'

'I'm sorry, Linda. But I keep thinking about you and Kabir. And what might have happened.'

'Just as I'm thinking about what might have happened between you and Tanya. Neither of us has been perfect and we never will be. But we've just got to get on with things.'

'Maybe you're right.'

'Remember a few weeks back when I was having my mini-breakdown?' He nodded, so she continued. 'I kept thinking about what things were like when we first met. The spark. The magic. How we used to get excited when we laid eyes on each other. How everything was new and thrilling and nothing else in the world mattered except the two of us.'

'They were good times alright,' said Rob. 'We were so in love. We couldn't keep our hands off each other.'

'I kept trying to get those feelings back. I wanted to feel that way again. To be excited and thrilled and to feel the spark. But over the last couple of weeks I've been thinking about it and I've come to a conclusion.'

'And that is?'

'That was then, and this is now.'

'Genius,' he said, smiling. 'And how did you ever get to that conclusion.'

'Smart arse!' But she was smiling too. 'What I mean is that we can never get the past back. We were two different people then. We were young and carefree. We had no children and nothing else to worry about but ourselves. Now we have a mortgage, two children and we're a lot older and wiser. We have to evolve. Things are different – some better and some worse. But we have to accept that the past is in the past and concentrate on making a good future for ourselves.'

Rob looked pensive. 'That's quite the speech. But I suppose it makes a lot of sense. And would you really want to have to do your tan, put on a face full of make-up, get your nails and hair done and shave your bits every time you saw me?'

'How do you know that's what I used to do?'

'Because I noticed. Back in the day when I noticed things.'

She smiled at that. 'And the answer is no. I wouldn't want to have to do all those things. But maybe I could every now and again. Just for the sake of the memories.'

'That would be nice.'

'So are we going to give it a go?' she said, looking at him hopefully. 'Things may not be perfect, but once we have love, we can conquer anything.'

'There you are,' said Alice, appearing beside them, out of breath. 'I thought I'd missed you. What time are you heading off?'

'What do you mean, Mum? Aren't you coming too?'

Alice shook her head and sat down in a chair beside them. Aidan is going away for a week and James won't be back for a while, so he's kindly offered for me to stay on if I want to. And I'm going to do it. Shauna has helped me change my flight and I'm staying until next Friday.'

'But what will you do here on your own? Won't you be lonely?'

'I've rung your dad and I've booked him a flight. He's coming over tomorrow.'

'Seriously?' Linda was astounded. 'Dad is actually getting on a plane to fly over to you? Alone. With one leg.'

Alice laughed. 'Yep. He obviously missed me that much. I think I've punished him enough and if the truth be known, I miss the old codger. I can't wait to see him.'

'That's great, Mum. I'm very happy for you.'

Linda suddenly felt a hand entwining into hers and she looked at Rob. He mouthed the words 'I love you' and her heart was fixed. He had a twinkle in his eye. The twinkle she loved. And she knew at that moment that everything was going to be okay.

Acknowledgements

Firstly, and most importantly, a huge thank you to my wonderful husband, Paddy. While I was writing this book, real life got in the way and on more than one occasion, I was going to give up. But he encouraged me as he always does, in his patient, gentle way, and I glued my bum to the seat and just got on with it. Paddy and I have just celebrated twenty-five years of marriage and I'm grateful every day for his love. He's my rock, and I don't know what I'd do without him.

My four children, Eoin, Roisin, Enya and Conor are the lights of my life, and I want to thank them for their help and support. I also want to apologise for all the nagging! Six of us and a crazy dog makes for a busy house, but I wouldn't have it any other way. It's a blessing to have them all still living at home and I realise every day how lucky I am. My beautiful children – having you all in my life makes my heart sing and I love you very much.

Two of my biggest supporters are two of the most important people in my life. My mam and dad, Paddy and Aileen Chaney, are the most wonderful people you could meet. They're sixty-four years married (imagine!) and still in love. I really look up to them and hope I've inherited even half their kindness, lovingness and zest for life.

Thank you to my brother, Gerry Chaney and my sister-in-law, Denyse Chaney. Having just one brother, I struck it lucky when Gerry married Denyse and I finally got the sister I'd always longed for. Gerry and Denyse are always there for me with encouragement and support and they're both integral in getting these books finished. Gerry helps me with all the technical stuff that I hate, and Denyse reads my first draft of the books and gives me her very honest opinion.

I want to say a huge thank you to my neighbours and friends – the wonderful Larkfield crew. I feel lucky every day to live amongst them. The support we have within our street is second to none and it's a comfort to know that there'll always be someone there if I need anything. Carmel and Derek are two of these neighbours and I have to say a special thank you to them. They introduced me to La Zenia, and while I was there last year with them, a seed of a story came to me and I knew I had the perfect place to take my characters.

A special thanks to Lorraine Hamm for the coffees and late-night phone calls, for the words of wisdom and the encouragement. And to Angie Pierce, who is always there and whose happy voice lifts my spirits. Thank you to one of my oldest friends, Rachel Murphy. She's always there for me, despite the distance, and I look forward to a wonderful adventure later in the year when I visit her and Lynn in Los Angeles. And to my two very special friends and partners in crime, Niamh Greene and Michelle Jackson. I live for our weekends away and our sneaky trips abroad. Honestly, the stuff we've done together in the name of research! Like finding ourselves on a lonely road in the middle of nowhere on the outskirts of New York, being followed by a gang of young guys joy-riding and wondering who'd be first to find our bodies. But we lived to tell the tale, didn't we, girls? And to the other wonderful friends I haven't named individually, please know I value your friendship and feel very lucky to have you all in my life.

Inspiration comes to me from various sources. Sometimes a thought springs to my mind and it becomes the basis for a new book. Sometimes I overhear things in restaurants or I people-watch on the bus or in a coffee shop. But the odd time, somebody will tell me a story and I know immediately I have to use it. That's what happened one day when I sat down with a friend after we'd played a round of golf together. (Yes, I said golf. Me. Playing golf. This is a thing.) So this friend, Joyce Boyle, told me a story about her son, involving a text about a buried body, a worried pensioner and eventually the police. Daniel is now twenty-one years old and has given me permission to tell his tale. Obviously, I've claimed literary licence and embellished it a little but yes, it did happen! So thank you, Joyce, for the priceless story and thank you, Daniel, for allowing your teenage prank to be unveiled for all to read!

And speaking of golf, I'd like to say a huge thank you to the Hermitage Golf Club, especially the ladies, for welcoming me as a member and allowing me to think I'm Tiger Woods. I was never really an outdoorsy sort of girl but being out on that course in the fresh air is where I get some of my best inspiration for stories. But all you golfers need to watch out – I feel a book coming on…!

I'm very grateful to all the professional people who work so hard to ensure my books reach you. Thank you to my lovely agent, Tracy Brennan, from the Trace Literary Agency. Thank you to my publishers, Hachette Ireland, and especially to Ciara Doorley, who's been my editor since the beginning. I was lucky to have two other people working on this book – Emma Dunne and Joanna Smyth. Thank you to both for making my words sparkle. Thank you to Elspeth Sinclair for her meticulous copy-editing and Aonghus Meaney for his proof-reading. And to all the team at Hachette Ireland – Breda, Jim, Bernard, Ruth, Siobhan, Elaine and Ciara Considine. It's a pleasure to work with you all. Thank you also to the book sellers, book bloggers and reviewers who are all integral in ensuring my words are read far and wide. I'm very grateful for your support.

I'm writing this on the day after my fiftieth birthday and I'm feeling emotional. We all become more aware of ourselves as we get older. Not only about the wrinkles and saggy skin, but about the fact that a lot of us are lucky. I've lost some friends over the years and I'm very grateful to be still here doing what I love. I want to briefly mention the late, great Emma Hannigan who, as well as being a wonderfully talented author and amazing human being, was a friend. I miss her a lot, but I know she'll be up there shouting, 'Book eight, Maria! Who'd have thunk it?! Bloody well done.' Love and light, Emma.

On a lighter note, when I turned forty I desperately wanted to be a published author. I spent years working in the bank and my dreams of writing a book stayed firmly in my head. But saying goodbye to my thirties gave me the nudge to do something about it and I set to work, putting all my energy into writing and looking for a book deal. I remember praying that I'd have a book published by the time I was fifty. I can scarcely believe that ten years on from that wish, I'm just signing off on my eighth. Never give up on your dreams.

And lastly, I want to thank you, my dear reader. You go out and spend your hard-earned money and trust that I'll tell you stories that will entertain you. I can't tell you how much that means to me. I love to read your emails and messages and it makes my heart soar to hear you've enjoyed one of my books. So please keep in touch. My email is mariaduffy2@gmail.com and on Twitter I'm @mduffywriter. I'm on Facebook too and I'm always dying for a chat. So thank you from the bottom of my heart for allowing me and my characters into your lives and I hope I can keep entertaining you in years to come.

Lots of love,
Maria x